Susan Sallis is one of the most popular writers of women's fiction today. Her Rising family sequence of novels has now become an established, classic saga and *Summer Visitors*, *By Sun and Candlelight* and *Daughters of the Moon* are well-loved best-sellers.

Also by Susan Sallis

THE SCATTERING OF DAISIES
THE DAFFODILS OF NEWENT
BLUEBELL WINDOWS
ROSEMARY FOR REMEMBRANCE
SUMMER VISITORS
BY SUN AND CANDLELIGHT
AN ORDINARY WOMAN
DAUGHTERS OF THE MOON

and published by Corgi Books

Sweeter Than Wine

Susan Sallis

CORGI BOOKS

SWEETER THAN WINE
A CORGI BOOK: 0 552 14162 3

Originally published in Great Britain by Bantam Press
a division of Transworld Publishers Ltd

PRINTING HISTORY
Bantam Press edition published 1993
Corgi edition published 1994

Set in 10/11pt Monotype Plantin by Kestrel Data, Exeter

Corgi Books are published by Transworld Publishers,
61–63 Uxbridge Road, London W5 5SA,
a division of The Random House Group Ltd,
in Australia by Random House Australia (Pty) Ltd,
20 Alfred Street, Milsons Point, Sydney, NSW 2061, Australia,
in New Zealand by Random House New Zealand Ltd,
18 Poland Road, Glenfield, Auckland 10, New Zealand
and in South Africa by Random House (Pty) Ltd,
Endulini, 5a Jubilee Road, Parktown 2193, South Africa.

Reproduced, printed and bound in Germany by
GGP Media GmbH, Poessneck.

Papers used by Transworld Publishers are natural, recyclable
products made from wood grown in sustainable forests. The
manufacturing processes conform to the environmental
regulations of the country of origin.

To my family

One
April 1850

Bridgetown was left behind in a flurry of dusty sand, and the two-handed curricle negotiated the hill on to the six-mile stretch of track to Speightstown or – as old Hanover Rudolf insisted on calling it – Little Bristol.

Charles Martinez was as entranced as he knew he was meant to be. The *Ulysses* had docked the day before and they had spent a stuffy day and night in Bridgetown. Charles had been unimpressed. Trafalgar Square and the new statue to Lord Nelson had struck him as poor; the smells had sickened him. The difference as they left the capital of Barbados was immediate.

The curricle and horses had been brought from England and the speed of their drive generated a breeze which took away the stinging heat from his skin and made him feel like a boy again. On the left there were occasional glimpses of the sea, intensely blue beneath the equatorial sun. On the right, the estates of the wealthy soon gave way to the sugar cane fields. At this time of year – April, when the rain was doubtless falling incessantly back in old Bristol – the long, sword-shaped leaves were already higher than their heads.

'You should be here for the cane cutting in the summer,' Hanover said loudly above the sound of hooves and wheels. 'It's like hacking down a forest. And the songs – the rhythm – nothing like it in the world!'

'I believe you!' Charles flashed a smile at the older man. 'But you know I have to be home by August.'

'For the wedding in September!'

7

Hanover grinned as if at a complicity, cracked his whip over the horses and said, 'Yet you have left your bride-to-be in order to see my plantations!'

Charles protested. 'You've been asking me to come here for two years! We share the *Ulysses*—'

'*You* share *my* ship! At excellent rates, I may add!'

Hanover laughed but Charles heard the warning bell. Charles' father, Carlos, had always warned him 'Watch the Rudolfs. They are fair-weather friends and bitter enemies.'

So Charles said smoothly, 'And after all, you came with me to Cadiz to see the vineyards. It seemed only fair—'

'That's the Colony Club. Down there in the coconut palms. If you want a white woman, that place is teeming with them. Governor's wife, daughter, niece . . . Bishop's six unmarrieds . . . They play tennis. Tennis is the thing for the girls. Croquet for the older women.'

Charles felt uncomfortable. The way the old man spoke made the trip seem like some kind of escapade. The three-week voyage had left him feeling strangely different; he had been sick for a week of that time and was doubtless light-headed now. That was attributable to the change of motion. It had been wonderful to set his feet on solid land again. He smiled, recalling the euphoria of sighting the island, watching it approach the ship, anchoring in Bridgetown Harbour and disembarking to the assiduous attentions of the boat and street peddlers. He had not wanted to come on this trip; he had not wanted to be parted from Harriet for so long. And he knew that since Carlos had died Hanover's avuncular interest in the House of Martinez had developed into a covetousness. Perhaps the Rudolfs had always wanted a share in the wine business. Certainly Hanover might imagine that with a young man at the helm, it was an opportunity to get a foot in the door. But when Charles had spoken to Harriet of his fears – and his unwillingness to leave her for even a few weeks

8

– she had smoothed her wide white collar and said judiciously, 'Dearest, I reciprocate your feelings entirely, but you must avoid an outright breach between the two families at all costs. I agree with your sainted father. Hanover Rudolf will be a good friend and a fearsome and unforgiving enemy. Indulge him as far as you can. You can go with him, admire his house, which I understand is truly magnificent – and still remain your own man.'

Harriet was so wise. And her father, Dr Beeching, the eminent Methodist preacher, connected to the Declivedens of Clevedon Court, even wiser.

'Hanover Rudolf may well have some idea of gaining a certain – influence – hold – over you, my son. Be wary.'

So Charles had come, and until now had been extremely wary. But now, with air in his face and the strange smells in his nostrils, he felt . . . somehow . . . different. After all, Hanover Rudolf had always talked extravagantly. And Harriet had been right; wherever he was, he was still Charles Martinez; his own man, son of one of the most upright citizens of Bristol. And now he was here, feeling so exceedingly fit, he might as well enjoy it all.

Even so, Hanover should know that this trip was by no means a last fling before settling down to marriage. The old reprobate was still talking robustly of the sexual options offered on the island.

'If you want to cut a few sugar canes of your own, the women on the plantation are less paltry.'

Charles had lost the thread of the conversation and could only repeat, 'Paltry?'

'The Colony Club females are concerned with either good works or parties, and both mean suitable clothes. Suitable condescension . . . God, man, you know what I'm talking about!' Hanover emitted his trumpet of a laugh and leaned back on the reins as they took a series of bends through a grove of bearded fig trees. 'My women are concerned with survival. They work hard and play hard. There's no special etiquette to be learned. It's wonderfully simple and . . . wonderful.'

Charles felt his 'own man' shrivel with distaste. He had been brought up to value loyalty, honesty, purity, above all things. He knew that since his mother died, his father had been faithful to her memory; he himself had been taught to revere the kind of women he would be likely to meet, and either to ignore the others or pray for their souls. He believed in the narrow public face of the new Victorian England: family values, the abolition of slavery . . . Yet here was Hanover Rudolf, head of the largest sugar company in the British Empire, speaking of his female cane cutters as if they were . . . commodities.

He recalled his father's warning with difficulty and said carefully, 'I might have sewn a few wild oats in the past, sir. But since meeting Harriet—'

The laugh interrupted him.

'Oh I know, I know. I'm bamming you, boy! You should know me better by now!'

Charles laughed his relief. He had been prepared to make a stand, but – Harriet had asked him to avoid a breach at all costs. And she was right. After all, he had known Hanover Rudolf all his life; the Martinez wine importers had used Rudolf ships for over one hundred years. The two families were bound together by business, always had been, always would be. The Rudolfs arrived in England back in 1714 with the new King George and – with him – had murky dealings in the South Sea Bubble disaster. They had emerged almost unscathed, with a plantation in Barbados and a great deal of expertise in trading. Old Mungay Rudolf had financed one of the first expeditions to capture slaves and had increased his holding around 'Little Bristol' to virtually half the island. His first *Ulysses* had put into Cadiz for water just when Carlos Martinez was seeking a vessel to bring his fortified wine to Bristol.

After that first shipment old Mungay had kept an

interested eye on Carlos. He had returned the empty
casks free to Cadiz and charged low rates for the next
shipment. The House of Martinez had been founded
just above Bristol's docks and had gone from strength
to strength. And the bond between the two men had
hovered uncomfortably between business and friendship.

Now, over a hundred years later, it seemed Hanover
Rudolf was making a real effort to develop the friendship
over the business arrangement. Charles' father had
visited the plantation in his lifetime and had told his son
that it was an 'earthly paradise'. As he was one of the
new Victorians – highly moral and suspicious of anything
that resembled a primrose path – this was not entirely a
recommendation.

Nevertheless, after his death, Charles had invited
Hanover to inspect the vineyards at the Castillo outside
Cadiz and had been pleasantly surprised by the old
man's obvious delight in the visit. But, after all, Hanover
had been a widower for many years and there were no
children. He was lonely.

It would have been churlish to turn down the return
invitation.

'See what you think of the island, my boy. Your father
liked it well enough. If you think it would suit, you and
your new wife would be most welcome to stay in the
Plantation House at any time.'

What could be more generous? And if the comments
on 'cutting canes' grated somewhat, Charles was only
too well aware that most men would relish them.

He smiled at his own thoughts and reassured himself
that he was indeed his own man. Soon to be Harriet's.
Till death. And even beyond.

And at the memory of her puritan loveliness, he
recalled his very private plan to build a house for her
in Clevedon, overlooking the Bristol Channel. If the
Plantation House was as beautiful as reported, then
he intended to ask Hanover's formal permission to

reproduce it. The old man would appreciate that. His smile widened. The air was truly like wine.

The curricle whipped around a large area where the chattel-houses were set around a village green. Children were playing here and turbaned women bent over a well, drawing water in a ritualistic way that made Charles think sentimentally of the women in the farms of Somerset back home. The children tried to run level with the curricle and Hanover cracked his whip when they got close to the wheels.

Charles forced a smile. It did not mean anything. The whip had not touched the children any more than it had touched the backs of the horses.

And now they turned inland and were climbing and the horses slowed to a lathering walk and tossed their heads.

'That was Little Bristol,' Hanover explained. 'That's where all the Bristol merchants landed their slaves.'

'No more,' Charles said thankfully. His father, a Whig all his life, had met Wilberforce during a meeting of the Clapham Sect in Bristol. Carlos, with no axe to grind, had been instantly converted to the anti-slavery lobby. He had preached to his friend, Hanover Rudolf, but had had no success until the legislation of 1834.

Hanover looked at him surprised.

'Haven't landed any slaves there for years, boy,' he said. 'No need. They breed like rabbits.'

It was not a reassuring remark. Charles was glad to spot a monkey leaping among the trees. The talk turned to the fauna of the island. And then Hanover spoke of his long-dead wife and how he had brought her to the Plantation House almost forty years before.

It was exactly as Hanover had described. The house had been built like the old cotton mansions of the Mississippi, hung with verandahs in delicate ironwork, and clothed with flowers. A long drive through the rustling cane led to a grove of palms and mahogany set in parkland. They drove beneath a stone archway and on to a gravelled drive, curving between brilliant rhododendron and hibiscus trees, and then the trees dropped away and there was an enormous sweep – 'Capable of taking a dozen coaches when we used to give dinners,' Hanover said. A boy, squatting in the sun, leapt up and ran with the horses until they stopped, tossing their heads, slightly lathered but obviously exhilarated. Hanover threw the reins to him and leapt out of the curricle like a man half his age. He waited for Charles to join him then bawled loudly, "Melia! Luggage!' and led the way into the house.

They stood in an enormous circular foyer, cool and dim as a grotto, a double staircase arching to a landing above. Servants scurried past them, bent almost double, and in the middle of the tessellated floor a tall Negress directed them in monosyllables.

'Bedroom blue. Flowers. Water. Quick now.'

Charles stared at her. She was a magnificent creature, almost as tall as himself – which was six feet – her head bound in the now-familiar bandanna, and a matching length of cloth tied beneath her armpits leaving burnished shoulders and arms free. There had been women in Bridgetown, of course, but none like this.

She must have been special because Hanover introduced her.

'Charles, this is Amelia, the housekeeper.' He went up to the statuesque woman, shrugging out of his frock-coat and handing it to her, then turned for Charles'. 'Take it off, man. We do not stand on ceremony here. No ladies present.'

Charles glanced at Amelia, surely the most womanly woman he had ever encountered. She looked past his left ear while holding out a long bare brown arm for his own coat. He placed it carefully into the crook of her elbow.

'Thank you, Amelia.'

Her eyes shifted and focused on him briefly. He took a quick breath.

'This is young Mr Martinez. You have seen his father before him, 'Melia.' Hanover took Charles' arm. 'Blue room as usual.'

Amelia inclined her head and waited passively until they moved past her. Hanover led the way beneath the arched stairway and opened a door on to another of the long verandahs which surrounded the house. From here the view was breathtaking. The land dropped away, clothed in all kinds of trees and flowering shrubs and the eastern side of the island was revealed. Charles saw that they were very high above the Atlantic seaboard. The west side had been calm, almost waveless, with curved sandy beaches and coconut palms almost to the edge of the sea. Here were rocky coves, high cliffs, rolling seas crashing on to jagged rocks. He stood looking out, taking deep breaths.

'This is magnificent, sir. Thank you for insisting on this visit.'

Hanover snorted his pleasure.

'Two very different coastlines, as you see. The gentle west – low plains. Raging Atlantic – cliffs, escarpments.'

The door opened almost silently and a tray bearing a tall jug and glasses was placed on a table. Charles glanced sideways and saw Amelia, but very changed in the ten minutes since they left her. Now she was in pale grey, a long dress hiding her bare feet, caught up at the back in a suggestion of a bustle. Rather like Harriet's best tea gown.

It did not suit her, but seemed to please Hanover.

'Ah. 'Melia. That's better. Caught you unawares, did we?'

The woman smiled discreetly. Hanover repeated, 'Did we?'

Her smile died. 'Yaas, boss.' She put her hands on the table edge. They were too big for the long-sleeved dress and her wrists stuck out awkwardly. She changed her tone subtly and repeated, 'Yes, sir.' And suddenly, perhaps catching an approving look from her master, she was voluble. 'We saw the ship through the telescope last night, boss. Thought it would be tomorrow at least afore you 'rrived. What with business in Bridgetown and hiring a carriage. Them's two fine horses brought you up, boss. Sir.'

Hanover grinned.

'From England, 'Melia. The curricle too. You should have seen the 'ninnies around Little Bristol. They tried to run with us.'

He laughed and so did she. Charles was relieved. So, old Hanover had been simply showing off his new racing curricle and the whip had been part of the show.

Amelia poured drinks and then withdrew quietly to arrange supper. The drink was rum punch, much loved by the Bajans, but it tasted mostly of nutmeg and was exceedingly refreshing. Charles felt his heart thumping unusually hard after he had downed a second glass but that was not unpleasant either. By the time they had gone indoors to a small dining-room and eaten the inevitable flying fish, cooked crisply and served with tiny fried bananas, it was dark.

He was used to the sudden and early equatorial darkness but it still made him think of retiring and by eight o'clock he was ready for bed. By nine, knowing he was drunk, he had to insist.

'It's either sleep in a bed or here, sir,' he said trying hard not to slur his consonants.

'Some more punch, my boy. And some of this fruit. Nearly two weeks since you tasted fresh fruit, and I reckon you've never tried mango.'

'I've eaten it at your house, sir. Delicious, it is. But – no – really—' He watched his tall glass being filled again with some dismay. One of the tenets of his upbringing had been that a man must hold his drink well. He knew that very soon now he would slip beneath the table.

That is what must have happened. He was conscious

15

of pressure on his elbows and armpits. Stairs . . . he had to lift each leg very carefully. Someone was laughing in his left ear and it sounded like Harriet Beeching and he turned and saw a beautiful sun-tanned face and then closed his eyes again. There was heat everywhere, tangible, another presence pressing in upon him. And at last, a bed. It caught his knee and he fell upon it and was delighted by the softness and the smell of fresh linen reminding him somehow of his long-dead mother. And then someone began to undress him.

He was instantly, if blearily, awake. Just once, ten years before when he had been eighteen, his father had put him to bed and undressed him. Carlos had told him categorically that it would never happen again, and it had not. Until now.

He rolled on to his back, striking something soft with his heels. And got up on his elbows.

'I'm all right. Really. Please leave me now . . .'

He forced heavy lids to lift and there were Amelia and someone else. Another female, but dressed as Amelia had been dressed in a colourful cotton bandage. A round happy face, smiling, white teeth, dark eyes, very white whites. Her skin was the colour of milky coffee.

'Oh God,' he said.

'This is Alice, sir.'

Amelia spoke in that low soft voice that was already familiar to him and very soothing.

He got his tongue off the roof of his mouth with difficulty and said, 'Go 'way now. Now.'

'Alice will stay with you, sir.'

And then he sat upright, appalled.

'What do you mean? You can't mean—'

'It is Master Rudolf's orders, sir. She is pure.'

'She is—' He looked at the girl in wild surmise.

Amelia said smoothly, 'I offered myself, sir. But Master wished for you to—'

The girl, Alice, said quickly, 'I am happy, sir.'

He transferred his gaze to Amelia. She was not happy.

16

He closed his eyes and let his breath go. Perhaps he was still drunk, but suddenly it was very clear to him that Hanover Rudolf was providing for his own ends. This was the kind of hospitality that might be offered to another . . . reprobate. But Hanover knew full well that the Martinez were not reprobates. The old man was relying on Charles' inebriated state to . . . to . . . what? Take advantage of this situation. Miles from home. But . . . Hanover never did anything without plotting for a return. So . . . he wished to get a hold over Charles. Over the House of Martinez.

Charles was terribly befuddled, but that was suddenly crystal clear. He could almost picture Hanover's cat-like smile as he asked for a share in the House of Martinez. 'Surely you do not wish your wife to hear of your escapades at the plantation, my boy?' Charles' imagination turned another notch. 'Especially as she is with child . . .'

He took a breath with some difficulty and said sternly, 'Go to your own beds. Both of you.'

There was a startled silence.

He repeated, 'Go. I am perfectly able to undress myself. Thank you for helping me up the stairs.'

They did not leave. After a while Amelia said haltingly, 'Sir . . . Master Rudolf wishes you to be happy on Barbados. He is honouring you with a gift—'

Charles said loudly, 'You are not objects to be given away. Do you not understand that you are no longer slaves?'

The girl said eagerly, 'We know that, sir. We are house servants and we are paid just as your servants are paid in England.'

'Then this is nothing to do with Hanover Rudolf. You are giving yourself. Is that true?' His anger was directed unjustly at the girl.

She was no more than fourteen. The whites of her eyes showed as she glanced apprehensively at Amelia.

Amelia said quietly, 'You can go to bed, Alice. I will join you directly.'

The girl turned and ran out of the room. He noticed her heels were whitish grey.

He said heavily, 'I do not wish to offend anyone, Amelia. I will wish you good night also.'

But she came slowly to the bed and sat on the edge.

'Sir . . . Martinez.'

'I am plain Charles Martinez.'

'Yes. But you are . . . important.'

He was revolted by it all, yet her beauty made him drunk again.

He said sternly, 'Not very. No.'

'You are almost as important as Master Rudolf.'

'Amelia, I wish to sleep. Please go.'

'But you are also kind. And if you do not let me stay, Master Rudolf will be angry with me tomorrow.'

'It is nothing to do with you. This is horrible. He is making you a procuress. *I* sent the girl away.'

Her beautiful eyes looked at the bed and she rubbed her fingers across the surface of the linen.

'You do not understand, sir. Alice is . . . his daughter.'

He swallowed. Now he felt ill. He wanted to be home so strongly that the thought of the three weeks between him and Bristol filled him with despair.

He said, 'The man is without normal feelings.'

'No. It is the best gift he can—'

'This is something you cannot understand, Amelia. He wishes to bring me down. To be able, when we return home, to call the tune.'

She frowned. No, she did not understand, and he had thought her so intelligent.

And then she leaned forward suddenly and took his poor aching head in her strong arms and cradled him.

He whispered, 'Amelia, please.'

She put her full mouth down to his ear and breathed, 'I will never tell him. Never. This is what I choose to do. Not what I have been told to do.'

He turned his head so that he could look into her face. And for a long time, he looked.

'I knew there was something between us—'

'When you came in, I knew it too.' She smiled and her teeth were brilliant in the darkness. 'You are so like your father.'

He did not have time to think about that remark. She leaned across and snuffed the candle between thumb and forefinger. If he was like his father, then she was like his mother. A provider, a nurse, an earth-woman.

He slept as he had not slept since his mother died. And in the wonderful clear morning, he awoke to a clear head and an enormous feeling of well-being.

The girl, Alice, brought him breakfast. Fruit and coffee and some bread that tasted strangely of melons.

She was subdued, her eyes could not meet his.

'Thank you . . .' She smiled and, incredibly, had a look of Hanover about her. He felt a surge of anger on her behalf. She had been born to slavery and did not even know it. What kind of man would use his own child so?

But he had played Hanover at his own game. He knew that Amelia would never say a word, he trusted her implicitly. There would be other nights and it would be their secret. So much so that somehow Harriet Beeching would never be betrayed.

Alice curtsied. 'Master Rudolf says, you go riding.'

'Very well. That sounds an excellent plan.'

He waited until the girl reached the door then said casually, 'Where is Amelia this morning, Alice?'

'She – she is in the room, sir.'

It meant nothing. It could have been the dining-room, the housekeeper's room, anywhere. He ate his breakfast and thought of Amelia and smiled.

When he joined Hanover later, he was still smiling.

The old fox was smiling too.

'So . . . you did not appreciate my gift last night, boy?'

Hanover trumpeted his laugh and led the way on to the gravelled sweep where two bay geldings – looking extremely lively to Charles' eye – were waiting.

Charles had already decided how to respond and laughed as well.

'Was that what it was all about? Children do not interest me, Hanover.'

It was not often Charles used the older man's forename and both of them noted it.

Hanover said, 'Well, no matter. I thought Amelia had put you off. She's a protective bitch.'

Charles put his foot into the cupped palms of one of the servants and mounted the fidgety horse with some difficulty.

He caught Hanover up and they galloped down the drive through the trees. 'Not at all,' he said loudly. 'She was most insistent.'

Hanover turned and made a glum face.

'Wish I hadn't been so hard on her now. Didn't realize you were celibate, my boy.'

Charles said, 'Hard on her?'

'Took my belt to her this morning and locked her in the cellar. Won't hurt her.' Hanover spurred his horse ahead then looked back over his shoulder. 'Thought she was jealous. Alice is her daughter, don't you know. And even when she sleeps with me she dreams of Carlos Martinez.'

Charles watched him disappear into the trees and made no attempt to catch him up. The blazing light of the Caribbean morning seemed to explode inside his head with his new knowledge. Amelia and Hanover? Amelia and his own father? Carlos Martinez who had been so moral and upstanding? It could not be . . . yet he knew it was. And that was why there had been that 'special feeling' between Amelia and himself yesterday.

He felt sick. It was as if the lid had been lifted momentarily from his neat box of morals and disclosed a writhing mass of snakes. Corruption, a kind of incest

. . . He closed his eyes tightly and held on to the saddle with one hand while his horse cavorted impatiently.

He heard Hanover shout to him to come on and forced himself to open his eyes and shout back. One thing emerged from this mess; he must not let Hanover know how he felt. Only then could he regain some kind of mental equilibrium.

And with that resolution came another. None of this was anything to do with the family of Martinez. Neither Carlos nor himself could be held responsible. It had happened because of Rudolf's plotting. Doubtless, when Carlos had been crazy with grief and Amelia a girl still in her teens, Hanover had . . . Charles swallowed fiercely and tried not to think of Amelia and Carlos. Or Amelia and Hanover. And especially not of Amelia and Charles.

Hanover had spoiled everything. Amelia was no longer a precious secret completely separate from Harriet Beeching. Charles could no longer look at her, or even think of her. And yet he had been responsible for her whipping. His disgust turned against himself. And in that moment he swore that he would live a life of completely moral rectitude. And somehow he would force Hanover to face up to his own degeneracy.

It was not until that night that he knew exactly what to do. They had spent the day visiting sugar mills and inspecting the canes. Dinner had been taken at the Colony Club and there had been a great deal of introductions, dancing, polite conversation. The ride back to the Plantation House had been silent; Hanover himself drunk, Charles never so sober in his life before.

And suddenly, as they climbed to the Atlantic Heights, it came to him.

He would bide his time. Wait until he was safely back in Bristol. There would be no 'favour' asked of the old man – Charles would build his summer residence in Clevedon on the lines of the Plantation House and damn permission from the Rudolfs. And then . . . he would drop a word in the right quarter. Here and there. Just one word linked to the Rudolf name and the Rudolf sugar plantation.

The word: slavery.

Hanover would get out of it, of course. But people would know that there was no smoke without fire. He would be disgraced. And he would know never to meddle with the House of Martinez again.

Two
September 1927

The Michaelmas Ball was in full swing.

Every year the Lord Mayor of Bristol held two balls; one was for children in fancy dress and was socially important, the other was for adults and was socially vital.

Not many parents could resist dropping a reference to the first into their conversation.

'Polka? Oh yes, Dora can polka excellently. She led the dancing at the Mayor's ball this year.'

'Edward is hopeless at dancing. But it didn't matter over-much. He went as Blackbeard and won the third prize so . . .'

There was absolutely no need to broadcast the adult attendance at the Michaelmas Ball. Everyone who was anyone was there.

It was one of the few occasions when the families of the Martinez and Rudolf households risked coming face to face with each other. Even so, it was possible to avoid actually dancing together by sitting out such dances as the new Paul Jones.

Austen Rudolf emerged from the refreshment room and surveyed the length of the Colston Hall with narrowed eyes. Ten short minutes ago he had found a seat for his sister and fought his way to the bar to obtain a Pimm's for her.

'I want the works,' she had commanded, her aristo-cratic Rudolf nose contracting in a special way she had which most men found irresistible. 'A cucumber slice, mint – everything!'

He had stared at her without pleasure. Maude was six years younger than he was, adored and spoiled by their father, rude and domineering to their mother.

'Very well. Stay there. Try to keep a chair for me.'

'Yes, brother dear.' Maude had twitched her nose again and smiled mysteriously. If it suited her she would do what Austen asked. She remembered him vividly when he came home from the war.

But the vegetable- and fruit-laden drink was now on one of the two chairs and Maude was nowhere to be seen. Austen scanned the dancers irritably. He had not wished to come this evening but his father had insisted.

'One of us has to keep an eye on Maude. If your mother and I cannot attend then it must be you.'

'I have not been invited, Father.'

Austen had returned from Barbados earlier than was expected.

'You will go on my invitation, of course,' Mungay said smoothly. 'Maude is using your mother's-ticket so—'

'Mother is too ill to go I suppose?'

Austen had felt a sudden, unusual anger. He knew that if his father used some tender persuasion, his mother would go out and about more often. But Mungay had other fish to fry.

Mungay was genuinely surprised. 'You know how she hates such occasions, Austen. And how much Maude adores them.'

'And why cannot you escort Maude?'

Austen knew the answer only too well. Mungay would certainly be going into Bristol on a visit of his own.

But the older man said smoothly, 'You should know, Austen. The ship that brought you home was fully loaded with sugar. I am going to the bonded warehouse on the floating dock to check—'

Austen turned away and stared out of the window at the familiar view of the Downs. He was sickened by it all. Sickened by his own experiences in Speightstown where he had behaved as all the Rudolf men behaved during their visits to the plantation. But at least he was not betraying anyone. Mungay continued to live as licentiously at home as he did on the plantation, although his wife probably guessed exactly what was going on.

So now Austen searched for his sister with mounting impatience. He strolled along the perimeter of the dance floor, his height enabling him to see across the heads of most of the dancers, and his long, dark, Rudolf face grew more saturnine with every step he took. And he was honest enough to know that his displeasure was centred deeply within himself and his own way of life. He hated Maude's frivolous, pointless existence because he hated his own. He was thirty years old, with a good brain and a love of beauty only partially satisfied by his growing collection of art. There had been no time for him to learn about such things; at eighteen he had been in the trenches and when he came home he had applied himself to learning the business. He had hoped that would be the way of salvation, learning the business like an art. The art of growing, refining, importing and selling sugar, literally from the roots. It had been expected of him and he had fulfilled all the expectations of his grandfather and his father. But something else had been expected of him. The climate and the way of life in Barbados had always encouraged a certain dissolution in the Rudolf men. It was called 'cutting their canes' rather than sowing wild oats. Austen had succumbed to every temptation offered to him, and hated himself at the same time. When he read *The Picture of Dorian Gray* he was physically sick. He recognized himself.

Suddenly, across the dance floor, he saw Maude. The dance was a foxtrot and her partner was an expert, which probably meant he was also a gigolo. His back was to Austen but everything about that back was personable; square-cut shoulders, long legs, tidy haircut – decent without being handsome. And then they did a quarter turn and his face became visible. It was Jack Martinez.

Austen shouldered his way through the dancers with minimal apologies. Maude had not seen him. Her head was thrown back showing a lot of throat. He supposed she was beautiful. And with her connections she would be a good catch. But Jack Martinez was not dancing with her for her beauty or her money. He was flouting the eighty-year taboo. He was a gambler and would one day be a roué.

He reached the couple and tapped Jack on the shoulder very politely.

'May I cut in?' He knew his smile was every bit as charming as Maude's. 'I believe this is a gentleman's Excuse-Me?'

He slid his sister away expertly and heard Jack's laughter in his right ear without pleasure. Jack Martinez cared for nothing. Austen looked into Maude's defiantly laughing face. He was no gambler himself, but he cared terribly that if he continued his visits to Plantation House he too might one day be a roué.

Harriet Martinez said, 'Jack, you are really naughty! You know very well it would upset Father and Aunt Caddie terribly if they knew you were flirting with Maude Rudolf!'

Jack could hardly control his laughter.

'She was flirting with me, little sister!' He tightened his mouth and pretended to look subdued. 'Let me confess all. I was standing with my drink, looking around for you and wondering whether to sign one of the programmes—' he indicated with his round chin the groups of non-dancers chatting vivaciously to each other and their attendant families. 'And she was sitting near by trying to get a cigarette into a holder. So what could I do but offer to help her?'

'Jack. You are incorrigible. When Father put me in your charge I nearly told him that the boot would be on the other foot entirely!'

'I haven't finished my tale.' He leaned on her slim

shoulder, suddenly helpless with mirth and then continued gaspingly, 'She simply chucked cigarette and holder on to the floor – it was jade, worth having a look around later – and stood up so that her Rudolf nose almost took mine off!' He controlled himself with difficulty. 'Sorry, sis, but it was a bit like that. And then she said, "Let's shock the whole bloody lot of 'em and dance!" And the next minute we jolly well were!'

'I saw,' Harriet said drily, 'and I cannot imagine that she would swear—'

'Honestly! She said exactly that!'

'Then she must be very fast indeed.'

'Oh, Hallie! When you go all pi on me I simply cannot bear it! She *is* very fast – everyone in Bristol knows that! Old Mungay can't control her – well, he's as bad himself – and her mother lies in bed all day and Austen has been in Barbados off and on since the war. Evidently he came back earlier than expected and . . .' He stifled another of his schoolboy giggles. 'Hallie, he was mad! I thought he might challenge me to a duel! Pistols at fifty paces in the dawn light on the Downs! Would you have been my second, little sister?'

Harriet said, 'Stop it, Jack. People are looking. You've done what you wanted, shocked everyone. Let it be.'

'Dance with me, sis.' Suddenly Jack was serious. 'I want him to see that my sister is . . . really beautiful.'

Harriet raised her brows. 'Jack? A compliment? You've had too much to drink!'

He held her gently and they side-stepped into the dancers.

'Yes, I have. But I'd say it again stone-cold sober.' He grinned. 'Hallie, one of your finest qualities is that you don't know about yourself. I hope the old man doesn't send you to that finishing-school place in Berne. They might spoil it.'

Harriet shook her head gently. 'Put a sock in it, Jack,' she advised in an exaggerated Bristol accent, and pulled him into a complicated step she had learned only the week before called the fish-hook.

Austen, guiding Maude back to the chair where he had left her Pimm's, caught a glimpse of the perfect oval of Harriet Martinez' face. It was a year since he had seen her last and that had been at her school during a Speech Day prize-giving when he had escorted his mother. She had been about sixteen, and had won what amounted to a consolation prize for being a 'good all-rounder'. He had thought then she looked a typical Martinez, good-looking without being striking. Brown hair, snub nose, freckles; surprisingly dark blue eyes. And long thin arms and legs which seemed to go in different directions.

Now she was different. He checked his stride and let Maude go on ahead. Her arms and legs were now perfectly co-ordinated and . . . perfect. Her bobbed hair and short skirt, lavender stockings and strap shoes made her look schoolgirlish still rather than flapperish. But there was something else, something he recognized with the essence of his being. It was . . . purity. She was a fashionable young lady, laughing and enjoying herself in this hotch-potch of pseudo-sophistication; yet she was apart from it. She was special. She was . . . pure. He could think of no other word.

He reached the table and Maude turned to him petulantly. 'My drink has gone! And I dropped my bloody ciggie holder. Can't see it anywhere!' She looked around her scornfully and said in an audible voice, 'What a den of thieves!'

For once, Austen could have agreed with her.

Mungay Rudolf emerged from the tall house in the Hotwells Road very late that night and walked to where he had left his Austin fifteen-horse-power car discreetly parked in the lee of one of his own warehouses. He stood on the runningboard and reached for the starting-handle. It was a glorious night; a harvest moon riding

28

just above the clutter of masts and spars in the river, the sky milky with stars. Mungay, scornful of most emotions, took time to stare upwards for a brief moment before feeding the handle through his hands and into the front of the car.

She came up first time; she always did – he had sworn by the internal-combustion engine right from its conception. He slid beneath the steering-wheel and pressed the accelerator encouragingly, smiled at the responsive roar, then settled back for the drive up the hill to the Downs. He felt good. After an evening with Lily Elmes he invariably felt good, but especially so tonight. Plans were afoot for enlarging the docks at Avonmouth. Lily had spoken with the County Planning Officer only the day before and it would seem almost settled. At present the Rudolf sugar was unloaded at Portishead and taken by dray to the refinery in the heart of the city. Mungay chugged up Whiteladies Road past the new University and planned a refinery in Avonmouth itself.

He arrived at the top of Blackboy Hill and struck across the Downs to High House, built by his father only sixty years before. His smile widened slightly at the very thought of the old man. A reprobate. That was the word for old Hanover Rudolf. When he had paid his fine and weathered the disgrace of the court case, he had turned over a new leaf with a kind of grim determination. At sixty-two he had married Grace Stuckey, the daughter of a Somerset farmer, with the sole intention of producing an heir to carry on the feud between himself and Charles Martinez. Mungay had not arrived until 1870 when his father was almost eighty and poor Grace forty. But Hanover had not died for another twenty years: long enough to instil his own loves and hates into his son. And to choose a suitable wife for him too: Florence was also from Somerset and in the same mould as her mother-in-law. She too took to her bed when she was forty.

Mungay pulled a face at the thought of Florence. With

Austen back from the Caribbean so soon, he would have to encourage her to come down for meals; maybe give a few tea-parties. Austen acted as if his father was some kind of gaoler. Well . . . the boy had a lot to learn.

He drove around the house to the stable block and saw that Sullivan's light was on. Sullivan had been a stable-lad in Hanover's day and had graduated reluctantly to being a chauffeur. Now he looked on the car as his own and resented the times Mungay took it into the city without him.

He appeared at the top of the steps which led to his room wearing a dressing-gown with his uniform cap perched on top of his bald head. Mungay straightened his face with difficulty and climbed out of the car to let the old man 'stable' it.

'Any trouble with them screen wipers, sir?' Sullivan asked as he hauled himself behind the wheel.

Mungay looked at the clear sky. 'It hasn't rained, Sully,' he said gently.

He smiled as he went indoors. So easy to be gentle with Sullivan; and Maude. So difficult with Florence; and Austen.

He frowned. It was odd that after each visit to the plantation, Austen seemed more withdrawn than ever. All the Rudolf men went to Barbados to relax. Why did it not work for Austen?

Jack said, half laughing, half serious, 'I did not steal the damned thing, Hallie!'

They were walking home: the Martinez family had always lived in the city within sight of their cellars.

Jack closed his gloved hand on the jade cigarette holder and pocketed it.

'I found it on the floor of the refreshment room!'

Harriet too laughed but still spoke sternly.

'You told me yourself she threw it down. You knew it belonged to her.'

' "She"? And just who is "she"?'

'You know very well! Stop treating me like a child, Jack!'

'But you are a child! Seventeen and never been kissed!'

'You know very well that holder belongs to Maude Rudolf.'

'Who threw it away!' he reminded her.

'Nevertheless—'

'Darling sis. You are such an innocent. Let me give you a lesson in flirtation. Maude Rudolf threw down that small *objet d'art* in order that I might pick it up and contact her with a view to returning it!'

Hallie was speechless for a long moment during which time Jack shortened his step to hers and minced along foolishly, still tittering.

She pulled her arm away and stopped in the middle of Park Street.

'You . . . you . . . philanderer!' she exploded.

'Ah, sis . . .' He took her by the waist and pirouetted her around. 'Come dance with me! Look at that moon – those stars – look at me! Can you honestly blame poor little Maude Rudolf for wanting to see such a handsome fellow again?'

'Her brother will kill you! His face was – was like stone tonight. And what about Father and Aunt Caddie? Have you forgotten the time Old Man Mungay drove them into a ditch across the moors? They *hate* us, Jack!'

'But we don't hate them, darling.' Jack stopped fooling and took her arm. 'I don't hate anyone in the world. And I'm certain you don't. You're incapable of hatred.'

She thought about that. The family feud had never bothered her, but she had thought it inordinately foolish until the incident in the motor car.

She said hesitantly, 'Of course our great grandfather did arrange for Mungay's father to go to gaol—'

'He paid a fine actually, sweetheart.'

'Well . . . it seemed a pretty dirty trick to play on him, I suppose. I mean, it wasn't certain that he kept slaves. It was just—'

'Darling, bearing that in mind, doesn't it seem to you that the feud ought to be over by now? And what better person to heal it than yours truly. Jack Martinez. Philanderer, gambler—'

'Don't say that, Jack,' Hallie put in quickly.

'Get your head out of the sand, Hal. Nothing wrong with gambling when you can afford it. And philandering – that's an art. Yes, I think I might be perfecting it!'

'Jack . . . you are . . .'

'I think you called me incorrigible before, Hallie.'

She gave in and laughed too. 'That's it, incorrigible,' she agreed.

Austen and Maude had arrived at High House almost an hour before Mungay. Maude was still petulant yet excited too. Austen, pouring himself some whisky at the sideboard, wondered whether she was drunk. Too much drink usually made his sister horribly sick and then horribly sober. Tonight her colour was high and she talked too much to be suffering from nausea.

He said, 'Time for bed, I think.'

'Not yet, Austen! Good Lord, it's not midnight yet! We should be still dancing!'

'It was you who decided to leave early,' he reminded her.

'And you were only too glad to get away.' She took the whisky bottle from him and poured herself a drink. 'Yes, I do drink whisky. Isn't it just too awful?'

'Not at all.' He refused to be baited and pushed the syphon towards her. 'In the islands, the white women drink rum or whisky. They think it kills any germs they might take in with the food.' He smiled. 'The Bajans are far cleaner than they are, of course. But they won't acknowledge that.'

'You love it out there, don't you?' She looked at him through her long lashes and did her nose trick. 'Tell me about it, Austen. I won't be in the least shocked, you know. I know what happens when the Rudolf men go to inspect the plantation. It's quite different from the times the women are there.'

He denied nothing. 'If you know, you do not need me to tell you.'

'I want all the gory details. I simply cannot imagine you . . . of all people. Daddy, of course. He followed in poor old Hanover's footsteps. But you . . . you've always been rather holier-than-thou—'

He snorted a laugh. 'Thank you, sis!'

'No, all right. But just tell me – is it still the same as when old Traitor Martinez went out there?'

He shrugged. 'How should I know?'

'Oh . . . *you*! I should know better than to pump you for any information! Pour me another drink and let's dance.'

She whirled to the gramophone and wound vigorously. He hesitated and then suddenly poured two more drinks and joined her. She had chosen the latest tango rhythm made popular by Rudolf Valentino. Their drinks held high they swooped and hesitated and bent and straightened expertly. Maude's eyes were brilliant and Austen could see that she was indeed aristocratically beautiful. He was proud of her. And probably over-concerned. He knew she was a flirt; the way she moved in the dance told him that, apart from her behaviour with Jack Martinez. She had too much Rudolf blood in her and not enough of Florence's. But it was the nineteen twenties: the jazz age. There were not many girls like Harriet Martinez. And probably by the time she had gone to finishing school she would be worse than Maude.

They whirled to the door just as it opened to admit Mungay.

He grinned hugely. Somehow, if he had a drink with his children and talked to them, he would be absolved from visiting Florence to say good night.

*   *   *

Charles Beeching Martinez, grandson of 'Traitor Martinez' as the Rudolfs put it, waited up with his sister, Cadiz, for the arrival of Jack and Harriet. They sat in companionable silence, either side of a low fire in the small morning-room of the house in St George Street where it was cosy and near the front door. The two servants, Mrs Yorke the cook and Rosie the 'rest', had been with them for a long time and had been sent to bed two hours before. Though Caddie Martinez knew only too well that Rose would not put out her light until she heard 'the children' arrive back home.

Cadiz Martinez was ten years younger than her brother and, at forty, was a handsome woman. Ever since the first Martinez had come over with his cask of fortified wine, the family had anglicized themselves in one way or another. Charles and his two children were both brown haired, blue eyed, round faced. Cadiz was the exception. Her name, for one thing, set her apart from the women folk of the Bristol merchants; the rest of her followed suit. Her black hair, worn in plaits coiled around each ear, was so glossy it seemed almost painted on her small neat head. Her eyes were black, her mouth wide and thin, her cheek bones high. She had spent a lot of time in the Castillo near Jerez in Spain, learning the business. If she tucked a flower behind one ear and picked up castanets she could have been a flamenco dancer. She looked foreign and she behaved . . . differently. She was therefore without a social life save that provided by Charles, and the children.

Now she looked up from the *Evening World*, removed her pince-nez and massaged the bridge of her nose. And Charles, his concentration disturbed by the rustle of her newspaper, looked up too and smiled.

'Go to bed, Caddie. They could be another hour.'

She said, 'I'm not in the least tired, Charles. And I want to know how Hallie got on just as much as you do!'

He laughed. 'She will have danced every dance and kept an eagle eye on Jack as well.'

Caddie smiled unwillingly. 'He is supposed to be chaperoning her.'

Charles merely laughed.

Caddie said suddenly, 'Charles, are you happy?'

He stopped laughing, surprised. 'Of course. You must know I am. No-one could have a fuller and more interesting life, Caddie. The business is doing well – because of you, my dear – I know I am no businessman. And our home life – also because of you – is tranquil and—'

'And you have been a widower for seventeen years. And I am a spinster.'

Cadiz never referred to herself as an old maid. Charles smiled, acknowledging that fact.

'We have both loved and lost, Caddie. And we know that the rest of the quotation is true. It is much, much better.'

'You have come out of it with your children, Charles.'

He was contrite. 'I know, my dear. But you share them. You love them as much as my Maria did. You must get a certain amount of pleasure—'

'They are my life, Charles. I know I am deeply involved in the business, but you and the children are my real life.'

'Ah. Caddie . . .' He was easily moved and closed his book to give her his full attention.

She said frankly, 'We are different, Charles. There is a strain in you – as there was in Father – of puritanism. I am not like that.'

He flushed slightly. 'You mean—'

'I mean that the love affair I had ten years ago is not enough for me.' She smiled slightly at his expression and went on, 'Please don't concern yourself, Charles. I am not about to bring another lover into the house. It was wartime then; Jack was away at school and Hallie was just a child. I would never be so indiscreet again. But

35

because of my . . . feelings . . . I know how Jack is . . . made.'

'You mean his gambling?' Charles asked, perplexed.

'It is not unlike business, is it, my dear? But I fancy Jack would not be a good businessman! I have to confess to you, Charles, that if there are any more fiascos like the one at university, the business will be strained to keep him afloat.'

Charles said, 'He promised me—'

'Take it from me, my dear, he is still gambling.'

Charles swallowed. 'I will speak to him, of course.'

'That would be good, I think. Make him realize that he has to finance himself from his allowance.' She sighed, knowing that Charles would make no impression on his volatile son. 'But I am thinking of something else. His emotions. There have been rumours—'

Charles said hurriedly, 'I will speak to him on . . . discretion.'

Caddie looked at him with her black eyes and said bluntly, 'Speak to him on the matter of birth control, Charles.'

'Caddie, really—'

She smiled. 'I'm sorry. You are such a dear brother. And you are right, we are happy. I am happy. Forget anything I have said which might seem to suggest anything else.' Her smile widened. 'I . . . am . . . happy. Dear Charles.' She flapped the paper open. 'And now. Take a look at this. Does it mean that the Avonmouth docks are to be enlarged? Because if so, Rudolf will be able to berth there and I would imagine he would build a refinery in Avonmouth itself.' She sat back. 'If only . . .'

Charles read the piece frowningly and said, 'I know. In the old days we used his ships, and an easy berth like this would be so advantageous to us. It would make a saving of . . . I don't know how much.'

'Has the time come to heal the breach d'you think?' she asked.

36

He sat back, folding the paper neatly.

'I am not sure, Caddie. Two generations separate you and I from that . . . incident. Only one separates Mungay. Hanover was his father. He was brought up on stories of betrayal.' He sighed. 'I am not sure.'

The door opened. It was Jack, laughing as usual. And Harriet tucked almost under his arm, pretending to struggle free.

She went straight to Caddie and kissed her.

'Did you have a lovely time, darling?'

'Oh, Aunt Caddie, thank you so much for giving me your ticket. It's quite different from the Children's ball, you know. It – it's sophisticated!'

'And did Jack take good care of you?' asked Charles, smiling up at his two children who were so . . . English.

Hallie looked at her brother and then said, 'He is absolutely incorrigible!'

But she would say no more. The Martinez were very careful about any kind of betrayal.

Three
January 1928

It was freezing hard. Even the river was frozen in places and a small tug snorted around the docks keeping it ice-free. It was too cold for snow but the frost rimed every object with delicate emphasis. Mungay, leaving the house before he could possibly set eyes on Maude, still found a space in his anger to admire the gorge, iced on both sides with spun silver.

Austen hurried out while the car was still clanking across the stable yard in its chains. He knew where his father was going and could guess why. The thought of any kind of alliance between the Rudolfs and Martinez was bitter as gall to Austen. Mungay had brought him up on the story of the Martinez betrayal and during the war he had only to think of it to renew his energy. Perhaps he had fought the Martinez rather than the Germans. But if he hoped to make a last-minute plea to Mungay, he was too late. His father stared stolidly at the back of Sullivan's head as Austen hammered on the window.

So he watched the car leave the grounds. He was still in his shirt-sleeves and hugged himself, shivering convulsively. There was nothing more he could do. He disassociated himself entirely from his father's actions. But as he turned to go indoors, he too could not help noticing the Downs in all their frigid glory. The wide heathlands rolled back from the lip of the Avon Gorge high above the city itself. A venue for circuses and fairs in the summer, now wrapped in a kind of narcissistic isolation.

He blinked his eyes and tightened his nostrils against the stinging cold and then realized he'd caught Maude's habit and stopped immediately.

He went inside.

Charles Martinez set out on foot. He owned a car – a box-like family-sized Morris. But it was garaged in the same livery stables as his four enormous dray horses, and was used for picnics in the summer and for transporting their luggage to Clevedon when they took holidays. Their town house was within easy walking distance of everything they needed.

He skirted the docks and struck up Baldwyn Street towards Christmas Steps. Rose had cautioned him to 'wrap the muffler twice around, sir dear, and get your nose right inside it' and though he had laughed, he did so now. His own breath was freezing his lungs.

He was more distressed than angry. And it was tempered with deep regret. Caddie had said rallyingly last night, 'Some good may well come out of this, Charles.' And of course he knew what she meant. Business. But Charles was a Martinez; the Rudolfs might – and did – go to Barbados to mix business with pleasure. The Martinez did not. It bordered on the immoral. Especially now. And yet that was what Mungay Rudolf must have in mind. Otherwise why would they be meeting at the Corn Exchange? Businessmen met in the Corn Exchange to seal bargains. Afterwards they went outside and struck the deal on the heads of the Bristol Nails. That was how it was done. There was no call to shake hands. No call for any physical contact. The Nails kept the whole business on an objective basis.

The two men sauntered side by side, hands clasping gloves behind their backs. They walked as far as the auctioneer's platform one side of the pillars, and returned on the other. Mungay opened the batting with a curt, 'I'm glad you came.' And Charles, his distress making him more sentient towards old Rudolf, heard the pain behind the fury and said simply, 'I'm just . . . so very sorry.'

Mungay's control slipped for just a second. 'Not half as sorry as I am!' he snapped.

Charles cleared his throat and said nothing. What was there to say? When casks leaked and wine spoiled there was nothing to be done.

But Maude was no cask and Jack was not a wine. And there was something to be done. He unbuttoned his great-coat and let it swing open. He always wore a morning suit for the office and the sight of it seemed to return him to normality.

He said pacifically, 'I take it by asking me to meet you here, you have no wish to . . . to . . .' He could not bring himself to talk about abortions and managed to change course in mid-stream. 'To ban Jack from – er – seeing your daughter – and even—'

Mungay interrupted bitterly. 'I had intended to pack him off to the plantation on some pretext. People disappear fairly easily out there.'

Charles swallowed and felt his blood temperature drop further still. Did Rudolf mean he would have had Jack abducted? Perhaps the stories handed down from the mid-nineteenth century were not so far-fetched after all.

Mungay swept on. 'Maude wants to marry the bounder. And as she has always had her way—'

'You mean you will agree to it?'

'That is why we are here. What sort of authority do you have over your son?'

Charles hardly knew. He had 'spoken' to him as he'd promised Caddie back last September, but he knew very well the gambling continued. Jack meant well; he always meant well. But he was so easily diverted.

'We are a reasonable family. But if I have to ask him to pretend to cast Maude off . . . he is deeply in love with her.'

Or so he said. Charles privately doubted if he knew what love meant. But Caddie believed him. Caddie said she and Jack were alike, so perhaps she knew better than he did himself.

'Does he wish to marry her?'

'He is determined to do so. Whatever the outcome of this meeting.'

Mungay glanced sourly at his companion. If the boy had felt any other way he would personally have sought him out and horsewhipped him. But the knowledge that he loved Maude honourably gave him no pleasure either.

'So there is no need for you to use your . . . authority.' Mungay made the last word sound insulting. Charles twisted his gloves behind his back and just for a moment his distaste for this whole affair simmered into sheer dislike of the Rudolf clan.

Mungay went on, 'There will be a good settlement, of course. And I have a property in Dowry Square which I will transfer into their names—' Charles made as if to protest but Mungay shook his head impatiently. 'I prefer to see my daughter settled properly. After that – we shall see.'

Charles thought it wiser to make no comment at this stage. He conquered his momentary burst of antipathy and listened as Mungay rolled on.

'Maude is headstrong. She will want her own way, but I understand your son is fairly amiable and easygoing.' Again there was a suggestion of a sneer in this description.

But Charles was suddenly heartened. If Jack was besotted with the girl then she might be able to get him away from the gaming tables.

He said, 'Above everything, he is kind. He will be a good husband. And I think a good father too.'

Mungay was silent, slightly mollified. They paced through the cast-iron archways and he too unbuttoned his greatcoat. It was an unconsciously conciliatory gesture. He was wearing a thick tweed suit, a heavy gold watch chain hung loosely across his flat stomach.

He said, 'Do I take it we are agreed on the marriage then?'

Charles said sincerely, 'With pleasure. I do not know your daughter, but Jack has described her in glowing terms.'

He should have let his first sentence stand alone. At the second, Mungay snorted derisively, shoved his hands into the pockets of his greatcoat and drew it over his watch chain.

Charles said quickly, 'I think . . . in time . . . you will come to . . . Jack is – well – as you said, easygoing. He will want to make your daughter happy—'

'He will continue to spoil her as I have done.' Mungay snorted again but this time with some amusement. 'Yes. Perhaps that will be best. She would not take kindly to any man who tried to restrain her.' He took a deep breath, turned and began the walk back. 'It should be soon.'

'The wedding? Of course.'

'The pregnancy has advanced almost four months already. It must have happened soon after that blasted Michaelmas Ball.'

Mungay was used to speaking frankly and was amused to see from the corner of his eye that Martinez was blushing. He despised him. Ever since that fiasco at the plantation, the Martinez family had pretended to be lily-white. Well, old Hanover had told him that 'Traitor' Martinez had indulged himself well enough when he had gone to inspect the sugar canes. And now this Jack had proved himself to be no pious celibate. Mungay felt a sudden twinge of sympathy for Jack Martinez.

He went on, 'It had better be a quiet affair. We can't stop the gossip – indeed I think Maude will decide to revel in it – but I am not going to be held up publicly to ridicule.'

'No.' Charles was fervent about this. Even if

everything had been perfectly above-board he would have wished to avoid the limelight.

Mungay continued to 'tie up the loose ends', as he put it, while they paced the hall four more times. And then, when it might have seemed that they had reached a conclusion, he paused by the dais and slapped his gloves on the dusty boards.

'I suppose . . . this will force our families to . . .'

Charles said gladly, 'Heal the breach?'

He was not thinking as Caddie had thought, about business. It was just that having to pretend the Rudolfs did not exist was so difficult and downright inconvenient.

'Well, bridge it at any rate. I cannot see that it will ever heal. After what happened between my father and your grandfather.'

'Umm . . . so long ago,' Charles mentioned.

'Not when such a disgrace has been visited upon—'

'But it enhanced his reputation!' Charles protested. 'Everyone knew he was a rogue—'

'Watch your tongue, sir!' Mungay slapped the boards again and dust rose coldly and acridly. 'My father was a normal red-blooded man. Much as your son is, it would seem!'

'I simply meant that in the end there was no harm done. You have to admit it, Rudolf!'

'I admit nothing. And as for the betrayal of a friendship. Your grandfather was like a son to—'

'But it's over and done with! And now our children – who obviously wish to forget it all – are to be married.'

Mungay simmered down and took a deep breath.

'Quite. I began to say . . . if we are to be linked again, it may be possible to turn the whole thing to some business advantage.'

Charles looked away down the hall. He did not like this. Somehow to him this *was* betrayal. But Caddie said they needed to retrench. She had told him exactly what

43

to say. And she had also told him not to beg. It was advantageous to both sides.

So he waited for Mungay to make the suggestion.

'We could return to the bad old days. The *Ulysses* could call directly at Cadiz then continue to Bristol with your cargo of wine.'

Charles said, 'I have to admit, that arrangement would suit us very well.'

Mungay snorted. 'I should think so!'

Charles continued smoothly, 'And of course it will suit you also.'

Mungay began to draw on his gloves. He had started to wonder if there was a core anywhere to this soft man. He was glad to find it. He inclined his head.

'I will give you times of sailing. You will arrange harbourage and transport to the yards.'

'Excellent.'

It was. The Rudolfs had always owned two ships; the Martinez had not wished to take on another business and had shipped their wine privately and expensively.

Mungay began to button his coat.

Charles said, 'I wonder, do you think your daughter would appreciate honeymooning at the Castillo?'

At last Mungay managed a small smile of genuine amusement.

'Perhaps you would suggest it. She takes nothing kindly from me any more.'

Charles thought of Jack who might be feckless but was warm and full of fun. And then he thought of Harriet, so like her mother. And was thankful.

Mungay said, 'Shall we settle on the Nail?'

'Very well.'

The two went outside and stood beneath the porticoed entrance shrugging themselves deeper into their coats at the sudden cold sifting up from the river. Opposite the Exchange a hurdy-gurdy man plied his trade; his monkey was visibly shivering.

They went to the first of the cast-iron bollards

where so many had 'paid on the nail'. Mungay laid a
clenched fist on the top and Charles brought his own to
meet it.

'On the nail,' he said.

And Mungay echoed, 'On the nail.'

When the car arrived at the Hotwells office Mungay
found Austen in the outer room where two clerks
were going through bills of lading with him. He did not
even glance up at his father's entrance. Mungay strode
through the room past the high-topped desks, his greatcoat making a draught that disturbed the papers. The
two clerks leaned temporarily on their piles of bills.
Mungay said curtly, 'My office when you're ready,' and
disappeared through the opposite door.

Sullivan appeared holding an umbrella and a brief
case.

'Not too bad,' he said to no-one in particular and
followed Mungay.

Austen's jaw tightened and he bent his head again.

'The consignment to the Birmingham warehouse is
not accounted for,' he said, checking a list in his own
hand. 'Bourneville will be needing their usual order after
Lady Day.'

'I think we have it here, sir. Loaded at the goods siding
on the overnight . . .'

Austen listened, checked, ticked his list and then
turned to the wages book.

'No hurry for this, sir,' said the other clerk. 'If you
want to get through to Mr Mungay—'

'We'll finish the morning's work first,' Austen said in
his smoothest voice. 'Pay day tomorrow, Golding. You
will need to go the bank this afternoon.'

'Very well, Mr Austen.'

They bent again to the books. The warehousemen,
loaders, and checkers all worked a nine-hour day including Saturdays. It had been discovered when men
came back from the trenches, that if they were paid on

45

a Friday they did not turn up for work on Saturdays. Therefore the Rudolfs paid their men on Saturdays. It meant keeping a great deal of money in the safe on Friday night. But Mungay never minded sleeping in his office once a week. Lily Elmes usually kept him company.

In his own good time, Austen closed his checking book and went into his father's office.

Mungay was sitting in front of a good fire, a glass of whisky at his side. Sullivan stood by the window, watching the drays being loaded with sugar sacks and muttering disapprovingly.

'You can go now, Sully.' Mungay looked at the old man and grinned. 'They can look after horses as well as you can, old soldier! But they can't drive a car! Go on – get it filled with petrol and be back here at three. I'll go home for tea – make my peace there – and you can drive me back down at eight.'

'Thank you, Mr Mungay.'

Sullivan grinned himself at the unexpected compliments and actually remembered to touch his cap as he left.

Mungay's grin broadened. 'Old reprobate. Didn't like it one bit when I got him to fill the coal hod and make up the fire! Who does he think he is?'

'A skilled man and a friend of the family,' Austen replied drily as he settled himself opposite his father. 'You can't treat Sully like you do Amos and Sugar at the plantation.'

Mungay actually barked a laugh. 'My God, Austen, the boot is on the other foot! Amos and Sugar tell me what to do!' He chose a cigar from the box on the mantelpiece and began the process of cutting and lighting it.

'You've guessed about Sugar, I suppose?'

Austen was immediately wary. Sugar was an old lady in her seventies, but he put nothing past his father.

'She's your cousin. Her mother, Alice, was my sister.'

46

Austen was not surprised. Sugar was the palest cream colour.

'That makes Amos my second cousin.' He smiled ruefully. 'In other words, if I don't have children, Amos's brood should inherit the Plantation House.'

Mungay frowned. 'Don't be absurd, Austen!' He saw Austen's expression and went on quickly, 'Anyway, Maude will have a son.'

Austen held his father's gaze. 'Ah yes. A Martinez. The new owner of the plantation.'

Mungay threw his cigar into the fire with the same petulance Maude had displayed at the Michaelmas Ball. He let out a string of curses until he exhausted himself. Then flung himself back in his chair.

'Damn you, Austen! I had no choice in the matter, did I?' He opened his eyes. 'It's up to you, son! You won't let that happen, will you?'

Austen said, 'I would very much prefer the place to go to one of Amos's children.'

But Mungay shook his head decisively. 'Once you start going the wrong side of the sheets . . . it won't do. You must have a family. And soon. Dammit, you are thirty!'

Austen shifted his gaze to the fire. He had vowed celibacy after the last trip to Barbados. And gradually, through the long English winter, he had attained some peace of mind. Until this business with Maude.

He said heavily, 'You had not thought this through, Father. It is not too late to change your mind.'

'It is.' Mungay took some deep breaths. 'It is, old son. We settled it on the Nail.'

It was Austen's turn to curse. He did so quietly but with more real venom than his father had shown. Then, unbidden, he had a picture of Harriet Martinez. Her face swam before him, naïve, ordinary, dominated by those violet eyes. Brown hair cut in the bob he had never liked; a boy's shape in one of the short shapeless dresses he hated. But those dark blue eyes and their sudden connecting stare . . . and the sense of complete purity.

47

He shivered and leaned forward to warm his hands. It was damned cold in that outer office; he wondered how the poor devils of clerks could hold their pens.

At last he said in his usual calm voice, 'I suppose you drove a good bargain?'

'I suppose you could say that.' Mungay too stopped staring and looked into the fire. 'However, I'm not sure whether the Martinez family won't come out of it better than we shall.'

Austen said sharply, 'We must make damned sure they don't!'

Jack said, 'I came as soon as I could, my darling. Pa returned for lunch and told me it was all right and I tried to look as though I actually liked toad-in-the-hole and cabinet pudding—'

Maude screamed with laughter. 'Toad-in-the-what?'

She looked like a handsome boy in a woollen shift, cut as a tabard, with the tall collar and enormous sleeves of a silk shirt worn beneath it. She drove him mad. He seized her and danced her around the morning room where the maid had shown him ten minutes before. They half fell on to the sofa and she held him against her and kissed him.

He surfaced, gasping. 'Oh God, Maudie – the child—'

'He's a tough little bastard – he'll come to no harm.' She drew his face down again and kissed him while he shouted his laughter.

'You're wicked! He won't be a bastard! We're going to get married!'

She pushed him away and pouted pretended petulance.

'How boring! I wanted to produce a bastard! I wanted to live in sin in some dreadful hovel by the docks and be ostracized by everyone and—'

He pulled her up, suddenly serious.

'Darling, be serious. You do want to get married really, don't you?'

She stared at him prolonging the intensity of the look until he was shaking. Then she said, 'I don't know any more. I only know that I want you. All the time.'

She reached for him and he said, 'Maudie – please – where are they?'

'Daddy? Austen? At the office. They'll be home for tea and we can have it all together.'

He was almost lost. He managed to say, 'And your mother?'

'In bed, darling. Where we should be.'

'Honestly, Maudie, you really are—'

'I know, darling. But what difference does it make now? Gather ye rosebuds, my angel-man. Just gather ye rosebuds.'

The flooded water meadows on the Wells Road were frozen hard enough for skating. That afternoon three of the 'old girls' from Saunton School met there with their skates. They had not seen each other since the previous summer: Harriet and Margo Adams were now eighteen, Tilly Hesterman nineteen next month.

'We're getting old, girls!' Margo announced as she struggled with her skates. 'And nothing is *happening*!'

'We shall have a season next autumn,' Harriet reminded her consolingly. 'And you've been to Switzerland and Tilly has been goodness-knows-where.'

Tilly was horse-faced in a charmingly aristocratic way, and very serious.

'Only London.' She tugged her laces unmercifully tight and slid down the frosted grass to the ice. 'Hard as nails, girls. And we've got it to ourselves!' She pushed herself off and glided over the ice while the other two cheered.

Harriet was next. 'You're an angel, Tilly,' she called. 'But if you keep on with the heroics you're going to die young!'

They all laughed. Harriet Martinez looked spiritual but was very down-to-earth.

'And what do you mean by that?' Tilly spluttered.

'She means—' Margo joined them pantingly. 'She means that you just had to be first on the ice to test it. And you're doing all this work in London at the Settlement or whatever it's called, putting yourself in the front line again.'

'Tommy-rot!' Tilly grinned and showed big square teeth. 'Someone had to be first on the ice. And someone has to help put things right. And anyway, girls, can you imagine me in white with a tiara . . . my bloody dance programme would be empty and everyone would be embarrassed!'

Harriet skated around her friend looking dismayed. 'Oh, Tilly! Are you going to back out of the season? It's not as if it's like London. We know all the local men and they're a pretty harmless lot!'

But Tilly did not want to talk about it.

'Take my hand – Margo, grab Hallie. Let's do a whizz!'

The girls began to rotate faster and faster. Margo on the outside of the radius screamed helplessly. When the spin was only just under control they slowed, their faces glowing with effort and cold.

'This is marvellous!' Harriet skated free, lifting her gloved hands to the metallic sky worshipfully. 'To be free like this! To be with you two who have seen me have nose bleeds and be sick and—'

Tilly said prosaically, 'And wet your knickers—'

Margo screamed anew. The girls came together again and skated sedately around the ice not unlike Mungay Rudolf and Charles Martinez had moved around the Corn Exchange a few hours before.

Harriet said, 'Tell us about the Settlement, Tilly. Could I come and work there?'

Tilly smiled delightedly. 'Why not? They'd think you were straight from heaven – they adore pretty girls and I'm a great disappointment to them.'

Harriet looked at her with disgusted disbelief.

Tilly went on enthusiastically. 'It's true, you know. They really love to see us in our fur coats and cloches. I wore my riding stuff the first morning – thought it was practical and would close the enormous gap . . . I soon saw it wasn't like that. They want to put us on pedestals, so that we can reach down and haul them up!'

Harriet said doubtfully, 'I don't like the sound of it. Being Lady Bountiful and all that. But . . . with Jack getting married I think I should do something with my summer.'

Tilly opened her eyes wide. 'Your Jack – your brother Jack? Getting *married*? Who on earth has managed to hook him?'

Harriet said, 'I thought you would know.' Her colour deepened. 'I thought everyone in the city knew. Maude is so . . . uncaring—'

'I haven't heard a thing. Remember I got home only yesterday. I would have preferred to spend my birthday in London, but Ma said my birthday concerned her just as much as it concerned me and I was to be at home or else!' Tilly laughed. She and her mother were very close. 'So, of course, I had to obey the matriarchal command. I simply cannot believe that Jack Martinez is getting married!'

Harriet said, 'He always liked you, Tilly. He said you were the only girl he knew who could talk to him properly.'

'Tommy-rot. I like a flutter on the horses, that's what he really meant!'

Margo, who had had a 'thing' about Jack Martinez since she was fourteen, said painfully, 'Is it true? The rumours?'

Harriet took her friend's arm.

'Margo, darling. I had forgotten how you felt about my wretched brother. It was just a schoolgirl crush though, wasn't it?'

'Of course. But – like Tilly – I didn't think he would

51

actually marry for years and years. And as for marrying a Rudolf . . . well, I just have to assume that what they say is the truth.'

Harriet spoke through Tilly's loud exclamations of further disbelief.

'Maude Rudolf is having his child, yes.' She seemed relieved to have spoken the words and smiled at both of them. 'It's not the end of the world, of course. But Maude is . . . well, almost brazen about it. I can't help wondering if she's doing it just to shock. That's unfair of me—'

'Maude was at Saunton with my sister,' Margo said. 'She was nearly expelled twice. It was the Rudolf money that kept her there.'

Harriet hastened to be fair. 'They're terribly in love. They've been meeting clandestinely all winter and I've been in their company twice. It's as if other people become invisible.' She paused. 'It was peculiar. I found myself feeling cold and excluded.'

'You mean you want to fall in love.' Margo squeezed her friend's arm. 'It'll happen. Next winter – just you see—'

'But a season . . . it's so calculated. Like a sort of slave market. We're put on show for the men to pick and choose.'

'I agree entirely,' Tilly said strongly. 'You really should join me, Hallie.'

'No. I have to do it. Daddy would be shattered if I didn't. And I want to help with the baby too.' She squeezed Tilly's hand. 'But I've got all the spring and summer.'

'Right. That's settled. Come with me. You can do the soup kitchen.'

'Really?'

'Yes, really. And what about you, Margo?'

But Margo did not like London, and she had a feeling there would be unpleasant smells at the Settlement. She hated unpleasant smells above all else.

'My sister is also having a baby, remember. Next month. I want to be with her.'

Tilly drew her mouth over her teeth, recognizing a flimsy excuse when she heard one. Harriet said, 'Let's forget all that. Let's pretend we're fourteen again. Let's do another whizz.'

And they did.

Four
May 1928

The block of mansion flats overlooking the river in Pimlico came alive about seven-thirty each morning when the small flower shop in the foyer had its first delivery from Covent Garden. The doorman appeared from behind the reception desk and the cleaners, who had been surreptitiously at work since before dawn, melted away to be replaced by two girls in very smart uniforms. The day had begun.

It was the first really summery day since Harriet had arrived in London. She and Tilly emerged from the lift and were greeted smilingly by the handful of people in the foyer. All Miss Hesterman's guests were 'real nice', all engaged in good works, some more quietly than others. But these two girls, Miss Hesterman's niece and her friend, managed to make the good works sound hopeful instead of despairing. Also the younger one was downright pretty, which made a change. Though not so pretty as when she had arrived. They were doubtless driving her too hard and she wasn't really up to it.

Harriet bought her usual small bunch of flowers; stocks this morning, cerise with the dew still on them.

Tilly shook her head helplessly.

'Honestly, Hallie! You don't give flowers to men! And I'm sure he'd rather have the sixpence for some breakfast.'

Harriet smiled, hung her handbag in the crook of her elbow and took her friend's arm with her spare hand.

'He'd spend it on beer, as you very well know! And he used to have a garden. I'm wooing him back to

54

Nature!' She laughed at herself and then paused on the pavement to draw a deep breath. 'Tilly, I know I don't fit in here – London is not my place – but I can see why you love it. On a morning like this, it's so fresh!'

Tilly smiled too, well pleased.

'I knew you'd like it eventually! And it's not just the weather – the freshness lies in the possibilities!'

Harriet lengthened her stride to fit in with her tall friend's. They arrived at the tube and began to descend. The freshness disappeared and Harriet felt her usual sense of doom. She tried to combat it.

'How do you mean?' she asked.

'Anything could happen here. The place is charged with excitement.' Tilly swept her spare arm around the grubby arch of the tunnel. 'This hole – the Settlement which isn't much better – everything is full of . . . of . . . *possibilities!*'

The train arrived while they were still laughing; they found seats and sat back with satisfaction. They were in good time. They would cut bread and butter and pour the tea for breakfast and then the bones would arrive from Smithfield and they would begin on the soup. Harriet thought of Cook's delicious winter concoctions and sighed. She had a nasty feeling she would never be able to tackle a plate of soup again. And her hands were absolutely done for. She drew off a glove and held the stocks in her bare hand hoping that the odour of onions might be neutralized by them.

Tilly glanced at her. 'Isn't it wonderful to have hands that look as if they've actually been doing something?'

They both pulled off their gloves and lined their hands up as if for inspection, and started to laugh yet again. And for a while Harriet forgot the hopelessness of the Settlement and even thought she might one day find fulfilment there as Tilly did. After all, old Walter always appreciated the flowers. So she must be doing some good.

* * *

Cadiz Martinez was early at the Denmark Street office too. The night before, she and Charles had dined at the house in Dowry Square. Mungay and his wife, Florence, had been there also and what between the family abrasions and the sight of Maude's fecundity, Cadiz had not slept very well. The early sunshine had promised instant rejuvenation and she found she worked better without Charles' presence.

She sat at his desk studying a time chart of picking, pressing, fermentation and 'laying down' and gradually realized that the oppressive ennui of the night had not gone. Something was the matter with her. Illness? The dreaded 'change'?

She sat back in Charles' chair and closed her eyes; the sunlight was too bright and there was a nagging pain above the bridge of her nose where her pince-nez clipped the skin. She removed the glasses impatiently, and with the sudden exquisite relief of the pressure she let herself think of Jonathan Pomeroy.

It was eleven years ago; she worked that out with something of a shock. And with even more shock she admitted to herself how rarely she thought of him any more. When he had been killed she had lived with the memory of him by her side; never an hour went by but his face came into her mind, his voice spoke to her, the salty smell of his sweat – a sweat of fear – was in her nostrils. And now, no longer.

She felt her eyes grow hot beneath the closed lids. As if she were a traitor. Yet another Martinez betrayer. And then, with complete reassurance, she knew that Jonathan had become so much part of her that she no longer needed to resurrect him meticulously into her thoughts. He was simply there.

In any case there would have been no future for them; she knew that also. She had been twenty-eight, already an astute businesswoman. Jonathan's commission had been purchased by his family; he was twenty and so raw he made twelve-year-old Jack seem sophisticated.

She remembered the first night he had been billeted on them. He had taken over the small morning room where she and Charles liked to sit in the winter. His regiment, the Somerset Foot, were training before embarkation. He was so frightened the whites of his eyes showed all the time.

She had gone downstairs for a book and heard him weeping. It had been natural – a sisterly act – to go to him and comfort him. But he had wanted more. There was a desperation about him that pushed him into completely uncharacteristic behaviour. He pulled at her clothing and mouthed her neck and ears, sobbing helplessly as he fumbled inexpertly. She never knew why she helped him. At first it may well have been pity. Later it became a grand passion that swept them both away.

For the remainder of that time he shared her room. She made no secret of it, and though Charles was shocked and stipulated that the children must not know, he too accepted the situation as another of her eccentricities and was merely fearful for her future.

There was to be no future. Jonathan Pomeroy was killed on Vimy Ridge in 1917. And though he was never spoken of openly, the children had gradually pieced together gossip and fact and knew that Aunt Caddie had 'loved and lost' and – they both agreed – was probably better for it.

Cadiz opened her eyes and smiled wryly. If only her frantic love affair had produced the same result as Jack's and Maude's.

And there, quite suddenly, she had the reason for her definite depression. She laughed aloud, surprised at the simplicity of the revelation and her own meanness of spirit. She was jealous of her own nephew!

She reached for her pince-nez and clipped them on firmly, refusing to wince at the return of the pain. And then she drew the order book to her and began to make lists of Christmas consignments.

At ten o'clock Charles arrived looking spruce. She surveyed him unsmilingly.

'Give me another half an hour here, Charles. I have everything where I can see it and work out—'

'Please, Caddie! Stay there all day if you wish. I am meeting Mungay for sherry at midday and we are lunching at the Club.'

Cadiz erupted. 'Charles – how could you? Last night was bad enough! We don't have to make the Rudolfs blood brothers just because Jack has married that hoyden of a daughter!'

Charles' blue eyes opened with surprise. He said, 'But I thought the whole idea was to bridge—'

'Which happened with that ridiculous marriage! And it's plain to see that once the child is old enough, Maude will be off with her old set again—'

Charles' face lengthened with disapproval.

'Really, Caddie. I think you are not giving the young people a chance. If anything was plain to see last night, it was that Maude is besotted with Jack. And Jack—'

'Is not besotted with her – don't try to fool yourself that far, Charles, for goodness' sake!'

'Naturally Jack feels a little oppressed at the mo—'

'*Jack* oppressed! It's Maude who is carrying that enormous child!'

Charles relaxed suddenly.

'Caddie, listen to yourself. You haven't a good word to say for anyone. First it's Maude who is on the point of straying. Then it's Jack who is being totally un-reasonable.' He leaned on the desk in his frank way. 'Listen, sis, you are still riddled with the old prejudices. Surely if Mungay can forgive and forget, you can?'

'I am not at all certain how deeply his so-called forgiveness goes, Charles.' She half-smiled at him be-cause he was right, of course. She knew she was being unreasonable. But apart from the self-discovery of an hour ago, she was also deeply disturbed by the vulnera-bility of Jack's marriage. 'He has come out of this business smelling very well indeed. You notice his son was not at the dinner last night? There lies the true Rudolf feelings. Of that I am certain.'

He straightened. 'Yes. You are right in that Austen Rudolf is determined not to compromise in any way. But do not be like he is, Caddie. It is not in your nature. Austen is a cold fish and you are not.'

She did not deny this and after admitting mute surrender with a deep sigh she waved him away. 'Go and enjoy your lunch. And if you get a chance to reduce the landing charges on *Ulysses*, for goodness' sake, take it!'

Charles, who had no intention of marring a pleasant summer lunch with haggling, smiled, nodded and was gone.

Caddie leaned back in his chair and removed the pince-nez again for a moment. She knew that Charles was right. She felt at odds with the lovely weather, with Charles, with herself. For the first time she was thankful Hallie was out of it all. It seemed to her to be a mish-mash of hypocrisy at the moment and it was souring her. She frowned at that word. Sour. She was forty years old and a spinster. Too late for children. Barren. Sour.

And then, because she was Caddie Martinez and possessed of a sense of humour, she smiled and mentally shook herself. As she said to the family, she was not an old maid. She had had her love affair. And it was part of her. It had made her what she was.

Maude smoothed her satin nightie across her abdomen outlining it unattractively.

'Of *course* the weather makes it worse!' she said bitterly to Jack as he came and went between the bedroom and dressing-room. 'It's bad enough when I can huddle into that ghastly silk raincoat! But when the sun is shining like today, it's going to be obvious to one and all that I am the model for the latest airship!'

Jack laughed, then saw she was not joking and straightened his face with difficulty.

'Darling. Baby. Honey. You're pregnant. If you weren't, it would be different. But everyone knows—'

'If I weren't pregnant and still the size of a house, I'd kill myself.'

Jack came to the bed and put his own hands next to hers. Beneath them he could feel his baby stirring. It was terrifying.

'I wish you wouldn't talk so extravagantly, Maudie. It cannot be good for you.'

She pouted. 'You used to adore the way I talked extravagantly. You said I was outrageous. And you loved me being outrageous.' She put her arms around his neck before he could take evasive action. 'Dearest Jack, don't go to that silly old office. Stay with me. Let's have a day in bed.' She kissed him. 'Let's stay in bed all day and make love every hour on the hour! Let's—'

He reached behind him and unclasped her fingers, managing to laugh as he did so.

'Sweetheart, you know I have to go in today. My father is lunching with your father. Which means I can get Aunt Caddie on her own and pump her for extra funds.'

'Some hopes! She doesn't like me and she hates the idea of the old feud coming to an end. She probably enjoyed it. It fed her in some way. Old maids are like that you know, Jack.'

Jack felt a now-familiar pang and refused to recognize it as dislike.

'Maybe a spinster, but never an old maid – that's my Aunt Caddie!' He laughed, standing up, still holding her hands but at arm's length. 'And you've got her wrong, my angel. Father does not understand me – he thinks he does but he and Hallie are so darned . . . *good*! Caddie and I . . . we're the wicked ones!'

'Oh, I'm not denying she is wicked. That is why she won't give you any more money.'

He put her palms together and went to the cheval mirror to knot his tie.

'Then pray for me, honey. Pray for us both. We need that five hundred pounds badly.'

He watched her in the mirror. He knew he was making a fuss about this debt and she knew why. She could have got the money out of her old man with ease. Mungay would give her anything she asked for. She could have made out she needed new clothes or a special piece of jewellery . . . But no. For some reason she refused to ask her family for anything.

Now she put her hands carefully on top of the sheet and leaned back on the pillows with her eyes closed. He frowned.

'Listen, baby, if you're feeling the heat so badly, shall I ask Caddie if you can go to the Flower House?'

'The Flower . . . oh you mean your summer monstrosity in Clevedon.' She opened her eyes then closed them dismissively. 'As if I'd want to go there where I don't know a soul. You're just trying to get rid of me!'

'Don't be absurd.' He had broken his thumb nail on his collar stud and gnawed at it irritably. 'You've just said you don't want to go out where you might be recognized! No-one would know you in Clevedon! And you could take someone with you – how about Stella Winters?' He deliberately named the fastest of her friends thinking she would jump at it. If only he could get a clear run of games he would soon recoup his losses. The trouble with Maude being pregnant was that she wanted his company the whole time.

But apparently Stella was the last person on earth she wanted at this moment.

'Surely you can see that in this state I need someone who is concerned. If only Austen weren't so set against us being married, he would be ideal. But he's hopeless! And your aunt hates me. I wish Hallie was at home. Now she'd be perfect. We could talk together – read – take walks – it would be marvellous.'

He was amazed.

'You hardly know Hallie. How can you possibly—'

'We had a long talk actually. Just before she went to London. She promised me she would come home for the birth. She was happy about it all. And . . . sort of . . . well, excited.' She stared at him. 'I like her. That's all. And I think given half a chance she would like me. She's open-minded. And fair.'

He stared back. 'Yes she is. But I didn't think she was your sort, old girl. I mean, like I said just now, she's so darned good. Almost goodie good.' He fiddled with his cuff-links. 'But if you want her to go with you to Clevedon, I can practically guarantee that she will. I'll phone her from the office if you like.' He frowned again. 'Are you serious, Maudie? Because if I get her back home and you won't go, I shall be . . . cross.'

She rolled her eyes in mock terror. 'And what will you do when you are . . . cross?' She laughed. 'Come here and let me do those cuff-links.' She fastened them expertly and he leaned down and pecked her cheek. She said, 'I am serious, Jack. Very serious. I think if I could spend these last few weeks quietly in Clevedon with Hallie, it would be wonderful. For me, and for the baby.'

He straightened and saluted.

'Your word is my command.' He grinned. 'How do I look?'

'You look beautiful.' She spoke yearningly as if she had already lost him. He waved, kicked his heels and was gone.

At the end of that day Harriet's bunch of stocks were still keeping fresh in a jam-jar on the shelf of the soup kitchen.

She said to Tilly, 'What on earth can have happened to old Walter? Has he slipped in when I was cooking d'you think?'

'No. I asked Aunt Hester to keep an eye open.'

Tilly's aunt had arrived at midday to help with the

serving. She was now upstairs using the Keating's liberally around the cramped beds.

'It's the first time he's missed a kitchen since I arrived,' Harriet said forlornly.

'It's the nice weather. He went down to the river and found someone to buy him a drink.'

'Yes. Probably.'

Harriet dried the last of the enamel mugs and hung them up. This morning's euphoria had gone with the sunshine. She felt cold and hoped that the tube would not be too crowded. Apart from old Walter the population at the Settlement was shifting and shiftless. She wondered what lasting good their work could possibly do.

Tilly said, 'Take the flowers up to Aunt Hester, Hallie. They'll brighten the dorm a little. Might make someone feel at home.'

Hallie smiled gratefully for Tilly's understanding and took the jam-jar through to the big community room. Several of the men were still sitting there looking at newspapers, and as she wound her way through the trestle tables to the stairs, they made token grabs at her skirt. Tilly said that sort of thing was just a sign of appreciation for a pretty girl, but Hallie could not get used to it and ran up the stairs red-faced and uncomfortable.

The big dormitory was at least empty of people, save for Aunt Hesterman who was sprinkling the end bed vigorously.

She looked up at Hallie's arrival and said sternly, 'Carbolic baths tonight, Hallie. This nice weather is hatching 'em out fast.'

'Oh, horrors!' Hallie felt her flesh creep and was immediately ashamed. With sudden cruel clarity she saw that she was not suited to this work. The romantic gesture – flowers for an old man who loved gardens – yes, that was her forte. When it came to carbolic and lice she was only just able to control her disgust.

Miss Hesterman knew too because she said, 'Don't worry, dear. I used to vomit quite regularly when I started. It doesn't take long to accept it all. Look at my Tilly.' Her voice was full of pride. Harriet wondered if she would ever refer to 'Tilly's little friend' in the same tone.

She put the flowers on one of the high window-sills and waited for Miss Hesterman to finish.

'I'm not going straight back to Pimlico Square, dear.' The older woman – though probably no older than Aunt Caddie – emptied the last of the powder over the floor and joined Harriet. 'There's a political meeting in town. You and Tilly might be interested too. One of the Pankhurst girls is going to be there.'

Hallie felt her spirits droop further. Tilly, of course, would jump at this chance; and the cause was good. It was ridiculous to limit the female vote to the over-thirties. But Hallie felt her very bones ache at the thought of a hot dusty hall somewhere, packed with women all rather smelly, shouting for their 'rights'. Sometimes she wondered whether anyone had any rights. Privileges maybe. But rights premised demands. Somehow Harriet found it impossible to make demands.

However, she was right, Tilly's eyes shone at the thought of hearing Sylvia Pankhurst. They packed up quickly and handed the keys to the warden and took a taxi to Russell Square where the meeting was to be held in the stationers' hall. Harriet had to admit it was interesting to identify such people as Clive Bell and Roger Fry, but when Tilly got caught up with a group of women who were arguing that God might just as well be feminine as masculine, she found herself thinking of home and going to Clevedon for the month of August. She was grateful to Jack and Maude for having a baby; the birth – about six weeks off now – provided an irrefutable excuse – to herself – for going home.

People settled on to the uncomfortable chairs and Sylvia Pankhurst came in and was introduced by Aunt

Hesterman. She was a woman of perhaps fifty with the dynamism of Aunt Caddie. Yes, there was something about her that reminded Harriet forcibly of Aunt Caddie. And increased her homesickness.

But this meeting was not going to take long after all. Miss Pankhurst was smiling; the other women on the platform were obviously excited. There was to be an announcement. Harriet's heart, already in the region of her strap-shoes seemed weightier still. There was to be another rally. Probably on Sunday which was their day off. They'd have to get up at the crack of dawn and assemble somewhere like Marble Arch and wave banners and shout and have people throw things at them.

Miss Pankhurst held up a hand and instant silence descended on the hall.

'Ladies, gentlemen.' Her smile was blissful and near tears. 'We have won! The property restriction has been removed. We have the same voting rights as men! Parliament has listened to the Women's Social and Political Union and—' Her words were drowned in the babble of voices from the hall. Someone started cheering crazily. Someone else shouted, 'Three cheers for Nancy Astor – hip-hip—' But the bulk of the audience wanted all credit to go to the WSPU and the Pankhursts in particular. Had they not suffered terribly under the Cat and Mouse Act in the war?

Harriet looked at Tilly. Tears were streaming down her face. Harriet wished that she too could weep; or at any rate could find some small pleasure in this triumph.

Someone touched her arm. It was a woman who worked alternate duties with Tilly and Harriet at the Settlement.

She had to shout against the euphoric hysteria.

'. . . know you had a special feeling for him. Body fished out of the Thames late last night. I was asked to identify . . .'

'Who?' Harriet shouted back and put her ear close to the other woman.

'Walter Skinner. The old man who used to be a gardener down in the West Country somewhere.'

'Walter?'

Harriet straightened and stared. People were jumping up and down around them. They were isolated by this tragedy.

'It happens,' shouted the woman. 'Quite often, you know. Suddenly it's not worth fighting any more. They simply get . . . tired.'

'Oh dear God . . .'

She was still weeping in the taxi going back to Pimlico and could not tell the others why. They assumed – quite naturally – that the emotion of the evening had at last caught up with her. She let them think that. Tilly teased her.

'Hallie, stop, for goodness' sake! We shall be thinking you don't want a vote at this rate!'

And because confession was good for the soul, Harriet burst out, 'I just want to go home! I'm sorry, Miss Hesterman – Tilly – I know I'm hopeless, but I can't be like you! I'm so terribly sorry . . .' and she howled like a dog.

They were wonderful. They told her that they too had had these moments of self-doubt. And when she convinced them that her self-doubt had been with her all the time, Miss Hesterman said gravely, 'Look here, Harriet. It does not matter if you never return to the East End after this. You know what it is like. You will never forget. You will never take things for granted again. And you will – whether you know it or not – spread the word!'

The thought of spreading any word made Harriet weep again. But when they reached the mansion block and heard the message that had arrived from Jack earlier in the day, her tears dried up. Jack had said that Maude needed her. No-one else would do.

So she was necessary. She could do some good in the world. She hardly knew her sister-in-law and had been inclined all along to doubt the wisdom of the hasty marriage. Now she thought she loved her. Positively loved her.

It was almost dark in the Denmark Street office and still Cadiz sat over the books. Below her in the Cellars, work had finished for the day. It was eerie in the old building knowing that, apart from the night-watchman who was probably asleep, she was quite alone. Most of all she missed the sound of the big horses snorting and stamping as they waited for their loads. She looked up momentarily and thought how loyal and undemanding were working animals.

It was a reaction from Jack's visit of course. The fact that he knew his father was with Mungay Rudolf disturbed her. She had said jokingly to Jack, 'Do you think I am a soft touch then?' And he had replied with his honest straightforward grin, 'Far from it, Auntie Cad. It's simply that on some wavelengths you and I run side by side.'

It was her own fault, of course. She should not have come out so openly in his favour when Maude's pregnancy was first announced . . . shouted to the house tops by Maude herself. And somehow, though he had been away at school at the time, he knew about Jonathan Pomeroy. He might look honest and straightforward, but he was as devious as . . . as she was herself!

A typically wry smile lit her face at the thought, and then was gone. She was devious in business. She would never be devious where the family was concerned. But it was not easy to produce five hundred pounds immediately – 'on the nail', as Jack had so aptly put it. And now it had to be disguised from Charles. He was so happy with the present arrangement, she was determined nothing would spoil that.

She closed the books at last and pushed them from her. If he discovered something she'd have to make a clean breast of it and take the blame on herself. But it was unlikely he would check anything after she had done it. Jack was safe. For another few weeks.

That was the real problem. What was going to become of Jack? Would fatherhood pull him together? Or would he go on squandering everything and be forced to turn to the Rudolfs for help? And he would probably get away with that too so long as Maude remained in love with him. But perhaps motherhood might affect her adversely.

Cadiz sighed. She realized she was getting into 'a state' as Hallie said when she massaged her aunt's neck to help one of her headaches. Thank goodness Hallie was coming home. Maude would adore being with Hallie. Things would go on very nicely for a while.

Cadiz stood up and went to the mirror to settle her hat. The fashionable cloches did not suit her narrow face and she had chosen a summer straw in honour of the lovely day. Now, with dusk bringing a chill, it looked ridiculous. She pulled on her gloves, gathered up her handbag and let herself out of the office. It was almost black on the narrow stairs leading down to the entrance and she took it slowly, feeling her way along the ancient banister. It occurred to her, absurdly, that if only Jack could have a small accident to confine him to the house, it would be the best thing that could happen to him! And she smiled again.

On an impulse she crossed the road at Park Street and went across the Green to walk by the river. Already skeins of gnats were beginning their summer dances; she thought of summer with intense pleasure. She had spent so long in Spain that the English weather was sometimes hard to bear.

There was a tow path in front of the old Rudolf warehouses and a full moon lit it clearly. She walked slowly, loving the feeling of the air soft on her face. Behind the stables she stopped and pulled off her hat, and, on an impulse, undid her plaits and began to comb out her hair with her fingers. She was filled with a curious yearning for something completely mysterious: could it be that she wanted to swim in the murky Avon? She laughed aloud at the thought of a middle-aged woman with long greying hair straggling behind her, being seen half naked in the river late at night. How the *Evening World* would love that!

And at the sound of her laugh, two shadows detached themselves from the door of the Rudolf offices; one of them started towards her.

For an instant she was terrified. It was Friday evening and that idiot Mungay kept a lot of money in his safe then. She had disturbed a pair of thieves who would now knock her on the head and throw her into the river. How the *Evening World* would love this particular incident! How simply dreadful for Hallie and Charles. And what would happen to Jack if she wasn't around to juggle the books in his favour?

The man came nearer and with a sob of relief she saw it was Mungay Rudolf himself. His face, illuminated suddenly out of the shadow of the warehouses was full of concern.

'Miss Martinez? Yes it is! I thought as much. What in heaven's name has happened? My dear girl, are you all right?'

She realized what she must look like, her hair, half unplaited, straggling around her face, her coat undone. Frantically she rammed on the ridiculous summer hat.

'I am perfectly all right, thank you, Mr Rudolf. I was simply taking the air by the river after working late and—'

'You've been working till this time?' He grinned wolfishly, accepting her *déshabillé* as perfectly normal. 'Cadiz Martinez – we are two of a kind! You know I work through the night on a Friday?'

'I had heard you sleep in your office. Yes.'

He laughed. 'I certainly do not sleep, my dear!'

She was terribly flustered; it was not surprising in the circumstances but she was rarely flustered and to be so

69

in front of this man was unbearable. She drew the rags of her dignity around her and began to move off.

'I will bid you good night then—'

But he was in front of her and there was not room on the tow path to pass him by.

'Excuse me, Miss Martinez. But should you walk across the city with your hair down? Believe me it looks charming but there may be others about who will see it as an invitation to – approach you and . . .'

She trembled with anger, certain he was laughing at her.

'I had a headache,' she said stiffly, bundling the hair beneath her hat. 'That is why I thought a breath of air from the Channel might do me good.'

'A headache?' He was behind her instantly and the next thing she knew her hat was off and his thumbs were into the nape of her neck, gently probing beneath her hair.

'Really, Mr Rudolf—' Her voice was faint with shock, and with something else. And she did not jerk away.

Unerringly his hands massaged, first the fingers easing upwards, then the thumbs rotating gently. It was like playing a piano *lento*. Beethoven's *Pathétique*, or the *Moonlight* . . . or . . .

'Is this doing anything for you, Miss Martinez?'

The laughter was still in his voice. He knew exactly what it was doing for her.

She turned as casually as she knew how and scooped her hair back on top of her head, fixing it firmly with her hat.

'Thank you, Mr Rudolf. You are very kind.' She tried to instil laughter into her own voice, as if it were all a big joke. 'I really must go now. Good night.' And she walked quickly away.

'Good night then, Cadiz,' he called softly after her.

She was still trembling, though no longer with anger. As soon as she could she drew into the shadows and looked back. And saw him emerge again, holding someone's arm. A woman. As they came into the moonlight, she saw it was Mrs Lily Elmes. At whose house Jack had lost a great deal of money, and probably more besides.

She found her way back on to the road and began to climb up Jacobs Wells. And as she turned into Park Street, she discovered she was weeping.

Five
June 1928

Harriet and Maude travelled from Bristol to Clevedon by train. Maude could drive but her father had forbidden it in her condition; Harriet had not yet expressed a desire to learn.

It was only a half-hour's journey even with the change at Yatton Junction, and they had no luggage. Aunt Caddie was driving down from the Cellars that evening with everything they would need, plus Bellamy the cat.

Maude, supporting her enormous abdomen with both hands, grumbled loudly as they alighted at Yatton.

'I really cannot see why we could not have waited and come with your aunt this evening. This is absolutely crazy – smuts and smoke – my mascara is absolutely ruined – and practically a whole day without any of my things—'

Hallie laughed. 'You thoroughly enjoyed poking your head out of the window and having all that lovely air about you! It's absolutely your own fault if your eyes watered and made that mess on your face!'

'Oh, Hallie, is it that bad? Darling, could you possibly . . .' She presented her face and a scrap of handkerchief and Hallie scrubbed protestingly.

'We should get over the bridge to the bay and into the Clevedon train.'

Maude started again. 'I can't possibly climb those steps! My God, Hallie, it's bad enough in this heat dragging myself along the level without having to scale a mountain!'

Hallie had, by this time, got the hang of Maude's

conversation. She had been spoiled for so long, that complaints had become second nature to her; simply an alternative form of communication.

Hallie said, 'Then I will ask Mr Jenkins to take us over the barrow crossing, like a load of luggage! In fact we can follow behind the strawberry baskets!'

Maude could accept such badinage from her young sister-in-law but when the station master, in an effort to console, said, 'We're used to traffic using the barrow crossing, miss. Had a circus unload here last week. Two elephants there was,' she said icily, 'I am quite capable of using the footbridge for humans, thank you,' and trudged up the steps one by one, her scrubbed face very red indeed.

Hallie settled her into the little push-and-pull waiting in the bay and said apologetically, 'Actually, Maude, we always went to Clevedon by train – I just associate it with summer holidays. I did not really take Cuthbert into consideration.' Cuthbert was the name Maude had given to her pregnancy bump.

'Oh . . . damn Cuthbert!' Maude actually smiled. 'He'll have to get used to me. And I do admit it was wonderful coming through Flax Bourton and Nailsea and all those lovely trees. It's just – my face looks ghastly!' She stood up and examined it in the mirror beneath the luggage net.

Hallie joined her. 'What rubbish! Your face is beautiful – you can see it better without make-up. Look at those bones. You're like a Roman goddess, Maude.' The carriage jerked as the guard's whistle sounded and the girls sat down suddenly. 'Oh golly! How is Cuthbert now?'

'Fine.' Maude was suddenly determined to like everything about this trip. 'How could he help but be fine with a Roman goddess for a mother?'

Hallie laughed. She was delighted to be going to Clevedon anyway, even more delighted to discover that she actually liked her new sister-in-law. She started to do what Jack had always called her 'Clevedon act'.

'On your left . . .' she strode down the ridged wooden gangway between the seats, gesturing extravagantly, 'you will see the water tower belonging to Hiscocks Farm. Where, as you will recall, someone called Boy Blue once blew a horn!'

Encouraged by Maude's laughter she broadened her vowels further and went on, 'And I do sincerely believe that them there buttercups and daisies – yes and them hollyhocks – originated from Miss Mary Contrary's garden! And that there well – see it over thur, m'flower – was the self-same one as Master Jack and Mistress Jill used afore they landed up in the Cottage Hospital!'

Maude gasped, 'Oh, stop it, Hallie! I'm more likely to have a miscarriage laughing at you than climbing them thar steps!'

Both girls were still giggling helplessly when the train drew into the Triangle station to find one of the old horse taxis waiting to take them up the hill to the Flower House.

It boded well for the next few weeks until Maude's lying-in.

When Mungay entered his office on Monday morning, he was still smiling privately at the memory of his encounter with Cadiz Martinez the previous Friday. It had coloured his whole weekend, making him feel young and irresponsible again. He had been tender with Florence, pleased for Maude to be going off with young Hallie to the Martinez summer residence in Clevedon; he had even tried to understand Austen's sudden absence. These had happened ever since the war, but he fancied they were more frequent of late. The boy would load his army knapsack with bread, cheese and beer and just set off into the blue. His bed had not been slept in on Friday night, nor since.

And now here he was, sitting at Mungay's desk, the petty-cash drawer in front of him and that infernal

74

checklist in his hand. The damned thing went everywhere with him; in the office, the warehouses, even down to Portishead to check the *Ulysses* cargo before it was off-loaded. This was the first time he had checked the petty cash by it. Mungay could guess what he had found.

He did not look up at his father's entry so Mungay did not greet him but flung his hat at the hatstand and made straight for the open window. He crashed it down.

'Too much fresh air is bad for the chest,' he announced. And then turned. 'And where might you have been all weekend?'

Austen looked up. Mungay rarely asked where he had been on his walks. The old man probably assumed he was womanizing and decided to be tactful about it. Austen smiled grimly.

'I took the Aust ferry. Walked through Chepstow into the Forest. Down to Gloucester yesterday. Took the milk train back to Bristol this morning.'

Mungay had not expected a detailed itinerary. He said, 'Oh.'

Austen continued to smile. 'Wanted to see the fan tracery in the Cathedral,' he said, certain his father would have no idea what he was talking about.

Mungay said, 'The ceilings in the cloisters? God. Years since I looked at them. I must have been about your age . . .' He sat down. 'I thought you might have gone to Clevedon.'

Austen stopped smiling. The old man was so damned surprising. Had there actually been a time when he had stood in Gloucester Cathedral and admired the ceilings? Was there actually something they had in common besides their licentious behaviour in Barbados?

There was a pause, then he said, 'Why would I go to Clevedon?'

Mungay opened his case and placed some bills of lading on the desk.

'To see your sister, of course.'

Austen said, 'I think there is enough fuss made of Maude, Father. Always has been, always will be.'

'And you don't care tuppence for her? Is that it?'

'As you know, I am as close to Maude as I am to anyone—' It was true. Maude had a way of crashing through his reserve and forcing a closeness whether he wanted it or not. 'But I believe Miss Martinez to be an excellent companion in the circumstances. I think they should be left in peace to get to know one another.'

Mungay made some grumbling sounds but, in fact, had come to the same conclusion himself. It had been a pleasant weekend knowing that Maude was in capable hands. He had heard that Cadiz Martinez had been taking their luggage down and staying with them overnight. That too had been a pleasant thought. A picture of her came into his mind suddenly; long hair bundled into a battered straw hat . . . rather like one of the Bajan women on the plantation.

Austen broke into his thoughts.

'Father, what has been going on with the petty cash?'

Mungay said, 'I've been fiddling it.'

'So I see. Are you going to tell me why?'

Mungay looked at him consideringly, then said, 'I suppose I am. And I suppose now would be a good time to say . . . certain things.'

He drew up a chair and sat on the wrong side of the desk trying not to feel like a schoolboy confronting his headmaster.

'Austen, you are a good son. When I compare you with someone like Jack Martinez . . . you are a good son. And this business will be yours. Soon. I have no intention of dying in that chair.' He stood up suddenly and went to the window. 'But . . . there are things you have to learn, my boy. And one of them is that to give way over an issue is not always to admit defeat.'

Austen said, 'The money has something to do with the Martinez?'

Mungay shrugged irritably. 'I am talking of something

bigger than the petty cash, Austen. I am talking of your sister's marriage. The renewed link between her husband's family and ours.'

'Which, as you know, I have been against from the outset.'

Mungay turned. 'Can you tell me why?' he asked.

'You know that already. The Martinez proved long ago that they are not to be trusted. They came within an inch of ruining us. They make Judas Iscariot look like a Sunday-school teacher.'

Mungay frowned. 'Who told you all this?'

'You did. And my aunt.'

'Your aunt?'

'Alice.'

Mungay made a sound of impatience. Austen went on, 'I was six when you took me to the plantation first. Mother was having Maude and I think you were fed up with . . . things. So you made the excuse that I should see where our sugar came from. When we got out there you were too busy with . . . too busy to pay much attention to me. So most of the time I was boarded out with Alice. Who – as you well know – was old Hanover's daughter by Amelia. Your half-sister. My aunt.'

He paused but his father merely frowned at him and made no comment.

Austen continued almost pontifically. 'Alice's husband had died by then and her daughter, Sugar, had been married to Martin up at the plantation for years and they'd had Amos – he must have been about seventeen then. None of them had much to do with Alice, so the old lady had no-one to talk to. Except me. So she talked. And she hated the Martinez. It was because of old Charles Martinez that Amelia got whipped once.' Austen smiled without mirth. 'You know all this from Grandfather, of course.'

'Of course.' Mungay's frown had deepened as Austen spoke. He said, 'Oddly, the old man was not as embittered about it as you.' He came back to the desk slowly. 'I wonder . . . Alice – my half-sister as you so tactfully remind me – Alice was turned down by Charles Martinez, you know. I wonder if it's a case of a woman scorned? She sounds almost vindictive about it all.'

'Life had been cruel to Alice, but she was very kind to me.'

'Cruel? How? She made a good marriage – she was almost white you know, and when she married that curate down in Speightstown, she came into her own. Looked after the local babies when they were ill – Bibles and bread-and-butter – you know the sort of thing.'

'She hated Sugar marrying Martin. She called Amos a child of the devil.'

'Good God. Why?'

Austen shrugged. 'When I went back just before the war, she was dead.'

Mungay's frown became a scowl. 'I don't understand it. Amos is the best man to come off the plantation. I made him manager . . . what is it . . . six years ago now.'

'On his birthday.'

'You recall it that accurately?' He leaned his hands on the desk and approached his face towards his son's. 'Are you jealous, Austen? Is that what this is all about? Jealous in case someone else gets a finger in our particular pie?' He straightened suddenly. 'I can understand it up to a point with the Martinez. But with Amos? What the hell is going on inside your head, Austen?'

Austen's colour was unusually high. He had never spoken to his father before of that time as a small child, banished to Alice Sheppard's house in Speightstown, first of all because his mother did not want him at home, and secondly because his father was too busy at the Plantation House. He had an unhappy knack of self-analysis and had known for some time that was when the estrangement with his father – with his family – had started. But jealous? Was it as simple as jealousy?

He said, 'Surely I have no reason for jealousy? Anger perhaps. Not jealousy. I spent more time with Amos than you, Father. We get on better than most brothers—'

'Because you think he is inferior to you?'

Austen's colour subsided. He almost laughed. 'He is inferior to no-one, Father. He is stronger, wiser, more intelligent than anyone I know. He taught me to swim, climb a coconut palm, fish, cut cane . . .' He stared his father in the eye. 'And run a successful sugar plantation.'

Mungay seemed to slump on his arms. He was silent for some time then said, 'You are saying I did not do those things for you?'

Austen had regained his composure. 'You were too busy, Father. And Amos was a young man then.' He had talked enough of the past. 'I am not jealous of any person. You must know that. I am jealous of what we have fought for. What is ours.' He pushed at the drawer lying between them. 'You have been donating money to the Jack Martinez gambling fund, I believe?'

Mungay straightened again, drew up a chair and sat down.

'You knew all the time, boy. You were playing with me.'

'I did not *know*. Now I do.'

'He needed five hundred pounds, Austen. I knew it was true, Lily Elmes told me. What could I do? Maude is giving birth in four weeks' time. She is low at the moment—'

Austen suddenly blazed with anger. 'And you know just how low pregnant women can get!' He looked at his father sitting back in the visitor's chair. The old man looked about ten years older than Austen himself in his summer suit and crisp white shirt. Probably the only person in the world he really loved was Maude.

His anger disappeared. He said gently, 'You know it won't stop at five hundred?'

But Mungay had thought further ahead than Austen. He leaned towards his son and spoke heavily.

'I might well have spoiled Maude, Austen. But I know her as well as you do. Jack Martinez is one of her crazes.

He is still. For the present. But in a year – perhaps two at the outside – the marriage will be as good as over. Whether our business arrangement with the Cellars will be over too, is impossible to forecast. Certainly gambling loans will be a thing of the past.'

Austen stared again, surprised at his father's objectivity.

And then he drew the cash drawer to him and began to replace the money in its various compartments. His father went to the door and yelled for Sullivan to make them some coffee. And Austen's thoughts returned introspectively to the surprising conversation of a few minutes before. Was it really so simple as jealousy? And if so, where did it stop? His brows came together; he knew it was more complicated than jealousy, it was deeper. It was rooted in his hatred of the Martinez family; nurtured in the forcing house of the trenches, maturing in this stupid marriage. And yet . . . and yet . . . he had to admit that the business alliance was advantageous. And the Martinez girl – Harriet – was good for Maude. He bit his lip, trying not to think of that wonderfully pure face framed between those crazy dancers at the Michaelmas Ball.

Sully came in with coffee, grumbling about leaving the car in the sun. And unbidden there came into Austen's head an idea. Jack Martinez' debt to the Rudolfs put him in their power. When the marriage ended and he was up to his neck in more debts to them, there may well be only one way to pay.

Austen stood up and let his father have his chair.

He said, 'I see no objection to covering that debt then, Father. But I do think we should charge a proper rate of interest. For Jack's sake as well as our own.'

Mungay sat down and shrugged. It had been an interesting and revealing morning.

He said, 'One thing, my son. I need never have any fears that the business will founder with you at its head!'

He laughed. And after a moment Austen did too.

And entirely without introspection or thought of any kind he said, 'And I think I'll go down to Clevedon and see Maude. Perhaps this coming weekend.'

Charles was thankful to see Cadiz back again. Jack had occupied her desk in the office, but his forte had always been in the actual business of blending and bottling. Paper work left him cold.

Charles looked at her as she fitted her pince-nez on to her aristocratic nose and settled down to correspondence. She was looking so well these days, the hot weather was suiting her. She had always worn her hair plaited over each ear, recently she had it in a complicated bun on top of her head. It was an old-fashioned style but it suited her well making her neck look very long and slim and emphasizing her high cheek bones. She should have married. She was a strong, passionate woman who would have been a wonderful wife and mother. But then she could not have been a wonderful aunt to his two. He smiled.

'Did you leave the girls all right?' he asked, knowing he had asked it before and not caring because he was so at ease with her.

She smiled back, understanding.

'Wonderfully all right. Hallie is so happy to be away from London! If we'd had secret fears that she might wish to live there, we can discount them, Charles. She talked about it – to Maude as well as to me – and it is not for her.'

Charles said, 'Does she feel she has failed?'

'Not really. She has learned her own limitations, which is always a good thing.'

'Does that mean she will go to Switzerland with Margo Adams?'

Cadiz laughed. 'Not so fast, brother dear! I don't think she knows what she wants. She is just happy – happy to be in Clevedon in the Flower House – that always makes her happy, of course. But happy to be of use to Maude. Yes, very happy to be needed.'

'She is like you in that, Caddie.'

'Is she?' Cadiz leaned back in her chair and one hand went to the nape of her neck.

Charles said sympathetically, 'Headache?'

'No.' Cadiz removed her hand quickly. 'Not at all. I feel well for my stay in Clevedon.' And she drew a letter towards her indicating that the exchange was over.

Maude lay in a steamer chair, an old cricketing hat pulled forward to shield her eyes, a shapeless cotton frock donated by the housekeeper, Mrs Hayle, who must be all of twenty stone, enveloping her lump in its general shapelessness.

She said, 'I hope you are satisfied, Hallie Martinez!'

Hallie, prone on the grass by her side, smiled blissfully. 'How could I not be? In my favourite place. The sun really hot. The sea breeze keeping us—'

'You know very well what I mean! Reducing me – a hated Rudolf – to this! No make-up. No perfume. A hat which Jack used when he played for the local cricket team. And one of Mrs Hayle's dresses which only just fits me!'

Hallie picked a succulent piece of grass and held it up and Maude took it gloomily. 'Of course. And no cigarettes. Because the smoke might spoil the wallpaper. I almost forgot that!' She stuck the grass between her teeth and chewed.

Hallie grinned. 'You almost forgot to add that you are content. You look great with no make-up, and you smell good too. Your baby doesn't want to look at a mask or smell perfume. And Mrs Hayle's dress adds to the Roman goddess look. As for the hat – you are honoured. Jack would never let me wear it!'

Maude let herself smile. 'He was rather sweet, looking it out for me, wasn't he? Like a schoolboy.'

'It gives him a real kick seeing you down here.' Hallie

rolled on to her back. 'We used to have such good times, Maude. You would have loved it. We'd wade out in the mud and pick cockles off the rocks and Mrs Hayle would wash them and boil them for us . . . we used to pretend we were on a desert island and could only eat stuff we found for ourselves.'

'Oh God. How perfectly awful!'

'Didn't you play with Austen?'

'He's six years older than me.'

'There're almost seven years between Jack and me. We still had such fun together.'

'Austen was away a great deal. Father used to take him off to Barbados every time he made a trip himself.'

'Well, Jack was away at school.'

Maude leaned over and changed her chewed grass for a fresh one. 'It's different in our family.' She stared at Hallie wondering why that was. She was unused to introspection. 'I think . . . I think we don't go in for contentment. We go in for excitement. And if we can't get it, we're pretty fed up!'

Hallie laughed, unable to take this seriously. She said, 'Well . . . you fell for Jack, anyway.'

Maude said frankly, 'That's sex. You wouldn't understand, Hallie. Sex is terribly exciting. The most exciting thing in the world. When two people sort of spark each other off, everything – every damned thing – is exciting.'

Hallie stopped smiling and swallowed. 'Oh,' she said.

'Sorry, old girl!' Maude laughed at her sister-in-law's obvious discomfiture. 'It'll happen to you. And then you'll think, Oh this is what Maude means!'

Hallie scrambled to her feet. 'Here's Mrs Hayle with the tea things. I'll run up for them, Maude. She won't be able to manage the steps.'

Maude spat out the second grass and relapsed in her chair. 'Why on earth you keep a dog and bark yourself, I'll never know!' she commented.

Everything was informal at the Flower House. After tea there would be three hours of evening, then supper and, immediately, bed. Dinner, or dressing for it, was left behind. They ate substantially at midday and after that Mrs Hayle supplied sandwiches and cakes and little else.

'The house was built in the 1850s,' Hallie said, in between bites of seed cake. 'It is modelled on those houses in Mississippi – all verandahs. Our great grandfather brought back the plans from—' She stopped suddenly and Maude laughed and sprayed cake crumbs everywhere.

'I watched you dig that hole and almost fall in it!' she crowed. 'Your great grandfather bloody well pinched the plans of Plantation House in Barbados and built this one!'

'Oh, Maude! I'd forgotten you were . . . I mean . . .'

'I know what you mean. And that's wonderful. You had forgotten I was a Rudolf. Well,' she made a wry face, 'I am not any longer, am I? I'm a Martinez.' For a moment, she looked almost frightened at the thought. Then she laughed at Hallie's anxious face and said, 'And I adore the Flower House!'

Hallie smiled too and went on chewing her cake and after a while she asked, 'Is it like Plantation House, Maude?'

'Yes. Very much. And Plantation House is on a hill too. There's a wonderful view of the Atlantic coast.' She sipped her tea. 'You'd adore it, Hallie. Shall I take you out there?'

Hallie paused, obviously struck by a thought. Then she said, 'Perhaps that is what we could do. Go to Barbados. Learn about the sugar. And then go to Cadiz and look at the vineyards.' She was suddenly excited. 'Maude, we could expand the businesses. Maybe even bring them together!'

Maude smiled and humoured the younger girl.

'What should we call it?'

'Ummm – what are you going to call your baby?'

Maude already knew that if she produced a male child

her father would want it to be called Hanover Rudolf Martinez. She would have a girl. She was determined on that.

She remembered tales from her father and said, 'Amelia. Yes, Amelia.'

Hallie laughed. 'Well! How does Amelia fine blend, sound to you?'

Both girls laughed. And then suddenly and unexpectedly, Maude leaned down and hugged her sister-in-law.

Austen arrived the following Saturday afternoon.

He found Lady Decliveden making a duty call to her cousin-by-marriage six or seven times removed. Hallie's great grandmother had been a connection of the Declivedons.

The three women, one so old she looked preserved in moth balls, the others young and resembling gypsies in clothes calculated to keep them cool, were in the shadowy drawing-room drinking tea. The flowers, for which the house was named, were invasive; nasturtiums trailed across the floor of the downstairs verandah and through the long casements; one tendril was about to wrap itself around a chair leg. Austen took the proffered seat and was surrounded by the sharp smell of the leaves.

'I knew you were in residence.' Lady Decliveden's nasal voice was not affected by the moth balls; it grated in Austen's ear.

'I was in the tower, bird-watching when I saw your Aunt Cadiz drive down last Saturday.'

Austen smiled and nodded and thought what a nosey parker the old girl must be. Bird-watching indeed.

'I don't really approve of motoring from Bristol when we have a perfectly good train service,' she swept on. 'Mollycot's cows do not give such a good yield if they have to stop for traffic.'

'Surely the cows are all right, ma'am.' In the past Hallie had tried 'Aunt' and 'Lady Decliveden' and had been told how to address her relative. 'I should have thought the geese were the most in danger.'

'Oddly enough, dear child, motorists slow down for geese. One of them flew up and into an open car once and did a considerable amount of damage.'

Everyone laughed. Austen was thankful his car was closed. He had slowed down for the geese and had noted the unpleasant glint in their eyes as they stalked past his bonnet.

Maude – looking halfway decent with her face washed and her hair looking soft and fluffy and innocent of marcelled waves – said, 'Didn't I read in the *Evening World* about somebody sueing a farmer called Mollycot?'

'You did, child.' Lady Decliveden smiled grimly. 'He was driving a Bugatti and edged it too close to one of Mollycot's herd. She was a nervous creature and the inevitable happened over his bonnet. He had the effrontery to engage in a civil action. Luckily he engaged Albert's cousin and naturally he lost the case.'

Maude laughed helplessly and Lady Decliveden said approvingly to Austen, 'Good to meet you. An excellent match if I may say so. The old feud has gone on far too long.'

Austen was amazed. Maude did indeed look charming with her head thrown back appreciatively. He turned his gaze on Hallie who had wrought this change. She was pouring tea, smiling and radiating that uncanny purity which had so struck him each time he saw her. How could this girl, so perfect, so untainted, belong to the Martinez family? Even the tabby cat curled around her ankles was looking up at her lovingly. Austen thought of Jack, superficial, weak. And the father, Charles Martinez, though perhaps a moral man, still shallow. And Cadiz; there were stories about Cadiz which – having met her now – he could believe.

How long before this girl grew up and was tainted by . . . everything. It hurt him to think of that. He would go to Barbados this winter and when he returned she would have had her first season and probably her first affair. Helped on the way by his own sister probably. Her life would be a round of parties, dances, clothes, hair styles, gossip. The purity would be gone for ever.

She straightened holding a cup of tea, stepped carefully over the cat, and came to him. Her startling blue eyes met his. She smiled. He did not look away and neither did she. She stopped smiling and went on looking. And then, quite suddenly, the teacup was on the floor, broken, and a river of tea streamed towards the trailing nasturtium, and the cat, imagining it was his fault, was running for the door.

Maude waited until Austen came to bid her good night in the privacy of her room.

'Listen, big brother. Don't let Hallie get a thing about you, will you? She's only a kid.'

Austen went to the window which led to the upstairs verandah and closed it firmly.

'Is that all you think about, Maude? Good God – as you say – she is a child.'

'There is a great deal to that girl. And I am fond of her. Got it?'

'I've got it. And I can assure you that if you are fool enough to make a match with a Martinez, I have more sense.'

She had been sore all evening that Austen could come to see her and Jack could not. She threw herself into the little spoon-backed chair in front of the dressing-table and began to brush her hair furiously.

'Sense has very little to do with it, Austen. As you may well discover one day.' Her bobbed hair clung to the brush with electricity and she herself felt near to sparking. Before Austen had arrived she and Hallie had been happy. Now she was not, and she had no idea why.

But he had noticed the contentment before it disappeared and said, 'You are different, Maude. This was a good idea – coming down here with Hallie Martinez?'

'A wonderful idea. For both of us. She has been working much too hard in London and I was becoming . . . stale.'

His eyes glinted with humour as he looked at her. 'You were your usual self. The excitement of seducing Jack Martinez and marrying him in the face of opposition has gone. That's all it is, Maude.'

She stopped brushing and stared at him. 'Is that how you see it? Yes, of course. You would.' She put the brush on her lap and stared at it. 'That was only part of it, brother dear.' She looked up and smiled brightly. 'Never mind. Where is he?'

'Jack? I would have thought you would have known more of his whereabouts than I could possibly know. At home, I suppose, in Dowry Square.'

She said, 'You could have brought him down with you!'

He looked out of the window again. The terraced garden dropped steeply to the black ribbon of Hill Road, and beyond that was the sea glimmering under a full moon. The sky over the Channel was a brilliant mass of stars. It was amazingly like Plantation House.

He said, 'I wish to keep as far away from your husband as I can.'

'Aren't you being a little old hat, brother dear? Just because his name happens to be Martinez—'

'That has nothing to do with it at the moment.'

She stared at his back. Then said, 'Ah. He has been gambling again. Is that where he is tonight?'

'I would imagine so.'

'He has no money. He had to borrow from his father to pay back . . .' Her voice trailed off as Austen turned and stared incredulously. She made a small sound. 'Oh no. He went to Father, didn't he? And I told him that was not on.' She swung round in her chair, the hair brush falling to the carpet. 'Damn!' She clutched the smooth rosewood of the chair back. 'Damn, damn, damn!'

He moved quickly to face her. 'For goodness' sake, Maude, don't get upset about . . . him! He's not worth it!'

She had her eyes tightly shut. 'I don't care! I love him! And I didn't want him to put himself into your power. And now he has!'

He said, 'You know me a little too well, Maude.' He squatted on his heels and touched her cheek. 'Sis . . . if I have some kind of hold over him, it would be used for your sake. For your protection. Don't you see that?'

'No. I don't see that. Because you're a cold fish, Austen. Things go on inside your head that no-one understands. No-one wants to understand.'

He said very quietly and slowly, 'I would never hurt you, Maude. You are my sister.'

She opened her eyes. 'There. You see? I am your sister. You do not say you love me. Just that—'

He said, 'I love you.'

She closed her eyes again, this time wearily. 'But you do not love Jack. And I do. And he promised me he would not go to Father.'

There was a pause. He spoke in the same quiet voice. 'And he broke his promise. You see?'

Another pause before she said, 'Where is he playing? Do you know?'

'At the Elmes' house, I think.'

'Lily Elmes. Father's joy and comfort. Is he sharing her as well as Father's cash?'

'Maude—'

'Well, you have proved to me that he cannot love me! So why he should not find—'

'Maude, stop it. You are dramatizing things as usual. I thought you had changed and I see that I was wrong.'

She rested her forehead on her arms. She was unbearably weary yet knew she would not sleep.

'Austen, I am tired. And as Mother used to say before she took to her bed, everything will look brighter in the morning.'

He stood up slowly.

'Shall I reopen the window?'

'Yes please.'

He did so and went to the door where he paused.

'Maude . . . sleep well.' He opened the door and as he went through it, he added, 'You know, sis, I want to understand.' And he was gone.

Eventually she undressed and stood in her petticoat by the open window, refusing to let the tears come, her eyes burning with them.

It was almost midnight when Hallie stepped out of her window further down the verandah. She did not see Maude until she was almost level with her, then literally jumped and clutched the balustrade for support.

Maude laughed and felt instantly better.

'Where d'you think you're going?'

'Oh lordy . . . for a swim . . . if my heart will start again!' But she was laughing too.

'You've got no towel – nothing. And it's dark!'

'Quite. Who wants to go swimming with those bathing-machine women pestering you, and the boys trying to get a glimpse over the Esplanade?'

'You mean you will swim in the buff?' Even unshockable Maude was surprised.

'Jack and I used to do it all the time. Come on, Maude. Come with me. No-one to see you. It's great fun and you'll sleep like a log afterwards.'

Maude hesitated, looked back at the bed which she was not going to share with Jack, and then nodded.

From further along the verandah Austen Rudolf watched the girls descend the fire escape and negotiate the paths and steps down the terraced garden to Hill Road. He had taken out his studs and cuff-links. He rolled up the sleeves of his shirt and followed them.

*   *   *

It was delicious in the water. Delicious to be free of clothes and to feel her abdomen supported and cherished by the muddy, milky liquid of the Channel. The bathing machines were behind them, dark sentinels on the shingle, and the incoming tide wrapped them almost immediately so that their feet could leave the pebbles and float behind them like mermaids' tails. Phosphorescence trailed them and when Maude lifted her bare arm and it dripped fire she knew a moment of ecstasy that surpassed anything with Jack.

She swam close to Hallie and whispered, 'I have become part of the universe!'

Hallie smiled whitely. 'I knew you would like it.'

They stayed a short time. They had no wish to be discovered and in any case, Hallie was anxious that Maude might overdo it. They huddled back into their bath robes and shoved their feet into sandals, giggling like schoolgirls.

Maude said, 'What an adventure! If only Austen could do this – it might help him to understand.'

Hallie said nothing. She had wanted to swim to get Austen out of her head.

The girls panted up Hill Road past the upturned shafts of the milk float outside the dairy and the blackness of the public gardens. And back in his room after running ahead of them, Austen watched them until they were at the top of the fire escape. And then, sweating, he went to bed and lay awake until the dawn.

And it was then, almost a month too soon, that Maude went into labour.

Six

Jack left the house in Hotwells Road at four-thirty just as dawn was oozing down the Avon Gorge. His eyes could barely focus, he was in debt again after promising Aunt Caddie . . . after promising Mungay Rudolf . . . and he was happy.

He took the same path as Cadiz had taken three weeks before, stumbling along between the banks of cow-parsley and foxglove, hearing the insidious whisper of the river just below him, conscious that all his perceptions were in top gear in spite of being drunk – perhaps because of it.

How could he be happy? He had been unfaithful to his wife three weeks before the birth of their child, and he had gambled with money that was not theirs. He was a cad. A rotter. He had no right to any kind of happiness.

Still he grinned, then halted his shambling walk to listen to a warbler down in the sedge. And spotted a water rat slipping into the water beneath him. It took him back to his times with Hallie . . . simple pleasures. Simple pleasures.

Perhaps that was why he was happy? Because he was a simple man and saw everything in that light?

His grin widened and he resumed his walk. There had been a time – just after Hallie was born and his mother died – when he had wanted a water ice. They had been in Clevedon, the adults concerned with other things. Someone – probably Caddie – had said no.

Everyone was unhappy. And all he wanted was a water ice from the man on the tricycle by the pier. So he had gone into his dead mother's room and found her hand-bag and taken money from it and bought his ice. He had known – at six years old – that it was a desperately evil act. And yet, as he sucked the ice and looked out to sea, smelt the seaweed, watched the donkeys parading the field . . . he had been happy.

Just as now.

He thought of his – what was it? – *dalliance* . . . with Lily. That's what it had been. A dalliance with a much older woman who offered comfort when he lost his money. His grin went from ear to ear as he recalled it. The dalliance had had such a delicious edge to it simply because Lily belonged to Mungay Rudolf. How Maude would appreciate that! He knew that one day he would tell her. She was that kind of girl. She would be angry and hit him and curse and then . . . she would laugh!

The tide was on the turn; it was light enough to see the depth of mud on the opposite bank. He halted again and stretched his arms above his head, inhaling deeply. It was going to be another hot day. How he would love to swim. Not here. In Clevedon. He could be there in a couple of hours. Have breakfast with the girls. And while they were at church he could walk right along to Woodspring Bay and bathe there at high tide. And perhaps while he was swimming he would be able to think what he could do about money. It might be possible to go to Spain and look at the vines. He was always lucky in Spain. Or . . . a sudden idea made him grin again. Perhaps old Mungay would send him to Barbados! He'd put it to Maude. A holiday in Barbados. What could be better for her and the new child?

Still smiling, he struck up to Hotwells and made his way to Dowry Square.

Maude made uncharacteristic whimpering sounds. Hallie had prepared herself for a stream of oaths, yells, anything . . . not whimpers.

'Darling, I've sent Mrs Hayle for Dr Mayhew. He's absolutely marvellous.'

'Something's not right, Hallie. Don't leave me, will you?'

'Of course not. Let me take your head . . . there, is that better?'

'Yes. Yes it is. Hallie, don't forget, if it's a girl. Amelia.'

'I won't forget. But you'll change your mind. It's so old-fashioned.'

'Everyone remembers Amelia. Hanover beat her. That is why your great grandfather reported him. He beat her.'

'Don't think of it, darling. It's gone now.'

'She was wonderful. She had a child, you know. Was it like this for her?'

Hallie felt the sweating forehead and wondered whether Maude was delirious.

'It'll probably be a boy. Father wants it to be a boy and so does Jack. Austen wants a girl. Because of the inheritance, you know.'

Hallie had no idea but she said, 'I know, Maude. Don't worry.'

'If it's a boy I said we'd call him Hanover. That's worse than Amelia, isn't it?'

'You could shorten it perhaps. Hans?'

'Or Hanny.' There came a weak laugh. 'Yes. Hanny. Hanny Martinez. Sounds like a jazz pianist.'

The pain was there again; Hallie could tell because of the sudden tightness beneath the voile nightdress. But Maude merely whimpered and turned her head into Hallie's neck.

And after a while, she whispered, 'You smell nice, Hallie. Like a little girl.' She started up, her eyes very bright. 'You should not be here! You are only a child! You should not—'

Hallie held her, stroked her face. 'If it had not been for the Settlement, you would be right. But I am not a child any more.' She smiled into Maude's eyes. 'Isn't

94

that wonderful, darling? God must have sent me to the Settlement for five months to prepare me for this.'

Maude's eyes swam with tears. 'Oh, Hallie . . .'

There were no more contractions. Maude lay with her head on Hallie's shoulder, waiting for the doctor to arrive; she seemed to recover. Mrs Hayle came in with a tray of tea and startled them both.

'Where is Dr Mayhew?' Hallie demanded blankly.

'Mister Rudolf's gone for him, Miss Hallie. He insisted. And I thought you might both like a nice hot drink.'

Hallie was about to tell her to remove the tea tray, but Maude said gladly, 'Oh, how lovely! Fresh tea! Is there toast, Mrs Hayle?'

Mrs Hayle smiled. 'There can be.'

It was wonderful, miraculous. Hallie poured two cups and they sat almost normally, drinking and talking.

She said, 'I did not think it would be like this.'

Maude smiled. 'Neither did I! I have to admit – just now – I thought I was for the chop, old girl. Sorry.'

'Think nothing of it!' Hallie's relief was enormous. She was able to voice her inner fear. 'Maude . . . was it because of the swim?'

'Who knows? I shouldn't think so, darling. I felt wonderful last night. I haven't felt like that before. Ever. At peace. With everything – I don't mean people. Things. The sky and the sea and . . . things.' She laughed and sipped and then put her cup down with a click. 'I say. It's coming again. But I think now, I can manage. You go, Hallie.'

But Hallie could not go. And this time it was as she had imagined. Maude gripped her hands until she thought the bones must crack and then, after a strangled cry, the tight mouth opened wide and a scream ripped the air apart.

Austen entered at a run. Dr Mayhew followed briskly but sedately. Mrs Hayle brought water and he washed his hands through the next contraction, and the next.

'My goodness, they are coming quickly. I think you are probably already dilated . . .' He sat on the bed. 'Mr Rudolf, would you take this young lady away. Mrs Hayle will help me.'

Hallie never knew whether the next scream was for her. Austen's grip on her arm was like a vice. He did not release her until they were downstairs in the drawing-room. And then he did so with uncomplimentary swift-ness and immediately walked away from her to the window.

'You must not blame yourself,' he said in an angry voice.

She stood, staring at his back, rubbing her arm where the impress of his fingers still burned. She knew sud-denly that Maude must have told him about the swim. She gave a strangled sob.

'How can I not? She would never have come . . . I asked her . . . insisted . . .'

He said as if he had not heard her, 'It must have been a wonderful experience. If I had realized what you were going to do, I would have joined you. But . . . that would have spoiled it.'

Her eyes ached with staring at his back. His shoulders were so wide; he had Maude's aristocratic neck and head.

She whispered, 'Spoiled what?'

'The baptism.'

She swallowed on a dry throat.

'I don't understand. We went swimming. Just swim-ming.'

'Maude has changed. Since being with you. Here. She has changed.'

'I know. Before coming to Clevedon she would have wanted . . . other things. What she called excitements.' She swallowed, remembering just what Maude had considered exciting and suddenly knowing exactly what she had meant. 'I mean – since we've been here, she's so enjoyed all the *ordinary* things. Only, of course, the swim wasn't ordinary. Not in her condition. And at night.' Her voice cracked suddenly. 'Oh, Austen, I am so sorry. She wouldn't have done it if I hadn't asked her. I shall never forgive myself.'

He turned slowly, almost unwillingly, and came towards her. She moved to meet him, stumbled against Aunt Caddie's footstool and reached out to him; and he took her hands and held her up.

They stood, holding hands, staring into each other's eyes with a kind of astonishment and then, from above, came another unearthly scream. Hallie sobbed and sat down abruptly on the footstool and Austen crouched with her, still holding her hands.

He said urgently, 'You have given Maude some of your innocence, Hallie. And when you took her into the water she was born again. That is why I called it a baptism. It was wonderful for Maude, and you must never regret it.'

She still had no idea what he was talking about, but his fingers were infinitely comforting on hers. So long as he was there, she believed she could help Maude.

Another scream ripped through the house and she said in a low voice, very fast, 'If it's a girl it's to be Amelia. And a boy . . . Hanover. And Maude thinks it might be good to call him Hanny.'

And he said conversationally, 'Amelia was a very, very old lady when I went to Barbados first. She doctored all the children, including me.'

'I wish she were here now,' Hallie said.

'Yes. She attended most of the mothers on the plantation.'

They looked at each other as Maude screamed again.

'Tell me about Barbados,' Hallie said.

And he began to tell her while she hung on to his hands and winced every time another scream came from above.

Cadiz woke Jack herself.

'A phone message from Austen Rudolf! Wake up, dear boy! Your baby is on the way!'

He struggled out of a sleep he had not intended. A shred of a dream whirled in his head. Maude, slim, beautiful, terribly erotic, holding him at arm's length. Lily Elmes . . . somewhere?

He said, 'Oh God, Caddie, I did not mean to sleep! What are you doing here?'

'I just told you, Jack! Austen tried to telephone you. Obviously you couldn't hear the bell through your drunken stupor, so he got hold of us instead, and I came round.'

He groaned, swung his legs over the side of the bed, groaned again and put his head in his hands. He remembered feeling so well and happy. Now he did not.

'Austen bloody Rudolf. Why is he in Clevedon?'

Cadiz was at the wardrobe, tugging out a suitcase.

'Pull yourself together for goodness' sake, Jack! Austen evidently took it into his head to go and see his sister – probably his father nagged him into it. But it was fortunate, as he was able to call old Mayhew out and take charge generally. Maude is in labour. Almost at the end of labour as far as I can gather.'

He had not undressed and looked blearily at his watch.

'Ten o'clock! My God. I was going to go down myself at the crack of dawn – take them to church and then have a swim!'

'Bully for you!' She was opening drawers and throwing things into the suitcase. Shirts, collars, ties, pyjamas. 'Where is your sponge-bag? And what about these ghastly plus-fours?'

'I suppose I'll have to stay for a while. Unless she comes back to town. She's booked into the Stanway on the Downs.' He shook his head perplexedly and then clasped it in agony. 'What'll I do, Caddie?'

'Go prepared to stay there. If everything is normal she won't want to leave Clevedon. Being there with Hallie is doing her good. And if she has to come up to the Stanway, then you simply come home again.'

'You come with me – yes, you come with me. You can look after Hallie then.'

'Hallie does not need looking after. And the business does.' She shut his case and walked round the bed to force him to meet her eyes. 'I juggled the books to keep that little transaction of ours quiet. I need to make certain they stay juggled.'

He was suddenly annoyed. Dammit all, Mungay hadn't gone on and on like Caddie did. He'd simply gone to the petty-cash drawer and taken out five bundles of notes.

He said, 'Blast it, Caddie. It's Sunday. And anyway, the whole shoot will be mine one day.'

'It will be your child's also. And Hallie's and her children. Stop thinking only of yourself, Jack.'

He was instantly contrite. 'Caddie, I didn't mean . . . I'm sorry. I'm an absolute rotter and you're an angel. But you don't need to keep an eye on things all the time. Come to Clevedon with me. You can have the car and drive back tonight if you insist.'

Caddie's gaze shifted imperceptibly. She went to the door. 'I've got other plans, Jack. Sorry. Love to Maude.'

He stared at the closed door. What other plans could Aunt Cadiz possibly have? She was at the disposal of the Martinez family. That was her *raison d'être*, surely?

He stood up and shambled into the bathroom.

There were periods of intense activity – boiling pans of water, searching for towels – followed by others when she and Austen did not know what to say any longer. Once that physical link had been broken, it could not be resumed, and the tales of Barbados had dried up long ago. She sat nursing the reluctant cat, he stood by the window looking down at the sea.

Mrs Hayle was attending Dr Mayhew until the midwife arrived which meant Hallie could at least make some tea. Bellamy the cat seized his opportunity to escape through the kitchen window. She watched him

99

while the kettle boiled. He oozed himself beneath the rhubarb leaves and lay doggo in the hot sunshine. She made the tea and waited for it to brew while she stared around the kitchen. The Sunday lamb, sprigged with rosemary, was sitting in the roasting tin. She lit the oven and put it in. 'Please God let Maude be eating this tonight,' she whispered. Then she took the tea upstairs.

Austen was waiting in the hall when she came back down.

'How is she?'

'Mrs Hayle sort of got in the way. But she said it won't be long now.'

'Thank God!'

He was blocking her and made no move. She cleared her throat and asked him if he would like some tea.

'I would prefer coffee. If it's no trouble.'

'I'm just boiling more water to fill the wash jug. And then—'

'Let me carry it up, it's too heavy for you.' He strode to the kitchen as if glad of the excuse to get away from her, and she followed him, shaking. Of course they hardly knew each other; it was no wonder they were nervous. In the circumstances. Yes, especially in the circumstances. Yet they had been so at ease an hour before.

The midwife arrived and was ushered into the bedroom. Hallie made more tea and took it up and Mrs Hayle emerged.

'We have to call the ambulance, Miss Hallie.' The housekeeper was visibly distressed. Her large figure filled the doorway but Hallie, side-stepping with the tray, saw that something had happened. There was blood; a great deal of blood.

She ran downstairs ahead of Mrs Hayle. She had to tell Austen. Austen would know what to do.

She found him in the kitchen measuring coffee into a jug. 'Austen – Maude is . . . oh dear God, we must get an ambulance!'

He looked at her face and ran for the phone without a word, just as Mrs Hayle came down the stairs saying, 'Doctor thinks perhaps the nursing home—'

'Mrs Hayle, what has happened?' Hallie was frantic.

'A sudden bleeding, Miss Hallie.' The housekeeper was white. 'I seen it once before. A rupture, it is. It was one of the housemaids up at the Court—'

Austen interrupted curtly. 'It's on its way. I'm going up.'

'No, sir! You mustn't—'

'I'm coming too.'

Hallie ignored Mrs Hayle's further protestations and followed on Austen's heels. He took the stairs two at a time but they arrived at the bedroom door together. Inside was a scene of carnage. Dr Mayhew was in his shirt-sleeves, blood-stained to his elbows. The midwife was supporting Maude's legs so that she was tipped backwards.

Hallie rushed to the head of the bed. Maude's eyes were closed. She looked untroubled.

Hallie whispered, 'It's all right, darling. You're going to hospital.'

Austen's voice was harsh. 'She's dead, Hallie. Can't you see that?'

'No!' Hallie cupped the calm face. 'No – she's asleep—'

'We have to save the child.' Dr Mayhew's voice was sharp with shock. 'There's just a chance we can save it.'

Hallie could not look. She held Maude's head as she had before and said – perhaps aloud, she never knew – 'Please God, please God, please God . . .'

Dr Mayhew's voice said, 'Never mind the cord, Sister. Clear the air passages – quickly. A great deal of blood . . .'

Hallie closed her eyes. Please God, please God . . .

Austen's voice snapped. 'Give it to me. I've seen this done.'

There were sounds, indescribable sounds. Gurglings,

someone spitting. Panting. And then, a thin, very treble wail.

Hallie looked round. The baby, hardly recognizable as a human being, was on Maude's stomach. Austen was kissing it. When he lifted his head, there came another wail.

Dr Mayhew said, 'It's alive. The cord, Sister.'

Austen straightened. His mouth was bloody; his eyes – just for a moment – wild. And then the shutters came down. He went to the basin and swilled his face.

Hallie said, 'It's Hanny. Maude, it's Hanny.'

He turned, soap lathering his mouth and stared at her. And Jack came into the room.

Cadiz had not been in the Royal Hotel before. There was a great deal of red plush, the wallpaper was Chinese and probably hand painted, the table covered with a white cloth so starched it knifed at her knees. The plate opposite hers was piled with roast beef, oozing pinkly in the middle of each slice. The vegetable dishes contained roast potatoes, summer cabbage, carrots, new peas. There was a silver plate of small Yorkshire puddings, and the ornate cruet contained lethal-looking mustard and horseradish sauce.

Mungay said, 'Can't I tempt you to some food, Miss Martinez? A plate of beef perhaps?'

'No thank you, Mr Rudolf.' Cadiz spoke with as much ice in her voice as the stuffy dining-room permitted. 'I was under the impression that your invitation concerned business.'

'Rather than pleasure?' Mungay's smile was charming, if wolf-like. 'I've always been able to combine the two, Miss Martinez. Always.'

She remembered his fingers on her neck and smiled involuntarily. He laughed.

'That's much better! Waiter!' He lifted his index finger and someone was there instantly. 'Beef for my guest. And a glass of . . . sherry?'

Cadiz decided on a humorous surrender as being the most dignified course of action.

'A very small plate, if you please. And a very dry sherry.'

'Excellent.' He did not wait for her but piled vegetables over his beef and used the mustard spoon to amazing effect.

'I'm delighted you accepted the invitation on any terms at all,' he confessed. 'I imagined – if you had been amenable – your brother would not.'

She had not told Charles. And she should have gone to Clevedon with Jack. She had convinced herself that meeting Mungay Rudolf superseded family duty.

'Charles is lunching with friends. The Hestermans.'

'And you were not invited?' His eyebrows were grey and bushy and lifted to meet his hair line.

'I was invited.'

'But my invitation had come along first?'

He was manoeuvring her into a corner. But he had reckoned without her honesty – which once before had proved to be almost brazen.

She smiled thanks as the waiter put a plate in front of her. Then she transferred the smile to Mungay.

'I said I was rather tired and would rest today.'

He was surprised and stared at her for two or three seconds before barking a laugh.

'So . . . this lunch is . . . clandestine?'

She cut her beef and lifted a forkful. 'Quite,' she said. And began to eat.

Jack was stupefied. The drive to Clevedon with the top of his new car down and the smell of the haymaking in his nostrils had been delightful. He had stopped at Hiscock's farm for a glass of milk and a chat. Everyone knew him; everyone loved him.

'Cricket 'satternoon, Jack.' The youngest Hiscock was Jack's own age. They had slid together off the same hay

ricks, stooked corn together, run after the same girls . . .
'Put you down for the team?'

'Wife's in labour, Billie. If she's going to hang about
for a couple of days you might see me!'

It was bravado, of course, but there had been just an
outside chance.

And now . . . he could not believe it.

'It's not true!' He had not released Hallie since his
arrival had coincided with the ambulance an hour ago.
'It simply cannot be true! Hal – tell me—'

'Pull yourself together, man!' Austen had sent the
ambulance away after talking to Mayhew. He had spoken
curtly to the doctor. 'Clear it up!' He had turned at the
door. 'You'll have to answer for this!'

Jack's total incomprehension, obviously stemming
from a hangover, infuriated him. 'You've got a son to
care for! As soon as they've finished—'

And at last Jack showed some kind of reaction.

'I don't want a son! I want my wife! I want Maude!'

He released Hallie and turned blindly for the door.
She called after him, her distress for him far outweighing
her own feelings.

But Austen put a hand on her arm.

'Let him go, Hallie. He needs to take it in – just as
we did.'

She looked up at him, her eyes enormous. It was
strange how she and Austen were bound together with
this shared experience. She would always see him, his
dark, unhappy face shadowing the baby's.

'You saved Hanny's life,' she said.

He said morosely, 'For what? A childhood without a
mother.'

But Hallie had known for some time now what she
would do.

'I will take him, Austen. Please let me. Jack . . .
he will be a loving father when he can be. But I can
be there. All the time. I know Maude would want it.'

He looked down at her. Her skin was transluscent with

tiredness and strain, but the purity was still there, shining through. The honesty. The goodness.

He said huskily, 'I know that.'

He knew he should squash the idea immediately. She was too young. The baby would become entirely Martinez. It was all he and his parents had of Maude. But he did not squash the idea.

She must have thought he would because her smile was wonderful to see and full of gratitude.

She said, 'Oh, Austen, I shouldn't have let her—'

He said, 'Don't speak of it. None of this terrible thing is your fault. That I promise you.'

She wished he had let her confess. But he had done even better; he had taken her guilt. Almost as if it were a physical burden he had lifted it from her.

Her smile was blinding. She did something that completely stunned him. She picked up his hand and kissed the knuckles.

'Austen, I thank you. I thank you from the bottom of my heart.'

And then she went to her brother.

Mungay drove Cadiz to Park Street in his car.

'This is ridiculous. I shall lose the use of my legs!'

But she loved it. The proximity to him – perfectly respectable – the air rushing through the open windows, the smell of worn leather. He drove to the end of St George Street so that they could look over St Brandon's Hill. And they were out of sight of the windows of number seventeen.

He turned and looked at her.

'If you lost the use of your legs, it would be a pity. Do you think dancing would help them?'

They had sparred all through lunch. It had been delightful. She wondered if it would continue delightfully or whether it would now come to a head. Mungay Rudolf was probably not a patient man. Well, she did not mind that.

She swivelled herself so that she too faced him. They eyed each other.

'I haven't danced for some time.'

'We should put that right.'

She imagined the gossip that would be engendered if they were seen at the Victoria Rooms.

'I don't think so. Do you?'

He smiled. 'Just the two of us. The rooms at the Royal are large. And they would let us have a gramophone.'

Her eyes widened slightly. He might be impatient but this was rushing things considerably. Perhaps after all it would have been better to go to Clevedon with Jack. Did she really want this to happen?

She said, 'Probably. But business first. Don't you agree?'

He held her gaze for a moment longer, still smiling that wolf smile, then he sat back.

'You may be right. I hoped in a way not to have to tell you. But you may be right.'

A little movement of unease fluttered her diaphragm.

'What do you mean?'

He shrugged. 'You may well feel less . . . independent. I would have preferred to have established – er – complete rapport before that happens.'

She took a breath and straightened in her seat to stare across the hill.

'You had better tell me,' was all she said.

'Jack is in my debt. To the tune of five hundred.'

She went rigid with surprise, annoyance, both developing rapidly into fury with Jack. How dare he put her in such an invidious position? And after she had 'arranged' to advance him five hundred from the Martinez books!

She said calmly, 'It will take me a week or two to pay you. I would prefer Charles not to know and as my money is tied up with his—'

He said brusquely, 'I do not want to be repaid.'

'Ah.'

'That is what I meant. I do not want to be repaid. In any way. You and I . . . that is something quite separate.'

She said angrily, 'Then why tell me about Jack's debt? Surely there was no need!'

He said, 'You are a businesswoman – the strength behind the Martinez throne. I know that. And since we have met again, I understand why that is. You have brains as well as beauty. You have common sense. You have a feel for things—'

'Don't flatter me, Mungay! Please!'

'I am completely sincere. It is why I told you. Because although I let Jack have that money for Maude's sake – and that was my only reason – my son discovered it and has condoned it for other reasons.'

She frowned. 'Austen?'

'Austen. He finds people . . . most people . . . abhorrent.'

'But . . . what has that to do with Jack?'

'Jack is a Martinez. Austen's anger with – everything – has centred itself into the old feud.' Mungay lifted expressive shoulders. 'I hoped . . . but it was not to be. Maude's marriage worsened Austen's hatred if anything. I am sorry, but it is a fact. And as a businesswoman you should know it.'

She turned her head, still frowning.

'Very well. I know it. Yet he condoned the loan you say.'

'Yes. And I understand why. At some time in the future, Austen wants to bring the House of Martinez to its knees. He sees the loan as a very small beginning.'

There was a pause, then she nodded slowly. 'I see.' She thought about Jack. He was a fool, but he would be able to grasp this. She would talk to him. They would find the money. It would be all right.

Meanwhile, Mungay Rudolf was sitting very close to her in this car. He had assured her this was a completely separate issue. And issue it was.

She leaned back and began to draw off her silk gloves finger by finger.

'Well. That has cleared the air considerably. I thank you, Mr Rudolf. I will certainly talk to my nephew when he has recovered from bringing his child into the world.' She opened her handbag and put the gloves neatly inside. 'About the dancing lessons . . .'

'They could start immediately.'

She looked at him and could not look away. His face was suddenly unsmiling and very serious. She felt exactly as she had done when he had put his hands on her neck.

She whispered helplessly, 'Mungay . . .'

And he said, 'Caddie.' And then, 'It's up to you.'

'Is it?' She remembered how it had been with Jonathan Pomeroy. Slowly she leaned forward and kissed Mungay Rudolf's wide, thin mouth. And then she took his hand from the steering-wheel and put it on her breast.

'We do not need to return to the Royal for this first lesson,' she murmured. 'We do this . . . and then this . . .'

His laugh tickled her ear. He said, 'I knew you were fast. I always knew you were forward. And very fast.'

She laughed too and although she could have swooned right away, she forced herself upright again to look at him. And at that moment, behind her, there came a sudden frantic tapping on the glass and she whipped around, startled, like a schoolgirl caught flirting with an older man.

It was Rosie.

Cadiz wound down her window.

'Oh, miss, I bin looking out for you. Oh, I'm that sorry, miss. I used the telephone for Mister Charles, but I did not know where you had gone and—'

'What has happened, Rosie? Is it Jack? Has he had an accident?'

Rosie's gaze went past Cadiz and alighted on Mungay Rudolf. Her eyes filled with tears.

'It's Mrs Martinez, sir. Your daughter. She's gone.'

108

'Gone?' Cadiz' mind filled with pictures of fleeing girls. 'Gone where? With Hallie?'

'She died, miss. Giving birth to 'er little boy.' Rosie broke down completely and used her apron on her eyes. 'She died in childbirth, miss!'

Stunned, Caddie turned to stare at Mungay. Her mind would not focus properly; she was still simply thankful that Rosie could not have seen . . . anything.

Mungay's voice was like a whiplash.

'What do you mean, girl? The child is not due to be born yet!'

Rosie's wails rose to a crescendo and Mungay gestured impatiently and half turned to feel for the door handle.

Cadiz said, 'Oh my God . . . I should have gone with Jack. It's my fault—'

'There's been some mistake,' he interrupted grimly. 'The girl is simple – she has got the wrong message.'

Cadiz clung to his arm. 'No. She's very sensible. Oh, Mungay . . . I am so sorry.'

He gave up looking for the door handle and turned on her fiercely.

'She cannot be dead. My only daughter! She cannot be.'

'Mungay – please—'

And suddenly he accepted it and his whole body was rigid, hands clenched into fists, eyes rolled to the roof of the car.

'I should have listened to Austen! Christ, I should have listened to him! The Martinez family are cursed for us – cursed! We should never . . . never . . .' His eyes came to rest on her again. There was no awareness in them now. 'And I am here. With you. When my daughter is dying!'

'Mungay, I am sorry—'

'Get out! Get out of my sight—'

Somehow Caddie got out of the car and almost immediately it moved away. She held Rosie and they went back down the street to number seventeen.

Seven
Christmas 1928

Rosie served lunch in the morning room because it was warm and cosy and offered the three friends privacy with a view of the street.

Margo said, 'Isn't this perfect, girls? Shall we sit by the window with our coffee and ogle the passers-by?'

Tilly sighed blissfully and caught Rosie's hand. 'It was lovely, Rosie. Thank you. I can remember making toffee with you in the kitchen when I was about two and a half and loving it. You never change, Rosie.'

'You never knew our Miss Hallie till you was eleven, Miss Tilly, so don't tell your fibs!'

But Rosie smiled, well pleased that her very special position in the household was known outside it. She drew a small table to the window-seat and laid out coffee cups.

'This is Miss Hallie's favourite place, isn't it, my lovely? She's sat here for hours a-nursing of that baby.' Rosie looked dotingly at the upturned face of her mistress and changed her tone slightly. 'Now come along. Here's Miss Tilly and Miss Margo come to cheer you up – face like a yard of pump water won't give them much of a Christmas spirit, will it?'

Hallie forced a smile. 'Sorry. It was just the thought of me sitting there each evening like Sister Anne—' She laughed. 'I honestly thought that if Jack saw us waiting for him once, he'd make a point of coming straight from the office each day. Ah well.'

Rosie clicked and bustled and Margo said, 'Won't he have anything to do with the baby at all, Hallie?'

110

'Well . . . it's not quite so dramatic as that.' Hallie looked at Rosie endeavouring to dismiss her without words, but Rosie hung on, mouth turned down, ready to put in her oar if Hallie strayed too far from the truth. So she changed the subject very obviously. 'Now. I want to hear about Berne, please, Margo. And I want to know every last detail about the Settlement, Tilly. And by then, Hanny will be waking up and you can come and see him.'

'Oh bliss!' Tilly was genuinely delighted. She adored babies and as she had said to her mother just that morning, 'I'd love to be Hallie. A baby without all the messy things that go before!' And her mother had said doubtfully, 'Well yes, dear, but it's a strange family for the child. Much better to endure the messy bits.' And then she had looked at her daughter and they had both collapsed with laughter and after that Tilly had said glumly, 'Trouble is, Ma, I'll have to find someone who is mighty short-sighted. I'm getting more like Aunt Hester every day!' And her mother had said stoutly, 'And what's wrong with that!' And they had laughed again.

But Margo was not terribly interested in babies. She said vivaciously, 'Oh, Hallie, it's just marvellous! I do wish you could be there with me! The city itself is beautiful and just outside the mountains . . . and the lake . . . and behind the parliament buildings the university students have sort of makeshift dances! If we slip away from mam'selle, we can just join in! Anyone can join in! It's – it's so *free*!'

Hallie was surprised. 'I had expected it to be twice as strict as Saunton.'

'Well, in some ways it is. We do silly things. Like *conversazione* and deportment and of course we still read like mad – classics in French and German aren't very funny – then we have to discuss them – but nobody pays much attention to that. Dancing is the best thing. And society.'

'Society?'

'We're taken into it, my dear. Like precious jewels we

are exhibited occasionally! If one of us goes home engaged to a count, the school chalks it up on the score board! But if someone else gets pregnant by a rag-tag student . . . oh dear God, death and destruction! Hell and damnation! The carpet is lifted and the offender is swept beneath it very quickly. In other words they are not even expelled – they are *expunged*!'

Tilly and Hallie laughed, thankful that Margo had not changed basically.

'What will happen to you, Margo?' Tilly asked.

'A count, *naturellement*. I've singled one out. He's German with a *schloss* somewhere or other. Goes back to the Hapsburgs. And . . .' she looked unutterably roguish, 'his mother actually likes me!'

Tilly threw up her hands in disbelief and Rosie, entering again with the coffee jug, said, 'And why shouldn't she, Miss Margo?' And Hallie, reverting to the schoolgirl, and influenced by her closeness to Maude, said rudely, 'If you'd slept with her, Rosie, you wouldn't ask that question!' And Tilly shrieked and said, 'D'you remember that frightful guide camp after she'd eaten the pickled eggs!' And Rosie made her exit, trying hard to look disapproving.

The girls gathered around the window in a mood of mild hysteria and heard Tilly's comments on life in the East End, and then Margo said seriously, 'What will both of you do? I mean, are you going to have a season? Or what?'

Tilly said an unequivocal, 'No.'

Hallie said, 'I don't think so.'

Margo was genuinely bewildered. 'What will become of you? How will you meet anyone? I mean . . . it's not as if the Settlement is a . . . a *career* exactly, is it? And Hallie . . . well, sorry, darling, but you're no more than an unpaid nursemaid! I know girls are sort of . . . doing things these days. Nancy Astor has a lot to answer for! But you two . . . Tilly is already twenty years old! And you're nineteen practically, Hallie!'

'On the shelf,' Tilly said gloomily.

'Dusty too,' Hallie agreed equally lugubrious.

'Be serious.'

'All right.' Hallie sipped her coffee and stared out of the window. It was raining. The people who passed were invisible beneath umbrellas. But she would recognize Austen. He was so tall. And he loped rather than walked.

She said, 'I'm glad I spent those few weeks at the Settlement, because I can answer for Tilly.' She leaned forward and directed her dark blue stare at Margo. 'What she does is so completely . . . worthwhile. Yes, that's the word for it, Margo. Worthwhile. Anything else would seem . . . rubbish. No, not rubbish. Irrelevant.'

There was a pause. Tilly smiled, embarrassed, pleased.

'A speech from Hallie Martinez! She could not have done that a year ago! So what between the Settlement and her job as unpaid nursemaid, she is coming out far more than if she went to Berne, or had parties, or met suitable—'

'If you're trying to make me feel useless, you are completely succeeding!' Margo looked exasperatedly at her two friends. 'But darlings, we live – the three of us – in a fairly useless sort of society! We have to fit in with what is expected of fairly useless women. And that is – make a good marriage and play bridge!'

'Speak for yourself!' Tilly protested vigorously. 'My ma can't play bridge! And she's not a bit useless. She cooks wonderful meals and keeps the house ticking over so that Pa can attend to his patients and never have to think where things are or—'

'She looks after her husband,' Margo put in quietly.

'And her daughter. And does it well. She makes a . . . blooming *art* of it!'

Hallie leaned forward, 'It depends on the marriage. It can be so exciting – every day something different. I think your parents are like that, Tilly.'

Margo and Tilly both assumed blank expressions.

Margo – who had been so quiet and conventional last year when they went skating, and was now almost brazen – said, 'How would you know that? Your father never remarried. Aunt Caddie is a spinster – a career woman if ever there was one! And Jack and Maude . . .' She stopped speaking. It had surprised her friends how very much Hallie had suffered at the death of Maude. And how dedicated she was to bringing up Hanny.

Hallie frowned, wondering why she was so sure of this thing. Then she nodded. 'I know. It was Maude who explained it to me. Golly, it was only last June. It feels . . . years ago.' She smiled wryly at the others. 'Knowing Maude was like a – a forcing house for me! We say what we think to each other – really speak our minds. But Maude . . . Maude's mind was so different from ours.'

'Tell us,' Margo demanded avidly.

Hallie laughed. 'It's difficult to do that. Because to a Martinez, Maude was typically Rudolf.'

'Selfish? Grabbing?' Tilly prompted.

'Yes. But perhaps most people are like that only it's not so obvious. No, it was much more than that. Mad. Passionate. Terribly aggressive.' She looked sharply at the window where a large black umbrella was passing. It continued to pass. 'Very complex,' she concluded.

Margo said thoughtfully, 'Of course, the mad Mrs Rochester in *Jane Eyre* came from that side of the world.'

Tilly said, 'The Rudolfs originated from Hanover in Germany.'

'But the plantation . . . you know what I mean.' She leaned forward confidentially. 'I heard my mother telling Lady Smythe that half the population of Barbados was entitled to the name Rudolf!'

'Balls!' Tilly said rudely.

The girls clapped hands to mouths and leaned back laughing and shocked. And just as Margo was telling Tilly that the Settlement seemed to be the real finishing school, the bell jangled in the hall.

Hallie leapt to her feet.

'Whatever is that!' she said.

Tilly leaned up and touched her hand. 'It's the front door, darling. I'm sorry. Did I embarrass you?'

'No. Of course not.' Hallie looked down fleetingly. 'I agree with you, actually. Whatever happened back in the Naughty Nineties, or whatever they were, is a thing of the past!' She started for the door. 'I'd better see who that is.'

Margo was amazed. 'Hallie – Rosie will go, for goodness' sake!'

'Rosie has quite enough to do . . .' Hallie was already gone, closing the door of the morning room carefully behind her.

Earlier that day, damp and cold in spite of her long trench coat and enormous umbrella, Cadiz arrived in Denmark Street to find Jack already there.

As far as she could remember it had never happened before and since Maude's death it had been unusual for him to put in an appearance before mid-afternoon.

'Darling boy!' She put her umbrella into the stand and reached down to peck his cheek. 'This must be my advance Christmas present! You look well. Your father will be delighted to see you.'

He looked up from the blotter where he had apparently been drawing spheres. His eyes, though not blurred by drink as usual; were dull and listless.

'Hello, Aunt. Thought I'd see you both before the day gets under way. Where is the old man?'

'Sleeping. We did not have a good night.'

'The kid? Why don't you get a nursemaid in, for goodness' sake? You can afford it.'

'You know why we do not.' Caddie kept her voice light as she filled her ink stand. 'Hallie wishes to rear the child herself.'

'It's ridiculous. She's just a schoolgirl. A sentimental schoolgirl.'

'Her birthday is next week, Jack. I hope you will not

115

forget it. And in a year's time she will be twenty. She is young, yes. She can be sentimental also. But she genuinely sees this as a sacred trust, Jack. I thought you understood that.'

He stared at her blearily. 'I don't understand anything much any more, Caddie. I don't understand why my wife died. Or why the child lives. Why I live. Why—'

'Bathos, Jack. Stop it.' Caddie spoke briskly, longing to take the boy in her arms. 'Your wife died because her womb ruptured. It could have done at any time and then the child also would have died. But—'

'She should have had an abortion! The doctor should have realized how thin the wall of the womb was . . . we didn't want children, Caddie! She didn't want them and neither did I! We would have been perfectly happy as we were.'

'Racketing around. Dancing. Drinking. Travelling. Is that what you want from life? Really?'

'I've told you, I don't know. I don't understand anything and I don't know anything. That's why I'm selling up and getting out.'

'Selling up? Your home?'

'I haven't lived there since Maude died, Caddie. You know that.'

'Then where were you last night? And three nights the previous week?'

'I was at Lily Elmes' in the Hotwells Road.'

'And Hallie sat in the window with the baby, waiting for you. We thought you had gone to Dowry Square.'

'*She* may well have thought that. You knew where I was. Probably Father did too. But you most certainly knew.'

She thought of Lily Elmes. And, inevitably, Mungay Rudolf.

She said heavily, 'Perhaps. I hoped you had gone to your own home. We all hoped that you might settle back there. Make a home for Hanny.'

'I have told you before . . .' He spoke slowly. 'I . . .

116

do . . . not . . . want . . . the child! Let the Rudolfs have him.'

'No!' She was vehement about this. 'Certainly not! Never! He is a Martinez and if you have forgotten that, we have not!'

He hung his head again and scribbled something on the blotter. 'Rudolf. Martinez. Who cares? It doesn't matter a fig, Caddie. I thought you of all people would see that.'

But Caddie had given up all pretence at arranging her desk for the day and was leaning on clenched fists, eyes closed.

She said, 'Mungay Rudolf blames you – and therefore the whole family – for the death of his daughter, Jack. I thought *you* understood *that*! I am sorry to be so blunt, but when you talk of handing over—'

'Oh God!' It was a cry from the heart and he did indeed look heavenward. 'Let it all go, Caddie! Let us be as we were – let us go back—'

'That is impossible, Jack.' Caddie straightened, opened her eyes and became her usual sensible self. 'Listen. We are not going to owe the Rudolfs any more than we do already. The business arrangements . . . they have permitted those to stand.' She sighed, seeing Jack's expression change to one of disgust. 'All right. If you will not accept any of those arguments, let me put this to you. Hallie promised Maude that she would look after your child. And Hallie is . . . Hallie. She sees it – as I said just now – as a sacred trust. She adores Hanny. We all do. How would he fare up at High House, Jack? Nannies galore. Florence, sickly and irritable. Austen . . . odd to say the least after his war experiences. And Mungay . . .' She swallowed hard. 'Mungay and his womanizing—'

'Mungay is all right,' Jack said. 'He might well blame me for Maude's death, but he has never said so. He could make it extremely difficult for me at Lily Elmes' place, but he never has—'

'You fool! Can't you see why? Because at Lily Elmes you are running up more debts! And debts to Lily Elmes are debts to Mungay Rudolf!'

He threw down his pencil and stood up. 'And that is why I am selling the house, Caddie. I can clear off every damned thing I owe and get out of the country. Start again somewhere.'

She stared at him for a long second, her dark eyes enormous. She wanted to tell him how much she would miss him. That, in spite of all his faults, he was loved by his family and would be loved by his son.

But something had happened to Caddie the day Maude had died. Some of her openness, her frankness which bordered on the brazen, had been destroyed. She had almost made a fool of herself with Mungay Rudolf. In future, she would take care.

So at last she said flatly, 'The house is not yours to sell, Jack. I think if you examine the contract you will find that it was given to Maude and in the event of her death, you, as her husband, can live in it until you either remarry or die.'

He said, 'Are you sure? I understood it was given to the two of us, which would mean that legally—'

'You can check easily enough. The Rudolfs' solicitors are ours also. Adams and Adams.'

'Margo's people. So it will be above-board.'

'Of course.'

He moved slowly to the hatstand and began to put on his outer clothing. 'I'll take your word for it, Caddie.' He finished buttoning his raglan and picked up his hat. 'Makes it easier in a funny sort of way. No business to be done after all. A clean break.'

Caddie was suddenly alarmed. 'Where are you going? You must talk to your father. And to Hallie. They have a right to know what your plans are.'

'I have no plans. But if I had, it would be best not to share them. My debts are . . . mine. And if I cannot be found—'

'You know your father will take them on, Jack!'

'No. I have already written to old Mungay. Whatever you say, Caddie, he will understand. He'll lay off the Martinez family.' He hesitated at the door. 'I'll go and say goodbye to Hallie. Sort something out with her about the kid.' He opened the door. There were sounds of footsteps on the stairs. He looked back and added urgently, 'No fond farewells, Caddie. Don't say anything yet. Please.'

She had a feeling it might be the last thing he asked of her. She drew her top lip in and held it between her teeth until it hurt. Then she nodded briefly and turned back to her desk.

She heard Charles' voice.

'Hello, my son! You're early this miserable morning!'

And Jack's reply, 'Thought I'd get a few facts and figures before I went down to the Cellars, Pa.'

They obviously passed on the landing. And then Charles came in.

'Everything all right with Jack, Caddie?' He asked, frowning slightly.

'Fine,' she replied and smiled, tasting blood on her lip.

Hallie opened the door and smiled her delight at seeing Austen Rudolf.

'I was half expecting you somehow. Isn't that strange? I often get a feeling just before you arrive.'

He smiled back at her, his long face lighting up humorously.

'Is that so surprising? I usually manage to slip in to see Hanover after I leave the office! And I did mention that if I could get some advice from old Adams about your guardianship of Hanny I would come to tell you.'

She laughed as she took his coat and hung it on the stand. If Austen had spoken those words to anyone else they would have been cutting. To her they were affectionate. She enjoyed his affection but knew it was because he saw her as a child. That was why his suggestion last week had been so . . . flattering. And apart from being flattering, so wonderful. As if Maude had officially handed over her baby.

She said, 'Actually, I haven't seen Jack for a couple of days now, so I have not been able to discuss your suggestion with him as yet.'

'Our suggestion, Hallie. I thought you were the one—'

'Oh, of course. Please do not think me ungrateful, Austen! I would be the . . . the beneficiary. I know Jack will trust me with Hanny – well, he is doing so already, isn't he? Any legal safeguards will be reassuring to him. I am certain of that.' For no reason at all she laughed up at him and he laughed back.

He said, 'There is no hurry with your brother, anyway. I simply thought I would tell you what kind of arrangements can be made – I've made a few notes – and we can discuss them together.'

She was practically certain that he was finding excuses for coming to see her. Because he . . . wanted to see her!

Her smile nearly split her face.

'Will you come into the morning room? My friends came to lunch and to see Hanny. But he is not awake yet so they have not seen him. Rose could bring him down now.'

'I don't want to intrude, Hallie.'

'You are not intruding. We have finished our gossiping.' She opened the door before he could object further. 'Girls, this is Austen Rudolf who is so kind and comes to see Hanny almost every day.' She could not stop smiling. 'And these are my dear friends, Austen. Tilly Hesterman – she is still working in the Settlement—' Hallie had told him about the Settlement and the old man who had been a gardener. 'And this is Margo Adams.'

'I have met Miss Adams,' Austen's smile had become formal but it was still in place. 'And I am treated by your

120

father, Miss Hesterman. A delight to meet Hallie's friends.'

Tilly and Margo plumped cushions on the sofa just as Rosie arrived with six-month-old Hanover Martinez. And after they had exclaimed and cooed and admired generally, they stood back and watched Hallie and Austen lean over the little boy together. As if they were the parents. And the girls looked at each other and opened their eyes very widely indeed.

He said, 'I should have left with your friends, Hallie. But I thought you would want to go through the possibilities of your guardianship in detail. I hope I am not taking up too much of your time?'

She was delighted that he had not gone with the others. The weather had closed in miserably, it was almost dark and the lamplighter was going down St George's Street with his pole.

She said, 'I am very pleased to have your company, Austen. But it may be as well if you explain the legal details to Jack himself. Or – if he is away somewhere – to my father. Or my aunt.'

Austen thought of the sharp-eyed Caddie and smiled gently.

'I do not think so, Hallie. In fact, although I know you are transparently honest, it might be better not to mention my name in connection with any of this. After all, I have simply been an envoy between you and your solicitor. Nothing more.'

Hallie could have sworn Austen had broached the idea in the first place. While they were still at the Flower House last autumn. But she could not be sure.

However she said, 'Austen, I want them to know how good and kind you have been. They simply have no idea—'

'Give them time, Hallie. You know how it is with that generation. They are completely prejudiced. And for so long they have set their faces against each other.'

'But surely anyone could see that your actions are entirely unselfish! My goodness, if – as you have said – this temporary guardianship by my father will lead to eventual adoption by me, then you have made sure he will stay with the Martinez family!'

'Of course. I know it is what Maude wished.'

'Oh, Austen!' She stood up and carried the child to the window to watch the lamp directly outside being lit. 'Your closeness to Maude mirrors mine to Jack. That is why I wish you would let me tell him at least—'

'I cannot stop you, of course,' Austen spoke smoothly, 'but I do entreat you to keep my name out of it. Jack is still in a state of shock and could react in a number of ways.'

She looked over Hanny's head and said, 'If you ask me to be silent, then I will be silent, Austen. Surely you know that?'

Her face was almost his undoing. It seemed to offer him . . . salvation.

He said, 'Come and sit with me then, Hallie. Let us take this clause by clause. You realize that this means nothing in itself. Jack must be the instigator. He must go with you and your father to Mr Adams and—'

She shook her head. 'I don't think he will do that, Austen. He is so . . .' She thought of Jack's complete indifference to Hanny and said apologetically, 'He is so lethargic.'

'Quite. He is – as I said before – still suffering from shock. That is why I arranged for Adams to draft this document. It gives your father – and eventually you – a kind of power of attorney. If your brother decides that it is in his son's best interests to hand over the legal guardianship, all he has to do is to sign just there, and he need not do anything else.'

She said doubtfully, 'It begins to sound rather . . . frightening, Austen.'

He chuckled reassuringly. 'Legal mumbo-jumbo is meant to intimidate, Hallie! But in this case it is meant to intimidate anyone who might lay a claim to the boy. It provides safeguards for him. And for Jack too.' He shuffled his 'notes' and pushed them into his pocket leaving the 'power of attorney' on the table. 'This bit of paper here is merely to save Jack all the business at the solicitors' office. It will then be left to you and your father to sort it out. And I will gladly help. You know that.'

She could have wept at his sheer goodness.

'You are more than . . . kind.' She would dearly have liked to ask whether he was protecting Hanny from any claims that might be made by his own parents. Was that why he had broached the subject in the first place? She bit her lip anxiously. 'So . . . my father will be Hanny's legal guardian. And when I come of age—'

'Or when you marry, of course.'

He heard her draw a sharp breath. But she said nothing more and after a moment she sat by him, the baby lively in the crook of her arm. He thought he had never seen anything so beautiful. A child mother. A virgin mother.

He said hoarsely, 'It is simply a beginning. Nothing can be done at all until we know that this is what Jack wants.'

She looked up smiling. 'I understand now, Austen. And of course any time Jack wished to resume . . . I mean, obviously I would never hold him to any piece of paper.'

He swallowed. 'Obviously.'

She said, 'Well. That seems to be settled. Let us take Hanny upstairs for his bath, Austen.'

And so they went upstairs together and into her room. He had seen it often before because this was not the first time he had helped to bath his nephew but still he looked around with unsatisfied curiosity. Her dressing table, where she brushed her short brown springy hair. He saw with a kind of alarm that there was make-up laid out there now. Mascara of the kind Maude had used, and an alabaster powder bowl. She was nineteen next week. Was he going to lose her before he had really discovered her?

She said, 'Could you take this sponge-bag? And he loves that celluloid duck . . .'

And when the baby 'swam' in the shallow bath, she stepped back and said, 'Oh, Austen, isn't he perfect?'

'Yes,' he replied. But he was looking at her.

After he had gone, Hallie sat in the window as usual. Hanny was bathed and powdered and in his long gown ready for bed. He could almost sit up on his own now and Hallie wedged his napkinned bottom between her thighs so that he was safe. His back was like a ramrod. He looked through the dark window, pointing with an inch-long finger at the gas lamps outside and then looking at her for approbation.

She said, 'Lamps. Pretty lamps, my darling. Twinkle, twinkle, little star . . .' He crowed and reached for her face and she kissed him and laughed with him. 'Hallie,' she said. 'Hallie and Hanny. We sound like a music hall duo. And probably that's what we shall be!' She sang, 'Hallie and Hanny Martinez, we'll make you laugh or cry all day!' He flung himself back, squealing and she pushed her face into his midriff and squealed herself.

And so they missed what they were watching for and Jack was upon them before they knew it.

Hallie jumped up, baby clutched to her hip.

'Darling Jack! We wanted to wave to you, didn't we, Hanny? Jack, how lovely! Come and sit by the fire and I'll ring for tea—'

'Please don't, Hallie.' He was still in his cap and raglan and made no attempt to take them off or sit down. 'I am in rather a hurry. I came to say goodbye.'

'Goodbye?' She had no prescience whatever this time. 'Where are you off to, brother mine? And in such a hurry. A train to catch?'

'I am going away, sis. Right away. I have to start afresh or go under. Try to understand.'

She was still, even the baby in her arms was still.

He said, 'Don't look like that, darling. I'll be back one day. And when I come I'll be different. You'll be proud of me.'

Her skin felt stretched over her face. She said, 'I am proud of you now, Jack.'

'No. You love me, but you cannot be proud of me, sis. I'm a wash-out and my one saving grace is that I know it.' He looked away from the pain in her face. 'Listen, kiddo. Will you look after the baby for me?'

She could hardly speak for tears. 'You don't have to – Jack—'

'If you're trying to say I don't have to go, you're wrong, Hallie. I do have to go. I owe a great deal of money and if the Rudolfs wished to, they could make life difficult for the rest of you. But if I just disappear, Mungay . . . the old man . . . will do nothing.'

'Oh, Jack—'

'Don't make it worse, sis. Just accept it, as I have. It's much the best.

'But, but where will you go? Now? When you leave here?'

'Probably not far tonight. But . . . don't tell anyone, Hal, but I'm going to head for Spain. I might even get work at our vineyard! That would be a neat bit of irony, wouldn't it? But I know one or two people out there. It's a bit like Clevedon. They'll accept me and give me something to do.'

'Then go to Clevedon! You could work on Hiscock's farm! Or Lady Decliveden would give you a job on the estate—'

'Hallie, that won't do. I have got to disappear. Just believe that.' He turned to face her again; he was smiling. 'And now. The kid. You're looking after him for Maude. And now you're looking after him for me. Is that all right?'

'Jack – you won't credit this – but I was going to ask you – tonight if you came home – whether you would agree to letting me have some kind of legal guardianship of him!'

He stared at her, then laughed. 'Hal! Talk sense! You are eighteen years old—'

'Nineteen next week! And of course it could not be properly legal until I become twenty-one. But meanwhile Father will do it. And it would safeguard Hanny. From . . . from . . . anyone!'

He went on staring then said, 'Caddie has put you up to this. To keep the kid out of Rudolf hands. Hasn't she?'

'No. As a matter of fact, she knows nothing about it.'

He frowned. 'Then Father . . .' He looked around the room slowly letting his gaze take in the marble mantelpiece with its carriage clock and massed photographs. His mother smiled down at him, gently. Hallie was so like her – in every way. Was that why Charles had made this suggestion?

Hallie said eagerly, 'I know Father will be all for it, Jack. And if you think Caddie would favour it too – then it would surely be the best thing?'

Jack said, 'I can't get my thoughts together. But if I am to be away . . . perhaps it might be better to make it legal.' He shook his head. 'Hallie, I have to go tonight. I cannot delay. There's no time to—'

'Do more than sign a paper.' She laid Hanny on the sofa where just hours before Austen had been sitting and plucked Austen's document from the top of the bureau.

'This is giving Pa a kind of power of attorney, Jack. Then he can see Mr Adams and fix it up properly. What do you say?'

Jack took the paper, amazed. The old man must have some inkling that he was leaving. There was no other reason for this. Had Mungay said something?

He blinked at the copperplate. He had never been able to follow legal jargon.

126

'Well . . . I know he could not have a better family.' He went slowly to the bureau and pulled down the writing flap. He was trying to read all the whys and wherefores. But if it had been concocted by Pa and old man Adams there couldn't be much wrong with it.

'Dammit all, I'll sign it. I've got to do something for the poor little swine, I suppose.' He lifted the silver top of the inkwell and thrust in a pen. His signature, 'Jack Beeching Martinez', still looked flamboyant. He thought wryly it was the only thing about him that did.

'So he's really yours now, Hal,' he said, waving the paper to dry the ink.

'Oh no. That is only your agreement. A lot more to be done. But it is the first step.' She waited until he had put the paper down then threw her arms around him. 'I will make sure he has everything he wants, Jack. Nobody could love him more than I do.'

Jack held her and over her shoulder looked at the child that he and Maude had so ill conceived. If he had ever had doubts about his paternity they were now gone. At six months Hanover was undoubtedly a Martinez. Brown hair, dark blue eyes and round, wilful chin.

He said, 'Don't spoil him, Hal. Make sure he has discipline too. It's all part of love.'

She wished she could tell him of Austen's involvement. Because Austen would provide the kind of loving discipline she knew Jack had in mind.

127

Eight
November 1930

It was Sunday morning and the first really thick frost of
the year. Hallie woke as usual at six-thirty and could
smell it seeping through the sash windows and coming
down the chimneys. She thought that as soon as it was
light she would go in to Hanny and show him the work
of Jack Frost on the glass. She smiled into the darkness
imagining his crows of delight when she let him draw
his own pictures in the rime. She was young enough
herself to remember the sheer magic of the first frost of
each year. Jack had demonstrated for her: Cadiz had
dried and warmed her numb forefinger. And she could
do both for Hanny.

Below, she heard Alfie Yorke open the cellar door to
fetch coke for the range. She heard Mrs Yorke riddling
yesterday's clinkers busily, then, not much later, the
clanking sound which meant the enormous radiators
were warming through. Charles had had them installed
only last year and they were proving a boon. Hanny
could run anywhere without getting cold and Rosie
could put his tiny nightclothes to warm each night – and
Hallie's larger ones too.

An hour later the squeak of the dumb waiter announced morning tea. Hallie was already up and dressed
and took it from Rosie at her bedroom door.

'No sound from Hanny?' she asked.

'Sleeping like a log, miss.' Rosie sounded cheerful but
looked gloomy. 'It's the radiators. They warm up just as
he would wake. Gives him an extra hour each morning,
I reckon.'

'Yes . . . Is it still the tooth, Rosie?'

'Ah. Giving me gyp all night.'

'You'll just have to see a dentist. I'll take you myself. This morning.'

'It's Sunday, miss,' Rosie said, satisfaction rising above the gloom. Rosie was petrified of dentists.

'Then tomorrow morning. Without fail, Rosie.'

'No, miss. They're nothing more than butchers—'

'Then would you see Dr Hesterman? Surely you trust him?'

'A doctor, miss? For me teeth?'

'You're not well, Rosie.'

Rosie fiddled indecisively with the rope of the dumb waiter and then a sudden nag from the offending tooth made up her mind.

'All right, miss. If you think he can help me.'

'Of course he will help you, Rosie.' Hallie smiled reassuringly. All Tilly's father would do would be to issue a royal command to attend a dentist. And Rosie would obey. Nobody ever disobeyed Dr Hesterman.

She carried her tea down the landing to the nursery and crept in. Sure enough Hanny lay supine in his cot, arms upflung, sturdy legs on top of his blankets. She stood above him, looking down smilingly. He was so beautiful in his ordinariness, and so sweetly familiar. Every line and indentation of his face was known to her and yet was never taken for granted. She often watched him while he was asleep, marvelling that such a miracle had come from such tragedy.

She went to his tallboy and sipped her tea while she sorted out his clothes for the day. A romper suit knitted by Aunt Hesterman, leather leggings . . . she went to the top drawer for the button hook that would fasten them. Brown strap shoes. A neat cloth coat and matching cap. They were going out. Immediately after breakfast Austen was calling for them in his new car and they were driving to Clevedon to see the sea. She was as excited as a schoolgirl.

She turned around and saw his eyes were open and on her. This was one of his many endearing traits. Just as she studied him so he studied her. As their eyes met he smiled and said very clearly, 'Mama.'

She came to the cot and put down the side. 'Hanny,' she said. And then she lifted him – not without difficulty because he was a big baby – and hugged him to her.

'Cold,' he mentioned. And she nodded.

'Very.'

She took him to the warmth of the radiator and wrapped him in his dressing-gown, talking to him all the time, telling him about Jack Frost and the winter windows of the house. And then she led him across the room and let him help her to pull back the curtains. And there they were, the whorls and squirls, ferns and flowers of winter.

'Pretty,' he said delightedly.

And again she said, 'Very.'

During the week he took his meals with Rosie and Mrs Yorke in the kitchen, but on Sundays his high chair was put into the dining-room and he ate with the family.

Charles and Cadiz adored this and spoiled him with bits of bacon or the yolk of an egg on squares of bread. Hallie made a point of standing back and letting them get on with it. After all she had the pleasure of his company all week.

Charles said, 'I know Austen likes to keep an eye on his sister's child, but don't you think it's rather cold for a trip to the seaside?'

'Hanny will be well wrapped up, Father.' Hallie smiled away his objection. 'And I understand the new car has a kind of heating system.'

'Yes. I believe hot air from the engine is taken through vents in the chassis. I hope the fumes are not bad for the child.'

Cadiz removed a piece of gristle from Hanny's teeth and offered him a toast crust.

'I'm sure he will be all right in the car, Charles. And the walk along the front at Clevedon will be bracing.'

Over the past two and a half years, Cadiz had come to realize that as far as Hallie was concerned Austen Rudolf could do no wrong. She judged that opposition to any of his plans would merely alienate her from her family. Cadiz prayed every night that Austen would do something that would show Hallie his true colours. It would have to happen soon. In a month's time Hallie would be twenty-one.

Pursuing her own tactics she added, 'I'm sure Austen would do nothing to harm little Hanny.' She smiled at the baby as she said this and he smiled right back at her. He was like Jack all over again. She felt her heart soften into blancmange.

Hallie said very seriously, 'He is doing his best to fill Jack's place. Well . . . even more. He is a wonderful person.'

Cadiz could not let this pass.

'Even so, Jack is Hanny's father,' she said quietly. 'And Hanny is a Martinez.' She saw Hallie's face and spoke directly to the baby. 'Definitely a Martinez, are you not, little one?' She glanced at Charles for support. 'He is Jack all over again, isn't he, Charles?'

'He certainly is. And he enjoys his food like Jack.' Charles handed over another unsuitable piece of bacon. 'I well remember when Jack was this age – you had come home for a holiday, Cad, and my dear Maria was not well . . . even then she was probably ill, you know . . .' He looked back into the past, remembering. Perhaps if they had not had Harriet, Maria might well have survived the consumption. But then . . . he smiled up at his serious-faced daughter, always thankful for her. He continued, 'And your brother wanted a boiled egg like his Auntie Cad! D'you remember this, Caddie?'

'I do indeed.' She kept smiling, willing Hallie to do likewise. Surely the girl was not *that* besotted with Austen Rudolf already?

Charles said, 'You refused to give him any—'

'That's not fair, Charles! I offered him a spoonful of yolk, but he wanted the whole egg!'

'Typical Jack,' commented Charles.

'Anyway, Hallie,' Cadiz looked up and saw a smile appearing on the full mouth, 'he leaned right over his tray – nearly fell out of the high chair – snatched my empty egg shell and shoved it all into his mouth!'

Hallie burst out laughing. She could imagine the scene only too well. Dear Aunty Cad doing her best to fill in for Mother . . . that was the trouble, of course. Caddie simply did not understand about children. She had been a wonderful aunt, but not a mother. Hallie thought she knew exactly how a mother felt. Maude had practically given Hanny to her. And Austen . . . had she given Austen as well?

Hanny looked very aristocratic in his cloth coat and leather gaiters. He sat on her lap in the front of the new car and kept pointing to the gear lever which had a bright red knob on its top.

'Wozzat?' he asked every five minutes. And every five minutes either Hallie or Austen would reply, 'The gear lever, Hanny. Gear . . . lever!'

Well used to such interruptions they maintained one of their conversations without difficulty.

Austen said, 'I've sent some of those paintings to a gallery in Park Street. If any of them sell I shall go up to London before my next trip and see what can be done there.'

From the corner of his eye he saw her face turn to him. It was eager, full of enthusiasm and interest. No-one had ever listened to him quite as Hallie Martinez did.

'Have you to put a price on them?' she asked.

'I leave that to the gallery owner. But I mentioned a base price. A kind of reserve. They mustn't go for a song. They are quite unique.'

'Oh yes – I've never been to the West Indies – not many people will have. But seeing those paintings makes you feel you have!' She laughed diffidently.

'How that would please Amos! Have I your permission to tell him?' Her eyes were like the Clevedon sky on the night she had taken his sister swimming. Almost indigo. Her face was shining and devoid of make-up. He had said to her just over a year ago, 'Your skin is too lovely to cover with anything, Hallie. And your lashes certainly need no mascara.'

She had remembered telling Maude how much better she looked with a scrubbed face. 'Then I'll never wear make-up again!' she had declared instantly. 'It's just that Margo was home from Berne and we sort of experimented together.'

He had said, 'Margo needs powder and rouge. You do not.'

And she had blushed and waited for him to say more . . . to take her hand . . . anything. But he had not.

She said now, 'Of course, you must tell him. It's terribly important that he should hear what people say about his work.' She gave her attention to Hanny for a moment or two then said, 'And another thing, Austen. Tell him it's humorous. Not many painters can paint things that make you smile. But he can.'

This was something new to Austen. He said doubtfully, 'You think the paintings are funny?'

'No! Not funny! Humorous. That's quite different.' She smiled at him, realizing he saw no difference. 'It's difficult to explain . . .' She often had to explain difficult things to Austen. Concepts which were apparently foreign to him. Like wanting to have fun without being silly or decadent. Like enjoying food without being greedy.

'I think he has made some of his figures quite comic. The cricket match – did you notice one old man is smoking two pipes? And the young mother with about fourteen babies? And their bodies are so . . . so . . . *wriggly—*'

'He would never poke fun at his own people, Hallie. This must be in the eye of the beholder.'

'He is not poking fun. Well . . . only with love. You need to love someone very much to discover their imperfections and – and – idiosyncracies – and still love them!'

He said slowly, 'As Maude did Jack?'

She was surprised. 'Yes. Yes, I suppose so.'

'And as Jack did Maude.'

'Probably. Although . . .' She did not wish to imply that Maude had had imperfections. She was, after all, dead.

There was a pause. They both spoke to Hanny at the same time and Hallie laughed and said, 'Austen is showing you the cows, darling. Look . . . the grass is frozen and they're going into the byre for their dinner!'

'Cows,' Hanny said clearly. 'Cows, Mamma.'

'Yes, sweetheart. Brown cows.'

Austen said quietly, 'I rather imagined it was entirely physical. For my sister and your brother.'

She stared at him, uncomprehending for a moment, then blushed violently and said, 'There must have been more—'

He said, 'It would be good to think that they – both of them – rose above their animal instincts.'

'Yes.' She remembered what Maude had said about the excitement of sex and added, 'I suppose so.'

'I worship purity.' He laughed, embarrassed too. 'I suppose, after the muck and mess of the trenches . . . and things that happened afterwards . . . a natural reaction . . .'

'I suppose,' she agreed.

Hanny jiggled on her knee and repeated, 'Cows, Mamma,' and Austen said, 'Does he call you Mamma all the time?'

134

The colour in her cheeks deepened. She could not deny it.

'I haven't taught him,' she said. 'And when he is old enough, of course I will—'

'But he should call you Mamma. He will be yours legally in just over a month's time. Had you forgotten?'

'No. Not at all. But I thought it might hurt you to hear him actually calling me his mother.'

'No. It gives me intense pleasure.'

'I see.'

She did not see. She thought sometimes she would never understand Austen Rudolf. But it did not matter. She admired him – had she known it, in the same way as he admired her. As someone beyond reproach. Beyond the taint of modern civilization.

They left the car outside the Nunnery on Marine Parade, and walked down to the esplanade with Hanny on his new reins. The sun was already melting the frost on the wide promenade, but the metal railings were silver with it and some of the pebbles above high water mark seemed crystalline.

Hanny was more interested in the jingle of the bells on his reins, but when Austen held him high, his round face was suddenly wide open with the wonder of the glinting sea. There was a moment of awe, then his ever-pointing finger – muffled in a fur mitten like a boxing glove – pointed outwards.

'Splash!' he said very clearly. 'Splash!'

'No, darling.' Hallie smiled up at him, sitting there so naturally on Austen's shoulder. 'Not today. Too cold. You splash in the summer.'

Several people smiled at them as they passed. It was obvious matins had finished and the churches were emptying. Hallie, Austen and Hanny made the kind of family trio that underscored the Christian values that had just been preached. Happy parents, happy child. When one elderly lady reached up for Hanny's fur mitten and said, 'Dance for your daddy, my little laddie!' Austen simply smiled and joggled obediently. And when they were alone again, he looked at Hallie and said quietly, 'Could it ever be, Hallie?'

She knew very well what he meant. The small episode had encapsulated her many fantasies; she had been in love with Austen Rudolf since the night she had spilled his tea two and a half years before in the Flower House. But she could not admit it, not even to herself, certainly never to him.

So she said, 'Could what ever be, Austen?'

He paused. Then reached up and lifted Hanny to the ground. They watched him toddle the length of his reins, jingling like a Russian sleigh. Austen had not intended to speak. Not until she was of age. But the day was so perfect, the opportunity so heaven-sent.

He said slowly, 'Could I ever be Hanny's father?'

Heat rushed to her face then drained away. She understood him, yet she did not. If this was a proposal of marriage it was strange indeed. Her brother Jack was Hanny's father.

She kept her eyes on the child and walked a little way as he tugged on the reins. If she were connected to him everything would be all right. Maude had asked her . . . Jack had entrusted her . . . she loved their son as if he were her own. She loved the daily routine of caring for him, bathing him, taking him for walks, playing with him, nursing him through winter colds – she had found her forte in motherhood.

She said in a small voice, 'I do not understand you, Austen.'

'I think you do. I think you know that I worship at your shrine.'

She gasped at his words. Worship?

She stammered, 'Please, Austen . . . be serious . . .'

'My dearest girl, I have never been more serious. The moment I saw you I knew you were perfect. Each time we have met since then, has only confirmed that first

136

impression. It has not been easy for either of us, Hallie. My father has wanted nothing to do with your family. He has consented to my visits only because he wishes to ensure that Hanny is being cared for.' He touched her arm as her eyes flashed up at him. 'I am sorry, Hallie. I have to be direct about this. You must have guessed how my father would have felt – his favourite child—'

'I did not think. Austen, I did not realize you were making such a sacrifice when you called—'

'It was no sacrifice to me. You are the only person in the world who understands me. We both are striving towards something good, something whole – haven't you felt this also?'

They were moving quite fast now as Hanny trotted by the band-stand. It must account for her quick breathing.

'Yes. Yes, of course.' She panted a small laugh. 'If we are to be direct, Austen, then I admit – I have lived for your visits!'

He could have wept. A grown man in a public place . . . and he could have wept. Her honesty was like a beacon in the darkness.

He said simply, 'Hallie, I admire and respect you more than I can ever tell you! I am old and cynical but – when you are twenty-one – next month – will you do me the honour of marrying me?'

She stopped dead and Hanny on the other end of the reins squawked with frustration and pawed the ground like a young bullock.

She said, 'Oh, Austen. Is that what you meant? That you wanted to get married? Oh, Austen, I love you so much! You remember when I dropped your tea? It's been like that ever since! Like Maude said . . . exciting and wonderful and—'

'And you will marry me?'

'Oh, I will!'

She flung her arms around his greatcoat and hugged him and Hanny sat down abruptly at the other end of

137

the shortened reins and yelled again. Austen picked him up and held him aloft and swung him until he laughed again.

'I *am* to be your father!' he said triumphantly to the cold blue sky.

And Hallie laughed aloud and wished they were on their own and somewhere very private so that he could kiss her.

He swore her to secrecy. Her birthday came and went and so did Christmas, and still he would not give her permission to tell a soul.

'I have to ask your father's permission officially. It must be done properly, Hallie. I want no-one pointing fingers – no gossip as there was about Maude.'

'How could anyone possibly gossip about us, Austen?' Hallie was bewildered. 'You have behaved so properly all this time. Supporting me as best you could. Calling once a week. Making certain that I was able to look after Hanny's affairs with the help of my father.'

'And now that help has to be transferred to me, my darling. If Hanny is to have a proper family again, he must see us as his proper parents. I need to see old Adams and have the documents drawn up in detail. We have Jack's agreement—'

'Only to my half, dearest. And how can we extend that permission? We have no idea where he is. Aunt Caddie nearly goes mad with worry sometimes—'

'Don't you recall, my angel? The document referred to you at your majority and your future husband.'

'I don't think I read it, Austen. It was so awful with Jack leaving that very evening.'

'Of course. I understand that. But it does make things much simpler now.' He looked at her, smiling. 'Unless you do not consider I am a suitable father, darling? You have the final say. That point is also made clear in the contract Jack signed.'

'Oh, Austen, how could you! You are already his

father – in his eyes.' She blushed as she so often did now. 'And in mine also.'

'Oh, Hallie . . .' They were alone in the morning room and he took her hand. 'Do you remember doing this to me once?' He put his lips to her palm and then covered it with his other hand. 'I have never forgotten that, Hallie. I almost fell to my knees before you then.'

She wished so much the kiss had been on her lips; her palm tingled with it.

She said, 'I wish you would find me a little less worshipful, darling, and a little more lovable!'

He laughed. 'Have I not told you you are the most lovable, adorable, wonderful girl – human being – in the whole world?'

She touched his face gently knowing that no-one else had ever heard him speak like this. She said, 'Why do you not let us tell the world then, Austen? Why do you not kiss me?'

He held her fingers against his cheek and looked at her, his eyes black with emotion.

'I do not wish to . . . sully you, my darling.'

'Sully me?' She laughed, outraged. 'For goodness' sake, Austen! I am to be your wife!'

He withdrew slightly. 'Dearest, I have felt that our love for each other was based on something far deeper – more enduring – than . . . a kiss! Do we need outward shows, Hallie? I certainly do not!'

She felt he was reproaching her and said quickly, 'Of course not. But surely, when we are married . . . married people . . . do you not want children, Austen?'

The door opened and Rosie ushered in Hanny who had just been for a shopping spree with his Great-aunt Caddie. The little boy thrust out his feet to display new shoes. Caddie, already halfway up the stairs to find herself a more comfortable pair, had a glimpse of Austen holding out his arms to the child and saying to Hallie, 'My dear, we already have a child!'

She almost ran along the landing to her room and once inside leaned against the door as if she expected intruders.

Had it all happened? Was it too late?

And below, Hallie watched Austen holding his nephew and felt her unease melt before such joy.

She said with her usual frankness, 'Austen Rudolf, you are a very unusual man. I feel sometimes I barely know you.'

His smile turned from the child to the girl. He felt a sudden surge of triumph. He had visited Barbados twice during the past two and a half years and both times had remained celibate. He had cemented the friendship between himself and Amos and encouraged the man to display some of his unusual paintings, so if there had been any jealousy he had overcome that too. And meanwhile, because of Maude's death and Hallie's ridiculous 'adoption' – which would cease to be ridiculous once she was married to him – he had succeeded in somehow preserving her. She had found something to do which fulfilled her and kept her safe at the same time. She had had no wish to return to the Settlement with the Hestermans, yet he knew her conscience might well have forced her there had it not been for Hanny. And as for joining Margo Adams in Berne . . . he shuddered inwardly. By forcing Jack out of the country and drawing up that peculiar 'contract of adoption' he had realized – released – her real strength. And he had preserved her innocence, that untouched quality which had so attracted him from the outset. And now – very soon now – she would belong to him. And Hanover Martinez would become Hanover Rudolf.

'Oh, Austen,' Hallie's face softened with love. 'You look so happy. Sometimes – when I see you looking so happy – I can hardly bear it!'

She loved him. She loved him as much as he loved her. It was incredible and wonderful. And he was now in a position to keep her as she was now. To stop time.

He was suddenly reminded of a butterfly preserved in resin. Trapped. And dead.

Then she said, 'We are going to have such fun once we are married, darling. I want to come to Barbados with you and meet Amos. He can give us painting lessons. How would you like that, Austen? Sketching trips? And we'll buy some bicycles and put Hanny on the back and cycle through Wales and—'

He blinked the butterfly image out of his head and wondered if it were possible to have this 'fun' she often spoke of. And above him, Hanny gripped his hair painfully and shrieked, 'Daddy! Dance, Daddy! Dance!' And the three of them cavorted around the small room like a gaggle of street urchins.

The next day he called at the house on his way to the office. Rosie announced him through gritted teeth.

Hallie was pouring tea for Charles, Cadiz had already left.

'Is something wrong?' She was more than alarmed. All night she had dreamed of him; her fantasy was coming true. She imagined he had changed his mind.

He smiled and put out an arm to stop Rosie leaving the room.

'Miss Martinez told me of your toothache, Rosie. I have made an appointment with my own dentist and have come to take you. The car is outside. Have I your permission, sir?'

Charles half stood, surprised then delighted.

'My dear boy . . . of course. Only too pleased! Poor Rosie has been in agony for so long. Rosie, you'll go with Mr Rudolf, won't you?'

Rosie turned a look of abject terror on Hallie and saw no hope there. Hallie's eyes were black with gratitude at Austen's thoughtfulness.

'Oh, Austen, when I mentioned Rosie's toothache, I did not dream—'

Austen addressed himself to Rosie. 'I have a horror of

dental treatment. But Mr Mallard is wonderful. There will be no discomfort at all.'

Rosie swallowed desperately and muttered, 'Very well, sir.'

'Get your coat and hat. I will wait outside for you. Good morning to you both.'

He was gone. And when Rosie returned an hour later her stiff face was lopsided with an enormous smile. Mr Mallard's ministrations had indeed been painless. And Mr Rudolf had now become Mr Austen. And Mr Austen was a very kind gentleman.

Mungay looked up from some papers on his desk. His dark eyes were dull; there was cigar ash on his tie and it drifted over his waistcoat as he lifted his head.

He said, 'I've seen what you have been doing, Austen. Ever since your sister died. I suppose . . .' He laughed emptily. 'I suppose Maude's death was quite an opportunity for you?'

'Father . . . you do not understand at all.' Austen drew up the visitor's chair, sat down and leaned across the desk. 'What you hoped for when Maude married Jack Martinez – that was an impossible dream. Because of the Martinez' weaknesses. Because of Maude's temperament too – face up to it. The marriage would never have been a success. The child would have been passed from one hand to another while they both pursued their pleasures—'

'They had warmth and passions. Stupid perhaps – both of them. Certainly Jack. But . . . dammit all, Austen, I understood them. I do not understand you.'

'Then try, Father. This marriage will work. It is not going to be based on the passions you so admire. It is based on respect. Deep respect. I care about this girl. I am not going to use her – exploit her – as most husbands do. I care about the child too. That is the difference.'

'A ready-made family, eh?'

'Exactly. Maude and Jack will live on in Hanover Rudolf.'

'She will not let you change his name.'

Austen said confidently, 'She will.'

'So. You will ensure that one day the House of Martinez will be yours. You will have an heir. And you will be able to remain completely uninvolved. No risk of pain, eh, Austen? You think you had enough pain in the trenches. You're making sure it will never happen again.'

Austen stood up abruptly. 'I do not have to justify myself like this, Father. I want your blessing for Hallie's sake. It will hurt her terribly if we do not have it.'

Mungay studied his son for a long moment. He was thirty-three; tall and upright and, Mungay supposed, good-looking in the Rudolf way – long aristocratic face, finely curved mouth. He was no darker than Maude, yet Maude's face had been vivacious and alive; Austen's was closed.

Mungay said, 'You won't make her happy, Austen. Does that not worry you?'

And, to his surprise, Austen's face flushed darkly.

'If I thought that, Father, I would not marry her!' He turned and went to the window. 'But . . . I am as certain as anyone can be in this world, that in spite of everything – the age difference, our family differences – perhaps because of those very things – I will make her happy!'

Mungay sighed deeply and reached for his cigar box.

'Then you have my blessing, my son, for what it is worth.' And as Austen turned gladly he added warningly, 'But you will never have the Martinez' blessing. I am certain of that.'

Austen resumed his seat, calm again. 'They are used to seeing me. I have been calling nearly every week. They must guess my intention.'

Mungay shrugged as he cut the end from his cigar. 'Even so . . . Charles, perhaps. He is sentimental. He will hope this will reconcile the families again. But

143

Cadiz . . . no. She has a mind like a razor. You will never convince her.'

Austen said, 'That is why I shall not ask her.' He saw his father's frown and said, 'Why should I? It is Charles' permission I need. Not hers.'

'She will be there when you make your request. I can practically guarantee it.'

Austen smiled. 'Father, I am going to take a leaf out of your book. We shall meet at the Corn Exchange. As you say, Charles is sentimental. He agonizes over the fate of Jack. If I repeat what happened three years ago – almost to the day – he will see it as pre-ordained.'

Mungay sat back in his chair. 'You are clever, Austen. But Cadiz handles all the appointments. Do you think for one moment she will permit her brother to meet you tête-à-tête—?'

'He is there today. Times are bad and his American importers have gone to the wall. He is auctioning their order.' Austen too sat back. 'I have arranged a very good deal for him. He will be mellow. As soon as most of the bidders disperse, we will meet accidentally.'

Mungay wondered whether he should try to stop Austen. But he was too tired to try. And he had to admit that the thought of Cadiz Martinez being bested by his son, gave him a little spurt of pleasure.

Nine
June 1931

They were married on Hanny's third birthday, and in view of the circumstances it was a very quiet affair. The bride's aunt was in Spain in a last-ditch effort to find her nephew and stop his son's adoption. Charles, when it came to it, had proved a much tougher nut to crack than the Rudolfs had bargained for. He attended the ceremony in Bristol's register office obviously burdened with forebodings. But Hallie had proved too strong for her father and when faced with his opposition had quietly pointed out that she needed no-one's consent. She was twenty-one, legally Hanny's mother. It would grieve her considerably if her father and aunt maintained their disapproval, but it would make no difference.

So Cadiz had gone to Spain because that was the only hope they had of finding Jack. And Charles donned tails and topper and took his daughter's arm as they went into the bare room where the Hestermans and the Rudolfs already waited. Tilly held Hanny on her lap; her pleasant horse face was very serious indeed. Margo was spending the summer in Hamburg with the family of her German *Graf*, but her father slid into a seat before the ceremony began. Austen had made sure that the signatures on the register would be biased towards the Martinez.

Hallie was wearing white; he had wanted that, though otherwise he made no stipulations. It was a hot day so she handed her wool coat to Aunt Hesterman and stood by Austen in the kind of simple dress she thought he would like. In fact, he had never seen anything like it.

145

It appeared to be two squares of pure silk joined at shoulders and sides, ending at her knees, and girdled around her hips with a silver cord. It was Grecian in its cut, but it was also – unrecognized by her – extremely provocative. The white silk stockings and cuban-heeled shoes beneath it and the thick springing bob of brown hair above, emphasized its terrific smartness. It was no coincidence that a great many young ladies in Bristol wore Grecian tunics that summer.

Austen found it very difficult to juxtapose the virginal and the allure in Hallie's get-up. Her straw saucer of a hat hid her face from him as they made their responses. He saw the rise and fall of the silk as she breathed – very fast – and imagined, just for a moment, what it would be like to smooth the bodice of that tunic and outline her hidden form. Like a sculptor moulding clay. And then she lifted her face to his and smiled; the dark blue eyes were innocent of flirtation, the mouth and cheeks unpainted. Her skin looked luminous. He knew it was because she was happy. He also knew that she was happy because of him. He felt shame at his stupid fantasy; he was, after all, her protector.

'I now proclaim you man and wife.'

The registrar smiled austerely and closed his book. Austen turned to her and put his hands on her waist. She swayed towards him, expecting him to kiss her. He smiled and whispered, 'Thank you, my dearest. My dearest wife.' And she whispered back, 'Oh, Austen . . . thank *you*.' And then he turned her to face the others and they were smiling at last; all of them. Except his own father.

They took Hanny with them to Cornwall. She had wanted to honeymoon in Barbados, but he had used Hanny as an excuse.

'He is rather too young, darling. Better to be within shouting distance of English doctors, don't you think?'

'Well . . . yes. Although you were young on your first visit.'

'Six. Twice his age. I was very homesick.'

'Oh, my poor darling!' She had hugged his arm, almost weeping at the thought of him taken from his mother all those years ago.

They caught the *Cornish Riviera* immediately after the ceremony. Austen had arranged a wedding breakfast at the Royal for one o'clock. When he had gone to his mother's room that morning to say goodbye, his father followed him, still expostulating at the tight schedule.

Austen kissed his mother's withered cheek. She smelled of wine. Charles Martinez had given her a case of sherry three years ago before relations had become strained again. Had she continued to order the stuff from him?

He smiled at her and replied to his father.

'The wedding breakfast is for you and the guests, Father. I have ordered lunch in the restaurant car for the three of us.'

Mungay exploded.

'This is the last straw! Your one aim is to alienate that girl from all of us – her family, friends, even your mother and me! And this is just one more—'

Austen had tried to reason with him. Had tried to explain that he wished to avoid all the innuendoes and jokes that were so unsuitable for someone like Hallie to hear – and young Hanny. His father had been able to see only that a wedding breakfast without a wedded pair would be a personal embarrassment to him.

'If your mother was there it would be slightly less difficult—'

Florence who had said nothing during the exchange made a sound that sounded like a laugh but had turned out to be a sob. Austen had tried to comfort her; Mungay had left the room.

Now, as they waved goodbye from the window of their

first-class compartment, Austen knew he had done the right thing. Hallie wanted to be out of it all as much as he did, and as for young Hanny, he could not wait for the King-class locomotive to begin its panting journey out of the canopy of Brunel's station.

'Wave the flag! Wave the flag!' he shouted to the guard and banged the leather window strap against the door like a drum.

Tilly stood on the running board and pecked Hallie's cheek. Aunt Hesterman held her hat against the strong breeze funnelling along the platform and said sternly, 'Stop that, young man!' Charles said, 'If only your aunt could have been here, I'm certain she would be reconciled to—' And Mungay thought of Cadiz and felt a sharp stab of longing for her acerbic words and sharp, Spanish features.

A whistle blew; the guard walked alongside the moving train and stepped casually aboard the van as it drew abreast. Hanny was speechless with admiration. Rosie suddenly appeared from nowhere, tore along the platform and hurled confetti through the window. Then the slipping driving wheels gripped properly and the train emerged from the station, enveloped in its own steam, and Austen pulled on the leather strap and pretended to help Hanny to close the window.

Hallie sat down looking dazed.

She said, 'Have we done it, Austen? Have we really done it?'

'We've done it. How do you feel, Mrs Rudolf?'

She looked up, momentarily uncomprehending. Then laughed. 'I feel wonderful, Mr Rudolf. Absolutely top-hole!'

Hanny clamoured for attention. 'Who is Mrs Rudolf?' he asked, jumping up and down.

'Allow me to introduce you.' Austen looked at him gravely and he stood still. 'Your mother. Mrs Rudolf.' He turned to Hallie. 'Mrs Rudolf . . . your son, Hanover Rudolf.'

Hanny said, 'That's not my name, Daddy. My name is Hanny Martinez!'

Hallie simply stared at Austen.

He said, 'How can that be? I am your father. My name is Austen Rudolf. Therefore yours must be Hanny Rudolf.'

The small boy was suddenly enchanted with the idea. He held out his hand and when Austen took it, he pumped both hands vigorously.

'How d'ye do, Mr Rudolf?' he said.

'Very well, Mr Rudolf, sir. And how d'ye do?'

'Not so bad. Not so bad at all, Mr Rudolf . . .' Hanny was a natural mimic. He turned to Hallie. 'How d'ye do, Mrs Rudolf?'

Hallie also took his hand but seemed unable to join in the game.

Hanny said, 'You've got to say—'

Austen interjected in a low voice, 'It will be so much easier for the boy, darling. Especially when he goes to school. If Jack agrees we can change it officially. By deed poll.'

Still Hallie did not speak.

Hanny pumped impatiently, 'You've got to say, How d'ye do, Mr Rudolf? That's me, Mummy. I'm Hanny Rudolf now! I'm Hanny Rudolf!'

Hallie forced a smile. 'It sounds strange, darling.'

Austen said stoutly, 'You'll soon get used to it, my angel!'

The steward appeared in the corridor and slid the door open.

'Are you first luncheon, sir?'

'I believe we are,' Austen said.

'Sherry is being served in the dining coach now, sir. Madam.'

'Then we will come along directly.'

He held out his hands for hers and pulled her to her feet steadying her against the swaying of the carriage.

'Darling, you don't mind, do you? I thought it would

simplify things so much for Hanny. Now he has a proper family.'

For a moment he felt resistance in her fingers. And then she stepped close to him and rested her cheek on his tie.

'How could I mind? You are the dearest most unselfish man in the world!' She lifted her face. 'Oh Austen, kiss me! Hold me close! I love you so much I can hardly bear it!'

He kissed her very chastely. Her eyes were still closed as he withdrew; her smile was blissful.

'I have never been so happy,' she said.

And they made their way down the corridor and into the dining car and met with the usual indulgent smiles from one and all.

The appalling thing was, Cadiz had found Jack, and he did not care.

She had begged and pleaded with Hallie; she had laid her cards on the table for Charles to see plainly what was going on, and when it became obvious that the marriage would, in fact, take place on June the first as planned, she had left for Spain on the twelfth of May in plenty of time to find Jack and bring him home.

Charles had been unconvinced.

'Caddie – my dear – what is the point of all this? Whatever papers Austen has signed, they will be null and void when Jack returns. It is quite obvious he is Hanny's father – they are like peas from the same pod.'

'But he will be called Rudolf! His name will be Rudolf!' She felt at times that she was going mad. Four years ago – three years ago – this marriage and adoption would have been as dreadful to everyone else as it was to her. Austen's careful wooing, his many small acts of kindness, his apparent acceptance of all things Martinez – had fooled everyone.

As if to confirm this, Charles said gently, 'We are talking of two very reasonable people, Caddie. Hallie and Austen. They will do whatever the boy wishes—'

'Exactly! Jack is a stranger to him!'

And Charles had said heavily, 'Whose fault is that?'

She had considered seeing Mungay. She had lain awake at night imagining walking into his office and saying coolly, 'May I have a brief word with you?' In the darkness of the night she had visualized him looking down at some papers on his desk; seen the top of his head – dark hair laced with white like the frost over the Avon Gorge in November. And then at her words, he would look up. Those dark eyes would hold her, that familiar mouth would smile sardonically at her and he would say, 'I rejected you once. Are you back for more?'

And at that point she always groaned with the shame of it and turned her face into her pillow.

So it was a relief to make the decision to go to Spain.

She told Hallie she wanted Jack to be at the wedding; it was half the truth anyway, but Hallie knew the whole reason for the trip.

'Listen, Aunty Cad. Hanny will always belong to Jack. You must know that. But . . . try to bring Jack home in any case.' She hugged her aunt's shoulders, suddenly shocked at their thinness. 'I miss him so badly. This will be the first time I've done something important without him being there.'

'Something catastrophic, you mean.' Caddie had long given up the pretence of accepting Austen.

Hallie released her. 'Oh . . . you have resurrected the old feud and made it worse! You weren't like this about Jack and Maude! I remember you supported them!'

'I thought of it as a business arrangement—'

'Not entirely! I remember Jack said you were the only one who understood about the – the passion!'

'Jack was different. And so was Maude. Crazy but not evil.'

Hallie was suddenly still. When she spoke her voice was low with sadness and anger.

'Is that what you think of Austen? You could not be

more wrong. He has not been a happy man – if he talked to you as he talks to me you would understand why. But to call him evil—'

Caddie stammered, 'I did not mean that he – personally—'

'I would hope not. Caddie, I love Austen. Go and find Jack. But believe that I am doing the right thing.' She moved away, terminating the discussion, but at the door she said very quietly, 'If I have to choose between Austen and anyone – anything – else . . . it will be Austen.' And she left.

Caddie remembered those words during the sea voyage on the *Ulysses*, when, as usual, she was horribly sick. She thought it quite probable, as she lay on her bunk, that she had never been quite so miserable as she had been since Hallie announced her marriage. She had grieved for young Jonathan Pomeroy, grieved terribly. But this was different. Her self-esteem was at its nadir. She had been proud of her independence in a world of dependent women, her business acumen, her ability to work twelve hours a day – they were all unusual qualities. And besides all that, she was a woman very much loved. Charles, Hallie, Jack and little Hanover all loved her almost as much as she loved them. Now . . . Jack was gone, Charles was bewildered and troubled, and Hallie – she had lost Hallie and her small great-nephew with her. Which showed her how wrong she had been about her independence. She was dependent on those people. Without them she was tired all the time and had made several mistakes in the office.

So she groaned and heaved and disembarked at the town for which she had been named, feeling, as usual, tired, lonely and . . . old.

Cadiz was not her favourite place by any means. The island, joined to the mainland by a dirty ribbon of sand, was a mixture of wealth and such abject and degrading poverty that you had to put it out of your mind or pretend you had strayed into a Hogarth painting. Crippled beggars lined the streets, the maimed led the blind, dogs snapped and growled underfoot and the whole area was swept by the heat of the sirocco blowing straight from Africa's enormous land mass. She wondered just why her parents had called her after this place. In her present state of mind she wondered whether they had anticipated her growing old so dismally.

But Spain was her second home. She said goodbye to the captain of the vessel as civilly as she could – sickness and a distrust of all things Rudolf, made this difficult. He was already supervising the unloading of empty casks for transport to the vineyards and had small time for the niceties. She planned to return with the full casks in ten days' time; and with Jack too. Everything would be so different then. So much better.

She secured a taxi without difficulty, collected her baggage from the customs shed and directed the driver to the Castillo in her flawless Spanish and with an authority he recognized instantly.

It was very hot and the dust enveloped them immediately. She pulled a chiffon scarf over her nose and mouth and held her hat with one hand. She was expected at the Castillo. Benita would be waiting with lemonade made with the ice-cold well water and a compress for her head. She thought of the stone floors and narrow windows of the Moorish fortress with gratitude. To be cool and shaded and lying down would be enough for now. Tomorrow she would start her enquiries. Dom Rodriguez, who managed the yards, would be able to tell her whether Jack had ever passed that way. She tried to concentrate on recognizing streets and houses. But they all looked the same; the cathedral rising from a huddle of square white boxes; the walls of tenements topping the medieval ramparts in places and seething with people on their galleries, much like a wasps' nest seethes with wasps. She closed her eyes wondering if she were really ill. It was a relief to smell the river smell of the Guadalquivir and know that soon they would be driving through the Andalusian peach orchards and then, within sight of the Sierra Moreno, the vineyards would slope upwards to the Castillo itself.

It all worked out so smoothly she might have guessed it was destined to end in failure. The Castillo was blessedly cool and Benita's lemonade froze the roof of her mouth delightfully. She rested and then talked to Benita about a light evening meal and heard the local news. Benita's daughter had had another baby. 'At forty years old, *señora*! There is still hope for you . . .' Said smilingly because news of Jonathan Pomeroy had reached the Castillo long ago. But Cadiz was in no mood for banter and said sharply, 'I am forty-three, Benita.'

There was goat's cheese for supper with the kind of salad she adored, thick with olives and bathed in oil. She slept like a baby, waking once to find bars of moonlight coming through the arrow-slit windows and turning her greying hair silver. She remembered smoothing it before she slept again, and in the morning knew from her salty face that she had wept.

She went to the kitchen and breakfasted with Benita, and four of her grandchildren, on melons and ginger.

'The children eat with me on their way to school,' Benita explained without apology. The Castillo had always been run as a family concern, and that meant Benita's family as well as the Martinez.

Then she walked down to the yards and into the shed which was Dom Rodriguez' office. He knew of her arrival, of course, and had lists of comparative yields drawn up for her inspection.

'But first, *señora* . . .' they all gave her the courtesy title just like the French '. . . you would like to see your nephew? Pleasure first then business, *si*?'

It was that easy. Jack had been working in the yards for the whole of the two and a half years he had been in Spain. He drew a labourer's wage and slept in one of

154

the adobe houses that old Carlos Martinez had had constructed for his labourers, itinerant or permanent. Everyone understood why he wished to live that way; young aristocratic dilettantes had reverted to living on the land before now. And Jack had always looked the eccentric Englishman with his big panama hat and silk cravat.

The hat was now unrecognizable, the cravat a knotted kerchief to soak up the sweat. But he was as open and casual as ever.

'Aunty Cad!' He embraced her thoroughly, lifting her off her feet and whirling her around as if she were still a girl. 'I didn't realize you knew where I was! Who has been telling tales? Rodriguez?'

'No-one. You mentioned to Hallie that you might do this and it was our only lead. So I was starting here. I thought it was a fruitless search. And here you are, as if we were together yesterday!'

She was almost weeping again. That too was a sign of age; weak maudlin tears.

'Come on, Aunty Cad! You didn't think I'd done myself in, did you?'

'Of course not! You're silly, but not that silly!'

'Why the tears then?'

'I'm just so very . . . p-pleased . . . to see you.' She was blubbing properly now, and he unknotted his kerchief and dabbed at her face making soothing sounds of comfort.

Rodriguez thought they had had long enough in private and came into his office.

'Ah!' He threw up his hands. 'Some catastrophe! I knew it! I said to Benita, the *señora* would not come all this way before the harvest unless there was a catastrophe!'

'No – really – I'm so sorry—'

'Is there a catastrophe, Aunty Cad? Sit down and have a sherry –' he laughed '– the Martinez panacea for all ills.'

'No catastrophe. Oh dear God, I never cry. I'm just so pleased to see you, dear boy. Dear, dear boy.'

Rodriguez withdrew discreetly and after Caddie was partially composed again, Jack armed her down the steep hillside, talking about the grapes, pointing out the new strain they were growing for next year's vintage.

She sniffed. 'It's good to be here. So long since I saw the blasted things actually growing. Nearest I've been to vines is the kidney bean patch Mrs Hayle has started down at the Flower House.'

He laughed. 'How is Mrs Hayle? I don't think I want to see the Flower House ever again, but she was good to Maude. She let her borrow one of her enormous dresses. And I fished out my old cricket hat. It was hot that summer.' He looked across the vine-covered slopes and into that recent past.

She said, 'Oh, Jack, I should have been with you then. You wanted me to come.'

He rallied instantly. 'Darling Aunty Cad. What good would it have done? No-one could have saved her. I talked to Doc Hesterman about it afterwards. Unless they could have operated about a month before, they could not have saved her. And if they had operated, the baby would have died.' He paused, then said with obvious effort, 'How is the baby?'

'He's no baby now, Jack.' She told him about Hanny and saw that there was no response in his face. 'If you saw him, I know you would love him. I just know it,' she concluded hopelessly.

'I think it is best as it is.' His voice was so gentle she knew he was sincere. There was no longer the tension of despair about him. The hard physical work of the vineyard was helping him to live again and she must not grudge him that.

She said, 'Jack. Please. At least let me rescind the adoption thing. I can talk to old Adams and have it destroyed. All I need is your signature on a letter to that effect.'

He was silent for a long time. They came to the top of the slope again and looked out towards the Sierra Moreno. They were sheltered here from the African sirocco; a heat haze hovered above the grapes so that they appeared to be shimmering under water.

He said, 'Caddie . . . you know I would do a great deal for you. But I wonder . . . it sounds as if this bee you have in your bonnet is because of the feud—'

'Jack, Austen Rudolf is the one who is continuing the feud—'

'Dear Caddie, please listen. Before I came here, during the six months after Maude's death, I thought and saw things very clearly.'

'You've always said that alcohol sharpens your perceptions, Jack. That is not true. You deceive yourself.'

He continued patiently. 'You were the one who backed my marriage into the Rudolfs. You were getting on well with old Mungay – yes you were, I remember one evening we all dined together and you and he sparked each other off amazingly—'

'Not true!'

'You did not even realize it. But it happened. And then, quite suddenly, after Maude's death, when everything was upside-down in any case, your attitude – hardened. I can't think of another word for it, my dear. You brought down the shutters. You put up the defences. You were so pleased Hanny looked like a Martinez and not like a Rudolf. You taught him our nursery rhymes. When poor old Austen called, you went out of the room—'

'Poor old Austen! He is devious and clever and ruthless!'

'And shell-shocked. It's true, Caddie. And Hallie is good for him.' He turned and faced her. 'And I think Hanny might be good for him too.'

'And what about Hanny?'

'You and Father still have a say in things. I remember

when I signed that piece of paper the responsibility was shared between the three of you until Hallie was twenty-one. Your influence will still be there. I know that.'

'But Austen will be her *husband*! It will be natural that he will call him father – I think he might already be doing so!'

Jack said, 'Good. I am glad, Aunty Cad. Let him think of me as an uncle. Austen will be a much better father for him.' He held her shoulders and shook her gently. 'Accept it, my dear. It has happened and you are fighting it all the way. This is no frightful Gothic tale of horrors. Hanny is very lucky. He could be living with a nanny in Dowry Square while Maude and I enjoy ourselves.' His face saddened. 'Somehow, there was never a chance for us, was there?'

And Caddie, looking into his honest English face, wept again.

Hanny adored the beach. He wore tiny khaki shorts with pockets which he loved to fill with shells and seaweed, and he waded through the rock pools and squatted on his heels so that the trouser hems always dripped sea water. The weather was not invariably fine but they went to the beach even in the rain because, as Hallie said, 'Wet is wet. And he is always wet anyway. And he does so love it.'

Austen hired a beach hut for the two weeks and he and Hallie would take breaks inside it when it rained and watch their son trail his spade and bucket down to the shore and begin his daily task of digging a channel and filling it with water.

'We'll come every year, shall we?' Hallie said, fiddling with the spirit lamp to make tea. 'It really wouldn't matter if it rained every day!'

Austen laughed and cleared the card table of sand to lay out Bakelite beakers and the tin of biscuits.

'It certainly doesn't bother him, does it?' He watched her pour water into the teapot and leaned down to turn off the lamp. 'I've never met a child so content before.'

Hallie was surprised. 'Don't you remember enjoying the shore, darling? Surely your parents took you to Weston-super-Mare – and you knew about this place anyway.'

'Yes. We came to Porthmeor before Maude was born. But, of course, I was not allowed to venture off alone. And Mother was not well . . . When we went to Weston we walked along the promenade.'

'Oh lordy.' She looked up at him, smiling ruefully. 'We really have got to start from scratch, haven't we?' She finished pouring and looked down at Hanny's figure almost shrouded in the misty rain. Two other children had joined him. They appeared to be digging a new Suez Canal. She said, 'It's one of the ways you have fun, darling. To do things – like playing on the beach – in unlikely circumstances. In other words, when it's pouring with rain.'

'You're teasing me.'

'No, I'm not, actually. When we've drunk this tea and given Hanny – and his new friends probably – a biscuit each, we'll do it ourselves.' She frowned judiciously. 'It might not work first time. You have to employ a certain amount of abandonment.'

He looked at her, smiling. No-one else in the world could talk to him like this.

He said, 'All right. I will bear that in mind.'

And when they joined the children an hour later, he understood exactly what she meant. The rain was cold on the back of his shirt, the sea was colder on his feet, the wet sand stuck to his hands so that when he scratched his face, it transferred to that as well. It was an unlikely way to have fun. Yet looking at Hanny, digging industriously and shouting to someone called Tom to fetch more water quick quick quick, and then at Hallie, who was working on a deep pit in which to store the water when it arrived, he felt the deep contentment of his marriage stirred by a strange little fizz. He wanted to laugh out loud, stretch his hands to the rain-filled clouds, and run for no reason at all.

The skies cleared the next day and two donkeys, grey and dusty, appeared at the West Head.

'Tuppence a ride!' bawled their keeper, whacking their sides with a whippy cane which woke them up for a moment and caused dust to rise into the sunlit air.

'Mummy – Daddy – can I?'

They walked by his side, living again the delights of being astride a living breathing animal and on the move. The channelling that afternoon was done from horseback, all the children galloping madly to the sea, slapping their own buttocks and yelling like maniacs.

Austen looked down at Hallie who was taking a siesta while he kept watch. Her eyes opened and dazzled him with their blueness.

He said, 'Am I allowed to choose something which might be fun?'

She was delighted. 'Of course.'

He said slowly, 'I would like us – just you and me – to come down to the beach at midnight and swim in the sea together.'

She blinked and her throat moved as she swallowed.

She whispered, 'Like Maude and I?'

'Yes.'

'But . . . although that was fun . . . can it be again? Ever?'

'I don't know. But it looked more than fun. Did you know I was watching you?'

She started up on her elbows. 'Austen! I thought Maude had told you! I did not know you were *there*!'

He nodded.

She was aghast. 'But we were – we did not have bathing suits and we were—'

'I know.'

She was genuinely shocked and he was glad.

He said, 'I am not suggesting we go without them tonight, darling. And obviously I was too far away to see you clearly.' He smiled and she subsided, slightly reassured. 'But it did look the most marvellous thing. You were both sort of coated in silver—'

'Phosphorescence.'

'Yes. Would it happen again?'

'I would think so.' She sat up. 'Austen, I am not sure about it. Will it make you think less of me? Will it come between us?'

He was surprised. 'Why should it?'

'I have always felt that it was the swim that made the baby come so quickly.'

'But, darling, surely you know that whatever had happened there would have been small chance of saving Maude?'

'So Father said. I did not believe him.'

'It is true.' He was filled with resolution. 'Listen. We will do it. Tonight. Definitely. And you will see there will be no pain. It will help you to overcome these feelings you have.'

She closed her eyes. 'Austen, you are so . . . wonderful,' she said.

They swam slowly and carefully through the moon-lit water as if afraid to disturb it. The waves were breaking close to the shore and the swell lifted them high so that they could see the whole of Porthmeor on its spit of land like a relief map in shades of darkness. Even the street lamps had been extinguished and the sensation of being the only people awake was overwhelming.

'Don't disturb the fish!' Hallie whispered. And he whispered a laugh back at her and lifted his arms high while he trod water. Silver fire dripped from them. He laughed again.

'You're right, my darling.' Her face was white as it

came close to his. 'This is washing away any guilt. As if Maude is here with us pronouncing absolution.'

But he did not want Maude to intrude in any way.

'I pronounce absolution!' he said, quite loudly like the vicar did in St Mary's on Sunday mornings. And he laughed to take away the solemnity and she laughed too.

'Say when you've had enough, Hallie.' He could have stayed out there all night, drifting with the wandering sea. The contentment that was always with him now, was increased by an enormous sense of peace.

She swam close and used Maude's words. 'Do you feel part of it? Part of the sea and the sky and everything?'

'Yes.'

'No. Not quite.' Her face was split with a grin and she held up her arm. From her hand a large soggy object hung downwards. 'Go on. Take off your bathing suit too. You have to if you want to become part of the universe!'

He trod water again, looking at her intently. As the swell lifted her he could see her small breasts, perfectly rounded, very white. She was laughing, waving her wet costume above her head, challenging him. He slid off his shoulder straps and removed his own bathing suit by jack-knifing his legs to his chest.

'Have you done it? Show me,' she commanded.

He could not speak. In spite of his mouth filling with sea water, it felt dry. He lifted his arm and showed his costume.

'Now . . .' she said. 'Now there is nothing between us and the elements.'

She floated, letting her head lie back in the water, staring up at the stars. He could see her body beneath the surface of the water; white, amorphous, moving and rippling, but *there*! And he felt as he had felt in Barbados so often – though not for the past three years. He hated himself. He knew it was lust. It was degrading. It put him on the level of the animals. He wanted that body.

He wanted to use it. And it belonged to Hallie, who was innocent.

He began to swim for the shore as if the devil were behind him.

Ten

Hallie lay in one of the twin divans next to Austen for the rest of that night and did not sleep. It was a relief when Hanny woke at four-thirty and demanded a drink and a story. There was no movement from Austen's bed; she put her finger to Hanny's lips and in the first pale light of another beautiful June morning, she dressed the two of them and they went downstairs.

They were not welcome. The cleaners were just arriving and there were sounds of crashing from the kitchen. She was reminded forcibly of the early-morning starts from the block of mansion flats at Pimlico. At least people had been pleased to see them. Here they were just in the way.

'I'se hungry, Mummy. Want a drink,' Hanny repeated as they went down the outside steps into the gravel driveway. 'Why couldn't we stay in bed and have a story?'

'I did not want to wake Daddy up, darling.'

She led him on to the wide sloping lawn in front of the hotel thinking how easily she had slipped into calling Austen 'Daddy'. 'Let's sit on the grass. I've brought your thermos of milk. You can drink that and we'll decide what to do.'

He drank then said, 'Why mustn't we wake Daddy?'

Austen had not minded being woken before. In fact, he had twice taken Hanny into his bed so that Hallie could go on sleeping.

'He had a bad night, darling.'

She recalled Austen's rigid form. He had not been

164

asleep, she was practically certain of that. What *could* have happened? She felt the flutter of panic she had felt when he ran up the beach last night. It had been so obvious he was trying to get away from her.

'Poor Daddy,' Hanny said, so mournfully Hallie would have laughed in any other circumstance.

Now she echoed, 'Poor Daddy.'

But why?

He said, 'Mummy, can we go down on the beach now?'

She glanced at her watch. It was five-thirty.

'It's very early. Breakfast won't begin for another two hours.'

'Is that time to go to the beach? We could start digging a river right up to the hut!'

There was nothing else to do. They were not wanted indoors and Hanny was not up to a long walk. So they trailed down the cliff path and she opened up the hut and took out the deck-chairs, hung towels over the back of them, fetched the bucket and spade.

It turned out to be the best thing she could have done. As she knelt in the sand digging industriously, the sun already above the East Head, she could feel the first prickle of sweat on her back. There was something wonderful in having the whole beach to themselves at the very beginning of the day. Hanny ran and shouted and brought water and she dug on and let her tired mind untwist itself gradually and begin to think properly again.

And as the channel grew longer so a memory was uncovered. This was not the first time Austen had run from her. It had happened at least twice before; both times after close physical contact. The first time was when he had hustled her out of Maude's bedroom at the Flower House and helped her downstairs. He had then released her as if she had become red-hot and moved away very suddenly. And the next time had been when she came down alone and he had accosted her at the foot of the stairs. Neither time had been so obvious as last night's dash up the beach, but there had been similarities.

She bit her lip, recalling again the awful shame of last night. Somehow Austen had got back into his costume, but she had lost hers somewhere in the shallows and had chased him right up the cliff path to the steps of the hotel, thinking he was ill, uncaring of her own nakedness until he stopped, head hanging and said coldly, 'Put on your costume.'

How had he known she was not wearing it? He had not looked at her once even though she had called him quite desperately.

She panted, 'I don't know where it is. In the sea somewhere.'

He threw her a towel. 'Cover yourself.'

She had done so. 'What is it, Austen? Are you in pain?' It was obvious he was not; no-one in pain could have sprinted as fast as he had.

He said tightly, 'We should not have left Hanny. We must be mad.'

She was bewildered. 'You know I asked that nice chambermaid to listen for him.'

'But he will have to cry before she goes in to him.'

'But he never does!' She remembered him telling her of his own feeling of rejection as a child; she tried to take his arm. He shrugged her away.

They had crept through the french door left open for them and padded upstairs where Hanny was sleeping soundly. Austen had scrambled into his pyjamas and got immediately in to bed. She had followed suit more slowly and then whispered, 'Good night, Austen.' He had said something, she hardly knew what it was. The silence had settled over them like a thick stifling eiderdown. Several times during the rest of that short night she had wanted to cry out just to break through it. It had been a relief when Hanny woke so early.

Her thoughts had come full circle. She took a scoop of sand and patched one of the channel's crumbling banks and sat back on her heels, trying to come to some conclusion. Austen loved her. She was certain of that. But he loved her only as a friend. Physical intimacy of any kind was repugnant to him.

She articulated the words in her head . . . 'physical intimacy is repugnant'. Quite simple. And she would prefer that kind of love anyway. Maude's kind was too all-consuming; even if Maude had lived she would not have been happy. Everyone said so, even Jack himself. Hallie remembered the three years of her growing friendship with Austen. It was good and wonderful. The very best kind of basis for marriage.

She screwed up her eyes against the sun forcing herself to be convinced. The excitement Maude had spoken of . . . yes, she knew about that. But it had nothing to do with sex as Maude had maintained. It had to do with the simple joy of having fun. As they'd had in the rain. And in the sea too, until she had been foolish enough to take off her costume.

She would have to be careful. That was all. She would just have to be careful.

Hanny interrupted her thoughts with a loud shout.

'Mummy – not deep enough just there!' And she came out of her reverie and waved, reassured by her own resolution and by the joy of being here in their special place. They had another week; in that time it would be easy to re-establish their friendship.

Then Hanny yelled, 'Daddy!' and Austen was there behind her and her heart leapt uncontrollably into her throat and then settled back into a very fast beat.

She was conscious that she was a mess. Wet sand everywhere, even dripping from the ends of her hair. She turned and squinted up at him and he smiled down at her. A wonderful, gentle smile.

'I saw you from the cliff top and thought you were two children playing together.'

She swallowed. 'We're digging a channel right from the hut to the sea,' she said.

He dropped to his knees beside her, uncaring of his flannels.

'Let me help.'

Hanny rushed up with more water and somehow they all got wet. Austen laughed while she scolded.

'What a way to begin the day!'

He said, 'But it's fun, isn't it?'

She almost wept. Her conclusions had been right. He was asking her for her friendship again.

She said quietly, 'Yes, it is.'

'If I'd had a bit more imagination, I could have done this down in Speightstown when I was not much older than Hanny!'

'What *did* you do?'

'Listened to Alice going on about Sugar and Martin. Telling me not to talk to Amos because he was a child of the devil!' Austen laughed.

She thought, This is how it was that time at the Flower House. Gentle conversation . . . and then those moments of awareness that pushed us apart. For three years, they had kept those at bay.

She went on with the conversation. 'She believed in the devil?'

'Oh yes.'

'But surely Amos was her own grandson?'

'Of course. She must have been crazy.' He laughed. Hanny brought more water and they followed the trickle of a river down to the water's edge.

Hallie thought, We must not ever risk our happiness again. The thought of repeating last night was terrible. They were together again now. Friends. She felt like a child, left outside for a long time in rain and cold, suddenly admitted to the warmth of a fire. She held out her salt-wrinkled hand and he took it in his and swung it companionably.

And then Hanny came galloping out of the shallows like a colt, swinging some object in his hand, scattering water everywhere.

'Look what I've found! Mummy's costume! Did you lose your costume, Mummy?'

Austen dropped her hand. She looked at him. His jaw was tight.

She laughed loudly. 'That's not my costume, Hanny! Throw it back in the sea, darling. It's nasty! Dirty!'

He looked at it doubtfully and she ran to him, took it from him and hurled it as far as she could. It soared into the air and hit the waves twenty yards away. It floated for a while, then disappeared from view.

'Gone,' she said. 'All gone.'

Hanny laughed. She looked around at Austen. He was digging the channel again.

Mungay was conducting one of his one-sided conversations in Florence's room. It could not be called a monologue because when he paused, she would flick him a glance from beneath her lids and he knew exactly what she would say if ever she spoke.

Since Maude's death she had rarely said more than one word and that was usually to Austen. He thought angrily that although he had been a poor husband, he deserved better than this.

Yet he spoke kindly enough in spite of his irritation.

'This man specializes in consumptive diseases, my dear. Hesterman has personally recommended him. If he says there is no trace of tuberculosis of the lung, then he is right.'

He waited and she opened her eyes wide enough to cast him a glance of pure loathing.

He said suddenly, 'Florence, I understand that you know all about me and find me lacking. I understand that you never wish to speak to me. But I have always given you the best possible care and attention money could buy. And by sending for MacLean, I am not trying to prove you a liar. You have been ill since the birth of Maude. I accept that. But if it is proved that there is nothing physically wrong, surely it will make you happy?

169

You could sit on the terrace today for instance – now – this afternoon. The children from Saunton School are going to do some country dancing for some charity or other. You could watch them over the wall and—'

The colourless eyes had filled with tears.

He went on quickly, 'All right. Perhaps Saunton reminds you of Maude. But what is wrong with that? We mustn't shut Maude up inside our heads as if she had never existed!'

She turned into the pillow. He realized he was being sidetracked.

'Listen, Flo. Listen to me. You are not ill. That is wonderful news. I'll send Meg up to you and you can dress.'

A sound like a sob came from the pillow. He wished he had not mentioned the schoolchildren.

'We'll go out for a drive!' he said. 'I'll go down now and ask Sully to get the car by the door. How's that?'

She reared her head like a horse and he encountered that basilisk stare again.

He went to the window and stared out. The girls were already being marshalled on the sward outside the wall of the kitchen garden. Several of them had the mettle-some air Maude had had as a child. He felt his own heart contract with despair. Maude had been so like him.

He said quietly, 'I would like you to know that since Maude died, I have not slept with Lily Elmes.'

A sound came from behind him. It could have been a laugh or a sob.

He clenched his hand on the sash and went on grittily, 'I have been unfaithful to you. Yes. Perhaps if you . . . I don't know. I was capable of a grand and passionate love, Flo. How can anyone say, now? Our lives are nearly over, my dear. Can't we become companions? Will you not take a drive with me?'

The silence behind him changed. It became taut as a violin note. It went on and on until he thought it would end with a scream. His. Or hers.

He looked around. She was propped on her elbow, the long hair that had so attracted him thirty-five years ago, was still dark and glossy; her skin was smooth. She had hardly aged. Yet the expression on her face was as old as evil itself.

'I hate you.' She spoke almost calmly. 'I hate you because after the agony of producing a son, you were not satisfied. I never wanted Maude. That night . . . you raped me.' There was a short pause. He gripped the window-ledge behind him, aghast. He could barely remember the night of Maude's conception. Had he really forced himself on her?

She went on slowly, deliberately, as if she had long rehearsed the words.

'You think I grieve for her? I never have. Because of her you took Austen away to Barbados. You taught him that the Rudolf men use women. You tainted him. He has never been the same since—'

He stammered, 'Flo – he was six years old! It was the war – the cursed war – that changed Austen.'

'When she died it seemed just to me. She had left a son. Another boy. But then you let those *people* – ' she spat out the word '– take the child. If it weren't for Austen—'

'Flo, please! All this bitterness – bottled inside you for a quarter of a century—'

'Well, I lived long enough to see another boy in the family. And because of Austen he is now a Rudolf. I can die now.'

'Flo, you are *not* going to die!'

'And I want you to remember that I have always hated you.'

She turned her shoulder and put her face in the pillow.

After a very long moment, feeling sick and very old, Mungay left the room.

That night when Meg took in the hot milk Florence sat up in bed and dropped in the sleeping powders she had hoarded for the last year. Ever since Austen had told her his plans for little Hanover Rudolf.

And then she settled down to sleep.

Hallie did not think Austen would be too grieved at the loss of his mother; she herself had seen Florence twice in her life and could feel a pang for Mungay but nothing on her own account. She had hoped for another week in Porthmeor; now that was out of the question.

The telegram arrived at midday when she was setting out the picnic lunch and still squirming inwardly from the thought of the swimming costume. The chambermaid who doted on Hanny came flying down the cliff path, waving the yellow slip, then waited apprehensively while Austen read it.

His eyes met Hallie's over the spread cloth.

'I'm afraid it's my mother,' he said briefly. Then glanced at the maid. 'Thank you for waiting but there is no reply. Will you give the boy this.' He handed her half a crown and she went off, still large-eyed, to report back to the hotel.

'Is she ill?'

Hallie continued to put out cardboard plates. After all, Florence Rudolf was an invalid and even if her life was ebbing to a close everyone had been prepared for that for a very long time.

'She is dead,' Austen said briefly. 'And there is to be an inquest. The doctor – Hesterman and a specialist – had visited her and pronounced her healthy. And now she is dead.'

'Oh, Austen! I am so sorry.' She half stood, wanting to take him in her arms, not able to. 'I am so very sorry,' she repeated haltingly.

'So am I.' He stared blindly out to sea to where Hanny, holding a crab, was chasing a small girl. 'She had a rotten life. Obviously it was all too much. I imagine she took it herself.'

'You mean—?'

172

'Yes.'

'Oh!' Hallie tried to hide the extent of her horror. Somehow it would reflect on Mungay – and Austen himself. She said, 'Your father – how will he take it?'

'On the chin, I imagine. They never got on.'

Shock was added to horror. She dared not even think of the awfulness of losing any of her own family, and felt a sudden sharp anxiety for Aunt Caddie still in Spain.

He said, 'We'll eat on the train, Hallie. We can catch the one-thirty from Penzance. Just. They will be serving luncheon in the dining car. Bundle all this up and I'll fetch Hanny.'

'But—' She watched him unfolding his length from the sand, then stared down at the wicker hamper containing their picnic. She had thought – after throwing away her costume just a few short hours ago – that they would have lots of time to be together and alone down here. She squatted there, still holding a cardboard plate, watching him lope down the beach towards the distant figure of their son, who was not their son, and – quite suddenly – she *wanted* him. She wanted to fuse their bodies as their minds had surely fused over the past three years. And after her careful conclusions and resolutions she was appalled at her own . . . what was it . . . looseness? Was she a loose woman?

She felt her face flame and began to pack up the picnic things as if her life depended on it. Perhaps, after all, it was as well Mrs Rudolf had died and their honeymoon was cut short.

They cleared out the beach hut in complete silence even when she caught her finger in one of the deck-chairs.

Hanny, struggling to deflate his beach ball, was the only one to notice anything was wrong with her. He said anxiously, 'Is you crying, Mummy?'

'Of course not. Mummies don't cry.'

And she was not crying. Not really. Her tears were tears of anger and frustration.

173

They caught the train but the journey back was delayed and miserable. A sudden downpour at Newton Abbot flooded the line and they waited on Teignmouth platform for an hour while gangers cleared it with shovels and buckets. The train crept along to Exeter at ten miles an hour and it was nine o'clock before they steamed into Temple Meads.

They had intended to stay in St George Street while they looked around for the ideal home in which to bring up Hanny. It had seemed sensible at the time and indeed Austen had been all for it – Hanny's things were still in the nursery there and her father was all alone. But Austen ordered the taxi to drive to High House in Clifton and settled back without comment.

She said, 'Will your father welcome visitors, my dear? It is late and Hanny needs his bed.'

'Visitors?' He looked round at her, surprised. 'We're hardly visitors, Hallie. In fact, there seems no point in staying with your father now. Obviously High House will be our home. I dare say Sullivan will have collected all your stuff.' He smiled, suddenly realizing that her fidgets all through the long journey were caused by grief for his mother. 'I know it will be sad for all of us for the first few weeks, Hallie. But the old place has long lacked a woman's touch. There is a place waiting for you there.'

'I—' She hardly knew how she felt and said lamely, 'My father will be very disappointed.'

'Dearest girl, he will be the first to understand. After all, his sister will soon be home again. And my father could not remain at High House alone. It is far too large.' He smiled and leaned across Hanny to touch her knee fleetingly. 'It is a family home, Hallie. Our family home. Surely you can see that?'

She knew she was being childish. She wanted to weep again.

And then he said, 'My father is very fond of you as

174

you know, dearest girl. I think your presence will make all the difference to him.'

She swallowed her stupid schoolgirl tears and smiled at him. The taxi ground up the hill past the Victoria Rooms and through the quiet squares that ringed the Downs. It was a beautiful part of the city, but it was not her part. She had always lived cheek by jowl with the Cathedral and the docks and the river. She thought suddenly of Bellamy: she wanted to see him stalk towards her, tail upright and twitching at the end, reluctant to admit his delight at seeing her. And her father – she wanted to see her father and get news of Aunt Caddie and Jack.

She swallowed and took herself in hand. She was a wife and a mother now: somehow being a wife made her an official mother, which was an interesting thought. She was also going to be the woman of the house. There would be things to do; servants to order and Mungay's likes and dislikes to consider. She would earn Austen's respect and perhaps . . . maybe . . . she let her thoughts go no further. She was becoming like Margo. Margo could think and talk of nothing else but . . . that.

She turned her head and smiled at Austen. He returned her smile. Two people, supporting each other through a time of crisis. Quite wonderful. But something happened. They did not look away quickly enough. Their gazes locked as they had that first time at the Flower House. Hallie drew a deep breath. She knew that had she been holding a cup of tea, as she had that time, it would have crashed to the floor of the taxi. Luckily she was holding nothing, not even the hand of their son.

The gaze went on as they rounded Blackboy Hill and headed across the high road above Avon Gorge. A full minute of complete absorption. It must end with . . . something. He would lean towards her and kiss her. She knew it. She waited with a kind of glowing confidence. And then they were pulling through the gates of High

House and Sullivan was running to open the door and welcome them back.

It was true that Mungay was delighted to have them with him. The shock of Florence's suicide had left him bewildered and confused. There was no note. He knew she had intended to make her death as uncomfortable for him as she could; he would have to live with her hatred now for the rest of his life. Guilt also. He had driven her to this. He was innocent of administering that sleeping powder, but not of causing her to administer it to herself. There was no question of any real suspicion falling on him: Dr Hesterman would vouch for her state of mind – she had barely spoken a word to him in all the years he had attended her. But there would be many in Bristol who would turn down their mouths, shrug, close an eye knowingly. Only Lily Elmes herself knew that he had not been to the Hotwells Road house in the last three years.

Meg's screams that morning had started a day that was like a bad dream. He had run into the bedroom overlooking the garden and had shaken Florence quite violently, still thinking she was play-acting. But she was already cold, her mouth open, her sightless eyes only half closed. And then there had been Hesterman's arrival, the removal of the glass containing the dregs of powdery milk, the removal of the body, the notification to the Coroner.

'Would you like a sedative?'

Hesterman had been unusually gentle; at times in the past his silence towards Mungay had been accusing.

Mungay had said, 'I'm not ill.'

'You are shocked. I'll leave you this. You may need it tonight.'

'I've wired Austen. They will be here this evening.'

Hesterman had lifted his brows. 'Is that possible? It is a long way and they may well be out when the telegram arrives.'

Mungay had felt a pang that was near to fear. He had

176

never been in the house alone. Florence had always been there.

'They will be here,' he said certainly, as if to reassure himself.

But as time went on and they did not appear, it seemed Hesterman's doubts were well founded. He worked out when the telegram would get there. Around midday. They may well have hired a car and taken the boy to Penzance. Or Falmouth. Or . . . anywhere. But if not, they could just about catch the one-thirty from Penzance which was due in to Bristol at six-thirty.

Eight o'clock boomed out on the grandfather clock in the hall. They must have missed the one-thirty. There was not another train that day.

Mungay paced the sitting-room floor, thinking of Florence alone here night after night when he and Austen were elsewhere. He half hoped that Hesterman would telephone Charles Martinez who would, of course, get in touch. Charles was on his own in the St George Street house; Cadiz had not returned from Spain yet. It was ridiculous, two men in separate establishments. They could at least meet for a meal.

But the telephone was silent and no-one called to offer condolences.

Mungay waited until eight-thirty and was on the point of leaving for Hotwells Road and the comfort of Lily's arms, when the taxi drove into the stable yard. He ran down the hall and was only just behind Sullivan. It was as if – just for a moment – they were a normal family. He heard himself laughing: he gathered Hanny into his arms and held him aloft until he screamed and then lodged him precariously on one shoulder while he hugged Hallie to him with his free arm and ordered Sullivan to get the luggage and put a move on, then turned to yell to Meg to put on a supper in the morning room and make sure Master Hanover's things were ready in the nursery. It was as if the more noise he made the easier things would become.

Hallie responded splendidly, putting her arms around his neck and almost sobbing. She lifted her head when he was giving out his orders. She looked dazed; her eyes were huge and blazingly blue, she continued to hang on to him as if she might be going to fall down. Austen was an unconscionable time with his head in the driver's window, paying him.

'Trouble, son?' Mungay boomed, every inch the patriarch. 'Let me – let me—'

But Austen said over his shoulder, 'Take them indoors, Father. I'll just help Sully with the luggage.'

Mungay felt deflated. Austen had often refused to look at him in the past. Marriage had not changed that.

They trooped into the morning room. High House had none of the cosiness of St George Street. It had been built to impress others, not to offer comfort, and even the warmth of the June day had not permeated among the stiff furniture and costly ornaments. Hanny was tired and put out at the sudden curtailment of his particular small Eden. At last, after holding out all day in the train, he began to grizzle.

'I want Grandad!' he said.

Hallie said swiftly, 'You've got Grandad. Come on, darling. Sit here and Meg will bring you a nice glass of milk and some biscuits.'

At the mention of Meg, Hanny wept anew. 'I want Rosie,' he said crescendoing into a whine. 'I want my proper Grandad. And I want Rosie. I want to go ho-ome!'

Austen, entering just at that moment, said, 'This is home now, son. Tomorrow we'll explore the garden. And then the Downs. It will be fun.'

Mungay lifted surprised brows but then sat down near his grandson and reached into his waistcoat pocket. 'Listen to my watch, Hanover. In just a few minutes it will chime.'

Hanny, temporarily diverted, stopped grizzling and

178

Austen turned to his wife. Mungay could hardly believe his ears.

'My father and I have a great deal to discuss, Hallie. Will you take the child to bed with you as soon as may be? I will see you in the morning.'

And even odder was Hallie's response. The amazing blue eyes were lowered as if she were an obedient child.

'Of course, Austen dear,' she said.

Mungay knew then. He wanted to go to her and hold her and let her weep on to his shoulder. He wanted to hit Austen and shout at him that he was a fool.

The watch chimed. He said, 'By the time you've eaten your supper, it will be ready to chime again.'

But Hallie said, 'We'll have our supper upstairs, Grandad. We're both very tired.'

So this was what happened most nights.

The body of Florence Rudolf was released for burial after a token inquest. She had taken her life while the balance of her mind was disturbed. It was no more than the truth, of course, but Mungay had business rivals who thought they knew more than the truth.

Florence had come from the village – now practically a suburb of Bristol – called Shirehampton, and there she went to lie in St Mary's churchyard. The church was large and Victorian but was crowded for the funeral. The June weather piled into a thunderstorm while they sang 'Abide with Me' and the heavens opened during the short walk to the open grave. Everybody crowded around, umbrellas clashed, the vicar's voice could only just be heard as he intoned, 'Dust to dust . . .', and Mungay threw down a single red rose before the earth was shovelled. He turned away immediately and looked into the faces of the assembled Bristol merchants. They all wore expressions of varying piety. They doubtless considered that he had been successful for too long – had become smug – needed some kind of come-uppance. Well, he had that all right. Suicide was always

179

somebody's fault. The Bristol merchants knew that as well as he did. They would have their ways of showing him just who they considered should take the blame. Florence would have her revenge for whatever he had done or not done during their marriage.

Hallie was surprised at how quickly she settled into High House and a new routine.

It was impossible to begrudge Mungay the pleasure he so obviously took in Hanny's presence. A few weeks after the funeral, on a Sunday morning in July, Hallie watched him take the small boy on a walk around the garden. Hanny was familiar with it now and would head straight for the brick wall at the end of the kitchen garden, where he kept a cache of snails.

She heard him say, 'Look, Grampy! two trails. They went for a walk last night!' And Mungay's reply, 'And they're not back yet. We'd better look around.'

It had been sensitive of Mungay to suggest to the boy that, as he had a grandad in St George Street, perhaps it would be sensible to have a Grampy at home. It had certainly pleased Charles.

She went through the french doors on to the terrace and called down to them.

'Who would like lemon caley with a straw?'

They both signalled enthusiasm in their separate ways, and she went back inside and made her way down the passage to the green baize door that led to the kitchen. Already she was used to this daily visit to check on the day's programme of work and meals. Already she was used to being called 'Mrs Rudolf' instead of 'Miss Hallie'. She could feel the change in herself; she had authority now. She was the only woman in this family. The last effective female had been Maude and she had been completely uninterested in domestic affairs. Hallie was interested. She wanted to make a home for Austen, for Austen's father and especially for Hanny. And in submerging herself in meals and the organization of the house, she could find another relationship with Austen.

Cook and Meg were putting the finishing touches to the galantine for lunch, cutting mint leaves into star shapes to amuse Hanover. She held up her hand to tell them to continue and went to make the lemonade herself.

'We'll have sherry on the terrace when my father arrives,' she said. 'Are there any straws?'

'Likes to blow bubbles, doesn't he, Mrs Rudolf?' Cook said dotingly.

Hallie nodded, laughing. 'And so does Mr Mungay,' she said.

Meg giggled. She watched Hallie's departure and turned to Cook.

'Diff'rent place now, isn't it?' she said. 'When I think of that ole mis'ry upstairs . . . best day's work she ever did taking them powders!'

'Now then, Meg,' Cook said mildly.

'Well . . .' Meg said. And they both smiled.

181

Eleven

Cadiz wanted to see something more of what she termed 'our Spain' before she went home. Jack, still basically lazy in spite of his manual work – perhaps because of it, was against the idea.

'I've made forays into Andalusia with the mule caravans. Rodriguez sent me looking for vineyards when I got homesick. You won't enjoy it,' he maintained.

But Cadiz was adamant.

'I want to see Seville again before I die,' she said rather dramatically.

'In July. The hottest month of the year.'

'We'll take two of Rodriguez' Arab ponies and go from village to village.'

She had a map and pored over it recalling the days before Charles' Maria had died and she had been a girl and had ridden over the plain like – like a warrior queen. Like Boudicca. She smiled at her own foolishness.

'I suppose I want to recapture my youth.'

'And do away with mine,' Jack said glumly.

But he was enjoying having his Aunt Cad with him. Rodriguez had taken him off the workforce so that he could be with her, and although he doubted the wisdom in this lapse of his routine, he and Cadiz had always shared a sparky comradeship. Nothing had changed between them; her acerbic comments on his life-style took him past the awfulness of his last years in England to his schooldays when she had been such an asset at things like school sports. And for the first time in years he felt he was able to help someone. During the time she had been with him, she had responded well to his policy of *laissez-faire*. When she first mooted the trip to Seville she had said, 'I don't want to be home when Hallie gets back from this so-called honeymoon – she won't belong to us any more – she'll be a Rudolf.'

And now, as she gave orders to Benita about their return in four days' time, she turned to him and said in English, 'And then I shall go home, dear boy. It will be good to see Hallie and your son again. I'm beginning to miss them quite badly.'

He had smiled at her and she had added, 'And please take that smug grin off your face! Whatever you say, she will still be Harriet Rudolf!'

And he had quoted, ' "A rose by any other name . . ." '

He was amazed at how small her pack was.

'Water and two of Benita's flat loaves and goat's cheese. First-aid tin.' She strapped the saddle-bags decisively.

'Clothing?' he asked.

'No. We'll be gone just four days. If I smell you must put up with it.'

'There will be other smells which will out-smell anything we can produce,' he forecast.

She was shocked at how right he was. They stopped at midday at a village called Cuerras. It was a collection of turf and earth dwellings, a cross between a collection of African mud huts and the earthworks still seen around Offa's Dyke. The plain shimmered around it and it sat like an obscene toad in the midst of the vapour, unable to reflect a glimmer from a window or any metal object.

A man emerged from one of the huts and announced his was the local inn. He was hospitable enough, producing wine from a cask in the corner of a single room, even flipping a rag over one of the rough tables before seating them. But as they rested the worst of the heat away, the other huts began to disgorge their beggars and cripples until Cadiz wondered whether the village was some kind of colony for the sick.

'This is Spain,' Jack said morosely, trying not to look at a filthy stump displayed by one of the children. 'At least here they bury their excrement.'

'Do you mean Seville—?' Cadiz did not think she could bear it if her beautiful Seville was desecrated by human filth.

'Seville is still Spain's shop window. Valladolid is the worst. Parts of Toledo . . . and Madrid—'

'It wasn't like this before the war.'

'You were younger also, Caddie. You were used to it. Less . . . democratic perhaps.'

Perhaps he was right. Boudicca had doubtless ignored the condition of her soldiers.

She watched a blind man picking at sores on his face and stood up. 'I will send money,' she said to the innkeeper. 'Come, Jack, I cannot bear this.'

'I warned you.'

That night they slept beneath the stars in a grove of trees by the river. Cadiz had planned to reach Seville during the evening but suddenly she wanted to arrive in the morning.

'It will be white and gold then,' she told Jack.

He smiled. 'I did not realize how romantic you were, Aunt Cad. You should have married.'

She shook her head. 'It would not have done. I am too bossy.'

They both laughed but then Jack said seriously, 'There must have been a man somewhere who would have been a match for you.'

She closed her eyes. There was, of course.

Seville was as she remembered it, although it had its share of beggars. The beautiful Moorish city with its echoing cathedral and many waterfalls satisfied something deep within her. For one thing it was always full of flowers, they fanned out amid their waterfalls from either side of the river, their houses embedded in them like diamonds. And there was gold everywhere, reflected in the water from the Toro de Oro and Giralda Tower and hiding in the bronze shadows from gates and gilded doors. She sighed with satisfaction, turning a blind eye on a beggar tugging at her stirrup with fingerless hands.

They put the horses in livery and walked around the streets, smiling at each other, buying fresh fruit and sitting by the river to eat it. Seville was fifty miles from the coast, yet Columbus and Magellan had both left from here.

They walked again, crossing and recrossing the river by its many bridges. Jack went off to find beds for the night and Cadiz stood alone looking towards the north bank where the old gypsy encampment still sprawled, seething with life. She was certain that she had roots in this place. She could almost feel what it was like to be one of the wives over there, squabbling over her cooking pot, slapping one of the panniered donkeys away from her children. It wasn't inconceivable after all; more than probable that the original Carlos Martinez had come from here.

What made it so easily imaginable was that nobody recognized her as English – Jack was instantly singled out for the attention of every beggar in sight. With her boots and leather skirt, her black hair beneath her sombrero, she was a high-born Spanish lady from some hacienda inland. She could come and go with impunity.

They spent two days there. On the first day a raggle-taggle mob of peasants driving poultry ahead of them, passed them as they were making for the Triano markets. Jack walked ahead of Cadiz to make a way for her; he was accepted as an English tourist, but she was taken for a land-owner and jostled accordingly and as the peasants passed, one of them turned and spat in her direction.

She was white-faced, wounded to the soul. She

185

wanted to call after them that she was one of them. But Jack hustled her away.

Later that evening, it was plain that an influx of peasants was coming to the city. There was a rumour of a political meeting in the Triano. A sailor came up to Jack begging a cigarette. He spoke in English.

'Hey. Johnny-boy. You want to see a war. Stay in Spain.'

Jack leaned forward. 'What is happening in the Triano?'

'The Communist is talking to us.'

'The Communist?'

'Zinoviev. It is better in Russia, you understand.'

Cadiz kicked Jack beneath the table to shut him up but he said, 'Could we attend?'

The man stared at Cadiz with contempt.

'You are welcome. No land-owners.'

'OK.'

As soon as he slid away Cadiz said, 'Jack, what are you thinking of? They'll string you up if the mood takes them!'

'Of course they won't. They want help from outside. They think I am a tourist. I must go, Cad. It is important to find out what is happening.'

She stared at him. Spain was changing him.

She nodded. 'Very well. But for God's sake, be careful.'

He seemed to be gone for ever. She spent the time in the cathedral. A girl stood before the Christ figure at the altar, tears running down her face. When she turned and saw Cadiz sitting quietly in a pew, she crossed herself quickly and almost ran into the Lady Chapel. Cadiz smiled wryly. It was more than likely that they had been praying for the same thing: the safety of the men over at the old Triano.

At last she stood up and went outside. It was quite dark but there were still cooking fires and flares over on the north bank. A few civil guard loitered on the bridges, but their rifles were still on their backs and they did not look like men who were expecting trouble.

She went slowly back to their inn and went to bed. She thought she heard Jack go into the room next door just before dawn.

They started back the next day. Jack had a hangover and was unclear about the real purpose of the meeting.

'Somebody from Russia had a lot to say,' he reported, pulling his hat almost over his eyes in a desperate effort to avoid the sun.

'Was it Zinoviev?' Cadiz persisted.

'Don't know. A representative of the Workers' Party, I think.'

Cadiz let him be until they stopped beneath trees for their midday siesta.

Then she said slowly, 'Jack, that sailor was right. There is going to be trouble. The country is still being run as if we were in the Middle Ages. Disease and poverty – even in Seville which is the tourist's delight – if the Communists are going to help to organize something, there will be a revolution. Their war cry is revolution.'

Jack slumped against a tree. 'I've got to sleep, Cad. There won't be fighting. Alfonso will come back and Zamora will . . .'

But Cadiz was not interested in what happened in the Cortes. She had seen the frightful conditions with her own eyes. Her concern was what would happen to their own vineyards.

Jack snored while she continued to talk to herself.

'The trouble with any fire over here – once it starts it is so hard to put out. The heat . . . the temperament of the people . . .' Jack stirred and she addressed herself to him. 'We have always been fair to our labourers. They have been part of our family almost. Rodriguez – Benita—'

He smiled sleepily and did not open his eyes. 'Darling Aunt Cad. After those two names you know no-one. You did not even know I was working in the yards. It was different when you were here. You knew everyone then. But old Carmencita and her brothers are long dead. And now . . . so long as the yields are good, no-one back home is interested in anything else.'

It was horribly true.

She said, 'But . . . if you were to take over, Jack. Live in the Castillo – it would be different.'

'No thanks. Once I'd got time on my hands again, I'd gamble it all away.'

She studied him, the lines of dissipation could still be seen on his handsome face. He was twenty-eight and looked ten years older.

'I could take over again. I don't really want to go back anyway.'

His eyes flew open. 'I should have to move on. These few weeks – fine. Not much longer. I have to sweat the gambling fever out of me every day.'

She frowned. 'Is it really that bad, Jack? You make it sound like an illness.'

'It is an illness. That is exactly what it is. A fever.'

'Oh . . . such rubbish!' She continued to frown at him. Then shrugged. 'In any case, I could not leave your father to run the Bristol end. We might manage without the Castillo grapes – we could import and make out own blends – but Bristol is where we sell the sherry.'

There was a pause. Then he said, 'There won't be any revolution, Cad. Take it from me. The Church, the landowners, they've been established for too long. The king will come back and then everything will re-settle. A few concessions here and there . . . nothing to worry about. Spain will always be the same.'

She did not reply. Jack had not felt the hostility aimed at the land-owners as she had.

He sat up and smiled, sensing her uncertainty.

'So. You are going home. In spite of the new Mrs Rudolf! You are going to stop sulking and skulking out here and face them all with a brave smile!'

'Stop teasing me, Jack!' But she smiled too and patted his hand. 'This visit has done its work. You have done your work. I honestly thought I was going mad when I arrived. I began to wonder who I was. Why I was on this earth.' Her smile disappeared and she concluded, 'It was ghastly, Jack. Ghastly.'

'I know. You have described my feelings exactly.'

'But I had you. You came out here to no-one.'

'They were good to me. Rodriguez. The others. They accepted me as I was. Mad English. You know. That's why I know there will be no revolution.'

She said quietly, 'You are not mad. Neither am I. But Hallie . . . even Charles . . .'

'Please, Aunt Cad. Don't start. Just believe that it is all for the best.'

'All right. And if it gets too bad, I shall come out to see you again, Jack. I give you fair warning. You are my bolt-hole. You and Spain.'

Just before he surrendered to sleep again, he murmured, 'Don't know about me. But Spain will always be here.'

But Cadiz stared down to the Guadalquivir and wondered.

They arrived at the Castillo early the next morning and found letters awaiting them from England.

Jack said, 'I did not realize how I longed to be in touch with Hal again. Just look at her writing – it's changed. She used to make everything so round. Now it's almost spiky.'

Cadiz was busy devouring a screed from Charles. Benita was pouring lime juice into tall glasses. The big stone kitchen was hung with herbs and vegetables. England seemed a very long way away.

Cadiz exclaimed, 'My God! Florence Rudolf is dead! Suicide!'

Jack looked up but said nothing. He was ahead of his aunt and knew that there were greater shocks in store.

Quietly he folded Hallie's brief note and took a glass from Benita.

Cadiz stopped reading. She looked up.

'He has taken over your child, Jack. The three of them are living with Mungay at High House. Hanover is now known as Hanover Rudolf.'

'Yes.' Jack sipped and fingered his letter. 'Hal explains it all here.'

'Well? What are you going to do about it?'

The acceptance, so hard-won by Cadiz, had gone; she was faced again with the awful situation at home.

Jack said, 'I'm not sure. I'll write, of course. Point out that nothing of this is legal and can only continue with my permission.'

'Which you won't give, surely?'

'No. But there is little I can do about it, Caddie. Unless I go back. And – darling Aunt Cad, try to understand – if I go back these last two years will be lost.'

She considered him, gnawing her lower lip. She knew she could push him into coming home with her. But . . . what then?

She said impulsively, 'We will take him! Charles and I! Bring him up as your son. He can go to your school—'

'He knows Hallie. He looks on her as his mother.'

It was true, of course. To take Hanny away from Hallie at this point would be cruel.

She stared at him, searching for alternatives.

At last she said, 'So you are prepared to give your permission.'

'I'm trying to think only of Hanny. I know – I absolutely know – that Hallie will not permit anything that will be bad for him.'

'She cannot see straight! Austen has so ingratiated himself – she came out of the schoolroom into mother-hood – and he was always there! She knows nothing, Jack!'

'I disagree. She learned a great deal from her time

with Tilly Hesterman. She knows her weaknesses. And her strengths.'

He put out his hand as she continued to rant.

'Hang on. I want to tell you something and then perhaps you will realize that Hallie is not a child and knows exactly what she is doing.' He took a breath. 'It's something Maude told me. I thought she was just bitching about her brother, but now . . .' He looked his aunt in the eye. 'Darling, Austen is impotent. That's what the bloody war did for him. He cannot have children. Don't you see, that is why he wants Hanover so badly? And Hal knows this. She is dedicating her life to looking after the two of them. It – it's her war effort if you like!'

He tried to laugh but Cadiz put her hands over her face and sat down heavily. Benita made clucking noises and put her glass on the table. Jack folded her in his arms and rocked her gently.

She wailed, 'I'm not going home! I'll stay out here and make sure the vineyard is safe—' But even as she spoke she knew they had already settled that question; there was little she could do here; everything she could do at home. And at least she had contacted Jack; she was not quite alone in this particular battle.

Sullivan pulled the car up outside the Adams' house in Queen Square and Hallie alighted nimbly, turned back and lifted Hanny on to the wide pavement.

'You did ought to let me come round and open the door for you, miss,' Sullivan said, drawing his upper lip down disapprovingly. 'We don't want Mrs Adams thinking I don't know my job!'

'I'm quite able to open doors for myself, Sully.' Hallie wanted to point out that by calling her miss, he was making Hanny practically illegitimate. She smiled beatifically. 'Can't you just smell the autumn?'

He sniffed. 'Someone's got a bonfire somewhere,' he admitted grudgingly.

'And the horse chestnuts are almost ready.' Hallie lifted her son and pointed out the spiky green fruits on the enormous trees that lined the square.

'Ah,' commented Sully.

Hallie made a last effort to cheer the old man.

'No need to wait, Sully. We shall be staying to tea. So if you could come back about five o'clock in good time for Master Hanny's bath—'

'You might be sooner. I'll wait.'

'Really, Sully, there is no need. You can pick up Mr Mungay and take him home then come back for me.'

'Master stays overnight on Fridays,' Sully reminded her grimly, 'and Mr Austen is always late now. I'll wait.'

It was true. Austen often arrived too late to say good night to Hanny. She gave up and climbed the steps to ring the bell next to the gleaming brass plate.

Mr Adams' clerk, Walter Hinch, opened the door.

'On my way out with some papers, Mrs Rudolf.' He paused and shook Hanny's hand. 'He's growing fast, isn't he?' With the solicitor's offices within the family house, Walter considered himself part of the family and had known Hallie since she and Margo had gone to Saunton School together.

'Great excitement upstairs,' he confided now. 'Two dressmakers – one especially for you, young man!'

Hanny jumped excitedly. His mother had shown him photographs of the Duke of York's wedding and he liked the idea of being a page-boy for his Aunty Margo.

Hallie said, 'We'll go on up then. Thank you, Mr Hinch.'

They took their time up the wide shallow stairs; Hanny was at the stage where he insisted on climbing stairs by himself and it was a slow job. Halfway up Margo emerged from one of the rooms on the landing and hung over the balustrade.

'Darling Hallie! I saw you arrive – Tilly's here already – I'm so nervous I can hardly bear all this tucking and pinning and tacking and—'

She gathered Hanny to her and whirled him into the large sitting room overlooking the square. Hallie followed, still smiling but thankful that Austen had insisted on a civil ceremony. Margo had arrived home four weeks ago to arrange her wedding to her Count in the cathedral, and there had not been a day since without some kind of crisis.

She set Hanny down in front of a small table where his white satin shirt and knee-length breeches were set out.

'What do you think, darling?' she asked.

Hanny nodded vigorously. He was not yet old enough to declare the outfit as cissy and the whole idea of dressing up appealed greatly.

In the corner, Tilly was already arranged in a long dress of peach silk. She was protesting about a coronet which Mrs Adams was pinning into place.

'We're ordinary people!' she said. 'They'll think we're minor princesses at least! Who ever heard of coronets!'

Margo flashed a look at Hallie, who said, 'Well, actually, darling, you can carry it off beautifully. It makes you look regal. Whereas on my crop it looks—'

'Terribly intriguing,' Margo said. 'It's a pity you are already married, Hal. My dear Otto has a brother who is absolutely devastating and almost as rich – a separate castle in Carinthia, no less. We could spend holidays together.'

She laughed but Hallie knew she was half-serious. Both Margo and Tilly knew that the Rudolf marriage was lacking in something.

The afternoon went very quickly. By the time tea was brought in, both girls were fully arrayed and Hanny was even more delighted by the addition of shoes with silver buckles.

'You'll hold my hand, darling,' Hallie said, bending to his level. 'You one side and Jennifer the other.'

'Oh no, darlings!' Margo was aghast at such a mistake.

'They hold each other's hand. You want to escort Jennifer properly, don't you, Hanny?'

Jennifer was Margo's niece and six months older than Hanny.

'Where is she?' he demanded.

Mrs Adams said prudishly, 'She's gone to look under the gooseberry bush for a little sister. Or brother.' She shook her head. 'Such a pity that Sybil cannot be at the wedding. My goodness, it seems only yesterday that she and Marcus were getting married. Not quite such a lavish affair, of course.'

'Now don't you start, Mummy darling. You sent me to Switzerland to make a catch, and I have. And now we have to impress the von Gellhorns. It won't be for long. All I ask is . . .' She proceeded to list exactly what would impress the von Gellhorns. Tilly made a face and Hanny yawned innocently.

'Oh, all right. I can take a hint!' Margo looked around. 'You look marvellous. I know you won't let me down.' She smiled a little tremulously. 'Forgive me – I am very nervous. Wish it was all over now.'

'Well, it soon will be.' Mrs Adams looked mournful. 'And then heaven only knows when we shall see you again.' She sighed gustily. 'Come on. You three have tea in here and I'll take Hanny down to the kitchen and see what Cook has in her cake tin.'

The girls changed quickly and gathered around the table by the window. They had not spent time together like this for almost three years and they were very conscious that it could be another three years before it happened again.

Tilly said, 'Well, girls, looks as if I'm to be the old maid among you. I'll be the one who comes to stay when you're having your children. Aunt Tilly, without whom no self-respecting family can exist!'

'Shut up, Tilly!' Margo commanded. 'You'll probably marry some learned professor who has written a treatise on unemployment in the nineteen thirties and you'll look down on us and never want to see us again!'

Tilly nodded. 'The filthy rich,' she agreed.

'Anyway,' Margo bit mightily into a scone, 'I'll take you up on your offer right now. The von Gellhorns will expect an heir within a year, so please accept my invitation to my "lying-in" here and now!'

Tilly made a face. 'Are they really like that?'

'Well, of course. All these family-types are.' Margo turned to Hallie. 'Are you pregnant yet, darling? I know the Rudolfs are devils for continuing the line.'

Hallie reddened. 'I don't know about that. Anyway, we've got Hanny to do that for us.'

'But he's a Martinez, so that doesn't count.' Margo grinned. 'No way out, Hal!'

'Actually . . . I thought I'd told you . . . Hanny's name is Rudolf now.' She felt very warm. 'It was Austen's wish that Jack's and Maude's child should – should—'

'You mean he doesn't want children?' Margo's eyes rounded incredulously. 'Hanny is a sort of ready-made heir?' She noticed Hallie's colour and sobered. 'Sorry, old girl. I didn't mean . . . Tilly and I noticed ages ago how close you were over Hanny.' She giggled foolishly. 'I'm glad. Really glad. I mean, I quite thought – when I was in Germany and Mummy wrote to me about the quick wedding – I thought you might already be pregnant!' The giggle rose frenetically and was cut off. 'Sorry, Hal,' she finished lamely.

Tilly poured more tea and said, 'It sounds as if you might be going to have a busy time, Margo.'

Margo drew her mouth down and said in a thick German accent, 'She might not be high-born, Otto, but her hips are excellent for child-bearing!'

This outrageous mimicry had the desired effect and Tilly and Hallie doubled over with laughter.

Margo said in her own voice, 'Actually, girls, you can understand why I'm so nervous, can't you? Not a baronet – not even a knight – in the family! And if I produce a girl – woe betide me!' She put her hand over Hallie's. 'You're the lucky one, darling.'

Hallie could tell Margo did not mean it. But she patted the comforting hand anyway. She knew she was lucky. Austen's way was the best.

It was six-thirty when she managed to drag Hanny away from the Adams' kitchen. Sully was buffing the head-lamps and immediately put his leather inside and came around to open the door for her.

'Thought you was never coming, Miss Harriet.'

Tilly was right behind her as she helped Hanny inside.

Hallie said, 'I saw you drive away. I did not see you come back. So I did not realize there was any great hurry.'

Her uncharacteristic sarcasm was lost on Sullivan.

'I went round to the office to see if there was any errands for me. Been back this last hour and a half.'

Hallie stepped on to the running board. 'Will you drop Miss Hesterman off in Park Street, Sully?' she said, ignoring his implicit complaint.

He melted immediately before Tilly's big horse-smile.

'With pleasure, miss.'

'It's Mrs Rudolf, Sully, if you please.'

'I was addressing Miss Hesterman, madam,' Sully came back suddenly as prickly as she was herself.

Tilly sat back and said in a low voice, 'Whatever's the matter, Hal?'

'Nothing. But I am supposed to be mistress of High House. And Sully will act as if I'm a child!'

'He acts that way with your father-in-law too. Stop taking everything so personally.' She gave Hanny her keys and added, 'It's Margo, isn't it?'

'This marriage is slightly worrying. I don't like the thought of Margo in some castle in the Harz mountains without anyone of her own—'

'Like you at High House?'

Hallie exploded suddenly. 'Oh, for goodness' sake,

Tilly! You sound like my Aunt Cadiz! How on earth can you liken my situation to Margo's?'

'Sorry – sorry, Hal. You're right, of course. It's just that . . . your revelation today made me think.'

'My . . . revelation?'

Tilly leaned over Hanny's head and breathed into Hallie's ear. 'The revelation that you and your husband do not make love.'

Hallie jerked away. 'I said nothing of the sort! And if it were true it would be no-one's business but our own!'

Tilly said, 'Hal – I'm sorry – I'm really sorry. How could I know anything about it anyway? Look – forget the whole thing – the whole conversation. You know how much I value your friendship. And Margo – well, quite honestly, old girl, if she couldn't marry Jack, she wouldn't really mind who she married!'

'Jack?' Hallie was diverted. 'That was just a crush. Margo would not consider Jack. No title, no money—'

'Quite. But she still loves him. Ah well.' Tilly gazed out of the window as they swept into Park Street. 'Perhaps I'm the lucky one after all. I know where I am with my gentlemen friends!' She smiled. 'We've got a man in the Settlement at the moment who was boot-boy in a very important household indeed. He has polished the urns and the saucepans till the old kitchen looks new. That's the sort of man for me!'

And Tilly was relieved to see a smile on her friend's face.

Austen came out of the back door as the car swept into the stable yard. His face was dark.

'It's seven o'clock, Harriet! The boy is supposed to be in bed by now!'

She waited until Sully opened the door for her and left him to help Hanny alight.

'I did not realize there was any hurry, Austen,' she said for the second time, and felt anger tighten her muscles. 'You are always late home from the office and we have been very busy with Hanny's outfit for the wedding.'

'Sullivan brought me home at five on the understanding that you were to be picked up at six.'

She glanced at Sully who had the grace not to meet her eye.

'We were delayed. And we took Tilly home.' She took Hanny's arm. 'Thank you, Sullivan.'

And Sully looked up and said, 'Sorry it took us so long, Mrs Rudolf. My fault, sir.'

Hallie acknowledged both the lame excuse and the form of address with a smile. She directed her anger at Austen by walking ahead of him with Hanny and straight up the stairs to the nursery.

'No bath tonight, darling, it's too late. Let's put on your pyjamas and I'll ring for Meg to bring some milk and biscuits.'

Austen said, 'I'll read you a story, old man. It's a long time since we had a story, isn't it?'

'Can we have the Bristol Giants, Daddy?'

'Whatever you say.' He came close to Hallie and said, 'Hallie, I'm sorry if I sounded—'

She turned and looked at him. For some reason she wanted to hit him. Instead she said tightly, 'Do not speak to me like that in front of one of the servants again. Ever. Do you understand?'

She saw his eyes widen with surprise, but all he said was, 'Yes. I apologize.'

It took the wind from her sails, and she did not want that. She wanted a row. She realized with a shock she wanted a row with her husband who was her best friend.

'I will go and fetch the milk and biscuits,' she said.

But the trip to the kitchen did not help. Mungay would be out of the house all night and the servants safely behind the green baize door. She planned how she would tell Austen that Margo had thought she might be pregnant. And she would laugh as she said it; she would laugh without any amusement at all.

And then as she came through the hall again, the door bell rang. She had just told Meg and Cook to take the evening off, so she put the tray on the hall table and opened the door herself.

Cadiz stood there.

'Oh . . . Aunt *Cad*!'

'My dear – dearest Hal!'

They wept and laughed as they embraced each other fiercely. The tray was forgotten.

'Come into the morning room. Tell me everything. I've missed you so *much*! How was he? How did he look? Is he coming home?'

'He is well. Better than he has been since school. He is content – not wildly happy but content. Tired out, sun-baked – he knows he is pulling his weight – he looks wonderful.' Cadiz drew back and looked at Hallie searchingly. 'But he is not coming back, darling.'

'I thought . . . What did he say? About Hanny's name?'

'He was taken aback, of course. But he knows you will always look after him. Perhaps one day . . .'

Hallie knew that Austen would have tied things so tightly that Jack would have great difficulty in changing the *status quo*.

She said, 'It is so good to see you. Margo is home to be married. And we have been for fittings and . . . oh, it's *good* to see you!'

Cadiz had not been so sick coming home. She had had time to think and perhaps to understand.

She said softly, 'I know it must be difficult, darling. But you are doing something quite wonderful. I was not able to look after my war hero. But you are.'

Hallie said, 'What do you mean, Aunt?'

'I realize the extent of his injuries, Hallie. Do not be embarrassed. Jack told me so that I would be more . . . sympathetic. At first it seemed to make the whole thing worse. But then – coming home – I thought that if he had lost a leg I would expect you to care for him.'

Hallie said, 'The war, you mean? Yes, it did leave him very withdrawn, but I think he is over that now.'

'I meant his impotence, darling.'

Hallie said, 'Impotence?' It was a word that had been bandied about at school with a lot of giggling. 'You mean . . .' She stopped speaking and stared at Cadiz as if she had seen a ghost. And then she flushed darkly.

Cadiz said, 'Do not be embarrassed, Hal. Maude said something to Jack and he put two and two together. No-one else in the whole world knows. Not even his father.'

The flush receded as quickly as it had come and left her deathly white.

Cadiz said, 'Hallie, don't look like that. Please. I realize it must hurt you to hear it spoken aloud. Yet surely we have always been frank and open—'

'You have been frank, Aunt.' Suddenly Hallie felt strong. Very strong. Everything was crystal-clear to her. How could she have been angry with Austen? She smiled suddenly. 'And I thank you for it. But you are right – no-one else must know. Certainly not his father, nor mine.'

'Of course not, dear child.'

'Darling, I have to go upstairs with some milk for Hanny. I had completely forgotten! Will you stay for supper?'

Cadiz, forgetting that it was Friday night and Mungay would not be there, said quickly, 'No, darling. I have to spend this first evening with your father. I think he has missed me. And I have certainly missed him.'

'And you want to talk business . . .' Hallie wagged her head humorously. Then hugged her aunt again. 'He certainly has missed you. And so have I. It was so good you found Jack – you were right to go in search of him. Now we know everything is all right.'

'Yes, darling.' Cadiz found herself in the hall and being ushered out of the door again. Hallie tore up the stairs, the tray still on the table.

Austen was creeping out of the nursery, finger to lips.

'He was too tired to eat anyway,' he whispered. Then stopped. 'Are you all right, Hallie? Can you forgive my unreasonableness?'

She stood close by him but did not touch him. Suddenly her eyes were bright with tears.

She said, 'I can forgive you anything, my dear. I love you. I love you very much.'

He was very still. And then he said, 'Thank you, Hallie. I love you too.'

Twelve
September 1931

Margo's wedding was resplendent; a spectacle that set
the merchants of Bristol by the ears. The von Gellhorns
wore shakos and tiaras and their side of the cathedral
glittered and shook as if a hundred exotic birds had
landed in the pews. The bride's side was gauzy with veils
and grey toppers. But when the bride came in with her
retinue she outshone everyone.

Margo had chosen a dress that was simplicity itself; it
was of ivory slipper satin, cut on the cross to swathe her
slender figure to perfection. But it was her veil that took
the eye. Over a thousand rhinestones had been sewn into
the twelve yards of net, anchored – very firmly – to her
head by a Suzanne Lenglen band of seed pearls. The
weight of the veil was taken by Tilly and Elisabeth
von Gellhorn. Behind them came Hanover Rudolf and
Margo's niece, Jennifer McKinlay, holding hands and
looking as if butter would not melt in their rosebud
mouths. They were very closely followed by Hallie, who,
at one point, separated their gloved hands and took one
in each of hers. It transpired later that the strength of
their hand clasp had become competitive; luckily Hallie
noticed their rigid arms and red faces before bedlam
broke out.

Hallie felt as if she was practically overflowing
with the tender love that Aunt Caddie's revelation had
generated. As she walked past Austen – who was an
usher – their gazes locked in a way that previously had
always ended in embarrassment. That was before she
understood. Now, she projected into her gaze something

that told him it would never develop into anything demanding. She loved him beyond any physical expression. She loved him as he obviously loved her. In a way that was so deep no-one else in the world could possibly understand it.

Everything was clear now. His deep need for a family, his love for Hanny . . . it was all part of a pattern. As she stood behind Margo's entourage and stared at the East window, she experienced a moment when it seemed as if everything that had happened had been pre-ordained, part of a wonderful plan. Even Maude's death. Though she did have to cover that particular thought quite quickly as it seemed so unfair on poor Maude.

But apart from that, it was a pure moment of epiphany and Margo's unnecessarily ornate wedding suddenly had a personal meaning that transcended all the trappings and almost welded her to Austen.

Afterwards she was presented to the von Gellhorns; the *Graf* and *Gräfin*, the handsome brothers, each with his wife and children. One brother was still unmarried and lingered over Tilly's hand with obvious intent.

Margo was thrilled.

'Tilly, just think! We could visit each other every week!'

It was the first time she had even hinted that she might well be homesick.

Tilly was genuinely amazed.

'What absolute tosh, darling! I'd just have to go to Berlin and do something worth while. D'you know that the statistics for prostitution in Berlin—?'

Margo said, 'Tilly, *please*—' and the subject was dropped.

Austen appeared, holding Hanny firmly.

'Are you all right, my dear?' He was looking tired, but – she was almost sure – more relaxed than before in their four-month marriage.

'Of course.' She sat on her heels, her dress billowing around her. 'Wasn't Hanny good?'

'Jennifer squeezed my hand so tight I—' Hanny began.

'And then you squeezed mine.' She gave the small boy a warning glance and he was just sentient enough to accept it. She wanted nothing to mar that look of happiness on Austen's face.

Charles said, 'Well, Caddie? What do you think of our German friends?'

Cadiz turned her head, trying to keep a weather-eye open for the approach of Mungay Rudolf.

'Not very much,' she said. 'They seem typical Prussian officers to me.'

'You're prejudiced, my dear. The war is over. There will never be another.'

'Don't be too sure, Charles. The National Socialists in Germany are thriving.'

'Who on earth are they? And how do you hear about things like this, Cad?'

'We have an expensive wireless set in the drawing-room at home. There are news bulletins three times each day—'

'All right, all right.' Charles was laughing. 'Let's get back to here and now. And I say Margo has done very well for herself.'

'I hope so.' Cadiz eyed the *Gräfin* who had the inauspicious name, Brunhilda. 'I do hope so. I thought at one time that she and Jack . . .'

'She had a schoolgirl crush. That was all.'

'Of course.' Cadiz had spotted Mungay, standing alone. That was not the usual state of affairs. She wondered whether he was being ostracized since Florence's death in June. She wished she could push her way through the crowds and talk to him; make a stand in his favour.

Then he looked her way and she turned quickly.

'Shouldn't we find our places, Charles?' she said.

*   *   *

That winter, Hallie and Austen took the reins of domestic life at High House and made it into the kind of family home old Hanover Rudolf had envisaged seventy years before.

Mungay had never been interested in it and his role as a father had been sporadic. Florence had left the running of the house to a succession of housekeepers until Maude was old enough to be the nominal lady of the house. Since then its running had been improvised almost from day to day. The last housekeeper had left in a temper, and Meg and Cook had limped along helped by various 'dailies' and outside caterers, until Mr Austen brought home his wife.

And then things were different.

Hallie was a natural homemaker. She went about things without even having to think about them. Planning meals to suit Mungay, Austen and Hanny held no difficulties for her. She filled the house with flowers and organized two ladies, prophetically called Gertrude and Daisy, into a routine of polishing, silver and brass cleaning and 'rough scrubbing' so that the whole house smelt pleasantly of beeswax, and gleamed accordingly. 'The man with the ladders' came every other Tuesday and washed the windows. The gardener pressed seasonal fruit, flowers and vegetables on to her because he knew she appreciated them. And Cook and Meg went around with smiles.

In December she was twenty-two. She wanted a photograph. All of them, Mungay, her father, her aunt, Hanny, Austen and herself. It all proved too difficult and finally they had to leave Aunt Caddie out.

'It's marvellous that our fathers hit it off now, isn't it?' she said to Austen as they drove back from the photographers. 'But I wish Aunt Cad could forget the old animosity. She hardly ever comes to the house. If I want to see her I have to go to St George Street.'

Austen said hesitantly, 'I hate to feel I have estranged you from any of your family, Hallie.'

She shook her head quickly. 'Dearest, that is certainly not the case. Jack talked to her, you know. He understands that we have done the best possible thing for Hanny. Her whole objection to our marriage was because we would be taking Hanny away. She loves him dearly.'

Austen said quietly, 'It wasn't only Hanny, darling. Your aunt does not like me.'

But she would not have that either. 'How could anyone not like you?' She was fierce in his defence, but then went on reasonably, 'Actually, darling, perhaps at one time she wasn't terribly keen. But I think your goodness is winning her round.'

He did not smile. 'I am not good, Hallie. I am in business and business rarely has anything to do with goodness.'

She told him how happy he made her. How happy he made their son. How content Mungay was now. And her own father. And she had heard that only the other day Austen had given all the draymen a rise in wages. And had allowed one of the clerks a Saturday afternoon so that he could play in a local cricket match.

He remembered the incident well enough. He had said to the clerk, 'Your time is my time and my time is all the time.' And then, as the man had turned away disappointed, he had had a look of Jack Martinez about him. Jack Martinez who had played cricket with his sister on the sands at Weston-super-Mare . . . And Austen had said briefly, 'Take two hours on Saturday. And lose the money.'

But Hallie had returned to her first contention.

'Something quite else is worrying my aunt. But . . . if she doesn't want to tell us, she won't.' She looked at him gloomily. 'And I know she won't want to tell us!'

And then, for some idiotic reason, they both laughed.

Christmas could have been awkward, so Cadiz went to Spain to see Jack. She had not managed to avoid Mungay entirely in all these years, but each chance meeting made her more determined to avoid another one. Everything about him affronted her. His dark eyes which saw right through her brisk façade and knew that inside she shook every time he looked at her. And his own . . . contentment. That could have been a comfort to her. She was practically certain he visited the Hotwells Road house rarely – if ever. The tales of domestic bliss at High House usually included 'Grampy'. He was obviously a reformed character. But however things had turned out, *she* could never have been content after that amazing confrontation in 1928. It had meant nothing to him. It had changed her life.

She returned home in February to open a new hospital wing at Hanham – a rare honour and very good for business. It had been snowing hard and as she drove down Old Market in the family Morris she was looking forward achingly to tea in the cosy morning room with Rosie clucking about her wet feet and the chance of Hal being there.

There were no chains on the car and she was creeping along in the centre of the road when suddenly she caught sight of Tilly Hesterman. The girl was dressed in a long astrakhan coat with a matching cloche, and looked like a Cossack. She was carrying something. Cadiz braked gently and the Morris waltzed sideways to the kerb.

'Tilly!' Cadiz opened the door slightly and waved. 'Tilly – it's me – Miss Martinez! D'you want a lift?'

Tilly glanced around startled, then shook her head violently. She lifted her hand and Cadiz saw that she was holding a banner. She waved it in the air and from inside the car Cadiz saw briefly a single word, WORK. And, as if at a rallying call, there streamed out from behind the cast-iron public lavatory ranks of men carrying similar banners.

Cadiz had seen it before in 1926. Grey-faced armies trudging silently from one place to another demanding – begging – for work. But that Tilly, only a year older than Hallie, should be one of the leaders was shocking.

Worse was to come. Tilly moved sideways, grinning, shouting something – probably inviting Cadiz to join them – when from the direction of Temple Meads came another column of marchers. These men were smartly dressed in police uniforms and walked like soldiers, armed with truncheons instead of rifles. They made an orderly line across the breadth of the Horsefair and stood there, implacably.

There were quite a few cars crawling along through the snow. One by one, spotting the police and the ragged army of unemployed facing each other, they came to a halt and their drivers emerged and disappeared hurriedly into the nearest shop. Cadiz remained at her wheel, still not anticipating any trouble.

And then the police raised their truncheons and in reply a stone sailed over the Morris.

It was not the sort of charge she had imagined from seeing newsreels of mounted-police attacks on civilians. The Bristol force was drawn from the ranks of Somerset yeomen, an easy-going lot on the whole. One of them went to the police pillar at the edge of the pavement and made a call while the front rank, perhaps a dozen men, began to advance purposefully towards the marchers.

Tilly faced them with apparent calm, then lifted her banner high and shouted, 'This is a peaceful march to the unemployment headquarters in Shepherd's Hall! No violence! There will be no violence.'

But behind her men were breaking their banners across their knees and brandishing the two pieces threateningly. Their mutterings were inarticulate yet unmistakable. If the police did not let them through they would fight their way to Shepherd's Hall. And the muttering grew as the thin line of policemen moved steadily forward; it began to sound like a lion's roar. The next moment the Morris was engulfed in bodies, the open door was wrenched off its hinges, people fell in on Cadiz as they slipped on the snow and the rest of the police ran forward.

Somehow Cadiz pushed her way clear and got her legs out on to the road. She shouted Tilly's name, but it was like calling into a gale. 'Get out the way, missis!' someone barked in her ear and she was swept aside and crashed over the bonnet of the car.

She wedged a knee on to the mudguard and managed to get a purchase on the icy surface and as she crouched there, hanging on to the roof for dear life, she spotted Tilly, banner gone, holding up her arms futilely against the mass of angry men.

She waved and shouted hopelessly, but something attracted Tilly's attention and she turned and saw Cadiz clinging precariously to the swaying vehicle, saw the door being used as a kind of battering ram, and fought her way towards her.

'Get in – get in—' Cadiz gesticulated frantically with her free arm. 'Drive the blasted thing – go on – I can hang on.'

Tilly did as she was bid, revving the car furiously, edging it forward into the fray, honking the horn the whole time.

Perhaps it was the strange sight of a middle-aged woman, hat gone, greying hair hanging loose, skirt somewhere around her waist, clinging to the windscreen of a moving car – it might even have been that the police felt bound to check that she wasn't actually driving it herself. Whatever the reason, a passage opened for the Morris, and Tilly drove through it and made for the Castle and Wine Street. And there she pulled up and Cadiz slid thankfully to the ground and the two women, hating themselves for their weakness, wept in each other's arms.

It became a wry, slightly hysterical joke between them afterwards. They went back to St George Street that afternoon and revelled in being pampered and clucked over by Rosie and, later, Charles. It was he who brought news that several arrests had been made and one policeman injured by one of the broken banners.

'It – it's so *pathetic*!' Tilly mourned. 'Grown men fighting with sticks like little boys!'

Cadiz said, 'Charles, we must do something. Take on more men. We could arrange shorter shifts which would let in perhaps half a dozen—'

'The draymen would not stand for it!' Charles objected. 'If work is taken from them—'

'I'm not suggesting a cut in money!'

'Caddie, you know yourself we're not like Rudolfs. We supply a specialized market—'

'Then we must expand. We must import from other places, blend new—'

'But we're not a philanthropic organization. And you said yourself that things were becoming difficult in Spain.'

'All the more reason for importing from France. And Germany.'

Tilly said enthusiastically, 'Perhaps Margo could help there.'

'Why not?' Caddie saw quite suddenly that she might be able to divert some of Tilly's energy into something less . . . dangerous. 'You're going out to visit her this summer, aren't you?'

Charles held up both hands.

'Ladies, stop it – just stop it there! You've had a shocking experience this afternoon and you are being carried away—' He was cut short by gales of laughter from both women.

'Carried away!' Tilly spluttered. 'Oh, Mr Martinez, if you could have seen your sister—'

'Did my suspenders show?' wailed Cadiz, eyes streaming.

'Absolutely, yes! Why do you think the police let us through?' Tilly sobbed back.

'Oh my God! My dear Lord! Charles dear, can you imagine it? Another story for the Bristol annals! Miss Cadiz Martinez, respected director of the House of Martinez—'

They clutched each other helplessly. And Charles, who was often worried about his sister these days because she so rarely laughed, joined in.

It was the start of a very solid friendship between Cadiz Martinez and Tilly Hesterman. And the start of something new for the House of Martinez too. In spite of all difficulties, hours were cut and new men were taken on. Cadiz became an eccentric yet popular figure in the city. She opened a new ward in the Infirmary to be named Martin Ward. She sent regular donations to the East End Settlement in London, and suggested to Dr and Mrs Hesterman that Tilly might open something similar in Bristol.

People laughed at Cadiz. But they were proud of her. 'Mad as a hatter,' they said dismissively when they saw her driving the Morris down to Clevedon for her Easter holiday. ''Eart of gold. But mad as a hatter.'

And Mungay, hearing reports of her escapades, smiled.

In September that year there was an attempt by the Spanish military to seize Seville. A letter came from Jack assuring them that it had failed and there had been very little damage done to people or property. But the premonition which had come to Cadiz as she stood on the bridge over the Guadalquivir was strengthened. Jack might tell her that once the Catalonian separatists had been satisfied, everything would be all right, she knew it would not. She had travelled extensively when she was younger and now knew that land reforms were a hundred years overdue in the whole of Spain. Their own vineyard might be an exception, but angry peasants were unlikely to concede any exceptions.

Tilly made her promised visit to Margo in time for her first wedding anniversary and the christening of her daughter. She came home impressed and yet apprehensive. Margo thought that she was already pregnant again, and if she was not she would soon be. The von Gellhorns adored baby Constantia, but needed boys for the New Germany. One of the reasons they had permitted Margo to enter their ranks was that she was pure Aryan.

'It's rather frightening,' Tilly told Cadiz. 'I was only just accepted as a visitor.'

'Why?' asked Cadiz.

'My name. Hesterman. It is so obviously Jewish.'

Cadiz had continued to listen to their new wireless in the drawing-room and she knew all about the Bavarian who had organized the Munich Putsch of 1923.

She said, 'You must not go again, Tilly. It could be dangerous.'

Tilly said, 'I shall go again, Cadiz. And I hope Hal will go too. Margo is going to need her friends.'

'Oh dear Lord. And I thought I was giving you a less risky goal in life!'

'As for that – there are vineyards galore on the south-facing slopes of the Harz. Margo is going to make discreet enquiries about shipping some samples over to you.'

'Will it be difficult for her?'

Tilly made a face. 'Depends how popular she is. Whether the next baby is a boy.'

'Oh dear Lord,' Cadiz repeated.

'Ghastly, isn't it? I shall never marry. I admire you for holding out, Cadiz.'

'That's not how it was,' Cadiz said wryly. 'But most husbands aren't like Otto, so don't you hold out!' She smiled. 'I take it the von Gellhorns would look down their long Rudolf noses at anything smelling of trade?'

Tilly laughed. 'Yes – they have got the Rudolf nose! And the *schloss* isn't all that far from Hanover!' She shook her head. 'No, they don't care for trade. But on the other hand, wine is rather different. I have told them the House of Martinez are connoisseurs. That puts a different face on it entirely.'

'Ah well. We shall see.'

Cadiz passed Tilly the latest news from Jack and settled back in her chair. Hallie was to have come down to tea and to meet Tilly. She would not come now. Cadiz could not quite believe in her niece's happiness, but she knew that by five o'clock, Hallie was waiting for Austen's homecoming. Nothing must interfere with that.

She sighed and looked deep into the heart of the fire. At least she was certain that Hallie would not go to Germany to visit Margo. Simply because Austen would not permit it.

1933

The first consignment of wine from the Harz Mountains arrived in Bristol the following year. Cadiz held a tasting in the office and for the first time invited Austen; which meant that Hallie came too.

Charles rolled his cheeks and lips expertly and then expelled the wine into the spitoon on his desk.

'Heavy. A feeling of claret. After-dinner stuff.'

Cadiz, still tasting, nodded.

Austen and Hallie sipped together. Hallie, experienced in such matters, took longer than Austen. He leaned over the spitoon and then said, 'Good. I would most certainly order a case of this. My father would enjoy it very much.'

Cadiz got rid of hers and said, 'Not only for men, I think. I agree, Charles, it is a little on the heavy side. But I think there is also a richness which ladies would enjoy.'

They waited for Hallie who was slightly uncertain.

'I'd prefer a lighter one myself. Shall we go on to the hock?'

They did so. Charles turned his mouth down on this one. Only Hallie liked it.

Austen said, 'Could you blend? I realize Jack was the expert on blending, but I am tempted to think an excellent wine could come of these two.'

Charles said, 'If you're not pressed for time, Austen, come down to the Cellars with me and talk to our blender.'

The two men drifted off and Hallie said, 'Let's think of a name, Aunt Cad! Something that will sound English and German.'

Cadiz smiled, well pleased by Hallie's enthusiasm. She did not entirely approve of her niece's total domesticity.

'Go gently with the German half,' she advised. 'I rather think all things Prussian will be anathema in a few years' time.'

'Oh, you and your portents of doom! I was going to suggest Harzland. But I suppose that won't do.'

'I'm not sure. It has a pleasant ring to it.'

Hallie nodded and then exclaimed, 'All right then. Heartland. How about that? It's near enough to Harz to please the Germans and sounds entirely English to anyone else!'

'Heartland . . .' Cadiz murmured the name several times. 'Yes. I see your point.'

Meanwhile, below them, Charles and Austen had talked to the blender and he had promised some samples within the next two or three days.

Charles said, 'Good of you to take an interest, old man. Good of you.'

Austen said, 'My opinion is worthless, I'm afraid. Where wine is concerned I know what I like and there's an end to it.'

'You know what Hallie likes too. And your father. There are three opinions!' Charles laughed. 'But that's not really the point. You are a businessman down to your socks and one business is much the same as another.'

Austen said, 'It is certainly odd that our importation is affected by unrest at the same time.'

'You mean, Barbados is having troubles also?'

'There is a great deal of talking – shouting – being done I understand. I really should go out and see for myself. It is some years since I was there.'

Charles looked at him. 'You would take Hallie, of course.'

'No.' Austen drew his brows together. 'Hallie would stay with our son.'

At one time Charles would have winced at Austen's appropriation of Hanny. Now he did not.

'You could take him, surely? A wonderful experience for a lad of five.'

'He is not five until June, Father-in-law.' Austen needed an ally in this. He smiled. 'I went out there at six years old and hated every minute of it. Hallie has you and her aunt. There is simply no question of subjecting her and Hanover to such an arduous journey.'

Charles was silent. Cadiz would adore to see more of Hallie and the child. But Charles thought that Austen was relying too much on his wife's acquiescence. Charles was certain that she would not be parted from Austen.

They began to climb the stairs again and Austen waited until he was at the top before turning and saying, 'My father knows far more of wines than I do. Perhaps you should call him in. As an extra opinion.'

And Cadiz, overhearing, looked around the office as if for a way of escape. It had never occurred to her that Austen knew of the seduction scene back in twenty-eight. Suddenly a new dimension was added to her nightmare fantasy: Mungay telling Austen how near he came to bedding the Martinez spinster.

She shuddered and Hallie said, 'Are you sick, Aunt Cad?'

215

Cadiz managed a smile. 'I'd better not be! Not after just tasting our newest wines!' And actually managed to laugh.

Austen had driven them into the city so that they could go home via Saunton School and inspect the new kindergarten. This had been opened only last September using the Montessori methods and Hallie thought it would be marvellous for Hanny to go there the following September. Austen was less certain.

'Saunton is known everywhere as a school for girls, Hal,' he objected. 'You know that better than I do. When he starts his proper education, how will it be received? Can't you just imagine the other boys—'

'Darling,' she interrupted eagerly. 'I do so agree. But there are at least six boys who are older than Hanny who have been entered for Colston. They will pave the way. And I heard that Marjorie Maxwell is sending Clive – same age as Hanny – and I know for a fact he is also going to Colston. So Hanny will have plenty of company.'

'Well . . . all right. Let's go and have a look around. I'm not at all certain about learning through play. But I'll try to keep an open mind.'

'It's all I ask, Austen dear. I've arranged for Hanny to go to tea with Clive, so we shall be completely free after this tasting.'

He gave her one of his wry smiles. 'The thin end of the wedge?' he queried.

'What? You mean Hanny going to tea with Clive Maxwell? But darling, they've been friends for ages. Marjorie and I used to meet up for walks with the prams when I lived in St George Street.'

'I know. I know.'

But in the event he could not possibly fault Saunton's kindergarten. The headmistress, a young woman in a boxpleated skirt and mannish blouse, impressed

216

him with her brisk manner, and the classroom or 'environment' as she called it, was colourful and as fascinating as Aladdin's Cave.

'We arrange things in various areas,' she explained. 'Here we discover how to tie shoe laces. Put on socks and gloves.' She looked sternly at them. 'You will doubtless realize that by the time we've done that, we can count to ten.' She added more kindly, 'Toes and fingers, of course.'

She led them to the 'painting area', the 'sand and water area', the 'special area'. Austen was amused to hear that the word 'learn' was obsolete here, and the word 'discover' took its place. But he liked it. He liked it for Hanny. Hanny was quick and intelligent but he had a resistance to work which he obviously inherited from both his parents. Hallie knew how to get around him; he had a feeling so would Miss Bush.

'Let's take a drive down to Clevedon,' he suggested when they were back in the car. 'Have dinner at the Rocks Hotel overlooking the sea.'

She was enchanted by the idea but had to turn it down.

'Meg is collecting Hanny at six. We must be there for him.'

'We could telephone.' He looked sideways at her. 'This is the first time we've been out somewhere on our own for . . . I don't know.'

It was true. But then, they did not have the kind of marriage that needed to be exclusive. She met his gaze and smiled. And then saw that he was serious; this was an issue for him.

She felt suddenly nervous.

'I – I don't know. If you think it's all right—'

'Of course I do. Sometimes parents do absent themselves. For one reason or another.'

She swallowed. 'Then . . . where shall we telephone?'

'I'll go into the office.'

He swung the car immediately along the Hotwells Road and down to the warehouses. As he got out he

217

looked back at her and smiled. 'Thank you, darling,' he said.

She hardly knew what to do with herself. Something had happened. Cadiz was wrong. Or perhaps Jack had misunderstood Maude. Or . . . anything.

He emerged, still smiling and climbed in beside her.

'My father was there. He will be home well before six and explain to Hanny.' He laughed. 'There are a few compensations in living with him, after all.'

She chided him gently. She had always got on well with Mungay.

'He loves Hanny as much as we do,' she reminded him.

'So he should. Named for him. His first grandchild.'

She said softly, 'Twice over, in a way. His daughter's son. And your son.'

He looked round at her. His dark eyes were almost black.

'Dearest Hallie. I love you so much.'

She laughed, nearly embarrassed, and drew his attention to the sprouting hawthorn.

'We used to call it bread and cheese.'

'You and Jack?'

'Yes.'

'You miss Jack, don't you?'

'A little.' She smiled. 'I am so lucky, Austen. I have so much. I feel Jack has nothing.'

He nodded. 'I feel the same. But he felt bound to go, Hal. And, listening to your aunt, I think he did the right thing.'

'If hard physical labour is what he needs, he could do that here.'

'Perhaps he needed more than that. To get back to his roots. To find out about his business.'

'Perhaps. Aunt Caddie has an enormous feeling for Spain. And she has always said that Jack is like her.'

'Well then . . .' He changed down to take the steep

218

hill to the Flower House. 'Darling, how would you feel if I had to go away?'

'It's different for us. I would come with you, of course.'

'Not if it were bad for Hanny, surely?'

She glanced at him, startled.

'Barbados? You are going over to the plantation? Well, of course, we will come with you!'

'No. I could not agree to it. But I should go. There is considerable unrest out there at present.'

'Then if it is dangerous for Hanny, I will come.' She dropped her voice. 'Surely you know that I would come, Austen? Hanny has a family here who will care for him.'

He had not anticipated this. He had thought that once he had convinced her of the danger for Hanny, she would give up all thought of the trip. He was touched, yet exasperated.

'I'm sorry, Hallie. I would not consider taking you with me for one moment.'

'I am equally sorry, darling. But I will not let you go alone,' she said.

He stared at her in astonishment until she exclaimed sharply and then he just avoided running into the bank.

'What on earth is the matter, Austen?' she asked.

'Nothing.' He began to coast down to the esplanade. 'It's just . . . You so rarely argue, Hallie.'

But she was not arguing; she was simply standing against him. And she had never ever stood against him before.

They took supper in the Rocks Hotel and he talked to her again. But she would have none of it. If he went to Barbados, she would go with him. In the end he surrendered.

'Darling, please think no more of it. I will not go to the plantation. Amos will sort it all out for us. I have complete faith in him.'

She did not look in the least pleased and after a while he was constrained to ask her what more she wanted.

'Well . . . nothing really. We came to Clevedon to talk about you going to Barbados, did we?'

He leaned over the table. 'I wish I'd never mentioned it. I can see it has spoiled your evening.'

'It's just that . . . I thought it was something else.'

'What?'

'I thought we came here to – to be together.'

He smiled, delighted. 'Well, of course we did. Dearest girl, that was the main reason. It was just that it seemed a good time to talk about whether I should visit the plantation.' He patted her hand. 'I have said – I will not go. There, are you happy now?'

He spoke to her as if she were a child to be indulged.

She said, 'Yes. Thank you, Austen.'

She stood up and waited while he fetched her coat. She sounded like a small girl being polite after a party.

It was dark in the car. She blew her nose quite often. He wondered whether she had caught a cold and cursed himself for bringing her so far on a cold March evening.

And she was angry with herself for feeling disappointed. Almost let down.

Thirteen
1935

The rebellion in Barcelona that year seemed to prove
Jack's theory that once the Catalan separatists were
satisfied all would be well. Cadiz allowed herself to
believe him. The general strike in 1934 seemed to bear
this out; Catalonia proclaimed independence, now all
would be well. But then the rising was crushed and in
the autumn of that year when the miners proclaimed
a Communist regime, they too were put down with
severity. Cadiz waited until after Christmas and the early
part of the New Year, and then in the April of 1935, she
went out to see Jack in an effort to 'assess the situation'
as she put it to Charles.

The German wines were doing very well and Charles
– who had not been to Spain since Jack's birth – was all
for selling up.

'We're all right now,' he said. 'I'm not saying it
wouldn't be a loss – a terrible loss. But we can continue
to import wine and blend it ourselves. Mungay Rudolf
is proving to have an excellent palate. After the Heartland vintage, I would trust his recommendations completely.'

Cadiz had no wish to depend on Mungay more than
was absolutely necessary. She had been unable to go to
Spain for two Christmases now and they had been forced
to spend a great deal of both festive seasons in each
other's company. Granted the rest of the family had also
been present, but she was so aware of him that they
might have been alone on a desert island. That would
have been . . . acceptable . . . perhaps . . . if he had felt

the same way. But he played with Hanny and pulled crackers with Hal and never once met her eyes. But then, just after last Christmas, he had encountered her on the dark stairs of the Denmark Street office and had congratulated her on her philanthropic work.

'I wonder what I am going to read next in the *Evening World*!' he had said with an emphasis she couldn't quite place. Did he think she was going soft in her old age?

She had snapped back something about being comfortably off and with no heirs.

'But surely we share Hanny?' He had sounded genuinely surprised. And when she had said nothing – because she thought she might faint and fall down the stairs – he had said, 'Besides a great deal more of course.'

She had gone then, knowing he was taunting her. And since then she had peered from the top of the landing each time she left her office.

So she said to Charles, 'Just at the moment we should get so little for the estate, my dear. The big landowners, who would have snapped it up in the past, are hardly likely to want to be seen taking on more land just at present.'

'Well, I suppose you will find out about that. I did wonder whether Rodriguez might be in a position . . . with a mortgage from us—'

'I'll see what Jack says. He has a stake in it too, remember.'

'Of course, my dear. And Hal.' Charles had smiled propitiatorily. Sometimes, in spite of her good works, Caddie was very prickly.

So she timed a visit to coincide with the *Ulysses* taking a ballast of casks on the way to Barbados, and for the first time was not sick and could write at length to Tilly who was at the newly opened Medical School at Bristol University training to be a doctor.

'I will not post this until my return, my dear,' she began, sitting on the deck and enjoying the sharp April breeze blowing straight down from the Atlantic.

'Perhaps my daily burblings will give you a better picture of what is happening in Spain than anything more considered. At the moment I am watching two negroes swabbing down the upper deck in time to some song – presumably Caribbean – and wondering if they are Mungay Rudolf's offspring! Is that wicked of me, Tilly? It is purported that Barbados is populated by Rudolfs! At least it obviates the need for soup kitchens, my dear. I believe you would call it a paternalistic society!' She looked up, smiling. The two sailors did not actually resemble Mungay at all, but Tilly expected her to be shocking. Ever since the incident in the Horsefair, they had developed their separate roles, Cadiz the outlandish, Tilly her disciple.

Cadiz, the town, was as awful as ever and she was glad that one of the same sailors secured her a taxi and loaded her two suitcases with supple ease. She planned that she would continue her letter with a suggestion that she and Tilly visit Barbados some time and see for themselves if everyone was as relaxed and happy as these two. If Tilly were to be a doctor, it might be a good area for study.

She was still smiling after they left Cadiz far behind and started on the long dusty road to the foothills of the Moreno. Beneath a grove of willow on the left, three men crouched, obviously waiting for transport. They half stood as the taxi appeared and as it went past without slowing, they ran by it, shouting at Caddie. One of them picked up a stone. The next moment, with the driver accelerating crazily, stones were rattling against the metal sides like machine-gun bullets. They outstripped the men easily, of course. Cadiz, shaking all over, peered through the oval rear window and saw them drop back and squat beneath the willows again. She folded her arms hard against her chest and closed her eyes momentarily. It was a horrible shock when the driver skidded around another bend, drew up at the roadside and indicated that she should get out.

'But I am English!' She protested. '*Inglesa!* They do not hate us, surely?'

'They do not know you are English, *señora*! There may be more of them along this road and they think you are high-born Spanish. And my taxi is my living. If it is damaged by stones I have no living! Out. Please out.'

She haggled in vain. At last he consented to take her luggage, but refused to be seen with her again.

'I would be stoned also for a blackleg,' he told her. 'I will send someone out from the Castillo. Sit here.'

He indicated another grove of willow further down the bank but Cadiz felt like a sitting duck beneath the swaying branches and after he had disappeared, she plodded stoically along the dusty road until Jack arrived an hour later in a closed car that looked like something from Chicago.

'Is it bullet-proof?' she asked bitterly as she climbed inside.

She was still trembling slightly so had determined to avoid hugging him and causing more concern. But it did not escape her notice that he did not get out of the car and once she was next to him he turned and made for home as quickly as possible without pausing for so much as a kiss on her cheek. They passed her taxi *en route*. Neither driver gave any indication of recognition.

'This is eerie,' she said to him, 'and stupid too.'

'I agree. But it is a storm in a teacup and will be sorted out quite soon.' Jack turned and flashed her his usual boyish smile. Then added, 'So if you have come to take me home, forget it.'

She was unwilling to mention the possible sale of the vineyard. He had looked on the place as a haven for so long.

'I have come to find out just what the situation is,' she said instead. 'Your letters tell me there is nothing to worry about. The newspapers prophesy disaster.'

'It depends on what you term disaster.'

She peered through the windscreen. The land fell

away to the river valley on her side of the car. Ahead it rose steeply towards the Castillo. They were passing the first of the yards. Everything looked absolutely normal. And, after all, she had encountered occasional animosity back in 1931. The stones just now had hit the taxi, not her.

She said doubtfully, 'Well . . . death. Destruction.'

'Then you can forget newspaper reports. A few stones will be thrown as you have discovered. And then Lerroux will go and there will be elections. The Socialists will get in. Land reform on a huge scale. End of unrest.'

She saw the fortress shape of the Castillo and breathed a sigh of relief. She wanted to believe Jack. Nothing had changed in the last four years; things were certainly no worse. Spain was not Russia. There would be no revolution here.

'I have to admit I am very glad to see you and the Castillo.' She smiled. 'Are Rodriguez and Benita still with us?'

He was not smiling.

'Not at the moment.' He drove the car through the archway which had once held a portcullis. 'One of Benita's daughters is looking after the kitchen while you are here. Come inside. I'll explain.'

He took her through the low postern into the kitchen where she nearly fell over her two suitcases standing just inside. The grotto-like room was still cool, still hung with onions and garlic cloves, still smelling of grapes. But the range was not lit and a kettle was standing on the small paraffin burner in front of it. Then at last, Jack hugged her and over his shoulder she saw a girl of about sixteen smiling and indicating the teapot with lifted brows. She nodded enthusiastically, disentangled herself from Jack and went towards the table.

'I am so sorry that your mother is ill,' she said in Spanish. 'I will go to see her tomorrow. I am sure I have met you before now. What is your name?'

The girl glanced up, obviously surprised.

'I am Carmencita. Benita was my grandmother.'

'Was?' Cadiz suddenly realized that Jack had not yet explained Benita's absence. 'Oh my dear . . . how awful—' She turned to Jack, who put an arm around her shoulders.

'Dearest Aunt Cad. You have known Benita all your life, haven't you? I did not want to tell you. But you must have realized that she was well into her seventies.'

Unexpectedly, Cadiz broke down on his shoulder. She spluttered, 'Oh God – I'm sorry – but . . . it doesn't matter two hoots about being stoned – damn the political situation! Benita . . . Benita was Spain!'

Jack hugged her and smiled at the girl. 'She would be pleased with that, eh, Carmencita?' He translated briefly. 'Your grandmother was Spain.'

The girl made clucking sounds and poured tea and after a very short time Cadiz could sit down and drink it as she had done so often before. Life would go on. Benita would want it to; the granddaughter would follow in traditional footsteps.

She said, 'I will show you how to light the stove, Carmencita. And I have some of your grandmother's recipes. We can work together for a few days.'

The girl did not speak.

Jack cleared his throat. 'Carmencita cannot stay, Aunt Cad. She is here to get a meal for this evening only.'

'Oh . . .' Cadiz tried to summon a smile. 'Then I thank you. But if you change your mind—'

Jack said quietly in English, 'If anyone guessed she was here, Caddie, there would be trouble for her. Since Benita . . . there has been no-one at the Castillo.'

She looked at him without speaking for a long minute. And he nodded.

She said resiliently, 'So. The Castillo must be closed. You have your own quarters, Jack. There is no point in this place being opened.'

He smiled. 'Well done. I might have guessed you

would be practical about this. The old place can always be reopened . . . later.'

'Of course.' She held his gaze. 'Just so long as you are right, and not the newspapers.'

'I am right,' he maintained stoutly.

She lifted her brows.

'Even though Carmencita must keep her work here secret from the villagers?'

He said steadily, 'Even so.'

They spoke no more of the troubles that evening and though Jack spent the night in the Castillo with her, she read very little into that: after all Carmencita left when it was dark and she would have been quite alone if he had gone back to the workers' bungalows.

But the next morning after a makeshift breakfast and quick clear-up, she asked to visit the yards.

'Why?' Jack seemed honestly surprised. 'In view of everything I would have thought it much better if you returned to Cadiz before the *Ulysses* left.'

'She will be docked for another day for the unloading. Besides, I rather hoped I could be with you for a week or so.'

He wrinkled his short nose.

'Is that such a good idea, Aunt Cad? You are seen as the land-owner hereabouts.'

She arched her fine black brows.

'You are a Martinez too, Jack!'

'But I have been here working for six years. They accept me as one of themselves.' He gave his charming smile. 'Come on, darling. You know what I mean. Surely I don't have to tell you that you look like a very beautiful high-born Spanish lady!'

'You . . . flatterer!' But she had to laugh at his obvious ploy. It was certainly true her Spanish looks were against her these days.

She said, 'There's still time to see the vines. Don't be shy. I remember how awful your little room was from before! Besides, I must have a word with

Rodriguez. He will think it strange if I ignore him.'

He hesitated then spread his hands. 'All right, I'll confess. Rodriguez is no longer here. In fact, Cad, I took charge of the place last autumn after the miners' strike. Sorry, I should have told you, but I knew you'd come flapping over and insist on me going back with you.'

Her brows had disappeared beneath her hair by this time. She said, 'Dead? Rodriguez? He was a young man. Younger than me.'

Jack laughed. 'Not a bit dead. His brother was taken by the Falange and he went to Madrid to sort it out.'

'His brother . . . the Falange? You mean the Fascist party? What would they want with Rodriguez' brother?'

Jack shook his head. 'Something silly. Mistaken identity. A church just outside Madrid was burned – the Communists see religion as the real oppressor here and several churches have been destroyed. But Rodriguez will make sure his brother is released.'

Cadiz was silent, staring at Jack as if he had grown horns. When she spoke her voice was level.

'How long since Rodriguez left? Last September?'

'October.'

'And now it is spring. When did you hear from him?'

'He's no writer. But news has filtered through. He is all right.'

She turned away.

'We'll have a look at the vines, Jack. I need to be outside. You should have told me all this long ago. If your father knew—'

'Exactly,' he said drily.

'You could have written to me privately.'

They walked through grass that could have been in an English meadow, and came to the first of the vineyards sloping down towards the river. Already the vines were as high as their heads and here and there blossom was forming. Cadiz walked between them looking for any sign of disease.

'They are good, yes?' Jack's English had a faintly

Spanish intonation. But he was justly proud of his stewardship. 'We used the old carbolic spray and a tar wash.'

She said, 'Vintage 1935 will be good.' She turned to him. 'And, I imagine, the last for the House of Martinez.'

He said, 'Don't talk like that, Caddie! It's our land! Our people grew grapes here two hundred years ago at least – maybe more!'

'Ah. So . . . you too are now a land-owner.'

It was his turn to stare at her. Then he said, 'Am I? Am I not one of the people any more?' He shook his head fiercely. 'I can be both, Caddie! All right so I had to take over when Rodriguez left – the villagers would have divided the lot up among themselves if I hadn't done something. But they let me! Don't you see – because I had been one of them, they let me take over!'

'Six years ago you would not have wanted to take over a single vine let alone the whole yard!'

His shoulders dropped in a kind of surrender. He grinned ruefully. 'No. I wouldn't, would I? So the seeds of ownership are in me after all. But Cad, I had to do it, for Dad – for you – Hal – Hanny . . . Oh God, you understand!'

'I do. And you have done well, Jack.' She walked on and when they came to the end of the row she stood looking over the valley. 'I can see that you will want to harvest this crop. But then . . . Jack, you must come home. Otherwise you will stop being one of the people and you will become wholly a land-owner.'

He frowned. 'What do you mean, Cad?'

'I mean, the people who will protect you will be the Falange. The same people who have got Rodriguez' brother. You will have to choose. To return home. Or to be seen as one of the Fascists.'

He was silent for a long time. She knew she was telling him something he had already faced.

At last he said heavily, 'What do you want me to do?'

'Try to find a buyer for the vineyard. But whether you find one or not, come home this Christmas.'

He thought of home and everyone treating him like the prodigal son. He thought of Hal torn between keeping Hanny and trying to introduce him to the boy as a new father.

He said, 'Trust me, Cad. I will come as soon as I know there is real danger. Leave it with me.'

She stared at him until her eyes hurt. She loved him in such a special way; perhaps as a mother loved a son. But she would never know that for certain.

She whispered, 'You have changed, Jack.'

'Yes. Don't make me change back, Cad.'

'Of course not.' She smiled brightly. 'Naturally I trust you. You have common sense and will use it.' She turned. 'I assume you are using Rodriguez' quarters? Let us go there and have something to eat. And then perhaps you will drive me in that gangster's car back to Cadiz and I will go home.'

He said, 'I love you, Cad.'

Hallie was cleaning the stair rods when she heard the car drive into the old stable yard. Sullivan was having a bad time with his arthritis and was being nursed by Meg, so the arrival of the car meant that Austen, Mungay or both of them were home.

Austen did not like to see her doing menial jobs in the kitchen and two years ago she would have bundled the rods into the flannelette dusters and removed the old kid gloves in which she worked. Now, without realizing it, her lips tightened and she continued to rub in the brasso with extra vigour.

They had both come home: she heard them enter the laundry room which gave straight on to the yard. It must be raining again because Mungay said clearly, 'Put the brolly over there to dry, Austen. We don't want Meg putting out her eye when she comes in.'

There was no response from Austen; presumably he

did as bidden. Mungay entered the kitchen first, un-buttoning his coat and flapping it energetically.

'Hallie! How very domesticated you look sitting there under the lamp!'

She glanced up smilingly. It surprised her sometimes how close she and Mungay had become.

'Hello, Gramps. You're nice and early. I'll put the kettle on in two minutes and we'll have tea.'

Austen came in holding his coat and hat. Unaccountably she felt irritated by his carefulness. Mungay was flapping and dripping everywhere making a fine old mess for Meg to clear up. Austen would carry his outdoor things into the cloak room with minimum mess.

He said, 'Why on earth are you cleaning the brass, Hal?'

She kept her smile in place. 'Because Meg is looking after Sullivan and Cook would be most put out if I asked her to do the stair rods.'

'I've told you before, dearest, we can take on more staff.'

His consideration was almost too much to bear. She wanted to tell him that Gertrude or Daisy would clean brass if she asked them: it so happened that she wanted to do it herself.

But he wouldn't understand her need to be needed, so she continued to smile and began to put away the cleaning things.

They took tea in the morning room as usual, then Austen went off in the car again to meet Hanny from Saunton kindergarten. Since Sully's arthritis had confined him to bed, Austen or Mungay had taken on the job of going to the school at four o'clock and usually Hallie went too. Today, under the impression that she was overworked, Austen said he would go alone.

'I like to come, Austen,' she protested, already gathering tea things on to the trolley.

But he pushed her gently down into her chair.

'I will take the trolley on my way out. I want you to rest, my dear.'

She stayed where she was, watching him as he stacked crockery, her blue eyes very dark indeed.

There was a silence after the clatter of the trolley receded into the kitchen. Mungay sat back, his usual cigar growing ash in his left hand. Hallie stayed rigidly where Austen had put her, her gaze now directed into the fire.

At last Mungay said, 'It is very natural that occasionally married couples feel a certain . . . irritation . . . with each other, Hal. Don't worry about it.'

She forced a smile and deliberately relaxed her shoulders.

'Of course. Austen is so good and kind, Gramps. It's just that . . .'

'Yes?'

'Nothing.'

'It's this business about Barbados, isn't it?'

She looked up at him wondering if that was it. Occasionally over the past few years, Amos had reported unrest. But never at the Rudolf plantation. Even so, Mungay always said, 'If only I were younger, I'd go out myself.'

Hallie said now, almost curiously, 'Why won't he take me out there, Gramps?'

'He does not wish to leave Hanover here on his own, Hal. That's all.' He anticipated her next comment and added quickly, 'He did not enjoy his first visit there, Hal. He won't inflict that on the boy.'

'I understand that. But you are here to see to Hanny's needs. And my own father. And Aunt Caddie.'

Mungay looked away from her and down at the Axminster. Hallie had refurbished much of High House, but the old rose-strewn Axminster was still there. He had loved it as a boy and now so did Hanny.

He said very gently, 'Your aunt may well bring your brother back with her, Hal. That possibility . . . frightens Austen.'

232

Immediately her sympathy was engaged.

'Oh, my poor Austen! I think he sees Jack as a bogeyman. Jack would never take Hanover back, Gramps. Not now.'

Mungay believed her. He failed to understand why Austen did not take her to Barbados. There had to be another reason.

She was silent again. He watched her tense up once more and felt his own muscles tightening. Suddenly he got up and threw the cigar into the fire.

'Hal, is there something else?'

He thought that if Austen had been messing about with other women he would kill him.

She did not answer for so long he thought she had not heard him.

Then quite suddenly she said, as if it had been wrenched from her, 'I want another child!'

Neither of them realized that she was assuming the parenthood of Hanny; it was not relevant at that moment. Mungay stared at her, longing to say simply, 'then why don't you have one?' but knowing from a long time ago that there was little possibility of Hal ever being pregnant by Austen. And yet, why not? What was the matter with the boy?

And quite suddenly, Mungay knew why Austen refused to go to Barbados with his wife. His amorous adventures were known well by Amos, probably by Sugar too. There was every likelihood that if Hal went with him, she would hear of them.

For a split second he felt some sympathy with his son. And then it went. Whatever devils hounded Austen, he had no right to inflict them on Hal too.

He sat down again slowly and leaned forward almost confidentially.

'I think you should go to the plantation with Austen, Hal. I think it would be . . . perhaps . . . a good thing for your marriage.'

She wished she had not spoken. She was letting

233

Austen down. How could she – even imply – any criticism of him?

She sat up and said rallyingly, 'We're back where we started, Father-in-law. Let's drop the subject.'

'No.' She was getting up. He seized her hands and held her still. She always called him Father-in-law when she wanted to push him away. He held on to her tightly, determined that should not happen.

'Hal, listen. I will talk to Austen. I will insist that one of us should go out there. He will agree to me going. And arrangements will go ahead. At the last minute I shall not be well enough to make the journey. And you . . . you will tell him that it is quite all right for him to go as you have been wanting to see Margo Adams – sorry – von Gellhorn – for a considerable time and this will be a good chance to do so.' Mungay smiled. 'Hal, I know my son. He will not permit you to go to Germany at the present time. His alternative will be to beg you to accompany him.'

She stared at him.

'It sounds . . . Machiavellian,' she said uncertainly.

'The Rudolfs have been likened to that gentleman before now, Hal.' He smiled, asking for a response. 'Think how cleverly Austen wooed you – when you were still in your teens – without seeming to do.'

She was startled. Her violet eyes widened.

He added quickly, 'You must realize now that he was always madly in love with you.'

She looked down at their linked hands. Of course, Mungay had no idea that Austen was impotent. He was doubtless thinking that a trip to the island would become a second honeymoon. Somehow it was all rather disturbing.

She said, 'Forgive me, Gramps. I have been making a fuss about nothing—'

'No, you have not. You never make a fuss about nothing, Hal.'

234

She smiled wanly. 'I cannot push myself on to Austen if he does not wish it.'

'You know that is not how it is.'

'It seems awfully like . . . tricking him.'

'He needs a holiday. You would be tricking him into taking a holiday. Together. Just you and him.'

'Oh, Gramps. You are so kind. He takes after you.'

Mungay could have hotly denied this. And yet – wasn't he practically as pure as the driven snow these days?

He grinned suddenly. 'Come on, Hal. Do something devilish for a change! You and Austen are always with Hanny. Porthmeor every Easter and Whitsun. The Flower House in Clevedon in August . . . splash out!'

He let his smile spread to an infectious grin. No-one could resist his grin – or so Lily Elmes used to tell him.

Hallie shook his hands conspiratorially.

'I'll take a bet with you. Austen won't fall for any of it!'

He said, 'Done!'

And at that moment the car could be heard outside and Hanny came rushing through the kitchen into the morning room.

'Guess what? I had a gold star for my story about Bellamy! And I done a picture to go with it and it's 'zackly like Bellamy!'

'I did a picture,' Hallie murmured automatically as she removed his cap, flattened his wild brown hair and caught his coat before it dropped to the floor.

'Miss Bush says it don't matter how we say things – we just got to *say* them!'

Hallie caught Austen's eye and they both smiled. Miss Bush's word was law these days and they admitted to each other that under her guidance Hanny was proving himself to be quick and intelligent. But the old adage of being seen and not heard was not for Miss Bush. And Hanny needed no encouragement to speak.

He accompanied Hallie back to the kitchen and ate an enormous tea and then announced his intention of visiting Sully. Austen, who had followed them, doubtless to keep an eye on the stair rods, warned him about tiring the old man.

'I got some jokes for him. And some riddles. Why has a camel got two humps?'

'Actually I believe—'

'Cos he's . . .' Hanny paused and thought hard, then said, 'I've forgotten. P'raps Sully will know.'

'Come back when Meg tells you,' Hallie said to his departing back.

He paused and turned at the door; his smile was very sweet. 'All right. I love you, Mummy. I love you, Dad.' And he was gone.

Austen said, 'I'll put him to bed, dear. Why don't you rest for a while?'

She looked at him. She loved him – at times with a tenderness that almost made her weep. And then, unexpectedly, she would feel this anger. She had to remind herself he was war-damaged.

Even so, as he turned away with that indulgent smile, she made up her mind. She would go along with Mungay's hopeless plan. She needed to be alone with Austen. She simply had to come to terms with this . . . sense of being wronged.

In the morning room Mungay cut and lit another cigar and made his own plans. By the time Austen and Hal departed for the plantation, Cadiz would be home. And the three of them – Charles, Cadiz and him – would be responsible for Hanny. If he couldn't break down her icy reserve in that time, then he never would.

He was halfway through the cigar when an unpleasant thought occurred. Cadiz had gone out to Spain to try to persuade her nephew to return with her. If she succeeded he knew that nothing on earth would make Austen leave Hanny.

For a moment he frowned into the fire. Then a slow smile spread across his face. If Jack came home, surely

Austen would immediately plan to take Hanny with them? Yes, that would get him out of the way quicker than anything.

Mungay's smile abated somewhat as he realized it wasn't quite what Hallie had had in mind. He would just have to hope that Jack stayed put at that crumbling old Castillo.

He leaned over to the radiogram and switched on for the six o'clock news. There was nothing about Spain.

He smiled again, and thought of Cadiz Martinez and her work around Bristol Docks. He would offer some help. A large donation. She would have to make some response to that. If she brushed past him once more he would just grab her and make her listen to him.

Perhaps that would be the best thing to do.

His smile widened at the thought.

Fourteen

On June the first, Hanover Rudolf was seven years old.
He still had his natural father's floppy brown hair and
blue eyes; suddenly it was possible to see that he was
also going to inherit his mother's long aquiline nose and
determined chin. He could be as easygoing as Jack and
as wilful as Maude. And, like both of them, he had an
unexpected charm that could get him practically everything he desired. Luckily, the Martinez trait of contentment was also there; his desires were well within
everyone's means. Cricket and the beach in the summer,
snowballing and sledging in the winter satisfied him
completely at the moment.

His birthday party was held in the large garden of High
House. Before tea there were traditional games intended
to make the disparate children integrate amiably. Unfor-
tunately Hanny and his best friend, Clive Maxwell, were
halfway through their introductory term at Colston's
and deep into the mystique of the boys' prep school.
They could just about accept Clive's younger brothers,
who, after all, would soon be leaving Saunton in their
turn and joining the elect at Colston's. Even Jennifer
McKinlay, who had tried so hard to crush Hanny's
three-year-old fingers at her Aunt Margo's wedding,
was bearable because she had been promoted into the
'proper' Saunton, but Jennifer's cousins from Germany
were absolutely beyond the pale. The eldest, Constantia,
was still only three years old but the same size as
five-year-old Clem Maxwell and twice as strong. She had
an unengaging habit of sidling smilingly close to Hanny

and administering a lethal pinch and then looking concerned and innocent at his yelp of pain. He had tried complaining to Aunt Margo just once; Constantia had turned her enormous blue eyes in the direction of Clive and said in her baby-voice, 'Naughty boy.'

Both boys were outraged by this. It was not just the underhandedness that appalled them, it was the adults' acceptance that they would resort to pinching. When they fought they used fists, never finger nails.

During Oranges and Lemons, Constantia managed two attacks on Hanny and no less than four on Clive. When Clive's four-year-old brother, Clarrie Junior, dissolved in tears and Clive was roundly ticked off by his mother, Hanny decided something must be done.

'After tea,' he promised Clive. 'Gramps and me have mapped out a jolly decent treasure hunt. We'll get her behind the potting shed.'

Margo, pregnant for the fourth time, reclined in Cook's chair and watched Hallie, Cadiz and Tilly turning out individual rabbit blancmanges.

'D'you know, I simply cannot remember a time when I wasn't in an interesting condition,' she said, mock-mournfully, and with a smug inflexion in her voice. After all, none of the women working at the table had ever given birth.

Tilly let out a yelp of laughter. 'What made you think of that, Margo? The rabbit blancmanges?'

Cadiz and Hallie glanced at Margo, not certain of her reaction. But she tipped back her head, entirely unoffended, and laughed too.

'I suppose so!' she spluttered. 'After all, I am a natural mother – Otto is a natural man – what could be more . . . *natural*?'

Hallie felt her face grow warm; somehow the remark was in bad taste. The young Margo had often been outrageous – and had enjoyed being so – but never tasteless.

Tilly shook another mould gently over a plate.

'I don't like the sound of it myself. Thank goodness the Red Cross have accepted my application to work in Madrid. I notice you don't say anything about Otto being a natural father. Just a natural man.'

'In Germany, life is so much simpler,' Margo explained. 'Women have their roles – the men worship them for it – and the men have theirs. If this one –' she patted her abdomen complacently, '– is a boy, then Otto will come into his own, of course. But *Grossmutter* and I will train the girls.'

Tilly stopped working. 'I always thought marriage – parenthood – was a partnership?' she said.

Margo smiled indulgently. 'Tilly, you cannot possibly understand—'

'But surely . . . look at Hal and Austen. They share everything concerned with Hanny.'

Margo's smile widened. 'Yes. Except his conception, of course.'

The awful thing was, she did not realize that she had just delivered an insult. Not until Tilly blurted, 'Doesn't that make it even better?' And Cadiz went on quickly, 'What about some angelica in front of each rabbit, Hal? To represent grass.'

And then she had the grace to stop smiling and say, 'Hal, I didn't mean – darling, we all know by now you cannot have children – nothing to be ashamed of, for goodness' sake! And you're still quite young. In a few years' time there might be an operation that could help you – who knows? Anyway, you're both doing a wonderful job with Hanny. Though I have to admit that if he were in Germany he would be disciplined far more strictly – but, of course, we've always been sloppy in this country, haven't we? When I think back to our Saunton days—'

The baize door swung and Austen came in.

'Dear, is it nearly time for tea? We've just played Grandmother's Steps and I'm afraid someone managed to step on little Clarrie Maxwell's foot quite painfully—'

Hallie turned to him, her face was bright red, her normally dark blue eyes, blazing azure.

'Darling, of course!' Her voice was unendurably gay. She flung herself at him so hard he had to put his arms around her to avoid them both crashing into the dresser.

She laughed. 'Darling, do stop it! My hands are covered in blancmange! I don't want to mess up your nice clean shirt!'

And she released him and went back to the table.

'If you could take one end of the trestle top . . .' She propped open the kitchen door and then the outer one. In the stable yard Sully could be seen arranging chairs. 'The trestles are all ready. I think we can manage to carry it out without spilling anything, don't you?'

Sully, a new man with the summer weather, took one end, Austen the other. The women followed with plates of bread and butter, the long board was fitted carefully on to the waiting supports. The children, led by Margo's sister, Sybil, and her husband, and restrained by Mungay and Charles, poured around the corner from the garden.

Tea commenced.

Walter Hinch was in charge of the von Gellhorn girls during the treasure hunt. He had always felt part of the Adams' entourage, but the three small girls defeated him with their obvious scorn. Constantia, at three and a half, spoke German at him, though he knew for a fact she could speak excellent English. Truda and Eva were still babies – Eva could barely walk – yet their air of superiority made him feel the servant he supposed, suddenly, he was.

'We have to follow the blue arrows,' he said. 'That one is orange, Miss Connie. Shall we look for the blue?'

'I want orange,' Constantia stated. 'And my name is not Connie. *Dummkopf.*'

'I beg your pardon, miss. And my name is not dummie-whatever-you-said.' Walter picked Eva up and walked in the direction of the blue pointer. 'Come on, like good girls. We have to play the game, you know.'

Truda took his hand obediently enough and seemed genuinely thrilled when they found the next blue arrow pointing to the rhododendron walk.

'Dragons,' she told him and he smiled, on safe ground.

'I'll save you, Miss Truda.'

He ignored young Connie. She could sulk and trail behind if she wished.

Connie did not wish. She watched them into the maze of rhododendron bushes, tall as trees and twice as thick, and headed off in the direction of the orange markers which led behind the potting shed exactly where Hanny had known she would come.

'Couldn't resist it, eh, Con-won?' he said. 'You knew we were orange, didn't you? And you thought we'd have rigged the hunt so that we got the prize?'

Clive smiled at her almost fondly.

'See, Con the Terrible, the English have got a few brains after all.' He pulled a regretful face. 'But then, of course, we've got round heads, not square ones.'

Both boys fell backwards into the grass cuttings, weak with mirth at their own jokes. And Connie turned to make her escape.

Hallie said furiously, 'Do you have to flinch like that every time I come near you? I can assure you I shall only do so when Margo is in view!'

Austen looked at her.

'What has she been saying?'

'Nothing. Leave all that mess – Tilly will help me later. We should be on the terrace by the tubs.'

There were four teams of treasure hunters and four tubs on the terrace.

'My father will be there. What did she say, Hal? Tell me.'

Hallie moved sharply away from the table loaded with a mess of blancmange and sticky cake.

'Nothing. Just on to me to go and stay with her when this new child arrives.'

Austen laughed. 'Some hope. What a ghastly set-up it sounds. The only good thing to come from the von Gellhorns is the Heartland vintage.'

Hallie agreed entirely but because of Mungay's complicated and stupid plan, she still said, 'I feel I should go. She is my friend. None of the family can go. Sybil and Marcus are—'

'Let Tilly go again.'

'She won't. It is becoming most unpleasant for her out there. Rather like it was for Aunt Cad in Spain.'

He said incredulously, 'Are you serious? Would you really go to Germany?'

'And leave you and Hanny?' Her voice had a sarcastic note he had never heard before. 'I've always told you that Hanny has two grandfathers and a loving aunt. As for leaving you – be honest, Austen – you wouldn't miss me that much now, would you?'

He was silent, walking one pace behind her across the lawn. Everything was blessedly quiet in the garden. Small groups of children could be seen dotted here and there with Mungay and Charles umpiring.

They reached the terrace. The flower tubs appeared full of some unusually exotic blooms. At close range these were obviously made of paper and stuck into sawdust.

Hallie stationed herself by them very casually.

Austen said, 'You are being deliberately provocative, Hal. You know I should miss you every minute of every day.'

'And every night?'

'What on earth do you mean?'

'Margo – and obviously Tilly and probably all of Bristol too – know that we shall never have children!'

'*What?*'

He was still staring at her and she was suddenly fidgeting like a schoolgirl under his intense gaze, when

243

screams broke out. Margo appeared from the gooseberry bushes and lumbered clumsily towards the potting shed, calling, 'Mamma is coming, *liebchen*!' Walter Hinch emerged from the overgrown evergreen walk clutching the two von Gellhorn babies and shouting, 'Connie, where are you?' Cadiz, Clarrie and Clem Maxwell popped up from the sunken rockery like twin jacks-in-the-box. As the screams continued and became more blood-curdling, children trailed from all over the garden in various stages of apprehension.

Austen and Hallie ran down the lawn together and met Margo as she half dragged, half carried Constantia from the compost heap which was fenced around quite stoutly with wooden stakes.

'Margo, how on *earth* did she get in there?'

Hallie took the child's free arm and they lifted her free.

She was weeping noisily, unhurt physically. Margo began to pick slugs from her clothes with loud shudders.

'Oh, my poor baby! Tell Mamma—'

Constantia obliged in a flood of German. Hallie said, 'I think a bath—'

Margo said, 'He should be whipped! If Otto were here, he would take a crop to him for this!'

They were by now the centre of a very interested group of children. Truda and Eva safe in Walter's stalwart arms, were laughing uncontrollably. Constantia's howls increased.

Cadiz said loudly, 'For goodness' sake, Margo, take her indoors and let Meg bath her.'

'Not before that boy has seen his filthy work! My God – he takes after his mother – Jack had a heart of gold—'

Austen said smoothly, 'Do I gather Connie is accusing Hanny of throwing her into the compost heap?'

'Certainly! How could she have got over the fence by herself? And do not call her Connie, please, Austen! Her name is—'

Austen opened his mouth. 'Hanover!'

244

He had not lifted his voice like that since the trenches. Everyone was immediately silenced. For an instant it was possible to hear the gentle hum of the bees over the fruit enclosure.

Then an upstairs window was lifted. It was barred because it was Hanny's room, but he still managed to push his head outside.

'Is the game over?' he shouted.

'I think it's up rather than over,' Austen shouted back. 'Will you come down now please?'

Hanny's head disappeared and Jennifer McKinlay's took its place.

'Me too, Mr Rudolf?'

Austen glanced towards Sybil and Marcus who both avoided his eye.

'Yes please.'

Another head appeared. Clive Maxwell's.

'An' me?'

Austen thundered, 'Who ever is there, kindly come here. At once!'

It took perhaps ten seconds for the three children to appear, during which time Constantia's sobs mingled with Margo's soothing croons punctuated by a giggle from Truda and a loud hiccough from Eva. It did not occur to anyone to move nearer the house. They were grouped like a set piece in a play, rigidly waiting.

The three miscreants arrived at a run and stood before Austen, panting.

He spoke slowly, with icy precision.

'Constantia could have been injured, Hanny. As it is she has had a very disagreeable experience for a three-year-old child. She is a guest in our house—'

Margo interrupted. 'If your Uncle Otto were here, Hanny, he would discipline you right now. I can see you're going to get away with a wigging – my God, when I think of Jack – how this would grieve him—'

Hallie looked sideways at her friend, incredulous that Margo had such a romanticized memory of Jack.

Hanny looked completely blank.

'What happened? Did she fall in the compost?'

'No. The fence is too high for that, don't you think?' Austen's voice was still iron-cold.

Jennifer said suddenly, 'I think I saw her on the roof of the potting shed, Hanny. When we were playing with your train set just now.'

Austen centred his attention on Jennifer. She did not flinch or look away.

'You have been playing with the train set?'

She said, 'I asked Meg first. She said I could go on up and she would find Hanny and—'

'And then Hanover and Clive joined you?' Austen persisted.

'They were already there. They knew where the treasure was and they were fed up with playing with the tinies, so—'

Austen said smoothly, 'That was most ill-mannered of you, boys. However, perhaps the hunt has gone on long enough. Let's go on to the terrace and see if we can find the treasure, shall we?'

Mungay and Charles uttered war cries and charged off. After an uncertain moment, the children streamed behind them all whooping loudly. Austen looked at Margo and she stopped patting her daughter and practically stood to attention.

'Short of calling Jennifer a liar, there is nothing more to be said here, Margo. Connie is obviously unhurt, except for injured pride. I think, in the circumstances, you should have a word with her. Explain about the meaning of retribution, perhaps.'

Margo bleated, 'Are you going to take Jenny's word for it? Constantia would never have climbed on to the shed roof – why on earth should she?'

Hallie said, 'Darling, let's leave it. Please. We simply must not fall out over childish quarrels. We've been friends since we were ten years old . . .'

Tilly said heartily, 'Who is falling out? Come on, let's

246

take Connie upstairs and give her a bath. It's going to be fun, isn't it, Connie? And I expect Aunt Hallie will bring you up your very special treasure . . .'

The child was partially mollified. She glanced quickly at Austen and said, 'I hate boys.'

Sybil laughed and looked at her husband. 'So do we, don't we, darling?' And the gaggle of females made for the house and the bathroom.

Milling around on the terrace examining their treasure, the children were persuaded one by one into cardigans and blazers and edged towards the stable yard where the wrecked tea had disappeared and cars were arriving for them.

Sybil beckoned to Jennifer who turned to Hanny very prettily and thanked him for a lovely time.

'And don't forget,' she murmured as she shook hands like a grown-up, 'you are now for ever in my debt.'

'You're a jolly good egg,' Hanny said fervently, and then discovered that he was quite unable to release her grip. When she decided to let him go there were tears of pain in his eyes.

Meg gave the von Gellhorn children some biscuits and milk in the kitchen while Margo enjoyed some Martinez sherry with the Rudolfs. Her brother-in-law would return for her as soon as he had delivered Sybil and the girls. Hanny had gone upstairs to put away his train set.

Margo sighed. 'What a day! Poor Con. I know – I accept – that she can spin fairy tales! My God, shall I ever forget when she told Otto she'd seen me kissing the bloody portrait painter!' She laughed. 'He was absolutely furious – sacked the man on the spot!' Her eyes sparkled at the memory, then she sobered. 'But she was so sure that Hanny threw her into that muck – all right, darling, I know he couldn't be in two places at once, and I agree Jennifer would hardly be likely to lie on his behalf. They never got on even at my wedding, did they?' She sighed again. 'Poor Con, she dreads this baby being a boy. Knows he will be her father's favourite, of course.'

Austen said, 'It's hardly likely at three years old that she would understand such things, surely, Margo?'

Margo looked very knowing. 'You'd be surprised. German women grow up fast.'

He heard that smugness and knew it was what had upset Hal. He looked at the two women sitting side by side, one gross, overfed, already Germanic after just four years. The other neat and girlish in a rose-coloured chiffon frock covered in penny-sized white spots.

He thought: She wants children . . . it's simply Nature doing her work . . . She is really above all that . . . surely she too will look at Margo and realize what sexual excess does.

And his heart ached for her.

He said that night, 'Hal. I wish I could make you happy. I've been thinking—'

She let him go no further. She too had looked at Margo and felt entirely unenvious. And Austen had been so marvellous with the crisis at the party and he was so good to her and she felt completely and utterly guilty for blaming him because she couldn't have just everything she wanted. She was a spoiled child. She should be ashamed of herself.

She said, 'Please, Austen. I know I have been cross – probably unbearable – but you make me happier than I have ever been – and I have always been happy! So you see you are making me happier than just happy! You make me feel special. And cherished. And – and—'

He laughed. 'Oh, Hal, you don't have to reassure me like this. I do understand that now and then you will want children of your own. But I know that underneath you realize only too well that our relationship is perfect as it is. *You* are perfect, my dear.'

She was sitting at the dressing table brushing her short thick hair and on an impulse he took the brush from her and began to brush it with a gentleness it was not at all used to. It curved around the brush and flew around his hand with its own electricity. Its softness was a caress.

She looked at his reflection. Her eyes were swimming with tears.

She said, 'Austen . . . forgive me. Today's pettiness was because Margo thought . . . it . . . was my fault.'

'It?' He frowned slightly.

She wished she hadn't mentioned it. 'Nothing. I mean – she thought – Tilly thought – they think – that I am a – a cold wife.' She tried to laugh. 'How petty I am, Austen! It irritated me, that is all.'

He continued to brush but held the recalcitrant hair down with his free hand.

He said in a low voice, 'Margo is so far from perfection, my dearest. It would seem unattainable to her. And therefore cold.'

Hallie blinked hard and the tears subsided. She smiled.

'When I think of that awful child in that mess of potato peelings and rotten fruit—'

Austen said, 'I wonder what Hanny gave Jennifer McKinlay to lie for him.'

'D'you suppose he did do it?' She was laughingly aghast.

'Oh, he did it! No doubt about that. But he knows that I know it. He will be very careful in future.'

'And she deserved it, Austen,' Hallie pleaded.

He laid the brush on the dressing table and went towards his bed. When he looked at her, his dark eyes were twinkling.

'It probably did her a great deal of good,' he said.

She twirled the stool, laughing helplessly. This was the Austen she loved most of all. The wise man with the sense of humour. And she knew with a small thrill of pride that she had given him that humour.

Suddenly he leaned forward in his bed, holding his knees.

'Hal, I know how I can make it up to you. Father has been worrying about the plantation again. He says he is going over this summer. Before the hurricane season. I know he's not keen, I can tell. We'll go instead.'

She looked at him, really aghast this time.

'But . . . you've always said—'

'I didn't want to go. Especially with you. I know all that. But it is beautiful, and you should see it before anything awful happens.'

'Awful?'

'There have been quite a lot of incidents. And civil war is inevitable in Spain. It has a habit of spreading.'

She looked at him. She felt like Judas Iscariot.

'I don't want to go,' she said definitely. 'If there are incidents it would not be safe for Hanny.'

He laughed. 'I want us to go together and alone. Hanny can stay with Clive for the school holidays. And as you have always said, the grandfathers are here. And Caddie will keep an eye.'

'Caddie? I thought you didn't like Caddie?'

He thought about it. 'I didn't, did I? I felt she saw through me.'

Hallie half smiled, hoping the conversation was turning. 'What a strange thing to say, Austen. Everything you have done has been for the Martinez family.' She sat on the end of her bed. 'You are a father to Hanny. You have helped us with the Heartland vintage. You give us excellent terms on the shipping transactions—'

He looked at his hands clasped around his knees. Then said, 'Hal. Dear Hal. You will come to Barbados with me, won't you? It is the only really unselfish thing I have done.'

She did not understand him at all, but she could not have stood against his sweetness. She thanked him, as she so often did, like a child at a party. And then she slid beneath the sheets of her bed and he put out the light.

Mungay had been wrong. There was no need for cunning to persuade Austen to take her to the plantation. He was doing it because he wished to do something special for her.

And she still felt like Judas Iscariot.

Fifteen

They travelled by a banana boat from Avonmouth at the end of July. It was agony standing on deck and watching Hanny, Clive and the two grandfathers waving frantically and growing smaller and smaller, but once they were well out into the Bristol Channel, sighting the two Holms and then Lundy was amazing – like making their own personal landfalls. The sun was shining, the air was exhilarating, and, after all, Hanny had not shed a tear and was looking forward immensely to staying with the Maxwells. Hallie decided she must put him out of her mind for the time being. Austen was tenderly protective as they moved around the ship, negotiating companion-ways and narrow passages. She began to feel an enormous sense of adventure.

There were twelve passengers in upper-deck cabins which, according to the captain, rivalled the *Queen Mary* for comfort and fittings. Hallie, who had thought that travelling by a banana boat meant hammocks and ship's biscuits, was like a child as she discovered each of these fittings.

'Darling, our own bathroom!' She emerged from a velvet-covered door, goggle-eyed. 'Come and see the taps! They must be gold! And they're shaped like fish-mouths—' She stopped speaking because the steward was there busy hanging their clothes in a very large wardrobe along one side of the cabin.

Austen smiled. 'You thought I was going to make it so tough, you'd never want to come again?'

The steward said, 'Most of our passengers come again,

252

madam. We go all round the Caribbean. It's an excellent cruise. I'm sure you'll enjoy it.'

Austen said, 'We're disembarking at Barbados. Picking you up again at the end of next month.'

'Well . . . perhaps another time you'll stay on board, sir. All the islands are worth seeing.'

'Perhaps we will,' Austen agreed. He was already wondering why on earth he'd made such a fuss about returning to Barbados. Those days of deliberate decadence were a thing of the past. He had risen above such excesses and attained real happiness. And they had happened so long ago. No-one would think they were of any importance now that he was married.

Hallie said a little more cautiously, 'One place at a time, dear. We must not be too long away from Hanny.'

The steward smiled and left and they sat down in the deep leather armchairs and grinned at each other.

Austen said, 'We should have got away together before this. It reminds me of when we were first married. And you taught me how to have fun!'

She shook her head at him teasingly. 'We must watch our ps and qs, Austen. We are, after all, pillars of Bristol society nowadays!'

He laughed obediently. Though actually he supposed they were. He wondered just how that had happened. And decided it was because they got some reflected glory from Cadiz Martinez. Certainly the Rudolfs were no philanthropists.

Cadiz had not gone down to Avonmouth to see them off. Knowing that Mungay would be there with Hanover, she had arranged her monthly visit to the hospital to fall at that time precisely.

Charles said, 'Caddie! You can't possibly let our little Hal go off to the other side of the world without a farewell from you!'

She said crisply, 'Of course not, Charles. I have already said *bon voyage* to them both. In fact, Hal and I went to see Tilly last evening and took leave of each other. Tilly is going to Spain, you know. The Red Cross has a centre in Madrid and she has volunteered to be one of the resident doctors.'

'Yes. I do know, Caddie.' Charles spoke gently. Sometimes he wondered if his sister's undoubted eccentricity was as deliberate as everyone assumed. 'If you recall, Tilly mentioned it just after Hanny's birthday party.'

'Did she? I had forgotten.' Cadiz rammed her hat over her plaits and knotted her long chiffon scarf like a man's tie. 'Anyway, my dear, I have no wish to stand on the dock waving to a ship. And I think it very unwise of Mungay Rudolf to subject little Hanover to such an ordeal.'

'Clive Maxwell will be with him. And we are taking both boys to tea at the Royal and then back to the Maxwells'. It's much better to make a treat of it rather than let Austen and Hal slip away furtively.'

Caddie smiled at him reassuringly. 'Yes, you are quite right. And it will be an all-male party. I am better out of it.'

'Caddie, you know that is not the case!'

'Charles—' She made her voice scolding. 'Stop nagging me! I am going to the Infirmary, and that is that!' And she pecked him firmly – something she rarely did – and left him to wait for Sullivan.

In spite of the August sunshine, it was a sad afternoon. Caddie knew at the back of her mind that Hal was leaving England for the first time. The West Indies seemed so far away and so potentially dangerous. She wondered, not for the first time, why Austen had held out for so long against taking Hallie to the Rudolf plantation. And then why he had suddenly caved in. Hal had told her some garbled story about a bet with old Mungay which hadn't come off. Caddie distrusted anything that smacked of Mungay interference. And she certainly did not believe Austen Rudolf was the saint

254

Hallie still thought him. He had got exactly what he had wanted from that marriage: a future stake in the House of Martinez, a ready-made son and heir, and . . . Hallie. The awful thing was, Caddie was almost certain he had not told Hallie right from the beginning that he could not have children.

She sighed sharply and tried to turn her attention to what the sister-in-charge was telling her. A wonderful breakthrough in the prevention of diphtheria. Eventually it could mean the complete redundancy of isolation hospitals.

'Research?' Cadiz knew what was coming. 'Naturally I would be delighted to be associated with such a worthwhile project . . .' Charles would hold his head. But what else was there to do with her share of the Martinez money? Hal and Hanover would have some, of course, but she dared not leave any to Jack.

She left the hospital and drove to the Hestermans' in Park Street, unable to face St George Street and Rosie's face as long as a fiddle because they had not been trusted with Hanny. Caddie decided to return at the same time as Charles. It would be six at least before he and Mungay had given the boys their tea and driven them back to the Maxwells at Clifton. And then Mungay would go home alone to High House. It would be unbearably empty up there on his own.

She told herself it served him right after the hours he used to leave Florence Rudolf alone. Nevertheless the thought of him in that great place without Hal and Austen and noisy little Hanover upset her enough that she parked the car completely askew at the kerb outside Dr Hesterman's and did not even notice it. She sat there for a moment wondering whether she could bear to suggest to Charles that they invite him to dinner.

Then she shrugged crossly. The old reprobate would doubtless find company and consolation down at Lily Elmes' house in the Hotwells Road and deserved no sympathy whatsoever. She got out of the car and ran up the steps to the front door, her scarf flying behind her. Her waking nightmares had grown less as time went by, but it was still a fact that Mungay Rudolf had repulsed her; and that she still trembled when he came near.

Dr Hesterman's nurse telephoned upstairs to announce her. Tilly and her mother were at home and delighted to see her for tea. Tilly came halfway down the stairs to welcome her.

'Caddie! I thought you'd succumb and go to Avonmouth.'

'I told you. I had to do my Infirmary visit. Talking of which, d'you know anything about a vaccine against diphtheria?'

Tilly led her into the large sitting-room overlooking busy Park Street. Mrs Hesterman took her other arm and they ensconced her in a comfortable chair with a view.

Tilly said, 'It's all the talk in the path lab. It will be some time before it is available, but yes, it's true.' Her dark eyes shone. 'Very soon, diphtheria will be a thing of the past.'

Mrs Hesterman groaned. 'Are you two going to talk shop? I thought we might gossip about clothes. Your aunt has only just gone back to the Settlement remember, Tilly. I have had my fill of serious discussion!'

Cadiz laughed. 'I've actually called to see whether Tilly would like a companion on the boat going to Spain. It is time I went and checked on Jack I think.'

'But you are barely home from the last trip!' Tilly looked at her friend with some concern. 'D'you think you should go again? For his sake as well as yours. If he is managing to sink into the background, you will put paid to that.' She smiled. 'You are very distinctive, you know, Caddie. Even when you are not standing on a car bonnet with your skirt over your head!'

They smiled, wonderfully comfortable in each other's company.

Cadiz said, 'That had occurred to me, actually. But . . . I am constantly anxious for Jack. The situation out there is going from bad to worse. And he is a poor correspondent.' She stopped smiling. 'Actually, I haven't heard from him for two months now.'

Mrs Hesterman said, 'For goodness' sake! If Tilly is going to Madrid, surely she can send you news of Jack?'

Tilly snapped her fingers. 'Of course. Why didn't I think of that myself? I might even be able to get down to the coast and see him, Caddie. Wouldn't that be wonderful! I haven't seen Jack since – since—'

'Nineteen twenty-eight,' Caddie supplied. 'He left just before Christmas.'

'My God.' Tilly was awed. 'Seven years. Where has all that time gone?' She shrugged. 'Ah well, he will scarcely recognize me, nor I him probably.'

'He hasn't changed,' Caddie assured her. 'And neither have you.'

'Seven years,' Tilly murmured. 'That sounds like a magic time-circle. Seven years.' She laughed suddenly. 'Oh my dear Lord – how furious Margo will be if I see Jack and she does not!'

They laughed.

So it was arranged. Caddie promised a map and wrote down the address of the Castillo. She explained about Rodriguez: he might have returned, he might not. Tilly said that she was bound to be able to find out. The International Red Cross was welcome anywhere.

It was past six o'clock when Caddie stabled the car in the old coachhouse in St George Street and climbed the steps above the area. Rosie let her in, all smiles.

'Good to see you cheerful.' Cadiz removed her hat wearily and then stopped, looking at Rosie questioningly. Sudden laughter came from the morning room. And the unmistakable ambience of cigar smoke hung in the air.

She said in a low voice, 'I'll go upstairs until supper, Rosie.'

But it was as if he knew that she had arrived and might try to escape, because as she made for the stairs, the door to the morning room was opened and Charles said heartily, 'Come and make our guest welcome, Caddie. We thought you'd deserted us for ever!' And, of course, she was bound to go inside and stand within Charles' brotherly arm and ask how the farewells had gone.

'Hanny took it well, I thought. Didn't you, Mungay?' It was obvious Charles had had too much before-dinner sherry. He was much too affectionate.

Mungay was sitting by the window – of course, that is how they had known of her arrival – wreathed in cigar smoke, apparently as expansive as Charles, yet with that curiously watchful look in his dark eyes that said otherwise.

'Excellently. Of course, he couldn't do anything else in front of the Maxwell boy. But I don't think he had to put on too much of a face.'

'Denver Maxwell – Clive's father – owns that enormous garage on the Cheltenham Road.' Charles spoke pedantically; they all knew Maxwell's and had in fact bought their cars there. 'He is taking the boys to Goodwood and will no doubt arrange for them to have a drive.'

Caddie moved away from Charles' fond embrace and said sharply, 'We know all that, Charles! And I hardly think, at seven years old, either boy will be able to reach the pedals of any car!'

'Maxwell will fix something for them, I'm sure,' Charles said grandly. 'Never a dull moment. All those children . . . good for Hanny, eh, Mungay?'

Mungay glanced at Caddie and said in the same tone, 'Never a dull moment.'

Rosie stuck her head around the door before Caddie felt the need to comment further on this. Rosie was beaming. It was the first time Mungay Rudolf had been entertained at number seventeen. Rosie had never quite forgotten seeing Mr Rudolf and Miss Cadiz sitting in that big car at the top of the street, just . . . looking. As if they had never seen each other before.

'Cook says will the cold beef do for Mr Rudolf, sir? With a nice lettuce sent up from Clevedon and some really hot horseradish, and apricots for afters from Lady Decliveden's glasshouse.'

'Well, I should think . . . What do you say, Mungay, old man?'

'Capital! Capital! English food in an English house-hold.'

Cadiz reflected grimly that no-one asked her opinion. And the Rudolfs were as bad as the Martinez for striving after Englishness.

But, in spite of her discomfiture, she had to admit the little dinner party was a success. Mungay was definitely not as drunk as Charles and he entertained them with stories from Barbados that had nothing whatsoever to do with the crucial visit of the previous Charles Martinez in the mid-nineteenth century.

'They're such a happy people,' he said, looking at Caddie because Charles appeared to be asleep. 'Hallie is going to love it. And I think it might help Austen to . . . relax.'

Caddie glanced at Charles then said flatly, 'I understand you never had any difficulty with relaxing when you were there.'

He laughed quietly. 'No. That is true. The Rudolfs have always sown their wild oats over there. A long way from home.'

'Except Austen.' For the first time Caddie was thankful for Austen.

Mungay raised his brows. 'You said that rather smugly, Caddie Martinez. Was it a criticism of me?'

He was determined to keep the conversation entirely personal.

She said lightly, 'Such conceit, Mr Rudolf! Why on earth should I criticize you?'

'You called me Mungay before. And if we are talking

259

of conceit, I remember a woman not far from here, on the bank of the river, her hair about her shoulders.' He laughed again, glanced at Charles who did not stir, and went on as if he knew her better than she knew herself. 'Caddie Martinez, you have always been very conscious of your appearance. Even when you allowed that artist's sketch of you to appear in the *Evening World* after the Unemployment March. That was clever, Caddie. It took the heat out of the situation. While people were laughing at respectable Miss Martinez, they couldn't get too hot under the collar about broken bones.' He smiled and added, 'Were you really wearing those awful bloomers?'

She lifted her coffee cup and put it down again. She was trembling.

He said in a voice low and urgent, 'Caddie, what has happened? You have ignored me all these years. I gave you time to get over Maude – dammit, I needed time myself – but then I discovered you were cutting me dead, making certain you were away whenever there were family occasions—'

She was amazed. 'You talk of *me* avoiding *you*?'

Charles woke at her outraged tone.

'And then what happened?' he asked. 'The horse bolted with the padre's wife?'

Mungay said smoothly, 'And the padre simply continued with the service as if nothing at all had happened.'

'My God – bit off, wasn't it, old man? What happened to his good lady?'

Mungay said, 'They found her in bed with the curate!'

Charles looked anxiously at Caddie, saw that she was looking very pink and bright-eyed and gave a guffaw of laughter to cover any embarrassment.

'You know how to tell a tall story, Mungay! I'll give you that!' He patted the back of Caddie's hand, distressed to discover it was trembling. 'Shall we turn in now, old girl? It's been an emotional day and I'm sure we could all do with an early night.'

Caddie stared at him.

He went on quickly, 'Did I not tell you? Mungay is staying the night here. We plan to take the boys to Clevedon tomorrow. The three of us. Sunday at the seaside. How does that sound to you?'

Caddie opened her mouth to make some kind of refusal and Mungay said, 'It sounds delightful to me. I'll bid you good night then. And my deepest gratitude for your hospitality. It's deuced lonely up at High House without the family.'

He was gone. Leaving Charles to work on his sister.

Bridgetown was a revelation to Hallie. Trafalgar Square with its monument to Lord Nelson, the shop fronts and the traffic were as she might have expected from a busy port with naval associations. But the intensity of colour and space almost stunned her.

She took leave of most of the other passengers with regret. Especially one lady who had confessed to having her fiftieth birthday during the voyage. Hal worked it out that her mother would have been fifty that summer had she lived. The woman's name was Mary and Hallie's mother had been Maria. It was one of those pleasing coincidences that made an enormous difference to their trip. While Austen was enjoying his after-dinner port with the captain, Hallie talked to Mary Anderson and heard that this was a voyage she and her husband had promised themselves on retirement. He had died last year. 'I am having the voyage for both of us,' Mary said with an unsentimental grimace. 'He probably thinks I'm a silly old fool, but I just had to make the effort.'

'I'm so glad you did!'

It seemed another bond that Mary Anderson was childless and they were both glad that they would be seeing each other again in a month's time.

Perhaps it was because of this new friendship or the strangeness of Barbados itself, but Austen seemed different here. He was used to the actual business of dealing with the hordes of pedlars, finding a taxi, superintending the loading of their luggage. He must be just as authoritative at home, yet Hallie never noticed it there. Sully was bossier than Austen.

He had already ascertained that she wanted to go straight to the plantation.

'We could stay a night in Bridgetown. There are some decent-enough hotels,' he said, thinking she might like to digest first impressions before embarking on others.

But she was adamant.

'It's such a small island, Austen. We can drive down to the capital often if you wish. I would really like to see your home.'

'Hardly that, Hal.' He made a face to remind her that the plantation had never been a real home to him.

She said, 'It's a bit like the Flower House for me. A summer place. A holiday place. Let's go straight there, Austen.'

And he had agreed because, after all, she had to see it all some time.

The road had not changed very much since the days of the first Hanover; the taxi bucketed along a sandy, unmetalled surface, hugging the West coast, stiflingly hot in the open and between the tall canes, cooler beneath the trees.

He pointed out the bearded fig tree which might well have given the island its name. And when the driver changed down and they began to climb into the hills, he stopped the car on a rise and got out to point out various landmarks.

She said, 'It's so – so – exotic, Austen! I mean, you've shown me pictures and Amos's paintings captured a great deal. But the smells and the heat and – look at that lizard – and the monkeys, I didn't expect it to be so foreign!'

He laughed and patted her hand with his old indulgence. He did not often do that now; she knew she had earned a large measure of Austen's respect over the years. So she would not allow herself to feel even a prick

262

of annoyance at this sudden appearance of condescension. After all he was the lord and master here; he knew every inch of the place; she was the visitor.

The cane closed in on them as they gained height and then suddenly gave way to a grove of palms apparently sitting on their haunches in a wide sweep of grassland that had the look of an English park. One or two enormous mahoganies shaded the road and beyond the trees the land dropped to the North-Eastern coast and the churning Atlantic. The air was suddenly fresh; Hallie leaned over the side of the car and drew deep breaths of it.

'Oh, Austen, marvellous – marvellous,' she said, head tipped back, eyes closed.

'We're here, my dearest. This is it,' he said and actually held her bare arm; he was excited. She was amazed. Austen was actually excited at seeing the plantation.

The end of the parkland was marked by a grandiose stone arch supported by gilded lions. They drove beneath it and on to a gravelled drive. Brilliant hibiscus and rhododendrons channelled them around a corner, and there, fronted by a huge gravelled sweep, stood a replica of Clevedon's Flower House. Hallie gaped.

'Oh, Austen! No wonder our families were so divided. Imagine my great grandfather copying this so faithfully! And so underhandedly! The verandahs, the roof – everything – it's identical!'

Austen laughed. 'Not quite the same inside. I remember while we were waiting for Maude to give birth . . .' He cleared his throat and went on determinedly, 'I remember thinking old Charles Martinez had slipped up as regards the inside. Our back verandahs actually overlook the sea.'

Hallie cast him a glance remembering that time in the Flower House too. She said practically, 'Of course, if we'd had verandahs at the back they would simply look out on the cliff.'

'Quite.' The car drew up with a spatter of gravel at the porticoed entrance and he leapt out immediately. 'I can't wait to show you around, Hal. Some of the views are quite spectacular!'

He was so rarely like this; once on Clevedon's sea-front when Hanny had been a baby, again at Porthmeor when they had taken that ill-fated swim. She could forgive him any kind of condescension for this.

He handed her out just as a tall angular nut-brown man appeared from the dark interior. Hallie would have known anyway it was Amos, but Austen made elaborate introductions. His courtesy was such that Hallie knew something was wrong somewhere.

She said, 'It's such a pleasure to meet you after all this time, Amos. I feel I know you through your work.'

She held out her hand and Amos took it after a moment's hesitation. He had a large thin hand, the fingers splayed from its palm like petals from a flower. When he released her and both hands hung at his sides, they looked ungainly. Not the hands of a painter at all.

He said, 'You and the master have been so good to me, Mrs Rudolf. I have made many sales from the Bristol gallery.'

'I know. It's marvellous, isn't it? I have seen some of them hanging in various houses. They bring everything to life.' She smiled around her. 'I realize why now. Even the rocks here seem to breathe.'

He smiled, delighted, and immediately she saw his negro roots. His grin was too big, too white for any European. But when he stopped smiling he looked like a taller, stronger Mungay, with black curly hair and more obvious whites to his eyes.

He gave orders about the luggage and led her in to introduce the staff. There was an enormous circular hall – she hardly took it in because a small gaggle of turbaned women and two men who looked dressed for a game of cricket were smiling and looking shy and obviously needed a lot of encouragement. She shook hands with

264

everyone, genuinely delighted to meet them and behind her she heard Austen say in a low voice, 'I thought we were Amos and Austen? What is this "master" business?'

She did not catch Amos's reply because an older woman shaped like a barrel was saying, 'I'm Dorinda, ma-am. And this is Cissy who helps me in the kitchen and will wait on table. She's worked at the Colony Club and knows how it's done.'

Hallie smiled and nodded at each name. She was conscious of Austen continuing a deliberately amiable conversation with Amos in the background. She remembered Mungay explaining that Amos was in fact his nephew 'on the wrong side of the sheets'. She wondered suddenly whether Austen's patronage was more than simply an interest in a talented, untrained artist. As she turned and saw him still chatting to the older man while the other two carried the luggage up the curving staircase, it occurred to her that such studied scrupulousness might well have something to do with guilt. Poor Austen. Was this the real reason he had never wanted her to come to the plantation?

He left Amos at last and came to take her arm and lead her upstairs where he flopped into a cane chair.

'Sorry, Hal. I'd forgotten about the *people*! I hardly notice Sully and the others back home. But there are so many here!'

She said, 'Oh, darling, never mind that. Come and see.' She took little runs along the verandah railing. 'What is that headland? Doesn't it remind you of the East Head at Porthmeor? And just look at those coconuts! I mean, I know they grow like that, but just *look*—!'

He took out his handkerchief and mopped his face, smiling again. It was delightful to see the plantation through Hallie's eyes. This was what he had somehow lost as a child. This wonder and exultation.

He stood up ponderously.

'Well, let's take it from that particular headland and

go south, shall we? We're in the parish of St Anne's and looking down to . . .'

She clung to his arm and he did not seem to mind. She knew that other people found Austen boring when he went into one of his lectures, but she never had. She loved his patience, his detailed explanations. If it occurred to her that he behaved like an avuncular schoolmaster with a favourite pupil, she never allowed it to spoil . . . anything.

Austen hardly left Hallie alone for two minutes. Even when she went into the kitchen to consult Dorinda about their meals, he was at her side.

'I'm perfectly used to managing this sort of thing alone,' she said smilingly. She found it touching that he was so protective of her.

'Of course, darling.' The respect he had always had for Harriet Martinez had taken surprised leaps when she became Harriet Rudolf and was pitchforked so unceremoniously into taking command of High House. He knew she would manage equally as well here. But . . . he was frightened to leave her alone. Amos was completely discreet, he had no doubt of that. But what if he had talked to Dorinda and Dorinda let something drop? It had been Amos who fetched him from the Bridgetown brothels and sobered him up and put him to bed and stayed with him when he raved and shouted.

He returned her smile, took her arm again. There was something so comforting about Hallie's hand and arm and if he did not prolong the touch it just escaped that awful physical awareness that he must avoid at all costs.

'It's just – the speech patterns are so odd at times. You might misunderstand. Or be misunderstood.' He was pleased with that and expanded. 'Sometimes these people confuse legend and truth you know.'

She continued to smile but moved away from his restraining hand.

'Trust me to know the difference, Austen.'

Her tone was light; it was the voice she used when she was making a stand. He heard it rarely but he recognized it, all the same.

He schooled himself to let her make her daily visits to the kitchen without him. At first it was difficult, but it became easier as each day her enthusiasm and obvious happiness continued to bubble out uninhibited by any gossip she might have heard.

He told himself that his sensitivity about those times after the war was exaggerated. He knew he had been living at the bottom of a dark and dreadful pit. He had escaped from the war with his life and all his limbs and felt guilty for it. Any kind of normal existence had seemed out of the question and he had tossed himself into the abyss of forgetfulness on rum and women in a way that had been satanic to him, but . . . just maybe . . . normal to the inhabitants of the island. His father had never remonstrated with him; in fact, had seemed almost relieved that he was 'following in father's footsteps'. He shuddered even now. However his behaviour had seemed to others, he knew he had grovelled in a pit of slime. And though he had exerted rigid self-control back home, he had returned to the pit time and time again. It was Hallie who had saved him. He must never forget that. Hallie. His symbol of light and purity. And she was saving him again; because the longer she darted around the house and took him on picnics to the various beaches and so obviously loved the life here, the more she cleansed it for him.

He said one morning, 'Hal, I know you used to ride at Saunton, but it must be ages since you were on horseback. Amos still keeps horses – easier to get around the cane fields – I expect he could find us a couple of passable hacks. What do you say?'

Her face was answer enough. 'Wait till we tell Hanny! He'll think we're proper cowboys!'

So in the mornings before the fierce midday heat, they rose and explored for miles around. Drax House,

St Nicholas' church, Sam Lord's Castle, they were all discovered on horseback. Hallie adored being high enough to see the cane-cutters at work and to feel those Atlantic breezes on her face. Already the September winds were starting to blow up. Sometimes a corner of a hurricane still caught Barbados.

'I just wish Amos wasn't so busy,' she said as they returned home one day. 'I wanted to get to know him better. I wondered about him coming to England to do some studying somewhere. What do you think?'

There was a time when he would have turned the plan down flat. But since Mungay's suggestion that he was jealous of Amos he had swung the other way.

'It might be a good idea. Although there's always a risk that his naturalness will be trained out of him. However, just a visit and a trip around some of the galleries in London would be good.'

'Could we take him with us tomorrow? Talk about it?'

'When the cane has been cut – he will have more time then.' Austen smiled. 'We have a festival. Dancing. Supper. Not unlike English harvest suppers. But more colourful. You will enjoy it, Hal. I've always wanted you to see it.'

'Then why on earth have we waited for so long?' she asked, halfway to exasperation.

He tried to give her part of the truth.

'There were so many objects . . . in the way. Hanny most of all. But other things too. I have always been frightened something would . . . spoil what we have.'

She said soberly, 'I know.'

He swung himself to the ground and took the two bridles to lead the horses into the stable. She was still mounted. He looked up at her, outlined in sun, dazzlingly beautiful.

He said, 'We must never let anything spoil what we have, Hal.'

She brought her leg forward over the pommel of the saddle in a tomboyish unthinking movement that exposed her bare legs to her thighs. He looked away.

She slid to the ground and hugged his arm.

'I know,' she said again.

And he moved away into the shadow of the stable yard.

She woke the next morning to the realization that something was wrong.

There was no sign of Austen. She slid out of bed frowning – he'd gone for an early-morning ride, or to see the cutters . . . nothing to fuss about. But when she went to the window the car was just pulling out of the drive and Amos was standing on the gravel sweep, holding his horse's head and visibly drooping. A faint acrid tang on the back of her tongue told her the worst. There was a fire somewhere.

She pulled on a summer dress and thrust her feet into sandals and ran down the stairs in two minutes flat. Amos was still waiting by his horse, his hat dangling from one hand. His coffee-coloured skin was streaked – she thought it was sweat at first and then realized it was blood.

She looped his horse's reins over the verandah rail and led Amos into the cool of the hall.

'What has happened? It's a fire, isn't it? Are you hurt?'

'No, Miss Hallie. Scratched a little, that's all.' He tried to smile. 'Fire started 'bout an hour ago. I came for Mr Austen and he's gone for the engine down in Speightstown.'

He swayed and put a hand on the banisters.

'Sit down, Amos, anywhere – here on the stairs. I'm going to get water and disinfectant.'

He protested but she was already gone. One of her first jobs had been to update the old first-aid box kept on a high shelf in the kitchen. She grabbed it now and called to Dorinda and Cissy to bring water.

She bathed a couple of long scratches on his head made by the cane leaves as he pushed his way out of the danger zone. He had lost some blood but it was the shock and the heat that had caused his momentary weakness.

As she put a long strip of adhesive tape over the lint she questioned him gently.

'How serious is this fire, Amos?'

'Bad enough if the engine don't get here real soon.'

'Don't worry about that. Austen will have them moving very quickly.' She smiled at him and after a moment's hesitation he smiled back.

'That's right, Miss Hallie.'

Dorinda wrung her hands. 'You can't go nowhere now, Amos! You should lie down. Don't you think that, Miss Hallie?'

'I most certainly do—'

But Amos was adamant. Austen wanted him to organize the cutters into some kind of a team. He was the only one who could do it.

Hallie saw that nothing would dissuade him, and made up her mind quickly.

'I'll come with you, Amos.' She flashed a reassuring look at Dorinda. 'I'll keep an eye on him, never fear. And if you could have plenty of cold drinks ready, we'll bring the cutters back here as soon as we can.'

Both women rolled their eyes; it was unheard of that cutters were fed and watered at Plantation House.

Hallie ran around to the stable and found the boy there already saddling her horse. Amos was waiting for her on the gravelled sweep and together they set off in the direction of a pall of smoke hanging above the trees.

If Hallie had needed any proof of Amos's ability to deal with a problem, she had it that day. The fire engine was not, in fact, long in arriving, but in that half-an-hour, Amos had rallied the frightened cutters and organized a series of human chains to the nearest spring. Hallie kept close to him, staying at the head of the line and helping him to direct the water so that a swathe of soaking cane was between them and the fire. The heat was intense and the sound of crackling wood quite terrifying. The women dropped back with screams of fright until they saw Hallie at their head.

Amos called, 'Let it burn itself out behind the water! The engine will be here directly and will deal with the fire itself!' He grinned whitely at the women. 'You've got the right idea! Fall back at each bucketful – put as much soaking-wet cane between yourselves and the fire as you can! Watch Mrs Rudolf!'

Luckily at that moment the sound of the fire bell split the still air and the Rudolfs' old car appeared on the track behind them, closely followed by the engine. The firemen were enthusiastic and amazingly well trained. Austen had had no need to be authoritarian. Cane fires were fairly common during a long hot spell and cane was indirectly everyone's livelihood on the island.

Austen put a restraining arm around Hallie.

'You've done a wonderful job, my dear. Come on, let me get you home now. Are you all right?'

'Of course – you can see I'm all right! And it was Amos who did all this—' She swept a descriptive arm around the lines of people who were breaking up now into small chattering groups. The arrival of the engine had taken the fear out of the situation and added entertainment value.

She shook herself free of his arm. 'I've told Dorinda to let them have drinks up at the house.'

Austen frowned at her, still trying to assess the situation for damage and loss.

'Is that wise, Hal? They're itinerants after all.'

She blazed at him. 'Very courageous itinerants who were trying to save your sugar cane for you!'

'Darling, I'm sorry. I didn't mean—'

'Look, I'm going to take Amos home in the car. Can you see to the horses?'

'I'll take you home, darling. I think Amos should go to his mother's house. He looks all in and there's no-one at the house who could look after him.'

'I could!' She hardly knew why she was angry.

'He wouldn't accept your ministrations, sweetheart.' It made it worse that he had no idea she *was* angry. 'And Sugar would doubtless come storming up to see him anyway.'

'Then I'll take him to his mother's.' She held out her hand for the car keys. 'Unless you think I'm incapable of doing that too?'

He looked at her for an instant, realizing, at last, that she was taking exception to everything he said. He murmured, 'Of course not, darling,' and handed over the keys. He was still staring after her as she collected Amos and bundled him into the front seat by her side.

'Tell everyone to come back to the house!' she called through the window. And then she smiled at Amos. 'Nothing like it, is there? Drives down to Speightstown to collect the fire engine and then starts telling us what to do!'

Amos glanced at her, startled at her sudden outburst. Then he too smiled.

'I reckon Mr Austen is a lucky man,' he said.

She said, 'All the Rudolfs are lucky to have you here, Amos. That's for sure.' She ground the gears horribly and waved defiantly at the watching Austen.

'I'm taking you home, Amos. To your home. Will you direct me?'

He did not argue with her but directed her down the steep slopes of St Anne's and into the small fishing village of Speightstown which the Bristol Venturers had claimed as their own so many years ago. 'I expect you know all about my mother.' Amos smiled ruefully. 'Mr Austen stayed with my grandmother when he was a very little boy. She did not approve of my mother. Nor me neither!' He chuckled. 'In fact, she called me the devil's child!'

Hallie was shocked. She remembered a conversation she'd had with Austen once; both of them had been puzzled by old Alice Sheppard's disapproval of her daughter and grandson.

'Why on earth should she say that?' she asked.

'Ah . . . she had her reasons, Miss Hal. None of them matters now. When she died she left her cottage to Ma, so she must have forgiven her at the end.'

'Well . . . I'm glad.' Hallie manoeuvered the car along a street of chattel houses, towards the parish church. John Sheppard had been the curate of St Peter's before his untimely death and the cottage had been ceremoniously handed over to his widow by the Bishop. It was a curious relic of Victorian days: built of local stone with narrow arched windows and a chimney stack built to resemble a castle turret, it was surrounded by a fenced garden which was a tumble of weeds. Hallie imagined the six-year-old Austen coming here to some peculiar old woman who believed in the devil. She shivered.

Sugar emerged before they could get out of the car. She was still tall though stooped now; and very slightly suntanned. With a shock, Hallie found herself looking at an elderly Maude.

'Amos! What has happened?'

'I'm all right, Ma.' Amos hurried around the bonnet of the car to take her hands and reassure her. 'There's a fire going on up in the fields. Miss Hallie and I got ourselves sooty before the engine came.'

Hallie looked down at her bare arms and realized they were streaked with black.

'I didn't know—' she said helplessly. 'I'm sorry, Mrs . . .'

'Sheppard. I use my mother's married name still.' Sugar took the blackened hand and leaned back looking at Hallie admiringly. 'Well. He's slow off the mark but he got himself a pretty wife in the end, didn't he, Amos?' She turned, interrupting the start of a remonstrance from her son. 'Now, you sure you're all right, boy?'

'We're both all right, Ma. Miss Hallie thought I might

273

do better down here for the rest of today. Dorinda might smother me.'

Sugar smiled unwillingly. 'You should marry the woman and make her happy, boy!'

She looked at Hallie again. 'My, but you are pretty. Will you come in and sit down for a while?'

Hallie thought of Austen still being concerned and paternal. She could not bear it just now. She nodded.

'I'd like that.'

They went into a room at the front overlooking the garden and stiffly tidy.

Amos said, 'Would you care to be first at the pump, Miss Hallie?'

'Certainly not.' She grinned at him conspiratorially. 'I must not return looking too spruce.' She laughed and turned to Sugar. 'My husband might think I've been out enjoying myself!'

The old lady enjoyed that. She waved her son away and went to make tea. When she returned, Hallie was settled in a chair by the window. Sugar sat down and poured just as her mother had taught her.

'Is the fire bad, Miss Hallie?'

'No.' Hallie accepted a bone china cup and saucer and sipped the contents gratefully. 'It would have been, without Amos. He had lost quite a lot of blood but the way he organized those people—'

Sugar lifted her shoulders. 'It's his home, child.' She dropped her eyes and added quickly, 'As good as his home, anyways.'

Hallie responded warmly. 'It is his home, Mrs Sheppard! I know that you and Amos are Rudolfs. It is no secret. My husband is very conscious of that fact. They get on so well – like brothers, of course!' She laughed to take away any embarrassment.

But Sugar was not embarrassed. She smiled warmly and again looked so like Maude it was almost shocking.

'An' you too, child. You and Amos – you get on well too.'

Hallie said warmly, 'Certainly. I admire Amos a great deal. His talent—'

'He would be . . . let me think now . . . a grand uncle to you?'

Hallie stopped in her tracks, confused.

'I think . . . perhaps . . . a cousin-in-law?' she suggested.

Sugar's grin erupted into a laugh. 'Through your husband – yes! But through your great grandfather . . .' She stopped laughing suddenly and looked at Hallie. 'You do know that your great grandfather and my grandmother Amelia had a son called Martin?' She misinterpreted Hallie's stunned expression and half closed her eyes, reminiscently. 'That was a true love match. Ma told me about it often. My old Uncle Martin he was a *real* love child!' She sighed deeply. 'Ma forgot to tell me all this before I met Martin. An' when I did—' She made an explosive movement of her hands and laughed again. 'It was too late! Amos was on the way and the weddin' had to be done in a hurry an' Ma never really forgave me!' She made a face. 'D'you know she called Amos a child of the devil! Just 'cos Martin an' me was cousins? An' she made my poor Amos promise he'd never have children himself! An' he's abided by that promise.' She pulled her mouth down. 'I tell you – you go ahead, son! Marry Dorinda – she'd have you tomorrow. But he tells me to mind my own business and he'll marry the woman when he's good and ready.' The mouth was an inverted U. 'And I know when that will be. When she can't have no more children!'

Hallie stared; shocked but also fascinated. She had been brought up on tales of her narrow-minded great grandfather. He had become a pillar of Bristol society; her own father had been named for him and she had been named for her great grandmother. And all the time he had been a sham! A typical Victorian sham.

She stammered, 'That's why I feel so close to Amos!

And all this time – the family feud – and the Rudolfs and Martinez had intermarried already!'

Sugar laughed again and drank her tea, obviously enjoying the effect of her disclosure.

'Well, bless my immortal soul – you didn't know! An' you can't hardly take it in! But child, you know how worry and grief can be eased by love, surely? When Master Austen's daddy, Master Mungay, came here, unhappy – ill with unhappiness – he found comfort with us. And after the war poor Master Austen . . . But it was diff'rent for him. He were like a crazy man.' She put her cup down with a click. 'An' now he's got you. A proper white woman for his own. An' he ain't crazy no more, eh?' She grinned knowingly. 'And when is that first baby going to be arriving, child?'

Hallie was suddenly very still; she felt her mind racing, things clicking into place. She remembered tales of Austen Rudolf – when she had still been at Saunton School. Was it possible that some of them were true? Was it possible that – like Great Grandfather Martinez – Austen had succumbed to the seduction of the Island? She felt the muscles of her eyes aching with the strain of concentration.

She forced herself to say, 'We already have a son, Mrs Sheppard.'

''Dopted. I know all about him! You should have children of your own! Then there won't be no wills contested in the courts, no trouble over who is rightful owner of the plantation.'

'Hanover is Mr Mungay Rudolf's grandson by birth . . .' She could hardly enunciate properly. She had to push away all thoughts that Austen might have – might well have . . .

Sugar leaned forward confidentially. 'Listen, child, there is some people on this island who want to change things too quickly. They could say they was Mr Austen's kin. Who can prove they ain't? They could cause trouble.'

Hallie opened her mouth to protest and then closed it again. What was she protesting? Austen's innocence? The unlikelihood of any future legal action? But Austen was patently not innocent. And in those circumstances what did it matter about anything in the future? What did anything matter at all?

She knew with sudden piercing clarity that she was about to faint and the knowledge jerked her to her feet.

'I really must go, Mrs Sheppard.'

'Now, child, you must have your wash and I must get you a clean dress—' At that moment Amos came back into the room looking almost his usual self.

He patted his mother's shoulder.

'She's been talking the whole time, I'll be bound!' He hugged Sugar with his good arm. 'She does love to talk.' He looked up. 'Will you wash now, Miss Hallie?'

'No. I have to go, Amos. Austen – my husband—'

Sugar said, 'Now just you give him my regards and tell him to come down and see Sugar at any time!'

'I will. I will.'

She could not wait to get out of the Victorian stuffiness of the cottage, and she barely remembered the drive back to the house. At the pillared entrance she stopped the car and stared long and hard at the gilded lion on the left.

Then she said aloud, 'Austen. How could you? How could you?'

And she drove slowly between the high banks of flowers and wished she were dead.

Sixteen

During the last week of their month at the plantation, Hallie discovered the full pain of betrayal. It ate into her soul in a way she could never have imagined. It made her feel an outsider, a pariah. Everyone had known. Therefore everyone was against her.

She withdrew so tightly within herself that she barely noticed what went on around her. The aftermath of the fire; the questions about how it could have started, the visits from other plantation owners and managers, the endless tales of previous disasters and the ways that future ones could be prevented . . . they all went over her head.

She arranged meals, provided iced drinks, smiled politely or shook her head as the occasion demanded.

It might have been different if Amos had been there. She felt a bond with him which she now realized was more than friendship; her great grandfather was Amos's grandfather. It was incredible and in any other circumstances would have been a thing to share with Austen. The fact that even as the Rudolfs and the Martinez began their feud, so the families were linked through children, made all that had gone on in Bristol ridiculous. The marriage of Jack and Maude had been pre-empted by Amelia's affairs with old Hanover and old Charles; by Sugar's marriage to Martin. Funny . . . absurd . . . the old Austen and the old Hallie might have found another link which bound them together. Except that they had never been together. It had all been a silly schoolgirl dream.

Hallie began to take a siesta every afternoon. It meant there was little time for riding any more. Business and politics took up the evenings. Amos made a brief appearance at one of these sessions. He wore a sling; it seemed he had broken his arm when he fell during the fire fighting and had not even known it. He told the owners that the cause of so much of the sporadic unrest in Barbados could be attributed to low wages. 'We are not politically dissatisfied as are the Jamaicans,' he said straightly. 'We have had coloured representation in the Assembly for over sixty years now. The troubles are social ones. We need better hospitals and doctors, schools . . . and wages.' The owners stared back at him without complete trust and Hallie wanted to shout that the plantation should belong to Amos . . . he was the rightful owner.

She retired early each evening, thankful for the first time that she and Austen had always slept separately. Within five days she had made that separation wider than it had ever been. Her eyes ached now from the strong colours of the island; she found them glaring and longed for the autumnal mists of England. One afternoon when Austen thought her resting, she rode alone to Speightstown and wandered along the beach leading the horse, staring out at the Caribbean unseeingly. A man was standing waist deep in the calm shallow water, a bowl and colander floating in the sea beside him. He grinned and called a greeting to her as they all did. She saw that he was cleaning fish, taking them from the bowl, gutting them with a flick of a knife, rinsing them and putting them in the colander all in one smooth movement. She stored it in her memory to tell Hanny. Hanny. Her lips curved in a rare smile as she thought of him at his birthday party. So like Jack. So unlike Austen. Yet he thought Austen was his father.

The smile disappeared and she frowned at the bland blue water. Austen and Hanny. It could not go on. She must get in touch with Jack – maybe through Tilly – and tell him what was happening. He must come home and take Hanny. However much it hurt her personally, she must not let Austen influence Hanny any longer.

And so the last day on the island arrived; the cane-cutting festival. The cane was being milled, the old leaves were piled ready for firing, the new shoots already thrusting through in places. Nothing stopped still for long in Barbados; there were no seasons, one crop was succeeded by another instantly. It was like a giant forcing house. Hallie, helping Dorinda clean and batter a bath full of flying fish, wondered – just for an instant – what chance the young war-shattered Austen would have had in such a forcing house. But the time had not come for understanding; there was too much pain. She took Dorinda's place at the fish fryer and dipped in a skillet. The small crisp fish were laid on a bed of green bananas and eaten with the fingers. There were rice cakes filled with pink crab meat. And rum punch.

It was probably the latter that got rid of collective inhibitions so quickly. The itinerants drank it like water before and during their meal, and then with the arrival of the tuck band the dancing began. For three hundred years the Africans in Barbados had made their own entertainment and most of it was through music and dancing. The tuck bands wandered from village to village, plantation to plantation, playing their music that sometimes sounded like an Irish jig, sometimes like a skirl of bagpipes, sometimes like a lament for their homeland. Hallie, dispensing food at one of the trestles which reminded her again of Hanny's birthday party, could not help being fascinated by it all. The dancers were now erecting a long bamboo pole in the ground. Lit by the flickering light of the fire, they could have been erecting a totem for some kind of war dance.

Dorinda said, 'You know this one, Miss Hallie. This is a maple dance.'

'Maple dance?' Hallie glanced at the full-moon face. Dorinda too had imbibed enough rum to make her glisten with sweat. Hallie said quickly, 'Why don't you sit with the others, Dorinda? No-one is interested in much more food and I can manage easily.'

'Very good, Miss Hallie.' Dorinda beamed gratefully. 'When you dance, I come back.'

'I am not dancing,' Hallie said firmly.

But Austen, at her elbow said, 'They will play specially for us, my dear. A waltz – they can all play "The Blue Danube". Or even a foxtrot.'

She did not look at him or reply. It would be easy enough to hand over to Dorinda in half an hour and melt into the darkness. She thought of her bed at the house as if it were a refuge. If only it weren't so hot and she could pull a sheet right over her head and stay there until it was time to go for the ship.

A voice said, 'How are you now, Miss Hallie?' And there was Amos, arm in a very white sling, looking at her with concern as if he knew exactly what was happening inside her head.

She asked politely about his arm in return.

He said, 'It did not hurt when I broke it and it does not hurt now!' He smiled. 'But I cannot dance either.'

Sugar appeared behind him her face thrown into a relief of angular planes by the firelight.

'There should be some compensation, Mrs Rudolf. He won't say anything to Mr Rudolf, but perhaps you—'

Amos said sternly, 'Be quiet, Mother. Sit with Dorinda and tell her all about it.' He turned again to Hallie. 'How are you, Miss Hallie? You have not been well?'

She said tightly, 'I know we are closely related, Amos. In the circumstances I think it would be less . . . condescending . . . if you called me simply Hallie!'

His smile disappeared. He said, 'That will be difficult. Surely you can see how difficult – how impossible – it would be?'

'No. I do not see that. You are my cousin. Or uncle or something. A talented man. The manager of a sugar plantation. I am a nobody with no talent. Perhaps I should call you Master Amos.'

She spoke without expression; there was no smile on her face or in her voice.

Amos looked aghast, then said in a low voice, 'Very well. Hallie. Perhaps, in private, it is not so impossible.' He cleared his throat and took a step as if to join his mother, but then paused and said, 'Well then . . . Hallie. As a cousin, will you tell me what is the matter?'

Dorinda's face swam up from the chairs.

'This is it, Miss Hallie. The maple dance.'

Amos laughed. 'A maypole dance, Hallie. Copied – caricatured by the old slaves, I expect – from your dances in England.'

She looked across the table of wrecked food. The bamboo had been twined with ribbons. The dancers were decked out in white bodices, full, gingham skirts. They began to untwine the ribbons with a zest never seen on village greens in England. Their bare feet stamped the dusty ground, their smiles flashed, the tuck band played furiously and the ribbons criss-crossed and made a new pattern. She thought her heart was breaking.

Amos said urgently almost against her ear, 'Hallie! Stop it! Everything is all right! Austen is here – I am here – nothing can hurt you!'

She did not look at him.

He took her arm. 'What has happened?'

His touch was like a Judas kiss. Amos was one of the family and the family had all betrayed her. Even Maude with whom she had forged that bond so quickly, even Maude was part of it. Everyone except Jack and Cadiz knew that Austen was a normal virile man. He had deprived his wife of children, used his sister's child to his own ends, and fathered who knows how many children out here.

She shook Amos off.

'You know what is the matter with me! You are a Martinez as well as a Rudolf and you too lied to me.

282

Your silence was a lie! How you must have laughed at me – and rightly so! How stupid I have been – how crass – how—'

Amos said, 'Hush. Hush, cousin. I do not know. That I promise you. And when the dancing is over, we will walk quietly along the avenue and you will tell me.'

She looked at him then, her eyes dry and smarting from the fire. She said helplessly, 'Tilly and Margo . . . they think I am barren. Amos . . . I feel . . . *barren*!'

For a long moment they stared into each other's eyes. Amos made no quick rebuttal; she made no attempt to explain her garbled words. Before them the country dance went merrily to its conclusion and the ribbons were twined again in perfect patterns around the pole. The music stopped with a last scrape on the fiddle and Austen's voice could be heard amid the clapping and shouting. 'Huzza!' It was all so English. So stupidly English.

And then two men scampered by with the pole and the fiddle started up again. A Viennese waltz. In the Caribbean.

Austen said, 'We'll lead this one, Hal.' He was bowing low before her, Dorinda and Sugar were laughing and clapping. The cutters were pairing up hastily.

'Austen, I don't feel—'

His dark face was laughing into hers. She noticed, not for the first time, the fineness of his features. Maude had been outrageous to the point of coarseness. Austen was like the cane, refined into something indefinably different. Maude had been heady, like wine. Austen sweeter than wine.

She took his outstretched hand as if hypnotized. He drew her to him and for a moment they were still, waiting for the right bar. She could feel his heart beating just above her own and she looked up at his dark silhouette and saw his hair apparently surrounded by a flaming halo; reflections from the fire. She felt as if she were, in fact, being held by a dark angel and that the last seven years of her life had been spent in thraldom to him.

And then he smiled down at her and whispered, 'Now!' and they waltzed sedately along the length of the dusty cane field and she was weeping and holding on to him for dear life because she had loved him so much and now knew that he had never loved her. She had been useful, maybe even decorative. She had brought an heir with her. She had brought the prospect of additional business – perhaps he had plans to oust Jack out of his inheritance and take over the House of Martinez. She knew now that Cadiz had been right all along.

Austen did a complicated double turn at the end of the field and lifted her off her feet.

'Darling,' he whispered urgently, 'what is the matter? Are you ill?'

She wanted so much to tell him how she felt and be comforted, be given some entirely rational explanation, be held by him, maybe have him brush her hair again. She wanted him to treat her as he always had done, like a much-loved and indulged child.

But she was not a child.

She said, 'I am very tired, Austen. Perhaps you would excuse me.'

'Oh, Hal . . . I'm sorry. I've had too much rum punch. And Sugar has been ranting on at me about compensation for Amos—'

'I think you should compensate him, Austen.' It was not the right time to be saying this. The flickering lights, the other dancers now crowding them on to the periphery of the field. But she might not be able to say it again. 'I think you should hand the plantation over to him.'

He definitely had been drinking because he laughed and said, 'You'll want me to call him sir at this rate! And touch my forelock.'

She stared at him and said, 'Yes. That is a good idea!'

And he continued to laugh so that her own eyes filled with tears and she could not bear it any longer.

She said, 'Austen – I must go. I am not well.'

284

She broke away from him fiercely; he staggered back among the dancers and someone caught him and whirled him round crazily. And in that instant she was away, out of the firelight into the humming darkness of the sprouting cane, on to the track and along the avenue leading to the lion-guarded gateway. It was there Amos caught up with her.

'Hallie – stop!' He was panting, trying to hold his plastered arm away from his body. 'Hallie – it is Amos. Austen is not in earshot but he will surely follow you home. Come with me. Let us talk.'

She hung on to one of the enormous leonine paws, bent her head, sobbing hysterically. He came to her side and put his uninjured arm over her oowed shoulders and waited.

When the intervals between the sobs lengthened, he spoke in a low voice. 'Hallie, we are related very closely. Can't you trust me?'

She knew suddenly that she could. She nodded dumbly.

'Then walk with me down to the shore. Let me tell you about the plantation. About Barbados. Why the troubles here have nothing to do with fighting against the white man. But for something else.'

She straightened slowly and leaned against his shoulder. What he suggested appeared to have nothing to do with Austen or herself. Yet in the four weeks they had been here, she knew that Amos was above all else, a thinking man. Perhaps his monastic existence had lent itself to philosophizing. He seemed to combine the black man's ability to live for the day and hour, with the white man's need to think back and then ahead and link everything into a pattern.

She whispered, 'Tell me one thing first, Amos. Do you think I am barren?'

'No.' His voice was steady.

She said, 'Did you know that Austen was cheating me?'

He shifted beneath her weight. 'It was not cheating, Hallie. Not in the sense that you mean it.'

She shook her head impatiently. 'I do not mean – I am not talking of his – his exploits in the past. Did you know that he has let me think – all this time – that he is impotent?'

She felt him stiffen with surprise.

He said, 'I did not know that.'

She moved away from him. 'Very well. Then let us walk to the shore.'

He did not move immediately and she knew he was still shocked at her disclosure. She turned and stared at him through the velvety darkness deeply thankful that he had not been part of the deception.

'Austen will probably arrive in the next two minutes, Amos.'

'Yes.' He joined her and guided her towards the thicket of hibiscus. 'There is a way through here, Hallie. Take care . . . Austen knows of it but it is twenty years at least since he took it.'

She ducked and passed under a mass of branches he was holding up with his free arm.

'He will go to the house in any case.' She held his belt. 'I'll follow you, Amos. Keep going.'

It was a difficult route but the best possible thing she could have done because she had to think for herself and for Amos whose arm was obviously proving a big handicap. The ground began to drop away quickly as they struggled through the foliage, leaves sprang back at her and she held her free arm in front of her face for protection.

They emerged quite suddenly on to a broad sweep of grass sloping to the cliff and then the roaring Atlantic. The grass was broken by outcrops of rock and it was to one of these that Amos led her. A cleft in the seaward side of the rock made a perfect settle on which two or three could have seated themselves comfortably and in complete privacy.

'I told Austen this was his little cave – a secret place for him when things went wrong with his father.' Amos sat back and drew his feet in. She heard a smile in his voice. 'He saw it simply as a seat in the rock.'

Automatically she sprang to Austen's defence as she'd done so often with Aunt Caddie. 'He was no good at imagining things then. He is better now.' She thought of the channel in the sands at Porthmeor. Tears welled again.

Amos said quietly, 'The burden of being a Rudolf outweighed almost everything else. So much was expected of him – it had been bred into his father – and his sister I think. But Austen . . . he was too sensitive.'

She said raggedly, 'I cannot understand him any more. All the time . . . I thought I did. Now, everything I thought was good, is not good. I'm sorry, Amos.' She took a deep breath. 'Tell me about your island. About you. And Sugar and your grandmother and grandfather.'

So he talked to her in his quiet, strangely English, voice. About Martin Martinez, his father, son of Amelia and the first Charles Martinez, who had inherited all his mother's gentle ways and capacity to love. And about Sugar who was a Rudolf through and through and saw Martin and coveted him. As Maude had coveted Jack. And how Amelia's daughter, Alice Rudolf, had called Sugar a daughter of Satan and had thought that Amos would be born with horns.

'Martin was Sugar's uncle, you understand, Hallie. And in *The Book of Common Prayer* that relationship is listed as incestuous. By rights – by all the laws of nature – I should have two heads or a cleft palate or—'

Hallie said, 'You are the most normal man I have ever met.'

'I was lucky. But that luck may well have run out. Had I fathered children, who knows? They could have been deformed . . . anything. But there are other things in life, Hallie.'

She breathed, 'Your painting . . .'

'Exactly.' He paused and scratched his nose consideringly. Hallie had seen her father do exactly the same thing.

He went on reflectively, 'I never knew my grandfather Martinez, of course. My father never saw him. But now I have seen you, Hallie, I feel as if I might recognize him in the next world.' He laughed gently but she did not join him.

She whispered, 'The whole thing is so terrible. So unfair. As soon as we return home I shall take steps to make it known that Hanover is not my child, nor Austen's.'

Amos made no comment on this but after a while he said ruminatively, 'My father told me it would be best not to continue the line, and I agreed. It would seem as if the plantation is destined to belong to both Rudolf and Martinez, however. Little Hanover should be at home here. That pleases me, Hallie. Do you not see a peculiar justice in that?'

She tried to think calmly about it.

'But . . . it does not make it just or fair for you, Amos. Nor for me. We are not permitted to have children.'

Her eyes were used to the darkness now and she could see his quick smile.

'But I do not mind that. Perhaps there *is* something wrong with me, after all.'

He laughed but again she was silent. So he began to talk of the island; and its displaced people. 'The whites from England, the blacks from Africa.' He leaned forward. 'The Rudolfs are not the only white men to produce half-caste children, Hallie. Samuel Jackman Prescod was our first representative on the Assembly. Old Hanover Rudolf knew him personally. He used to take supper at the plantation and my Grandmother Amelia made him the waistcoat which you see in his portrait in the House.'

He spoke of Grantley Adams and Charles O'Neal and

288

the fight for better wages and conditions in many plantations.

And then he said gently, 'You see, Hallie, here, on this small island, we are so closely knit. Families spill over into each other, whites, blacks, coloureds, cousins . . . I am an example.' He leaned forward. 'Dorinda's children think of me as their father. One day I shall marry Dorinda and that will become true.' The whites of his eyes flashed. 'Just as true as little Hanover belonging to you and Austen.'

She looked at him.

'So in the end, this is what you have been saying.' She smiled wanly. 'You are a clever man, cousin Amos. As clever – and as devious – as Austen. But . . . you are also honest. And he is not.'

'You do not know that, Hallie. Honesty is a personal quality. To be honest to oneself can mean being dishonest with someone else.' He slid off the rock. 'I think when you are back in England, you should talk to Austen and persuade him to talk to you.'

She took his hands and slid down herself. Her feet, dangling for so long, tingled painfully. She stamped on the ground while she studied her watch.

'It's past midnight, Miss Hallie. Unless you want the servants sent out to look for you—'

'You are missing also. He will know I am safe with you.'

'But this is long enough.' They began to walk towards the rhododendron thicket. And as he held the first branch back he said gently, 'You see, Hallie, I am also Austen's cousin. I love him too.'

She ducked and began to fight her way back up the steep path.

Cadiz found herself like an uncertain girl – something she had never been. That night she half expected him to knock on her bedroom door. When he did not she was a little affronted but mostly relieved. Seven years ago she had been prepared to fling her bonnet over the windmill after a few hours sparring with him; things were different now. She was fast approaching fifty years of age: Mungay must be nearly seventy. And she was practically a public figure in Bristol. At forty she might well have been prepared to cock a snook at her immediate world, just as she had with Jonathan Pomeroy. She could no longer do that.

In any case the Sunday in Clevedon seemed to put their renewed relationship on a different footing. With Hanny and Clive, Mungay was totally grandfatherly and expected her to be totally great-auntly. She was glad to see the boys, but there was no chance to follow up the previous night's conversation with them shouting and running like puppies all day long. Grandfathers and great-aunts had quite well-defined roles. They ate a picnic, played cricket on the Green Beach, swam in the afternoon and had a bumper tea at the Flower House where Mrs Hayle recalled sadly, while the boys were washing their hands, the tragic circumstances of Hanny's birth.

Charles rallied her quickly.

'No unhappy memories today, Mrs Hayle! I have a treat for you. As Mr Austen and Miss Hallie are away and Hanover is staying with his friend, I thought you might like to take a holiday yourself.'

Mrs Hayle looked terrified. 'Where would I go, sir? My daughter wouldn't take me in and my sister has just lost her hubbie—'

'Then take her away, Mrs Hayle. I'll gladly stand the cost for you both. How about a nice hotel on the front at Sidmouth? Devon is such a pretty county.'

Mrs Hayle said doubtfully that she would talk it over with her sister. She went outside to call the boys in for their tea and hugged Hanny as if she might never see him again.

Mungay said, 'That was good of you, old man. I ought to do the same for Sully.'

'Had to stop her in her tracks with that ghastly dirge she loves. Thought it might spoil your day,' Charles said.

Cadiz looked at Mungay and he looked back.

Charles went on bluffly, 'Look here, Rudolf. Move in with us while the children are away. No need to rattle around in that great place on your own.'

Cadiz looked away and after a moment, Mungay said, 'I'll gladly accept your invitation for tonight. It will be dark by the time we've got back to the city and returned the boys. And then . . . we'll see.'

Cadiz poured more tea and waited while the boys settled themselves at the table and gloated over the spread. Then she said, 'I might give the office a miss tomorrow, Charles. I would like to see Tilly again with some things for Jack.'

She did not look at Mungay again. He knew now that she would be at home if he wanted to see her.

But the next morning when she came downstairs he had already left for the office, or so Rosie told her.

'He's a nice gentleman, miss,' Rosie said sentimentally. 'Like father like son, I always say. D'you remember the time Mr Austen took me to the dentist when I had rampin' toothache?'

Cadiz said, 'Is Mr Rudolf about to do the same thing, Rosie?'

'No, miss!' Rosie laughed indulgently. 'An' well you know it! But he thought he'd put us out like. Stopping the two nights. So he gave Cookie and me a guinea each. Wun't that kind?'

Cadiz smiled briefly and took a slice of toast from the rack. Although she was half relieved at Mungay's absence, half of her was also disappointed. Their conversation on Saturday night had been fascinating. And unfinished.

He stayed away for a week during which time Tilly left for Spain. Cadiz began to feel exceedingly isolated. And very nervous. Charles asked her if she was coming down with something and she snapped his head off.

'Pardon me for living!' he said. It was a line from a film they had both seen recently and should have made her smile. Instead she said, 'Don't be absurd, Charles.'

A letter came the following week. It was addressed to Charles but she recognized Mungay's hand as she sifted the envelopes lying on the salver in the hall. She studied the postmark wondering if he had gone away. It was indecipherable.

She could not go to the office until she knew what it was about and as Charles was late down these mornings, she had to pretend to send off an urgent letter herself. She wrote to Tilly in much the same way as she had last spring.

'I am missing you. And Hallie. And Hanny. And even tall and ascetic Austen! I must be getting soft in my old age. But if you meet someone in Madrid and decide to stay out there I will never speak to you again!'

Luckily, Charles entered the morning room at that moment and saved her from further drivel.

'Not at the office then?'

'I wanted to talk to you, Charles.'

'About what, my dear?' He glanced at her mail. 'Have you had a letter from Jack? An offer for the Castillo?'

'No, no. If only . . . But also there is nothing from Tilly. I should have thought . . . by now . . .'

'Caddie, dear. She has been gone barely a week!'

'I am so anxious about Jack.'

'Is that why you have been such a cross-patch?' He smiled his lovely, forgiving smile and she wished so much Maria was still here for him. She stood up from the bureau and kissed his cheek.

'Charles, you are such a good man. Forgive me if I have been a cross-patch. I – I appreciate you very much.'

'My God! You are certainly sickening for something, Cad!' He pulled out a chair. 'Come and have a proper breakfast with me.'

'No. Open your post. I will finish this tonight.'

She went to the door certain that she did not care

what Mungay Rudolf had found to write to Charles. But he stopped her.

'Wait. Here is a letter from Rudolf. Let us see what he has to say.' He used his fish knife to slit the envelope and removed a single sheet of paper. 'Oh . . . nothing important. He suggests we take the boys out again. To lunch. Today!' He raised his brows. 'Rather precipitate. But he is precipitate.'

'I don't think I can manage lunch today,' she said, already fluttering with panic.

'Well that's all right, old girl. It's at the club. Gentlemen only, you know.'

'What about children?' she asked crossly.

'Well, they are both males.' He smiled at her. 'You must accept that men have to have some privileges, my dear!'

She did not answer but swung into the hall and picked up her hat. She hadn't wanted to lunch with him anyway, had she?

He was waiting for her when she emerged from the office at one.

She blinked in the strong August sunshine unable to believe her eyes.

'I thought you and Charles . . . The boys . . .' she stammered.

'I ensconced them at a table and left them choosing a huge menu. I was called away urgently.' He smiled at her. 'I thought it was time we took lunch together again, Cadiz.'

She conquered an impulse to run down Denmark Street and over the docks. 'We lunched together last week. At Clevedon. Have you forgotten?'

'I mean together and by ourselves,' he explained and took her arm.

He had his car parked right outside the offices so even the draymen would know that Miss Martinez was going off with him. She felt so hot she thought she must

293

explode. Mungay Rudolf could make her blush by simply looking at her. Cool Cadiz Martinez. Indeed.

He said, 'I was tempted to make it the Royal again. Dancing lessons, you know. But then I thought not. We are past dancing lessons now, wouldn't you say?'

She simply did not know what to say, which was another non-characteristic of Cadiz Martinez.

He went on blithely, 'I thought after Clevedon the other week – when I behaved beautifully, you must agree – I thought a tête-à-tête would be in order today. We broke the ice and—'

She burst out, 'That was over a week ago! Eight days in fact! We haven't seen hide nor hair of you since then! If that is breaking the ice—'

'Caddie – my dear Caddie – I wanted to give you breathing space. That Sunday was the first time we have been in each other's company properly for seven years. Surely you needed to think it over? And I knew Tilly Hesterman was leaving Bristol last week and you would need to see her—'

'And now you turn up and whisk me off without so much as a decent invitation! In fact, just the opposite because you led me to believe you were lunching with Charles and Hanny—'

'You came down the stairs with me. You got into the car. I did not have to push you once.'

'Why the underhandedness? Why could you not simply invite me to lunch?'

'Because embarrassment might have made you say no. You would have been forced to tell your brother.' He glanced at her sideways as they negotiated the traffic around the docks. 'I did not want to lose you again, Caddie.'

She said swiftly, 'You never had me! A brief flirtation lasting perhaps three hours hardly counts for much!'

'It counted a great deal for me. And I think for you too.' He ground the gears execrably and then said, 'Why did you cold-shoulder me for so long, Cad?'

She was silent until they took the Weston Road to Long Ashton. Then she said in a muffled voice, 'Have you forgotten what happened? You told me to go. You blamed me . . . and you were right, of course. I felt responsible for Jack not being with Maude at the end. He wanted me to go to Clevedon with him, you know, but I had already arranged to meet you . . . I acted like a silly schoolgirl. I hated myself.'

The car bucked a protest. 'You could not act like a silly anything, Caddie. And had I thought for one moment that you had chosen to see me above going to Clevedon with Jack, I would have been . . . more than flattered. Honoured.' He cleared his throat. 'I hardly remember that part of the day, but you must have known – surely you knew – that what I said was simply an involuntary reaction? I had to blame someone and the Martinez have been whipping boys for the Rudolfs for many years.' He glanced at her. 'I understand now why you have avoided me like the plague. Ah, Caddie . . . I am so sorry.'

She made a sound in her throat and a dismissive gesture with her hands.

He said, 'Another start, Caddie. Please?'

It was such a relief to be able to be honest again. She sat back and let her knotted muscles untie themselves one by one and said simply, 'Yes. That would be good.'

She wondered what would happen next.

After a while she said, 'Are we going to Weston?'

They were just going past the Smythe Arms. He said, 'No. I thought we'd go back to Clevedon. That is where things went wrong for everyone. Somehow Hallie and Austen have retrieved so much . . . I wondered if we could do the same.'

She murmured, 'It was pleasant enough that Sunday. There were no ghosts.'

He nodded. And then said, 'And today there will be no Mrs Hayle.'

She sat up again very straight. 'I'd forgotten! Charles

has sent her off to Sidmouth! The house will be empty!'

He said, 'Yes. I do hope you have the keys.'

She turned and stared at his profile. He was an old man. She was an old lady. It was ridiculous.

She said, 'Such . . . conniving! I cannot believe that you began to plan this over a week ago!'

He shook his head. 'I thought you knew me well, Caddie. You met my eye and I could have sworn that our thoughts were running together.'

'I can assure you—'

He laughed. 'All right. But do you agree with me that we should start at the Flower House? If we can be happy there, then we can be happy anywhere.'

She sat back again. She was trembling once more. The trouble with Mungay Rudolf was that he was constantly surprising her. And he did not look like an old man. And she certainly did not feel like an old lady.

She tried to speak judiciously. 'It is a logical idea I suppose.'

'And very romantic?'

'I am not sure that you and I have much to do with romance, Mungay.'

'Because you want me? And I want you? And we have waited for so long? That makes it romantic to me. I have never waited long for anything in my life, Caddie. I would have waited another seven years for you.'

She gasped and put a hand to her throat.

The confusion went on and on. They opened up the front room, pulling back the shutters with some difficulty and removing a few dust-sheets. She made tea in the pristine kitchen and found a tin of water biscuits and some Gentleman's Relish. They ate at the kitchen table, and she felt so awkward and embarrassed she was certain that the whole stupid situation was doomed.

But then he led her into the sitting-room where, seven years ago, they had sat so guiltily and heard from Dr Mayhew and a tightly furious Austen exactly what had happened. This time he pushed her gently down on to the sofa where she had sat that afternoon and he went behind her and began to massage her neck.

'This is where you tighten visibly every time I come near,' he said. 'Do you remember the first time I massaged your neck?'

She remembered vividly. His fingers moving upwards, the thumbs in the rear rotating gently. She remembered she had likened it to piano playing. Beethoven's slow movements.

He said, 'Even then I planned that I would begin your seduction by massaging your neck.'

She gave a sound like a sob. 'Was I so very . . . obvious, Mungay? Am I like Lily Elmes? A woman of easy virtue?'

He did not flinch or pause. He accepted that she knew his reputation. His hands flattened on her shoulders and slid towards her waist beneath her satin brassière.

He said, 'You are honest, Cadiz. I am a devious man and it is your honesty and lack of deviousness that is so . . . disarming.'

She closed her eyes. 'What are you doing, Mungay?'

He was still so expert at the mechanics of it all and her dress and underclothes fell to her waist without any struggle. He stood back looking at her.

'You are beautiful, Cadiz Martinez. Your dark, Spanish skin, your thin shoulders, your little breasts—' He knelt before her and began to kiss her. Everywhere. Her smallness, which she had always thought made her a typical spinster, was suddenly gloriously feminine. She felt her body stretching, responding, proud and . . . yes . . . beautiful.

And then, quite suddenly, he drew back.

'No. We must not. Cadiz – I am sorry – but this is not right.'

She was appalled; thrust out of a paradise of sensation into cold and cruel reason. She had forgotten where they were. And he had not.

'What is it, Mungay? Shall we leave – go to an hotel—'

He stood, his face was closed and hard.

'Cover yourself, Cadiz. This is wrong. We must control ourselves.'

She made no attempt to pull up her clothes. Suddenly she was so angry she wanted to kill him.

'How dare you? You are in the middle of a seduction and you tell me it is wrong! How dare you behave in this caddish and dreadful way? Are you trying to make a fool of me?'

He turned towards her and he was actually laughing. It was too much. She launched herself from the sofa, her hands like claws, striking for his face. He caught them easily and held her wrists while she screamed like a fishwife and tried to kick him with her hobbled legs.

They fell together on to the sofa and the weight of his body momentarily winded her. She felt stupid tears begin to form in her throat.

He looked into her face intently.

He said, 'This is something neither of us thought possible, Caddie. A grand passion at our age. But we want more, my darling. We want to be together all the time. A few days in an empty house will not be enough.'

She whispered, 'I can't help it. I love you. It is not wrong – it cannot be wrong—'

He said quietly, 'I want you to marry me, Caddie. I want this . . .' He kissed her gently. 'And I want other things. To share my meals with you as well as my bed. To walk together on the Downs and be able to say good-evening to people. To go dancing together. Properly. At the Mayor's Ball.' He kissed her again tasting her tears. 'Cadiz Martinez, will you marry me?'

She started to weep just as the door bell jangled imperiously.

They were frozen, staring at each other in wild surmise.

Then Mungay, who was still almost fully clothed, scrambled off her in the most undignified way and crept to the window.

He looked back at her, his dark eyes apprehensive. 'It's Lady Decliveden!' he whispered.

'Do nothing. She'll go away,' Caddie whispered back.

'My God. She's clambering over the railing. She's going to walk around the verandah and look in!'

'Come here!'

He ran to her and lay by her side and she dragged the dust sheet over the two of them and held him closely. It was stiflingly hot. Sweat trickled between her breasts; she could smell Mungay; a wonderful male smell. She found a gap between the buttons of his shirt and ran her lips over the hairs on his chest. He whispered, 'For God's sake, Cad . . .'

They heard Lady Decliveden try the window. Then she called, 'It's all right here, Denver. Obviously Mrs Hayle forgot to do the shutters on this room.'

Then a male voice said, 'Nothing at the back, m'Lady. No sign of a break-in.'

'Very well. I'll have a word with Mrs Hayle myself when she returns. Help me over . . . Thank you, Denver.'

Their straining ears heard the gate squeak to a close.

They began to laugh helplessly, falling off the sofa, tangled in the dust sheets, kissing each other almost frantically.

And much later, Mungay said, 'Darling Cad. You did not answer my question.'

She murmured sleepily, 'What was it? I've forgotten.'

'I asked you to marry me.'

'Oh. Of course you did. And of course I will.' She kissed him again and looked at his narrow Rudolf face with tenderness. 'Oh, Mungay, it will be so lovely. And such fun!'

Seventeen

The five weeks with Clive Maxwell did not seem to have done young Hanover much good. It was the second week of September and Hallie proposed to him that they should visit the outfitters in Park Street and collect his school suit and a set of shirts.

'I don't want to go back to school,' he said, sticking out his lower lip aggressively. 'It's going to be hard and I can't do Latin.'

'Of course you can't, darling.' Hallie forced a smile with some difficulty. 'No-one can do anything much until they've been shown how.'

'You can breathe. You can eat things. And no-one taught me how to read – I just done it!'

'Did it, darling. And actually Miss Bush taught you to read—'

'No she never! We never had to say words out of a primer like other kids!'

'That is because she is a very clever woman and taught you without you even realizing she was doing it.' Hallie realized the boy had inveigled her into one of his long and pointless arguments. 'Eat up your porridge and we'll see if Sully is back from Bristol and can take us to the shop.'

'I don't want—' Hanny caught her eye and changed tactics. 'I don't like it here without Gramps. And I don't like him marrying Aunty Cad. And poor Grandad is going to be lonely living in St George Street by himself.'

'He has Rosie,' Hallie said sharply, her lack of sympathy caused by the same feelings exactly. 'And it's just marvellous that Gramps and Aunt Caddie are married. You must stop being selfish and be happy for them.'

'I'm not selfish!' Hanny was very red in the face suddenly. 'I like them being married but why can't they live with us?'

'Because married people like to have their own homes and they both feel it would be good to live in Dowry Square where . . .' She ran out of explanation. After all, as yet, Hanny knew nothing of his parents and their ill-fated marriage. And she had been as surprised as he was that Mungay and Caddie elected to live in a house of unhappy memories. In fact, the whole thing was so staggeringly unexpected, she could not quite believe in it. Mungay and Aunt Caddie. Aunt Caddie and Mungay.

She hugged Hanny suddenly. 'Darling, I miss Gramps as much as you do. And I miss Auntie Cad too.'

'But Auntie Cad doesn't *live* with us!'

'No, but I lived with her for a long time. And I feel now as if – as if—'

'She has been taken away?' Hanny offered.

'Well, perhaps not quite so—'

'Well, that's how I feel about Gramps. He's been taken away.' Suddenly he turned and clung to her. 'I'm frightened you will be taken away – or even Daddy!' He gave a small hiccough. 'I feel lonely, Mummy! Clive has got two brothers – they're the most frightful bores, but they're there! And even Jennifer has a sister! And Gramps was sort of like a brother for me and now he's gone!'

She tried to laugh into his floppy brown hair. His sudden insecurity came as a shock. She realized she would not be able to tell him about Jack and Maude just yet. 'Aren't we being silly, darling? Of course he hasn't gone. Nor has Auntie Cad. They'll be here most days, or we shall be there. Whatever is the matter with us getting so depressed?'

'Is that why you're cross all the time?'

She swallowed on a dry throat. 'I don't mean to be

cross, Hanny. I'm sorry. I'm happy to be home and with you again.'

'You're not really cross with me. You're cross with Daddy, aren't you?'

She held him very close. 'Only a little bit. He was busy all the time on the ship coming home. He wants to lobby the Government to send out a Commission—'

'What's lobby mean?'

'Persuade.'

'And when he has finished persuading will you stop being cross with him?'

'I'm not cross with him really. I think I'm like you, a bit lonely. I'm missing Aunt Tilly too.'

'It's awful, isn't it?' He added fiercely, 'But I'm not crying, Mummy!'

'Neither am I, Hanny. And we're not going to, are we?'

He said reluctantly, 'All right. But do I have to try on my suit in front of Mr Goatman?'

'You can go into the changing alcove by yourself and I will talk to Mr Goatman outside and when you are ready you can come out. How's that?'

'Not bad. But I bet you a million-trillion pounds, he'll find something wrong and he'll fiddle about with his measuring tape and we shall have to go again next week.'

'We can't, darling. School starts on Wednesday. So right or wrong, we take the suit.'

He nearly told her again he did not want to go to school, but in the end all he said was, 'Good.'

Austen felt her unhappiness as a pain throughout his chest cavity. He refused to think of it as heartache. It was indeed a physical pain. Like indigestion.

At first he had attributed it to her maternal yearnings again. And then, thinking about it on the night of the cane-cutting festival, when she had not been in the house or the grounds and no-one had seen where she had gone, he realized it had started after she had taken Amos home and talked to Sugar.

The knowledge that she had probably heard an un-expurgated account of his past behaviour in Barbados was iron in his soul. He simply could not bear it. His shame was so great it curtailed any natural behaviour. He had heard her arrive home very late that night and had told himself he would have to take his attitude from hers. If she spoke of it then he would try to talk to her and explain. If she did not, then he must abide by that too, he must suffer with her. It would be his punishment and must be taken in silence.

It might have been easier if Mrs Anderson had been on board the returning ship. She and Hallie had got on so well; Hallie might have been able to tell her . . . There might have been a chance of expiation for Austen. But Mary Anderson had died in Jamaica, laid low almost immediately by malaria and living for only two weeks afterwards.

Hallie was heart-broken. She had gone about the ship like a small ghost inappropriately sun-tanned and healthy-looking, but so obviously isolated and lonely it hurt him to look at her. He had already decided to make a request for a Government Commission to visit the island and offer some help and he shut himself in the cabin drafting proposals and discarding them daily.

It seemed worse when they arrived at High House to the news of his father's marriage. He could believe it of Mungay; he was making certain of the House of Martinez. He had probably planned this move for years; had seen Cadiz Martinez as the brains behind the wine firm and had accordingly made her his personal goal.

But Caddie . . . how had he duped her with such an obvious ploy? Surely she could see through it? And then to move into Dowry Square where Jack and Maude had got up to heaven knew what. It made Austen feel physically sick to contemplate it. He hated his father and himself and all the Rudolfs for this side of their nature.

On the day that Hallie was taking the boy for a fitting at Goatman's, he decided to visit Charles Martinez.

He had no real idea of why he was calling on his father-in-law. That it was the natural and friendly thing to do after being away for a month, seemed irrelevant. Austen wanted to see him for other reasons. One of which was that Charles Martinez was almost the only man he knew well, who had been faithful to his wife in life and death.

He found Charles sitting at Cadiz' desk going through some old ledgers and frowning prodigiously.

He stood up and reached for Austen's hand immediately. His manners were charming. Like Jack's. But, at fifty-eight he looked an elderly gentleman, whereas Mungay still looked . . . a rake.

Austen pumped the proffered hand gratefully. You knew where you were with Charles Martinez.

'How are you, my boy?' Even the tone was predictable: bluff and hearty. 'And how is Hallie? And didn't you think young Hanover had survived rather well?'

Austen gave the expected answers and added a quick sketch of the voyage and the cane-cutting and the fire.

'You must come to supper, Charles. Tonight. Yes, tonight. Can you?'

'Of course! I am as free as a bird now.' The ruddy face dropped slightly. 'Going to be rather too free I imagine. What do you make of my sister and your father?'

'We were astounded.'

'So was I. Though I did think perhaps a match might be made there one day . . . When you were in their company, there was certainly something in the air between them. But then, it was so sudden. Mungay left me eating lunch with the boys . . .' He sat down, Austen did likewise, the story of Caddie's and Mungay's 'elopement' was expounded at length.

'The best of it is, my boy, I hear from Lady Decliveden

that she actually called during the afternoon of their arrival at the Flower House! One of the shutters was open and she thought the house might have been burgled!' Charles laughed fruitily. 'Of course, they were there! But they lay doggo and she went away!'

Austen could imagine it only too well and swallowed hard.

Charles continued, 'I'm glad about it, Austen. Caddie . . . she had an affair with a young subaltern in the war. He was killed, of course. But she is not like me. She is a very passionate woman. Wasted here—' He gestured towards the ledgers and frowned again. 'D'you know anything about this, Austen?'

Austen accepted the ledger and scanned a column of figures.

'At the bottom. A sort of personal note. Dated 1 June 1928. The day Hanny was born.'

The ink had faded to sepia but in Caddie's unmistakable copperplate was written, 'I.O. £600. Mungay Rudolf.'

He looked up. Seven years ago. That was before Jack went to the Castillo. He was still gambling and he had borrowed the money from Mungay to repay debts. Austen recalled it only too clearly. The fact that Caddie had been so determined to pay it back probably meant that she and Mungay had already been together then, and had split because of Jack.

He said, 'As a matter of fact I do happen to know. Jack borrowed the money from my father. He must have told Cadiz. She took on the debt.'

There was a silence, both men thinking their own thoughts. Eventually Charles said, 'So. That was when the romance started. Seven years ago.'

Austen, who had been remembering that he had seen the debt as a lever in the door of the House of Martinez, looked up, then nodded.

'I wouldn't be surprised.' He smiled briefly. 'It doesn't matter now, of course.'

'No.' Charles took a deep breath. 'I am afraid we shall not see Jack again.'

Austen looked up sharply. 'You've had some news?'

'A letter from Tilly. Cadiz told me to open all her mail, especially from Tilly. The Red Cross have been trying to contact him. They know he left the Castillo to go to Madrid. Looking for Rodriguez, I shouldn't wonder. He has not been heard of since.'

'That is no reason to suppose he is dead, Charles!' Austen forgot his own misery for a moment and leaned across the desk to clap his father-in-law on the shoulder. 'Come on, man! If he has had to go undercover to find Rodriguez then obviously there can be no news.'

Charles, always the optimist, accepted this comfort gladly. 'You're right, of course. And Tilly is taking over the administration side of the hospital. She'll have ways of getting information.'

'Well then . . . how about lunch?'

Charles stood up immediately. 'I have a feeling you've got good news for me, Austen. Am I right?'

Austen led the way down the dark stairs and into the sunshine of Denmark Street. 'The crop was a good one. But I told you that in one of Hallie's letters to you.'

Charles laughed as they strode towards Park Street.

'Don't fob me off, Austen! I'm an old hand, remember! You went to Barbados on a second honeymoon and I hope very much that next May the crop will be excellent!'

He laughed so heartily Austen had no need to answer.

He and Charles duly admired the new suit before supper. Hanover stood before them drooping sulkily while they rallied him on the cut of the trousers, the line of the jacket.

'It scratches,' he told them.

'It's Harris tweed, Hanny,' Charles told him. 'It's supposed to scratch.'

'It makes my knees look funny.' Hanny stared at the

306

gap between the hem of the trousers and the top of his grey woollen socks. His knees, thus highlighted, did take on an odd look they hadn't before.

'You've been wearing short socks. That's what it is,' Charles said. He looked across at Austen for support. Austen had barely spoken a word since they sat down to lunch earlier that afternoon. Charles wondered whether he had lost weight during the holiday; his face looked almost gaunt.

Hallie, coming in at that moment to tell them supper was ready, said, 'Change into your pyjamas, darling. Your knees look quite raw.'

'See?' Hanny looked wildly around at them.

Hallie said, 'Enough showing off, dear. When you're ready for bed you can put on your dressing-gown and come downstairs for some biscuits if you like.'

It was compensation enough. Coming downstairs when Grandad came to supper, meant an extra hour, perhaps sitting on his knee, listening to stories or telling jokes, or working out riddles.

Charles said, 'He's not been like this while you were away. I wouldn't want you to think so.'

Hallie did not look at Austen. 'He told me today he was lonely. All his friends have brothers and sisters. He has none.'

Charles glanced sharply at his daughter, then across at Austen who still remained silent. He said briskly, 'I expect it's all about Caddie marrying your father, don't you, Austen? Spot of jealousy there, I wouldn't wonder.'

Hallie took her father's arm and led him into the dining-room.

'How about you, darling? You're going to miss Caddie frightfully. Would you like to move up here with us?'

Charles reflected that there was a time Hallie would have referred to Austen first before issuing such an invitation.

He said, 'Of course not! I shall be perfectly happy in St George Street. I've got enough cronies who will call during the winter evenings. And I'm there if any of you need a bed after some function in town.'

They sat around the table chatting about domestic arrangements. And still Austen said nothing.

Hallie pretended to be asleep when he came to bed that night. He was a long time in the dressing-room and she watched him through her eyelashes as he emerged, took off his dressing-gown and got into his bed.

As time went by her confusion and pain seemed to be gathering into a bitter anger against him. She wanted to cry out childishly that he had no need to don a dressing-gown simply to walk from dressing-room to bed – she would not deign to cast a glance at him!

She had left Amos that night with one thing clear at least: she would inform Hanny that his true father was Jack and his mother was Maude. But in view of Hanny's unsettled emotions at the moment, she could not even do that. If only Mrs Anderson had been able to consider the whole mess through her clear eyes, she might have been able to find a solution. As it was, Hallie felt she was becoming more and more isolated every day. Tonight with her father chatting and laughing amiably with Austen the feeling had been trebled.

She lay on her back, rigid with lack of sleep, and thought that there must be something she could do. Some decision was waiting to be made, some action waiting to be done; but she could not think of anything. For Hanny's sake she could not leave Austen.

And with frustration came more anger.

And then towards the late dawn, she thought of one small thing she could do.

She would go to the Harz mountains and see Margo.

She expected opposition. Remembering what Mungay had said, she was certain that Austen would oppose her plan. She was determined to fight him. When he said quietly, 'Perhaps that would be a good idea,' she was not as pleased as she should have been. He wanted her gone, that was obvious. He found her presence as difficult to bear as she found his.

The following Wednesday she dropped Hanny at school and went straight to the office in Denmark Street.

Charles was much more concerned.

'Go to Germany? But why? Margo comes over here every summer and she is our contact out there! There is simply no need for you to go, child!'

'I'm not going on business, Father!' Hallie found herself irritated with her father as well. She enunciated her words very clearly. 'I'm going to visit my friend Margo. I was at school with her if you recall. I still do have some friends, you know!'

He stared at her in astonishment.

'Darling girl. I'm sorry. Obviously . . . Margo is giving birth at any moment, I suppose?'

Hallie had completely forgotten that Margo was pregnant. The thought of being there for the new birth was not pleasant, but did offer a proper reason for going.

Charles said, 'I don't like the idea of you being in Germany at the moment, my dear. What does Austen think?'

'He is quite agreeable.' She laughed. 'Perhaps he hopes I won't come back!'

Charles was further aghast. 'How can you joke about such a thing, Hal? I am amazed that he has agreed to you going.'

'Ours is not a Victorian marriage, Father. I do not have to ask Austen's permission to go where I like when I like!'

He began to look wary. 'Of course not, Hal. I did not mean . . . and after all we only have Tilly's account of what it is like out there. And as she so often points out, her name and appearance are both Jewish.'

'I did not come to discuss my visit, Father. I came to ask if you would move into High House while I am away. To be there for Hanny. I'm afraid he is feeling slightly

309

insecure and I think he might take my absence hard.'

'Of course! Of course, my dear girl!' Charles beamed again, delighted to have an excuse to see more of his grandson. 'And I can take him to school. And meet him.'

She frowned. 'Can you? Without Aunt Caddie here I thought you would be very busy.'

'Caddie makes work. You know what she's like.'

'Well . . . if you're sure.'

'I'm sure. Just let me know when you're going and I'll get Rosie to pack a bag.'

She left him making plans, and thought suddenly that if Austen went anywhere he invariably packed his own things. Austen was strong and independent and . . . did not love her.

She took a ferry to Wilhelmshaven and wept bitterly as the English coast melted into a grey blur on the horizon. And then, surprisingly, she felt better. A man wearing a dog-collar asked her if she was all right and was she travelling with her parents. She managed a smile and shook her head and he said severely that young people were allowed to roam the world quite indiscriminately these days.

Realizing he thought she was a schoolgirl, made her want to giggle. She planned how she would recount the story to Margo.

Then she wondered whether that was why Austen did not want her, she was too young, she simply did not have that unknown quantity known among the flappers as 'it'.

There was a chauffeur to meet her at Wilhelmshaven; the black limousine bore a crest on its door and flew a small black-and-yellow flag from its bonnet. If Margo were trying to impress her, she was succeeding. Hallie watched the chauffeur stow her well-worn leather case in the boot with obvious disdain and tried to thank him with the few words of German remembered from Saunton days.

'It is a pleasure, *gnädige Frau*!' the chauffeur spoke in thick English and clicked his heels. Hallie, who had tried so hard to dissuade Sullivan from ushering her into the Morris, crept past the German as he stood to attention by her door. She had already gone beyond being impressed: this was ridiculous.

A glass partition between the front and back of the limousine let her off having to find conversation. She discovered an up-to-date copy of *Sporting Life* in the map pocket, and an inset shelf contained a thermos of coffee and some *petits fours*. She nibbled and sipped away the miles to Hanover. They went through unmarked towns and villages: she identified Bremen from the sign over the enormous railway station and tried to remember buildings and landmarks so that she could question Margo later.

She peered around her as they threaded the narrow streets of Hanover. She had no idea where the original Rudolf had originated, but he had come to England at the same time as the first King George Hanover. The place must have some significance.

It was pretty in the way the English expected German towns to be pretty, like an illustration from a fairytale by Grimm. The shop windows bowed into the cobbled streets and the roofs were pointed and many-gabled. Hallie craned her head upwards looking for storks, but there were none.

And then quite suddenly they were out of the town and the car began to climb into the Harz mountains. It was October and any vineyards were fallow for the winter so it was impossible to see where the Heartland vintage came from. She sat back again, thumbed *Sporting Life* and gazed upwards to the rounded tops of the Harz. Through the window on her right the land was wooded, dropping into the Leine valley. The car took a right turn and began to run through groves of willow, birch and then dense conifer. And, quite suddenly, above them, commanding a view of woods and river, a turreted castle seemed to grow out of the hillside. Hallie rolled the *Sporting Life* into a tube and gripped it hard. It might look romantic; it also looked terribly foreign.

The limousine purred across a stone bridge and took to a gravelled drive which led through an archway into a cobbled courtyard. If she imagined she would alight here, she was wrong. They swept the length of the courtyard and through another archway to a stone terrace carved out of the mountain and looking over treetops into the valley far below. Its height, and the fact that it was in the midst of a land mass, made it more spectacular than the view from Plantation House. It was Olympian. Hallie felt she had stepped into a Wagnerian opera.

But before the chauffeur could come around and help her alight, the enormous studded door set in the stone of the *schloss* opened and Margo lumbered towards her. If she had looked cumbersome at Hanny's birthday party, she looked almost grotesque now. Gone was the slim, vivacious girl of Saunton days. Margo von Gellhorn was the typical Prussian matriarch.

But she enfolded Hallie as warmly as ever and was obviously delighted to see her.

'Oh, Hal – darling Hal – you never change – never! Thank God to see an English face – it's all right he doesn't understand a word—'

Hallie glanced at the chauffeur; his English had sounded fluent enough to her.

'Margo, it's good to be with you. Everything seemed strange and now . . . here you are!'

The two girls walked slowly through the studded door and into what appeared to be a baronial hall. The effect was chilling. Glass cases held serried ranks of rifles and swords. Other medieval weapons adorned the stone walls. The enormous hearth held a slack fire that smoked sulkily and gave forth no apparent heat.

'*Grossmutter* is here to superintend my lying-in,' Margo said, not even giggling. 'But I can't tell you the relief of having you. I know you've not had a baby yourself, but you were with Maude Rudolf, weren't you? You'll take it seriously! The trouble with being German, you're supposed not to feel pain!'

Hallie's heart sank again. She had forgotten *Grossmutter*. And Margo's aptitude for the barbed remark too.

But she said cheerfully enough, 'This is the fourth time, darling! Surely you know the ropes yourself by now?'

'Eggs . . . ackly!' Margo said, and at last gave her well-remembered Adams giggle.

It took a long time to haul her bulk up the stone stairs at the back of the hall, but once on the first landing, things changed. Here were thick rugs laid on glowing floorboards, the walls were panelled, pictures replaced weapons on display.

'Downstairs is the sort of front parlour of the house,' Margo explained. 'We have kind of receptions there to impress people. We have our apartments up here. Much more civilized.'

It certainly was. As Margo flung open various doors, Hallie was reassured. Even allowing for *Grossmutter* she was at least going to enjoy a luxurious stay.

'My room. Otto's room, only obviously he is not here!' She spoke with some bitterness. 'Our sitting-room. His study.' She pointed across the hall. 'The guest rooms are all on the other side. *Grossmutter* is there. The suite next to hers is kept for Otto's brother and his wife. But they are not here either!'

'But surely at such a time—'

Margo snorted. 'I don't need visitors. But to leave me alone with *Grossmutter* is the end, Hal. If you hadn't been arriving today I don't know what I'd have done!'

Hallie decided it was good to feel needed. She had not felt needed for a long time. Even Hanny had acquiesced in her decision to come away. He was well settled at school and the prospect of having Grandad at High House had been compensation enough.

She said apprehensively, 'Am I having that suite next to *Grossmutter*?'

Margo laughed a second time. 'Certainly not! I have put you next to me. Just here.' She opened another door and led the way into a large light room with windows overlooking the terrace. 'I knew you'd love a view – you were always crazy about views. And there's a connecting door here. Look.' Margo lifted a curtain to reveal it. 'I've got a feeling this is a lovers' room!'

She laughed again, fast reverting to the Margo Hallie knew. They opened the door and went through into Margo's enormous bedroom which was dominated by a canopied bed mounted on a platform; the whole thing the size of a railway engine at a station.

Hallie was stunned. 'You had the other three here too?'

'Connie was born in a posh clinic near Magdeburg,' Margo said, hauling herself on to the platform and pulling a cord which opened the curtains. 'But the other two . . . Otto wanted to go to the clinic again, but hardly anyone spoke English and Tilly came out to be with me . . .' She looked down at Hallie. 'How is Tilly?'

'We heard from her last week. She's in Madrid at the big hospital there. No sign of Jack.'

Margo sighed. 'I never thought I'd envy Tilly.'

'It's hard out there, Margo. She's not exactly on holiday.'

'But she's useful. And she might be able to help your Jack.'

'Yes.' Hallie was always surprised by Margo's penchant for her brother. 'I hope so. My father seems to think he's disappeared for good.' She shook her head and moved to the window to study that view again. 'I don't think so. I want to tell Hanover that Jack is his father, but I must wait for news. And for other things.' She stared at the forest of conifers which appeared to be giving off a faint blue mist. 'I can't think why everyone is so pessimistic. There was supposed to be trouble in

314

Barbados, but when we got there it was perfectly all right. And there's no war or anything in Spain.'

Margo watched her back consideringly, then said, 'But there could be, you know, Hal. The Army could rebel. They are like the Prussians over here. The old school. They hate the way things are going.'

Hallie said idly, 'You know a great deal about it.'

'Yes. Well . . . we are helping them.'

Hallie turned, frowning. 'We?'

'We. Us. Germany. Otto.'

'How on earth . . . ? What do you mean?'

'Well, you know about Abyssinia?'

'The war with Italy? The League of Nations will put an end to that.'

'I don't think so. Germany is helping Italy. With ammunition. Things like that.'

Hallie was wide-eyed. Foreign affairs were to her simply that. Foreign.

'How do you *know*?' she asked.

'The von Gellhorns have enormous interests in Krupps. Otto has told me. He is in Rome at the present negotiating an arms deal. It's – it's business, Hal.'

Hallie continued to stare and at last said, 'I cannot believe this!' And then, 'Are you telling me that similar negotiations are happening in Spain?'

Margo got off the bed and stepped down to hug her friend's arm.

'Don't look like that, darling! Politics – they're nothing to do with us! And it doesn't mean that there will be a war! Of course not! And anyway we shall always be friends!'

Hallie patted Margo's hand. 'Of course . . . of course.' She looked at her. 'It's just . . . oh, Margo, what about Jack? And Tilly?'

Margo had run out of reassurances. She put her forehead on Hallie's shoulder. 'I know,' she said.

There seemed nothing else to say on the subject. After a moment, Hallie turned and put her arms around the bulk of her friend. And then she said, 'Show me the nurseries. Let me see Constantia and Truda and Eva.'

'All right.' Margo drew away and sighed deeply again. 'Oh I do so hope this one will be a boy!'

England had never seemed this far when they had been in Barbados. Hallie, sitting next to Margo at the enormous refectory table that evening, looked across at *Grossmutter* and thought of the long dead Amelia who had been grandmother to Rudolfs and Martinez. It was a strange role, grandmotherhood. Somehow grandfathers had more defined limits. They had little to do with serious matters and everything to do with recreation and enjoyment and spending money. Grandmothers would seem to take the brunt of most of the unpleasantness.

Even making these definitions and consequent allowances did not endear *Grossmutter* to Hallie. The older woman could speak English but made no attempt to do so. Translated by Margo, she made a few statements. It was quite unnecessary for Harriet to have journeyed so far when Margo had the support of her family. It was very apparent from Harriet's size that there was not enough food in England. And Harriet was indeed fortunate to be in a place like Germany with a family like the von Gellhorns.

Hallie replied in kind: it was a pleasure to come to see her old friend and indeed *Grossmutter* herself. There was ample food in England, though she and her family inclined towards simple tastes; and she was indeed fortunate to be in such wonderful surroundings. She thanked Margo pointedly for her hospitality and turned her smile on *Grossmutter*.

Grossmutter said grudgingly in English, 'You are truly Aryan. Margo's other friend was not so.'

Margo said hastily, 'Darling, have some more meat with those vegetables. And have you noticed the wine?'

'Yes indeed. My father will be most interested.'

316

Hallie hoped very much that Margo would give birth quite soon. Threesomes like this one were going to prove difficult.

However, in Germany things were nothing if not orderly. The next day it had been arranged for the three children to be taken to Hanover where a distant von Gellhorn would introduce them to the delights of dancing, singing and social life while their mother got on with things at home. They had no sooner departed in the limousine than the medical entourage arrived. One doctor and two nurses in another limousine were unloaded in the court-yard and ushered through a side door and up to Margo's room.

Hallie had voiced her surprise at breakfast.

'The baby is not due until Thursday, Margo. And it could be much later – you've gone full-term each time, haven't you?'

'Certainly. But I thought this time I would have it on your first day when perhaps I shall be able to show you around a little in a week or so.' She smiled at Hallie. 'Darling, no mystery. They give you an injection and you go into labour.'

'Is that . . . wise?'

'It's no more than people taking castor oil at home.'

'I suppose not.'

And so it happened. The injection was administered just before lunch, Margo went into labour at three in the afternoon and the baby arrived just before dinner.

Hallie was amazed and delighted. She had held Margo's hand with terrible apprehension, terrified that she brought bad luck to such occasions. But beyond some panting and straining and groans of, 'You're better off without this, Hal!' the child was born without incident.

Hallie viewed it incredulously as it was held up by one of the midwives, covered in slime and ugly as a baboon but, blessedly, male.

317

'My God, Margo . . .' It's a miracle,' she whispered.

'No it's not.' Margo said prosaically. 'It's a logical sequence of events.' She grinned tiredly. 'That's what Otto tells me if I grumble.' She sat up with difficulty. 'Thank the lord it's a boy. I might get some peace now.'

The implications behind that were unthinkable. Hallie hugged and kissed her and told her she was wonderful.

The next day she was sickeningly smug just as she'd been at High House last June.

'He said I couldn't do it. He said all the English could produce were girl children. But it's nothing to do with the woman – did you know that, Hal? It's the male sperm which determines the sex of the child.'

'So Tilly told me. So much for Henry the Eighth getting rid of his wives—'

'But I shall take the credit all the same!'

She talked vivaciously of how delighted Otto was going to be.

'He'll make such a fuss of me, Hal, you've no idea. German men absolutely worship their wives. We'll travel. I long to go to Paris and see some of the exhibitions.' It was hard to remember that Margo had been 'good at art'.

Yet still Otto did not return from Rome to see his wife and heir in spite of a telegram being despatched that first day. Over two weeks drifted by. *Grossmutter* spent a great deal of her day resting and the two girls sat talking or taking walks around the estate. Or cuddling the new baby when he was brought in by his wet nurse. It was very restful. It was also boring. Hallie told herself she was homesick; she wanted to see Hanover and her father. She wanted to see Austen. But she felt unable to return home until Otto arrived.

When he did come it was like a warrior of old returning from the battle. Hallie happened to be descending the stairs into the hall when she heard the blast of a car horn. She retreated to the top step and watched. The footmen at the *schloss* rarely put in an appearance for the women of the household, but they must have been alerted of Otto's arrival because one of them was standing by the studded doors and opened both of them at the sound of the horn. There were some exchanges abrupt and one-sided outside, and then Otto entered. His coat was flung across his shoulders like a cloak and he twitched it off with one hand and swung it towards the footman without casting a glance in his direction. It was caught neatly and without fuss while Otto continued into the hall, bellowing at the top of his voice. It was all in German but Hallie caught the words '. . . *dein Mann ist zu hause . . .*' and something about '*der Führer*' from which she deduced he was announcing his own arrival as husband and head of the household.

Grossmutter passed her at a trot not even seeing her. Halfway down the stairs she stopped, rose to her full height and said something declamatory. Otto clicked his heels and bowed and then met her on the stairs and embraced her as any son might embrace his mother. And then Hallie moved back along the upper hall and into her own room. Otto was home and she knew it was time for her to leave.

It had been a strange interlude: she had gone ostensibly to help Margo through her latest lying-in, but in the event there had been absolutely nothing for her to do. Enforced idleness had been restful up to a point. The idle gossip with Margo, who talked of people she did not know, was not of much interest. And in some ways it distressed her to see how Margo was being absorbed into this life. At times it was hard to imagine the stalwart German *frau* was slim Margo Adams whose aim in life had been to have a good time.

With Otto's homecoming there were other things too. She had been surprised that Otto kissed Margo perfunctorily long after he had been shown the baby by a proud nursemaid. She knew Margo had not expected this. She had expected instant adulation.

In fact, as soon as he had gone to the nursery with his son Margo begged her to stay.

'He can't be here long. He has to go to the factory as soon as he has seen the girls tomorrow.' Even Margo knew that with Otto in the castle, Hallie could not stay.

'He might stay longer if I am not here,' Hallie said. 'Really, Margo, it is not right – I have to go. It will be almost four weeks by the time I am home again.'

That night, through the connecting door she heard Otto come to Margo and heard her protests. And his coarse laughter. She pulled the bedclothes over her head.

When she went in to say goodbye Otto was lounging by Margo's side, his arm possessively around her shoulders.

'We shall look forward to your visit next year, darling.' Hallie tried to include them both in her smile. 'Your mother will simply adore little Otto. The first boy in the family.'

Margo was back to being smug. 'Yes. I beat Sybil at something at long last!' she said.

'We hope we do not have to endure another three girls before the next son!' Otto said, laughing loudly.

Margo tipped her head to look at him adoringly. 'Otto, you are insatiable!'

Hallie said quickly, 'Will you have the christening in Bristol, Margo?'

Otto shook his head. '*Nein.* Next year the Olympic Games are to be in Berlin. We shall be seated with the Führer's party.'

There it was again. The Führer. The leader?

It meant something to Margo. She sat up within Otto's arm. '*Liebe Gott*, Otto! Is this true?'

He smiled at her. '*Natürlich.* Herr Hitler is exceedingly grateful to me.'

Margo turned to Hallie. 'Darling, you have no idea what this means. Hitler is the most wonderful man! He's rescuing Germany from all the degradation, making the most of the old nobility – it's difficult for you to understand – but take it from me, this is an honour!'

Hallie said, 'I am glad for you then, Margo.'

She hesitated about leaning over the two of them to kiss Margo farewell, but then, suddenly, Margo swung her legs out of bed and put her arms right around her friend.

'Dear Hallie. So naïve! You are a comfort to me, darling – you have not changed one iota since Saunton!'

Hallie thought how untrue that was, but she returned Margo's hug and kept her smile in place. They stepped down from the platform and walked to the door together. And there Margo said in a low voice, 'Darling, keep in touch about Jack. I might – just might – be able to do something.'

And she kissed her fingers and turned back to her husband.

Eighteen
1936

She returned home to find great jubilation. Tilly had discovered Jack. There had been a scuffle with the Carlists and he had been injured and taken to a hospital where Tilly was in charge. She wrote to Caddie who passed the letter on to Hallie.

Don't worry, he had simply gone to ground with a group of people who are trying to discover just what General Molo has planned. He hoped to hear news of the Falangists and to find where Rodriguez is. In fact we could not find him because he did not wish to be found! As simple as that. This was a scuffle and he tells me he was what he calls 'an innocent bystander'! As it turns out, it is a blessing in disguise. He is not badly hurt and was brought in to the Red Cross hospital because he appears to have no papers! I won't let him be involved in the horridness which is boiling up over here. It only needs a spark to set it alight, but luckily at present, the main force of troops are in Morocco under General Franco – he was in the war over there. With him out of the way nothing can happen really. I hope to get Jack back to you before anything really happens – if it is going to happen.

Hallie read the letter several times. She made up her mind that she would wait until Jack's return before she told Hanny anything about his true parentage. And at least this would keep Margo out of the whole thing. She wrote to tell her of Tilly's latest mission and knew from her reply that she was disappointed.

The visit to Germany had solved nothing. If Hallie had imagined that her absence might make Austen's heart fonder – or even her own – she had to think again. That winter of 1935 saw their marriage founder almost completely, and by Hanny's eighth-birthday treat, even Caddie, starry-eyed and optimistic with her own amazing romance, had to admit that Hallie and Austen were very unhappy.

She said to Mungay, 'I wonder what happened in Barbados, my darling? They had something so special, those two. Not crazy – like us – but steadfast and secure. And it's all gone.'

They were eating breakfast together in Dowry Square and he caught her hand as she passed him the toast rack and drew her fingers to his lips. He could not believe his good fortune and had to touch her continually to reassure himself.

'I suppose everybody is prophesying doom for our match,' he said taking the toast as an afterthought. 'It's just as unlikely as Austen's and Hallie's – maybe more so. Twelve years between them, twenty between us. Common sense for them, nonsense for us.'

They both laughed, completely secure in the knowledge of their own rightness. Mungay buttered the toast, took a bite from it and passed it over the table to Cadiz. She accepted it as if it were a precious gift and sighed ecstatically.

'Oh darling, why did we waste all those years?'

'We didn't waste them, my beautiful girl. All that time we were doing our courting.'

'Courting? D'you call that – that – vacuum – courting?'

'That's what it was. A look. Your picture in the newspaper. Hearing about your latest exploits from Charles or Hallie. I knew one day we would be together.'

But Hallie's plight was making her insecure and she said, 'But darling, we haven't that much *time!*'

'That's why it's so wonderful.' Mungay was genuinely surprised. 'That's why we live here where Maude and Jack had so little time.'

She touched wood quickly. 'Don't say that, Mungay.'

He leaned across and kissed her, toast and all.

'Caddie. Don't you see? We are living for them – we are so like them.'

It didn't make sense but she didn't care. She clung to him and knew that she would be late for the office again, and when she got there none of her ledgers would add up properly and she wouldn't care about that either. They stood up in unison and made for the bedroom.

He had been insistent that Dowry Square was where their married love affair would take place. And he was proving to be right. He was so often right she trusted his judgement more and more. He said, 'I want to bring happiness back into the house. I want to bring happiness . . . full stop.'

She had loved that; it sounded like a mission. The sort of mission she might undertake; or, more especially, Tilly might undertake. But the happiness was so obviously missing now from Hallie's life and when they came back downstairs and got ready to go to their respective offices, she returned to that theme again.

'Dearest, could you talk to Austen?'

'I could. It's never had any effect before. But I could.'

'And I'll talk to Hallie.' She went down the hall to see Mrs Hayle who had moved up from the Flower House to look after them since their wedding.

Mungay opened the door to find patient Sully waiting in the car outside. The cold weather was once again taking its toll on his health.

'How long have you been here?' he asked.

Sully looked dour. 'Since I dropped Mr Austen,' he said. 'Not as long as usual.'

Mungay grinned and got inside and a few seconds later, Caddie joined him.

"Morning, Sullivan!' she said brightly.

' 'Morning, madam,' Sully said and if he made the title sound improper that was all right by him. Hussy. That's what she was. A hussy. She must be a hussy because she had lured Mr Mungay away from High House. And since then the young people had gone downhill with a vengeance.

'How is Master Hanover this morning?' she continued.

The really annoying thing about Miss Martinez – or Mrs Rudolf now – was that she had no conception of his disapproval. On the other hand the master had never looked so cheerful. He glanced at him in the mirror and thought he could be taken for a man half his age. She'd done that for him.

'Young Hanny is fine,' he said and his sepulchral tone lifted in spite of himself. 'Took him to school early this morning. Cricket practice.'

'He is so like his father,' Caddie said fondly.

Sullivan was about to tell her that Mr Austen had never been that interested in cricket, but she was off again on a fresh tack.

'Which reminds me, we haven't heard from Tilly lately. I must ask Hallie about that. In fact, it will be my excuse for going to see her.'

'You don't need an excuse, my love,' Mungay said fondly.

'I do in this case. I am, after all, proposing to interfere.'

She caught Sully's eyes in the driving mirror and thought – just for a moment – that she detected a smile on his face.

In the event she could not concentrate on the business of wine and after a brief call into the Hotwells Road office, where Mungay signalled to her that he was taking

Austen to lunch at the Royal, she took a taxi to High House and sat on the terrace with Hallie, sharing some cheese and tomatoes.

'As I say, I wondered if you'd heard from Tilly lately.'

She had already said it too, but Hallie had a disconcerting habit of not always responding to indirect questions these days. Her dark blue eyes appeared to be looking inwards as if contemplating her own unhappiness. Caddie could have wept; or shaken her niece hard; or simply run back to Mungay where happiness sprang like a fountain.

Hallie smiled slightly, took a small tomato from the bowl and began to eat it like an apple.

'You are the one who hears from Tilly,' she said. 'The only person I hear from is Margo.'

It was probably true. Hallie was in a curiously isolated position especially now that Hanny was at full-time school and terribly involved in his own affairs.

'And how is Margo?' Caddie asked.

'Well . . . she is not pregnant again.'

'Thank goodness,' Caddie said.

'Why thank goodness?' Hallie came out of her reverie completely and narrowed her eyes at her aunt. 'She is perfectly happy with her brood. She is fulfilled.'

'Oh, come now, Hallie! Less than five years of marriage and four children? That is rather too much fulfilment!'

'You think it is better to be as you and I are, Aunt Cad?'

Caddie was still, looking across the metal garden table.

'And how – exactly – are we?' she asked slowly.

'Rather unfulfilled I would have thought.'

'Darling girl—' She leaned across to take Hallie's hand but it was withdrawn quickly. 'Hallie – my dear – Austen cannot help it! Surely your understanding and love can compensate for his lack? You have Hanny after all!'

'We do not have Hanny. As soon as Jack returns I shall insist—'

'Darling, Jack would prefer to keep the *status quo*. For Hanny's sake and for his own.'

'Then I shall tell Hanny. In fact, I shall tell him quite soon. I do not wish him to think he belongs to either Austen or me. As for Austen not being able to help it – he probably has children in Barbados. Did you not know that, Aunt Cad? No, I don't suppose you did. Maude told Jack some cock-and-bull tale about Austen's war damage and Jack chose to believe it—'

'Hallie!' Caddie sat back amazed and appalled. 'So that was what happened in Barbados. We knew something had!'

' "We"? You mean you and Mungay? You talk about us quite a lot, do you? How interesting that must be.'

Caddie regained her composure with some difficulty and closed her eyes for a moment. She should have recognized Hallie's symptoms a long time ago. Her own happiness had made her selfish.

After a long and fraught silence she said, 'What are you going to do? Are you going to divorce him?'

'That would be difficult. I have no proof.'

'He would admit it. He would give you a divorce.'

Hallie was silent, accepting the truth of this. Then she said in a small voice, 'There is Hanny.'

'You have just told me that you are returning Hanny to Jack—'

Hallie burst out, 'I do not know what to do!'

Caddie said nothing and after another moment Hallie said, 'I'm sorry, Aunt Cad. You are so happy – I mustn't burden you with this. I shall work it out. Come to terms with it.'

Caddie leaned forward again and this time captured one of Hallie's hands.

'I would rather see you angry as you were then, than in this mood of silent bitterness. Do you and Austen have arguments – rows?'

'Oh no! We have never . . . We are always polite.'

'Oh dear God.'

Hallie removed her hand. 'Please, Aunt Cad. You cannot possibly understand – Austen and I are completely different from you and Mungay. And we shall sort something out.'

She stood, dismissively, and Caddie looked up at the girl who had been more than a daughter to her. Her short hair still flopped over one eye, her skin was unlined and slightly transluscent. And yet she had changed. Her features were set. She might have practised in front of a mirror to attain an expression of acceptable neutrality, and having achieved it she kept it in place.

'I expect you want to get back to the office, Aunt,' she said pleasantly. 'And I shall have to go to meet Hanny.'

'I . . . yes . . . you're right.' Caddie found herself scrambling up and taking her leave. She thought of going home to Mungay and being comforted by him and then, of course, making love. Their marriage was founded on deep physical attraction and she was proud of it. Or she had been proud of it until she saw the expression on Hallie's face. Mungay was not home when she got there and she lay down on the bed like any other middle-aged woman having an afternoon nap. And discovered she was crying. She never cried.

She sat up and blew her nose irritably, then said aloud, 'Poor Hallie. Poor, poor Hallie.'

On 17 July General Franco's manifesto was broadcast on Spanish radio and was quickly picked up by the BBC. Fighting broke out in isolated pockets all over Spain while the transport of the Moroccan army was arranged from one continent to another.

By October, horrified at the Fascist intervention in a domestic war, the Russians began to supply arms to the Republicans. Suddenly the war was full-blown and instead of being an army revolt against the elected government, it became a fight between ideologies. Republicans versus National Front. Communists versus

328

Fascists. Democracy versus dictatorship. It depended on viewpoint only.

Tilly wrote to Hallie at last.

I am worried that your aunt will come out here as she did before and hope you will be able to stop her. The situation is very volatile and she could possibly do more harm than good even if she could get into the country, which is not at all certain. I am sorry to tell you that Jack has joined a group of Republicans who are trying to form themselves into some kind of resistance outside Madrid. I have not been able to dissuade him. But I should be able to keep in fairly close touch with him. I am now medical officer for the two hospitals which are entirely under the International Red Cross control. I am also in close touch with other hospitals. It is a ghastly muddle out here, Hal, and nothing is certain, but you may rest assured that I can do more to protect Jack than anyone else. And I will do it. There is one thing you could possibly do. English or American currencies are the only valid ones at present and money is very short. The Red Cross will be sending out supplies next month. My father will have the address in London. If you could send some money, wrapped as bandages, it would enable me to go in for bribery and corruption! Not an enormous amount, my dear, it may never reach me. Perhaps a hundred pounds. I will leave it to you. If it seems too dangerous, please forget it.

The nights were drawing in by six o'clock and Gertrude was coming in every morning to light fires. Hallie moved into the room next to Hanover; she had a slight cold and arranged for the fire to be lit in there. She took Tilly's letter to bed with her at nine o'clock and sat by the fire reading it for the third time.

She did not think for one moment that Caddie would want to rush over to Spain when she knew what was happening to Jack. Caddie was much too wrapped up in her affair with Mungay – for that was what it was, an affair. For quite different reasons from Tilly's, Hallie decided to keep the letter to herself.

But if she could not ask Caddie for the money she could not ask her father either; he would be frantic with anxiety. She thought vexedly that she should have arranged ages ago for some money to be put in her own name. It was ridiculous that she had to beg for it from someone else. Her husband.

She bit her lip. It came down to Austen. She would have to ask Austen.

She undressed slowly, wondering why everything was such an effort these days and just as she was about to get into bed, there was a knock at the door.

'Come in.'

It would be Meg with a hot drink. Meg acted as if Hallie were really ill and had been delighted to arrange a 'sick room' for her.

It was Austen.

He stood inside the door, practically fidgeting.

'I didn't realize . . . Hanny told me you had a cold. I didn't know it was flu.'

Hallie said briefly, 'It is a cold. I am very tired. That is all. Thank you.'

He did not leave. She discarded her slippers and slid into bed and he was still there by the door.

He said slowly, 'Is this how it happens?'

She was rigid beneath the sheet. 'How what happens?'

'Invalidism. Like my mother. A day in bed here and there and then . . . all the time.'

She put her hands beneath the bedclothes and clenched them hard.

'Are you criticizing? Is something lacking in the house? Your meals not on time?'

He said in a low voice, 'Shut up, Hallie. Please.'

'Then what do you mean? I am guilty of something, that is obvious. What is it?' Her voice rose shrilly.

He said, 'I was merely wondering if invalidism is a solution to an unsatisfactory marriage.'

She said, 'I have a cold!'

He turned, as if she had defeated him. 'I know. I am sorry.'

She said desperately, 'Your mother was hiding from Mungay's infidelity!'

He paused and stood there, head hanging as if waiting for punishment. When she said nothing more he whispered, 'Hallie . . . can't you forgive me? I was trying to drive away the devils. They came at me all the time. I thought if I did what the Rudolfs had always done . . .'

She gripped the sheets and pulled them frantically to her neck.

'Do you think it's *that*? Do you think I could not understand and forgive *that*?' Her voice rose. 'I thought you couldn't – I thought you were impotent! And I could forgive you *that* too! I could still believe you loved me and it was as much a torture for you not to be able to – able to—' She choked and lowered her voice with an effort. 'When I knew that that wasn't the case at all, then I knew the whole truth. You never loved me, did you Austen? All you cared about was getting Hanny. And later, through Hanny and me, getting the House of Martinez! I was so blind – so young and stupid – thinking we were soul-mates!' She spat the words derisively at him and then reared up on her knees. 'I wish I could say I couldn't care, Austen! I wish I could retire into this bedroom and let you lead your own life! But I can't do that! Do you know why? Because I hate you! Because you have used me and now you keep me around to look after Hanny and the house and make everything easy for you! I hate you, Austen, because you've trapped me here! My friends are gone. I can't worry my father because he's on his own. And Caddie has been seduced by your father – I hate the Rudolfs!' Her voice rose again hysterically. 'I hate them all! But you – I hate you especially—' and with a cry she launched herself at him from the end of the bed.

He caught her easily, just as Mungay had caught Caddie, but he could not ward off her clawing hands. He tried to hold her against him but she was a tigress, fighting off the long months of loneliness and bitterness, beating at him as if he were fate itself; cruel and utterly indifferent. She hammered as she might have hammered at a locked door. And all the time she screamed and panted, 'I hate you! I hate all the Rudolfs! I hate you, Austen Rudolf!'

They swung around the room as if executing a complicated jerky, tango-like dance. He heard his own voice, sobbing above hers wordlessly, begging her to stop, begging her to love him as he wished to be loved and as he wished to love her. Begging for the sterile calmness of pure love, of spiritual love, of the kind of fun and friendship they had had before.

But she did not understand what his choking sobs meant and she could not stop. Not now. With that rigid politeness gone, she was unable to control herself. She twisted and turned and when he pinioned her hands she threw her head back, screamed once and then buried her teeth in his upper arm.

He was wearing a brocaded smoking jacket and a shirt beneath that, but he felt her teeth and as he jerked away he saw that her lips were drawn back from her mouth in an animal snarl.

It seemed to him then that something snapped in his head. He could feel it, hear it. His hands which had merely held her, tightened suddenly into an iron grip. He pushed her backwards to the bed and flung her on it. Had she begged for mercy he would not have heard. Just as the private war in Spain was escalating into something barbarian, so Austen's and Hallie's private differences flared into uncontrollable rage. And the passion that followed was aggressive and furious, without any tenderness but with an energy which swept away the stagnation of those past months. He held her on the bed with the pressure of his mouth on hers while he tore at her nightdress, and when he would have raised his head she held it to hers by hanging on to his hair.

It was painful for Hallie. She was still a virgin and he was not gentle. She screamed and tore the shirt from his back and then suddenly held on to him as if she were drowning.

They lay silent after that, but there was no peace between them and after a very short time they made love again. There was still no tenderness; neither of them knew anything about the tenderness of love-making. They struggled frantically towards a mutual climax and reached it pantingly as if it were another battle.

And then, quite suddenly, Hallie began to cry.

Austen was frantic.

'Oh God . . . I've hurt you! Hal, speak to me – say something – anything—'

She whispered, 'I didn't know it would be like that.'

He got off the bed. He was suddenly unutterably weary. And he felt old.

He said, 'I know. I understand.'

She gave a low moan. 'I wish I could talk to Maude.'

He did not reply. He gathered together his discarded and torn clothing.

'Do you want me to go?'

'I don't know. If only . . .' She tried to sit up. Her body was aching everywhere. She picked up Tilly's letter from the table. 'If only I could talk to someone who knows. If only Jack were here.' She put the letter down again, and rolled on to her face. 'Take it,' she said in a smothered voice. 'I was going to ask you . . . take it and go.'

Very quietly Austen picked up the letter and crept from the room.

The next morning embarrassment made a wall between them.

Hallie felt really ill; her cold had worsened throughout a restless night and she still ached in every limb, but to stay in her room would be – somehow – admitting defeat.

She and Hanny were in the middle of their breakfast when Austen appeared. He looked so washed and brushed and shaved it was as if he was pared down to the bone. His dark eyes appeared black and sunken.

'Hello, Dad.' Hanny had taken to shortening the babyish 'Daddy' since this second year at Colston's. He looked up sideways from his porridge. 'I'm being given a trial today. Third rugby side.'

'Very good!' Austen said heartily in imitation of his father-in-law. 'Don't let games take over from your academic studies, will you, old boy?'

'Acky what?'

Hanny spoke through a mouthful of porridge and Hallie reprimanded him sharply.

Austen said, 'I meant your other lessons. Especially maths.'

Hallie said, 'You'll need to be good at that, Hanny. To take over the Rudolf business.'

Austen's pallid face turned dusky red. He said nothing.

Hanny finished his porridge with much scraping of his plate and began on a long tale of his prowess over Clive Maxwell in everything except 'drama'.

'We had to start drama this term,' he said scornfully. 'It's good fun if you don't take it seriously like Clive.'

'Perhaps Clive wants to be a famous actor.' Austen suggested taking a piece of toast and buttering it industriously.

'Yes, well, he does, ackcherly. He wants to go to Hollywood and see Greta Garbo.'

The scorn was now withering and seemed to affect both Hallie and Austen. There was a silence that penetrated even Hanny's preoccupation with his chances for the rugby side.

He said apprehensively, 'What's the matter?'

'Nothing.'

Hallie and Austen spoke in unison but did not laugh about it. Hallie went on quickly, 'We'll be late. I'll call Sully and we'll get off to school.'

Austen said, 'Hang on just a minute. I want to say something to you both.'

Hanny looked more apprehensive than ever. Hallie was still, her hand on her napkin ring, her eyes on her plate.

Austen said, 'I don't want to make too much of this. I am going to Spain.' He put Tilly's letter next to the toast rack. 'I'm going to take some cash over for Tilly to use as she thinks best. And I'm going to do my utmost to bring Jack home.'

Hallie looked up. She was very pale.

'Why?' she asked.

Hanny said, 'Spain? I thought there was a war in Spain?'

Austen looked across the table. 'Because it's the only thing to do.' He turned to Hanny. 'There is a war over there. We have to get Jack out of it.'

'But Uncle Jack lives over there. He won't want to come home,' Hanny said sensibly.

'He must,' Austen said.

This time it was Hanny who asked, 'Why?'

Austen took a deep breath. 'Because he is your father. And he should be here with you.'

In the silence that followed, Hallie could be heard breathing.

Hanny looked at her.

'What does he mean, Mummy?' he asked in a little boy's voice.

Austen said, 'We adopted you when you were a baby. It's never been a secret, Hanny. We've simply thought of you as our son. Just as you thought of us as your parents. Well, your mother died. But your father is still alive and must come home.' He stood up abruptly and went to the door. 'This is his rightful place. Not mine.' He looked around the morning room with distaste. 'I have no place here.' And he walked to the door and left.

Hanny made a whimpering sound in his throat.

'What does he mean, Mummy?' he repeated.

Hallie looked across at him. Her head thumped alarmingly and the chill which had enveloped her throughout the conversation with Austen, suddenly exploded into heat. She closed her eyes momentarily.

Hanny repeated more loudly, 'What does Daddy mean? Is he really going to Spain? I want him to stay here!'

But she knew that at least Austen had been right in that. She said in a low voice, 'He has to go, darling. And he might as well go to Spain as anywhere else. Especially if he can bring back your father.'

Hanny began to sob tearlessly.

She said, 'I'll telephone the school. You had better take today off while you get used to the idea.' She thought of her plans to break this news gently to Hanny. And Austen had simply thrown it at him, like a rock into a pool.

He said desperately, 'I've got the rugby trial! I have to go to school!'

She smiled suddenly, reassured.

'Very well. I will explain everything to you quickly and then we can talk tonight.'

She looked at the door. It was not like Austen to throw a stone and not wait to see where the ripples went. And this had been a rock. She should have felt bitter about that too, but somehow she did not. If it was the price she and Hanny must pay for his absence, then they must pay it. And last night she had voiced a longing to see Jack. It might be the solution to . . . everything.

She said, 'Are you too big to sit on my lap?'

He rushed around the table and half-strangled her as he took his place.

She began to tell him about Maude and Jack. And

about how she and Austen had been there when he was born. And about how she had promised Maude that she would look after him and call him Hanover. And about how his father had been so wildly unhappy he had gone away. And how Maude's brother, Austen, had loved him too and had wanted to marry her so that he could be Hanny's father.

He accepted it as Jack would have accepted something similar. There was a silence after she finished speaking, then he said, 'But you and Dad – if you adopted me you're still my parents. That's the law, isn't it?'

'Who told you that?' she asked.

'Jennifer McKinlay. Her Gramps is a solicitor and—'

'I know, I know.'

In other circumstances Hallie might have laughed. As it was she let Hanny slide from her lap and go for Sully.

By the time she returned from the school, Austen had left. She thought at first he had gone to the office as usual. But then she found some of his clothes were missing.

She stood by the window looking over the garden to the edge of the Downs where the Avon Gorge cut its way to the sea.

She said aloud, 'He couldn't stay. Not after last night. If he hadn't gone, I should have had to go.'

She was going to add, 'And I hate him.' But she did not. Instead she went back to the small bedroom and made up the fire. She would take some aspirin and try to sleep. As Florence Rudolf must have done so often in the past.

Nineteen

Austen arrived in Madrid when the seige was under way. It was like returning to his own special nightmare: the trenches, hastily dug on the south side of the city, were awash with a recent rainstorm; the men were ill-equipped and looked undernourished.

It had been amazingly easy to reach his destination. He had left the house that October morning and gone straight to Park Street to see Dr Hesterman who had telephoned· ahead to the British Red Cross headquarters in London. Austen never knew what was said, but when he arrived at the austere building near Charing Cross, he was shown immediately into a private office where a man in a dark suit, umbrella and bowler hat on the nearby desk, was looking out of the window.

He turned. 'Travers. Board of Trade,' he introduced himself.

He indicated the only visible chair in the room.

'We understand you represent the firm of Martinez, wine importers of Bristol.'

The man, Travers, held out his hand in a friendly way that – for Austen – labelled him instantly as untrustworthy.

Austen said cautiously, 'Actually, I am hoping to act as a courier for the Red Cross—'

'But you *are* an agent for the House of Martinez, Mr Rudolf?' the man insisted.

Austen made sounds of prevarication which seemed to satisfy Travers.

'You doubtless realize the difficult position we are in at this time—'

'We?' Austen queried.

'The country. Britain.' Travers indicated the chair again. 'Do sit, Rudolf, old man. You've had a tiring journey I do not doubt.'

Austen said drily, 'First-class compartment from Bristol. Taxi from Paddington.'

'Quite. Well . . . as I was saying. Difficult position at present . . . we would normally support the elected government of the country unequivocally. Naturally. But as things are . . . you have doubtless heard that the International Communist Party are recruiting brigades to fight for the Republicans. It puts things on rather a different footing. One wonders whether Communist influence would persuade the Republicans to nationalize our Spanish interests . . . in the event of them winning this war.'

'Quelling an over-ambitious *coup* by the Army,' Austen qualified quietly.

For the first time in the last twelve hours he managed to block out his particular mind-picture of Hallie. Her eyes had been black with pupil, tiger's eyes, and they had stared at him in the firelight as if he were a stranger. And he had been a stranger; forcing himself on her, trying by sheer physical strength to weld their bodies and souls into one. Just as Franco was doing in Spain.

Travers smiled, unruffled. 'It depends on how you look at it, surely?' He took a turn around the small room. 'I think it is more than possible you can see it from both viewpoints. You have interests in Spain which you may well lose. Yet you – quite obviously – sympathize with the Republican cause.'

Austen said, 'I am against the elected government of a country being overthrown by the Army. I would have thought that viewpoint was also yours. And every democratic Englishman's.'

'Quite. Or rather, not quite.' Travers' smile was

339

genuinely amused. 'And until we know for certain which viewpoint to take, we need someone to observe. Someone such as yourself. Someone who has an axe to grind. Or a vineyard to protect.'

Austen said, 'I understand Cadiz has been occupied by the rebel forces. The Martinez property is near Cadiz.'

'Quite. You will have a diplomatic passport. Also Red Cross credentials. There will be no difficulty in landing at Cadiz and hiring transport to reach the Castillo—'

Austen frowned. This man knew there was a Castillo. Since Hesterman's phone call there had been a lot of homework being done.

He said heavily, 'I wish to go to Madrid. A friend of the family is working in the Red Cross hospital there.'

'Which will mean you will travel through Nationalist-held towns – Seville, Toledo – there will be ample opportunities for you to assess the strength of Franco's forces. And the extent of aid from Italy and Germany.'

Not for the first time Austen felt a prick of his old terror. It was one of the reasons he was going, of course. To expiate last night. But the old devils were still there, waiting for him and he said quickly, 'I'm sorry, Mr Travers. My mission is purely personal. I cannot undertake to spy for you.'

Travers threw up his hands. 'My dear sir! I am a humble civil servant! Is it likely that we would send out spies? We simply need to know what is happening to English-held interests in Spain! And if you are going there in any case, where is the harm in keeping your eyes and ears open?'

'It is a matter of principle, Travers.'

Travers said a rude word and laughed in a manly way. Then he said, still smiling, 'If you do not accept my offer of diplomatic status, I am afraid you will be unable to go to Spain at all.'

Austen stared at him for a long moment. The smile

340

slowly disappeared from Travers' face. He looked cold, soulless.

Austen was about to say, 'I cannot fight a war again, whether it is as soldier or spy – not ever again,' and then remembered that the only possible way to banish Hallie's pain from inside his head was to replace it with his old enemy, fear.

He said even more heavily, 'Very well. Tell me what I must do and how I am to do it.'

Travers smiled and went behind the desk where, hidden from view, there was another chair. He sat down and opened a folder. After a moment's hesitation, Austen moved the other chair to the desk too and sat on it.

Travers began, 'The Government has warned all our merchant shipping to obey Franco's blockade. Therefore we run a gunboat along the coast occasionally to make sure no-one breaks the rules. You will land at Cadiz from the gunboat.'

Austen looked at the map that was inside the folder. The Nationalist-held towns and villages were marked in black. Malaga . . . Marbella . . . whole tracts of land into Granada. Madrid was ringed in red. For Communists.

The irony was he was taken to meet the gunboat in a merchant ship carrying supplies destined for the beleaguered towns in the north.

The captain nodded briefly at Austen's diplomatic papers but was brutally candid.

'We shall land this stuff in Bilbao the night after we've transferred you.' He grinned. 'Quite possibly your gunboat will follow and protect us.'

Austen was astonished. 'Is this a personal rescue mission? Are you Spanish?'

'No! We're not Fascist either. First Abyssinia. Now Badajos. It'll be us next. You see.'

Austen tried to imagine rows of trenches along

341

Porthmeor beach where he and Hanny had dug their channels down to the sea. He felt sick.

'I hope you're wrong,' he said fervently.

'So do I,' said the captain.

The transfer to the gunboat was the most dangerous part of the trip. He was swung across in a bosun's chair in choppy seas on a very dark night and was quite obviously not welcome. Austen gathered that the gunboat's diversion to land him in Cadiz harbour would cost them a day's sailing around the Cape. And perhaps that would mean the loss also of the merchant ship carrying much-needed food stuffs to Bilbao. It was indeed a very tricky situation and for the first time Austen felt a pang of sympathy with the delicate path trodden by the diplomats back home.

By this time the combination of dread and misery was making him feel very ill. He spent the rest of that night in the heads vomiting until he felt his stomach must turn inside out. The officer who knocked on the door to announce breakfast in the mess, sounded amused. He obviously thought Austen was a typical landlubber. Austen knew that his sickness was not *mal de mer*. He wondered what the crew would say if he announced that he was sick unto his soul. Probably nothing; probably turn away embarrassed at such lack of British phlegm.

The commander of the Nationalist troops in Cadiz greeted him warmly. After all, England and France were lagging behind Germany and Italy and Portugal in recognizing the 'New State'; visitors like Austen carrying diplomatic papers as well as Red Cross credentials must be a hopeful sign.

The day after his arrival, three thousand Italians disembarked at Cadiz to swell the Nationalist ranks. Austen was taken out to the Castillo in an armoured car and had a view of them being marched to the barracks from the docks.

He had never been to the vineyard and had no idea

342

whether the gaunt old castillo had been pillaged or not. Many of the narrow windows were broken and bird lime spattered the stone floors, but there was still furniture in some of the rooms and the store cupboard next to the kitchen contained a barrel of flour and rows of spice jars. He walked the spiral staircases slowly while the car waited in the courtyard, the driver sprawled anyhow on the front seat smoking a cigarette. Austen tried to imagine Cadiz here as a young girl. She had described the part of her life when she had learned the business 'root and crop', as she put it. He knew she had worn a big black hat, knotted loosely beneath her chin with leather thongs. And she had been 'a bit bossy'. Yes, he could imagine that very well. She would have run up and down the narrow stairs, calling for the servants as if she were rallying them to war. There must have been plenty of young men in those days too. And she had chosen his father. A typical Rudolf.

He went to see the vineyards. They were derelict, rotten grapes everywhere, the vines trodden into the ground. The row of huts used by the pickers – and probably Jack too – was razed to the ground. No-one was about.

The car driver straightened hurriedly at his return and took him to the village. He enquired for someone called Carmencita. He was told she was dead. Her whole family had been shot by the *Falangistos*.

'Rodriguez?' Austen hazarded.

'Dead.'

'And Jack Martinez?'

'Who knows? Probably dead. Perhaps in England.'

Austen said in his execrable Spanish, 'He is not dead. And he is not in England. He has stayed to fight for Spain.'

Nobody wished to hear this. They glanced at the driver of the car and then away. Austen was reminded of French villagers in 1917; their co-operation had been strictly limited and their eyes had never met those of their English 'saviours'. Tomorrow it may well be the Germans who were the saviours. And this was much worse. He was the only foreigner here; both sides were Spanish.

He made his way north, following the Guadalquivir as Jack and Cadiz had done in 1931. The towns and villages held by the Nationalists were by now subdued and orderly. The massacre of Badajoz had happened over two months ago and the autumn rains had washed away the stench of dried blood which English newspaper reporters had said hung everywhere. The people went about their business with their eyes down. Every morning the *Africanistos* paraded in the square. It was the dreaded Spanish–Moroccan army who had eventually overcome the resistance at Toledo. Austen remembered the highly emotive newsreels showing the emaciated survivors of the Alcazar claiming victory for God and the Catholics. They saw this war as a crusade, well worth hardship and even martyrdom. Austen watched Franco's crack troops from Morocco as they drilled on the parade ground and knew he had seen men just like them before. Some of the German troops, trained until all personal will had gone, had had similar brutalized expressions.

He wondered if he would meet Franco himself in Seville, but the Generalissimo had made Burgos his winter headquarters and was preparing for the final onslaught on Madrid. So Austen made his way slowly via Cordoba and Merid to Toledo. He had been given a list of British-held interests in this area and made cursory trips to factories and fruit farms. His reports were unequivocal; if the Nationalists won this war as they seemed to be doing, foreigners would be out of Spain. The Republicans may well be supported by funds from the Communist Party, but they were still the elected government and the British had been safe with them for the past few years. It was Franco and his army who were the revolutionaries.

His car approached Madrid from the south. There

had been heavy fighting quite recently in this area and in the village of Esquivias the Red Cross ambulances were still picking up the wounded. He had been told at Toledo that he would have to make his own contact once he was at the front; the *Madrilenos* had a fearsome reputation. Austen left his driver and made his way down the rubble-strewn street to the first of the ambulances.

'English? Does anybody speak English?' he called as he approached.

His enquiry was ignored. He was not surprised, the men who were carrying stretchers were obviously much too involved in their work to bother with what they must assume was another journalist.

He made his way to the head of the small column. The driver of this ambulance was just recognizable as female. She wore an old army greatcoat and a man's cap, but her hair was long and the face small and pinched.

He tried French and German on her and was turning away when someone inside the ambulance swore violently and in English.

Austen stuck his head through the driver's window.

'Are you badly wounded? Can you talk to me?' he called urgently.

One of the stretcher bearers looked up from a crouched position. 'Blimey, it's a Tommy officer! What the 'ell are you doing here, sir?'

Austen said 'I'm not an officer. I'm supposed to be an observer. But I have to get to the Red Cross hospital in Madrid. I've got papers – money – can I get a lift with you?'

'Not this trip, sir. Too many wounded. Unless she'll let you stand on the step.' He shouted at the girl driver, 'Step! 'E wants a lift. Stepo!'

Incredibly, she seemed to understand and after a quick frown she nodded. Austen ran back to his car and grabbed his bag.

'Thanks – here—' He shovelled English money into the driver's ready palm. 'I'll see you later. Perhaps.'

And that was it. Clutching his bag on one shoulder, clinging to the ambulance door with the other, he entered Madrid on the step of the Red Cross ambulance, flanked by a woman who looked as shell-shocked as he had been twenty years before and heartened by shouted encouragements from the old soldier inside.

The Red Cross had taken over the isolation hospital to the east of the Casa de Campo, out of the line of fire from the Nationalist artillery and with a view of the city across the river. The buildings were mostly wooden frames on brick foundations and some extra corrugated huts had been hastily erected to provide storage and billeting for the medical staff.

Austen dropped off the step of the ambulance at the entrance to show his papers to a Swiss soldier on duty and was immediately waved through towards the main building. Washing lines were strung between two of the huts and a woman was hanging out sheets and waving to the ambulances, her mouth full of pegs. Austen had been struck often during the last three weeks by the juxtaposition of the horror of war and the spurious normalness of domesticity, but never more so than at that moment. Simply because the girl was Tilly.

He called to her and she turned, screamed at him – losing her supply of pegs – and then ran towards him. It was a moment of decision for Austen. He had held Maude on occasions, cradled her when she wept as a girl, danced with her sometimes. But she had accepted his undemonstrativeness as Hallie did. If he did not catch Tilly now and hug her, it would be a most decided rebuff.

She opened her own arms. Her skirt flapped around her legs nearly tripping her. She screamed, 'Austen Rudolf! Oh my God – how wonderful—'

And without another thought he ran to meet her, caught her, swung her around and then held her to him.

She was sobbing, quite unlike the Tilly he knew through Hallie.

'Oh, Austen – I am so glad – of all people – I could have wished for no better rescuer. Oh, Austen – Austen, it is so awful. The bombs . . . the Condors bombed us last week – and there are no more beds and we have to nurse the Italians – Franco's Italians as well as the Brigaders! Oh, it is such a mess, Austen. It is such a hopeless *mess*!'

He said, 'War always is a mess, Tilly.' And then, 'Look, is there somewhere I can put my bag? And can we sit and talk together? I have your money.'

She withdrew slightly and scrubbed at her eyes with her knuckles.

'Oh Lord. What must you think of me? Listen – I have a sort of cupboard to myself. All the doctors do. You can share it. It's in that hut over there.' She pointed to one of the corrugated buildings. 'Ask anyone. I have to see to this laundry and then I will join you.'

'Why is a doctor doing the laundry?'

'I have just finished in the operating theatre. We do our own laundry,' she said simply.

He said, 'Then I will help you.'

She did not protest. He realized she was exhausted. He took the pegs from her and hung out the sheets and some overalls and then they walked across a compound and into the hut.

The door opened on to a central passage, broken by doors either side, which ran the length of the hut. Roughly halfway down the hut, this passage opened into a space where a pot-bellied stove was providing the only light. Clothes had been draped over the flue to air and someone was busy with a kettle and beakers.

Tilly raised a hand in silent greeting and moved along to the fourth door on the left.

'It's divided into cubicles.' She opened the door to reveal a space, perhaps eight-by-eight, containing a bed and a tall locker with a shelf which served as a table. It reminded Austen of a nun's cell; it suited Tilly. They sat side by side on the iron-framed bed. He glanced sideways and saw that her long face was scored by lines running downwards from her eyes and mouth. She was terribly thin. And she kept glancing at her hands; they lay one on each knee, long-fingered, raw-knuckled; the tools of her trade.

She said, 'It's mostly bullet and shrapnel wounds. Shrapnel rips them apart. Dr Benedict – French – he does the amputations. I make sure gangrene is kept at bay . . . It's all right, I'm more objective when I'm actually working. But there's no glory out here, Austen. Spain wanted a Republic and elected themselves a Republican government. The Nationalists want to keep the old order. They talk about a religious crusade. And this is how the old Crusades must have been. Bloody and cruel. What terrible sins are committed in the name of Christ!'

'Tilly, it's all right. It's simply a group of madmen trying to seize power—'

'They'll do it, you know. The German air squadron – the Condors they call themselves – they're terrifying, Austen. They call it a blitzkrieg. They don't bomb military targets at all – the Post Office is still intact – you can see the tower from here. They go for the people. Homes. It's a psychological thing. Demoralize the populace and they surrender.'

He said gently, 'Don't you think you've done enough here, Tilly? Why don't you let me take you home? Your own people need you, my dear.'

She looked at him briefly, then back to those chapped hands. 'I can't leave Jack,' she said simply.

'But that's why I'm here. He has to come back home.' He placed his hands next to hers as if demonstrating his sincerity. 'It's something I have to do for Hallie. Bring him back. And . . . drop out. Myself.'

She looked up at last. Her face was scoured of all

defences. She said, 'Is this something to do with Rudolf pride, Austen?'

He smiled slightly. 'Far from it. This has to do with . . . humility. Penance even. But more than that. Justice. Hanover must know his real father.'

'Yes. You're right. And if Jack won't come for me, then perhaps he will come for his son.'

She returned his smile and quite suddenly put her hands over his.

'Oh, Austen, when I saw you, I knew you were the right one to come out here. And now I know why.'

For a week they used the room Box and Cox. When she was on duty he slept in the narrow bed. When she returned, he got up and washed himself and went to peg out her laundry and talk to the medical officer in charge, in the hope of taking one of the ambulances into Madrid.

The *Madrilenos* had their own hospitals, however, and the Nationalist troops were by now camped all over the Caso de Campo. The officer in charge was afraid that an ambulance seen to be crossing the river into the city would be the target for artillery fire.

Austen accepted that he would have to mark time and feel his way cautiously. He was a neutral agent and the Red Cross were seen by both sides as angels of mercy, yet if he took advantage of either status he could ruin things for himself and many others.

At first he was embarrassed to use Tilly's bed and live with her cheek by jowl so that when she suggested he work on the wards, he agreed, simply as a way of being useful and out of her way. Yet, after a spell of duty in the hospital, he discovered he slept soundlessly. The devils seemed to retreat. Strangely, he began to come into his own.

For one thing there was so much to do. As a medical orderly he was at the beck and call of everyone in the main block. The sights he saw were all horribly familiar but whether he was harder now or more deeply

349

compassionate, he found he could deal with them. There were no dreams; not even of Hallie. In the no-man's land between sleep and waking, he visualized her moving around the kitchen at High House; playing with Hanny in the big walled garden, sitting on the verandah at the Flower House in Clevedon, with old Bellamy on her lap.

One night in the short spell of her arrival off duty and his departure for the wards, he found himself talking to Tilly as she talked to him. As if tomorrow they might be dead.

She put her hands palm to palm this time, as if considering his comments. Or as if praying.

'Perhaps it is quite simple, Austen. Perhaps it is simply because you are helping people now. When you slide a bedpan beneath a pair of buttocks I have heard you. You have a way of murmuring reassurances. Whatever language is spoken matters not. You – you—' She laughed as the old Tilly had so often laughed, self-deprecatingly. 'You positively *exude* compassion.'

'Is that how you cope with it all?' he asked curiously.

'My training helped, of course.' She pressed her hands very firmly together. 'I still have nightmares.'

'Oh, Tilly – oh, my dear – I am so sorry.'

She looked up at him. Her nice English face contorted suddenly and agonizingly. She whispered, 'I love him, Austen. I dream of him being terribly maimed. I dream of going into the theatre and finding him there before me. Of having to dig into that flesh to take out bullets. Of suturing pieces that I have had to gouge away.' She began to sob and he gathered her to him and held her against his shoulder. And as he rocked her into hiccoughing quiescence, he knew a kind of triumph that he could hold a woman against him and comfort her without . . . without sin.

And even as the thought crossed his mind, he smiled at himself. What a fool he was. And what a fool he had been. And if he could not explain it to himself, how could he hope – ever – to explain it to Hallie?

There seemed no way to contact Jack let alone to see him. They knew he was with the British Battalion attached to the Eleventh International Brigade and that they were manning the outer ring of trenches around the city. Austen now felt that if only he could get Jack and Tilly out of this hell, it would be much more than a worthwhile rescue. It would give the two of them time – precious time – together. And it would demonstrate to Hallie that although his motives had always been pure Rudolf in the past, he was capable of something altruistic now.

At the beginning of the second week on the Casa de Campo the German air raids intensified and there was a constant pall of smoke hanging over the city. Austen came off duty one morning just as the grey of dawn paled the incendiary fires. He was so tired that the walk across the compound to the iron huts looked endless. But during the night he had had an idea.

He sat on the bed trying to clear the dullness in his head, watching Tilly dress and comb her hair beneath her cap and don a white overall.

She glanced at him, concerned.

'I'll fetch us some breakfast,' she said.

'No. Wait. Let me tell you . . . it's our only chance.' He glanced at her. 'Presumably the money I brought you . . . you intended to bribe Jack out of any prisoner-of-war camp he might land in?'

She nodded. 'I hoped that might happen. But the way things are . . . it's stalemate, Austen. They won't surrender. He will be killed by Nationalist fire or bombed by the Condors.'

'Listen, Tilly. Before I arrived Franco's brother-in-law was in Madrid. Trapped there, I suppose, like so many other Nationalists. He escaped.'

'Yes. Most of them are repatriated by the Red Cross. But he made his own way through the defences.'

Austen said, 'Could we offer that money for

information? If he got out then people can get in.'

She almost laughed, then said soberly, 'Austen, think about it carefully. Is it likely that the Nationalists will divulge a way into Madrid if there is one? They would be relying on it for their own agents. They'd arrest us for subversion – we are supposed to be strictly neutral remember – probably our bodies would be discovered in a ditch at some time.'

He looked up at her without hope. 'But if we lay our cards on the table, Tilly – if we're together – they can't shoot both of us, surely? We tell them we want to take Jack back home. That would be a good thing to them, I would imagine. They might even blow it into halfway-decent publicity. For their crusade.'

She returned his gaze without speaking for some time. He was exhausted after a night on the wards. Her tiredness was a permanent state now. How far could their judgement be relied on?

She said at last, 'Let me think about it today, Austen. I'll try to get off early. Can you be around at mid-afternoon?'

He rolled on to the bed. 'I'll be here.' He managed a smile before closing his eyes. She thought of breakfast and then decided against it. Sleep was more important.

They agreed to go during the evening when, hopefully, the commanding officer would have eaten and the artillery would be silent. They agonized about who to approach. Tilly wanted to go for the top man. She had met him twice when he had come to the hospital to identify his dead. He had some English and seemed less autocratic than many of the Spanish officers. On the other hand, Austen argued, he had brought only five hundred pounds in English money. What was that to an officer in the army of the Spanish New State? Austen thought someone much more lowly would be tempted by the sum. Perhaps the C.O.'s batman? From his own experience as a soldier, Austen knew that batmen knew as much – sometimes more – than the officers they served.

By the time it was nine o'clock – when they had decided to take an ambulance across the vast parkland to the Nationalist headquarters – they had not made up their minds. Tilly was stupid from lack of sleep, Austen still fairly refreshed. It was he who came up with what he termed 'a typical English compromise'.

'We ask to see the officer in charge. If we're taken to him immediately, fair enough. If not, we have a message for his batman.'

'All right.' Tilly felt dejected from sheer weariness. The plan was half-baked, too loose and formless; it stood no chance. And then the precious five hundred pounds was gone.

Outside it was raining; somehow another bad omen. They went back inside for stronger shoes and, of all things, an umbrella. Huddled beneath it they made for the ambulance pool. The ambulances were all out; there was a car but they did not dare risk going across the Campo in an unmarked vehicle.

They were still waiting by the barbed wire, eyed suspiciously by the soldier in charge, when one of the orderlies came panting up behind them.

'Visitor for you, miss. Doctor.' It was the elderly Cockney stretcher bearer Austen had met on his arrival.

'A visitor?' Tilly looked up at Austen wildly. 'It's news of Jack! He's been wounded! Killed! Oh God—'

Austen would have questioned the man, but Tilly was dragging him across the wet compound as fast as she was able. They stumbled into the hut again and there, waiting by the door of her cubicle, was Jack himself.

Austen stood aside while Tilly flung herself on him, weeping and embracing him almost frantically. He had not seen Jack Martinez since the birth of Hanny. He had hated him them. He had been the cause of Maude's death. He had already shown signs of over-drinking; he had been wild; excessive in everything. Austen had known he was visiting Lily Elmes with Mungay and had hated his father for accepting such infidelity. And had been afraid of all of it because it represented the baser side of Austen himself; licentiousness.

But after Jack had gone he had come to see the other side of him; the side that Hallie loved. The boy who had enjoyed beachcombing with his small sister; the boy who had played cricket for local village teams, who had been loved by everyone.

Neither of those men was apparent in the gaunt figure who held Tilly close to him, burying his face in her neck, sobbing with her. But he was just as identifiable to Austen as the other two had been. This man was shell-shocked. His eyes, when they showed above Tilly's head, were unfocused and wild. He was visibly shaking. And he was unclean; Austen could smell him from six feet away.

Tilly said, 'Oh, Jack, we were just – oh, this is an answer to our prayers. Oh, Jack!' She wept, held the filthy face between her rough hands and kissed him frantically.

He said, 'There's hardly any food. And gangrene – next to me a man has gangrene – and it is rumoured we are to mount an offensive in the East very soon. I had to see you, Till . . . I had to see you once more!'

'You'll see me often now, my darling. Everything will be all right now—' She became the doctor again, propping him on her shoulder and feeling for the door behind her. 'Come, my dear. Come and rest. Austen, can you—?'

For the first time, Jack noticed Austen. He stared above Tilly's head and then said, 'Austen Rudolf. By all that's holy! Do you always have to be with me when I fall to pieces?' He tried to rally his voice into some semblance of jocularity but it cracked and with it, his knees gave way. He would have fallen and dragged Tilly with him if Austen had not leapt forward and held both of them up.

As he laid them gently on the narrow bed, cradling Jack's head, murmuring to Tilly, he thought wryly, Now I am embracing two people.

Jack had merely fainted and came around almost immediately. Austen sponged him while Tilly went for food. Jack allowed himself to be washed, staring up at Austen silently.

Austen kept up a monologue that had more than usual significance.

'You will be proud of him, old man . . .' He had started with Hanny as being the most likely to hold Jack's mind. 'He's eight now, of course, and very like you. Medium height, brown hair, blue eyes—'

'Mad?' Jack whispered.

'Sometimes. He chucked Margo's eldest daughter in the compost heap last year.'

Austen was rewarded with a twitch of Jack's tight lips.

'The thing is, Jack, he needs you.'

There was another long pause then Jack whispered, 'Tell that to the marines, old man. He might be curious. No more. He's got you and Hal. How is Hal?'

Austen took one emaciated leg, laid it on a towel and soaped it thoroughly.

'Not too good. My fault. I . . . let her down.' He looked up. 'She wants you back. She asked me . . . as good as asked me . . . to bring you home.'

'Spanner in the works, eh? Is that what you're trying to do, Brother-in-law?' He did not sound angry; almost amused. 'My God, you're like your sister. How she loved to do that. Throw a spanner – a monkey wrench if possible – into the works!'

Austen was too astonished to reply immediately. Was that indeed what he had been attempting to do? He concentrated on Jack's leg, sponging away the soap and drying it with all the tenderness of a woman.

Above his downbent head, Jack sighed. 'I'm tired and I can't sleep, Austen. Is that how it was for you?'

Austen did not look up. 'Yes.'

'How did you deal with it?'

He remembered how he had dealt with it. In Barbados. He said nothing.

Jack breathed, 'Women, eh? I thought you were a cold fish.'

Austen began on the other leg. The silence went on for so long he thought Jack was at last sleeping. He looked up. The very blue eyes were fixed on him.

Jack's whisper was suddenly intense. 'You are. With Hallie you are a cold fish. Oh Christ . . . poor Hal . . . Why, Austen? For God's sake, why?'

Austen could not answer him but his expression must have said it all because the intensity of Jack's gaze subsided gradually.

'You fool.' The thread of a voice was entirely without anger. It was pitying. 'Hal can give you . . . so much. Gifts like that . . . rather bad manners to turn them down. Don't you think so, old man?'

Austen swallowed. Jack was asleep so there was no need to find any more answers. Yet still he whispered back, 'Damned bad manners, Jack. Damned bad manners.'

He wrapped the naked body in one of the rough army blankets and covered it over with several more. By the time he had done that Tilly was back with a billy of soup. Together they roused him and fed him. He smiled gratefully, swallowing with difficulty.

'Cold,' he whispered when the soup had gone. 'So cold.'

Tilly did not even glance at Austen.

'I will warm you, my dearest boy,' she said.

Austen crept away. And outside in the rain again, he wept and did not know why he was weeping.

Twenty
1937

Tilly and Jack were married by a Lutheran minister four days later on 2 January 1937.

The stalemate of trench warfare created a kind of no-man's land in which they could live together in a curiously normal way. The wounded from the October battles around the city were being shipped out to hospitals in the south and Tilly was given a week's leave. Jack had simply walked away from the Eleventh Brigade five days after Christmas. Nobody came after him. The Red Cross compound was a sanctuary for them both. Sometimes they went out of the barbed-wired gates and wandered across the rolling parkland of the Campo where once deer and game of all kinds had provided sport for the Spanish kings. Occasionally during the day the Nationalist artillery would open fire on the besieged city and some retaliatory fire was returned. And then, apart from the smells, it was as if nothing was amiss. With the New Year the weather improved; there were some bright frosty days. The medical staff continued to wear stars in their hair; the decorated wards and small, candle-lit nativity scenes helped to make it seem like any hospital anywhere. The French sang their carols. The Swiss played glockenspiels. It was not only because of Christmas; the wedding made everyone feel good.

Austen wanted to go back home while this lull gave them easy passage. With the marriage certificate from the minister and their Red Cross and diplomatic papers, it should be possible to get Jack through to Bilbao where British merchant ships were reported to be landing illegal food supplies. But neither of them could bear to break the fragile bubble of happy security which encased them.

Tilly said privately to Austen, 'He won't come yet. Give me a little more time. I can persuade him, but I need time. He is shocked beyond logic. You understand that, Austen.'

'Yes.'

Of course he understood, and tried hard to quieten the terrible sense of urgency he felt.

He said, 'Listen, Tilly. It's hopeless – the three of us sharing that cubicle. I'll leave you. For a week. I can go towards Valencia – there's a mining area financed by the British – obviously still being run by the Republicans. It will give my report a more balanced look.' He grinned wryly. 'I've tended to overlook that part of my trip.'

She said anxiously, 'Is it safe? If you're going for our sake – then don't. You've been sleeping on the wards anyway. We are glad and thankful to have you here when you are off-duty.'

For some reason that made him want to weep. It must be a diet deficiency; he wanted to weep quite often.

He said sincerely, 'I feel privileged to have been here for your wedding, Tilly. I was representing Hallie too.'

'I know. I know that.' She hugged his arm in a way Hallie had and he swallowed fiercely. She said, 'Stay with us, Austen.'

'Well . . .' He cleared his throat. 'No, my dear. You will be able to persuade your husband to leave here more easily if you are alone.'

To talk of them being alone in these rabbit hutches was ludicrous. Yet they had created their own privacy.

He did not wait for her reply but kissed the top of her head gently.

'I think I must go, my dear. For Jack's sake. I am a Rudolf.'

'Oh, Austen.' She looked at him sadly. 'You carry that

358

name like an albatross these days. Remember too that makes you Maude's brother.'

He managed a proper smile. 'And in the circumstances, is that entirely a good thing?' He picked up his bag from beneath the bed. 'I've arranged with your medical director to take a Red Cross car along the Jarama Valley.'

'On your own?'

'Safer that way.' He showed her his arm band. 'With this, and all my papers, I can't go wrong.'

'So . . . just a week, Austen?'

'As near to a week as I can make it.'

By Christmas Hallie knew, beyond doubt, that she was expecting a baby. She told her father and was overwhelmed by his enormous joy.

'Oh, my dear girl! I began to think – silly old fool that I am – oh, Hal, I am so delighted! Absolutely delighted!'

Hallie, after seven weeks of sickness, with three formal letters from Austen and the knowledge that she had cheapened herself beyond belief, was genuinely surprised. And then reduced to tears of weakness.

Charles was terribly concerned.

'My dearest girl! You must send for Austen at once! Are you ill? Why did he not return the minute he knew—?'

'He does not know,' she sobbed. 'And I do not wish him to know. Oh, Papa, I am so glad you are glad! Austen will not be glad and I have felt so rotten – I don't think I have felt glad – not once! And you are!' And she wailed as she had done when she was hurt as a child, and, just as then, Charles gathered her up and rocked her and told her what a brave girl she was and how everything would be better in the morning.

And, in fact, she did begin to feel better after his ministrations. He insisted on ringing for Rosie, although it was her afternoon off and when she came and was told, she too wept and then went immediately to make tea and butter scones.

'Oh, Pa, I should have told you as soon as I knew!' Hallie wiped her eyes smiling at her own childishness. 'But I was so *miserable*! I couldn't think straight.'

'Cadiz and I thought you'd had a row,' he said soberly. 'When Hanny came to tea the week after Austen's departure and told us Jack was his father, we guessed it was something awful. But really, Hal, he has a right to know about this child. He is your husband.'

Just two hours ago it would have been salt on all her wounds to know that Aunt Caddie – and that meant Mungay too, of course – had discussed her with Charles. Now the sense of family support was like balm.

She said, 'Oh, Pa . . . I can't explain it all. But I think my marriage is over. Caddie was right all those years ago. Austen is a true Rudolf.'

'But my dearest girl, of course the Rudolfs have faults. So have we! So has everybody. And as for Caddie – she has married a Rudolf and is very happy indeed, as far as I can tell!'

'Caddie is so strong, Pa. You know that. And I am not. I cannot stand against Austen.'

'I hardly think Caddie has to do battle with Mungay, dearest girl!'

'She could if it came to it! But she is clever too. She can – can channel his – his—'

Charles took her hand. 'I know what you are trying to say, my dear. Caddie is a match for Mungay. They have similar . . . passions.'

She flushed dark red and pulled away from him. He frowned, worriedly.

'I was anxious about it at first, too, Hal. But I promise you—' He stopped. She was shaking just as Caddie had shaken that night last summer. He cleared his throat and continued in a stronger voice, 'Whatever you think about your aunt, Hal, you must know how precious you are to her. She has been your mother – just as you are Hanny's mother. And you need a mother now. Go and see her. Talk to her. It could be that she can help you.'

Rosie brought in the tea things before Hallie could respond.

She went to see Cadiz because there was no-one else. Marjorie Maxwell was away and in any case they were not confidantes. With both Tilly and Margo out of the country she had to face up to the isolation in which Austen had somehow cocooned her.

Her aunt's delight at her news was tempered by other considerations.

She said tentatively, 'Would it be silly of me to say this will heal everything?'

Hallie looked at her without speaking.

Cadiz said, 'But . . . obviously you two . . . I mean . . . oh, dammit all, Hal, you made love! After five years of that stupid platonic business, then your terrible sense of betrayal when you discovered that Austen was by no means impotent after all – you came together! It's no good looking at me like that! You are pregnant! You must have made love!'

Hallie had been to see Dr Hesterman that morning and was still sore and somehow humiliated.

She said wearily, 'And then Austen left. Does that not tell you something, Aunt Cad? He won't come back. Not to me. He'll bring Jack back home and probably I shall look after Hanny down in St George Street again and he and Jack will gradually get to know each other and Austen will sort of fade away.'

'Why?' Cadiz asked straightly.

'Because he wanted me to be pure. And he made me impure.'

Cadiz leaned back in her chair, astonished.

'What absolute rubbish, Hal! You must realize yourself that the fact that Austen made love to you, shows he is normal. Somehow he has overcome that awful time – how long was it, probably ten years?' She narrowed her eyes. 'You hated it? Darling, of course you hated it. You were scared – it was the first and only time—'

'It happened twice,' Hallie said levelly.

'Even so, my sweet – you feel he practically raped you—'

Hallie's bark of laughter cut her short.

'Oh, Aunt Cad. It wasn't like that. Not one bit like that. If there was any rape then . . .' She put her hands to her face. It was hot again. Whenever she thought of that night she almost combusted.

She said through her fingers, 'I told him how I felt. It wasn't what he had done in Barbados – not at all. It was the fact that he had treated me like an object. A precious artefact. Kept me in a glass case – I have no real friends now you know – and deprived me of – of—' She sobbed and lowered her head. 'I – I forced myself on him, Aunt Cad. I screamed like a fishwife and jumped at him and tore his clothes and – I cannot bear to think of it!'

There was a long silence. Then Cadiz spoke quietly. 'And the second time?'

'I don't know. It just happened. I don't know.'

'Oh, Hal.' Suddenly Cadiz was on her knees by the chair, removing the fingers one by one, exposing Hallie's ravaged face. 'Darling Hal, don't you see? That was the only way to break through Austen's reserve? And having broken through – that second time—'

Hallie stood up almost tipping Cadiz back on to the carpet.

'You yourself have always said he was a typical Rudolf! Now I can see it! Plotting to get Hanny because he thought there would be no children for us! Don't you see, by the time Hanny is old enough to take over, Amos will be dead – he will have the whole sugar plantation and the Martinez business as well!'

'Darling, you are not talking about some stranger! It will be *Hanny* doing these things! Hanny is a Martinez

362

and a Rudolf by birth. Wouldn't it be the best thing that could possibly happen?'

Hallie said wildly, 'Why did he keep me in purdah like that? When all the time – all the time—'

'One thing at a time, darling.' Cadiz came behind her and held her shaking shoulders. 'Maybe he *was* impotent—'

Hallie shook herself furiously like a dog. 'I know he wasn't! I've told you – Sugar – and Amos – said he was a true Rudolf!'

'But then – afterwards – when he met and loved you, he wanted to keep you—'

'So he talked himself into being impotent? Is that what you are saying?'

Cadiz said, 'Hal, I don't know. Maybe Dr Hesterman could talk to you and explain—'

'And if he was suddenly cured, why did he go the very next day to find Jack? He has left me, Caddie! Austen has left me!'

'Darling, when he knows about the baby—'

But Hallie was past reason or hope. 'He must never know. I am not having him back from a sense of duty.'

'Or a sense of happiness? Fulfilment after the long years of—'

Hallie controlled herself with an effort and said in an almost normal voice, 'Aunt Cad, I disgusted him. And I disgusted myself. That is the root of all this. I am . . . disgusting.'

Caddie was distressed now. She tried to tell Hallie about sexual love, but women did not talk frankly to each other and it was difficult.

She said lamely, 'Listen, Hal. Austen has been fighting against his own inheritance. His Rudolf passion. He has hated it – can't you see that? He hated it more because he thought you had none of it. He has been two people all this time. The man he would wish to be. And a Rudolf.'

Mungay's voice came from the doorway. Neither of them had seen him enter.

He said, 'I agree with Caddie.' He came into the room and put a proprietary arm across his wife's shoulders. Hallie was aghast and turned to the window.

He said, 'I thought we were friends, Hal? But, of course, I am a Rudolf. There is no doubt of that.'

Caddie said quickly, 'Darling, I did not mean—'

'I know.' He grinned down at her, revelling as he always did in her thick hair piled at the back of her head, her thin Latin face and dark eyes, her sheer daintiness. 'A Rudolf is good for you, Cadiz. Not for Hal. Is that it?'

'Darling, it's not simple. And I think Hallie would prefer not to explain—'

'I don't want to talk about it any more!' Hallie said fiercely from the window. 'I don't want you to talk about it either!'

Mungay said very quietly. 'Hallie, I think there is something you should know. And then you can tell Austen. I kept it quiet all these years – for Florence's sake. But surely it was obvious? No-one could be more unlike a Rudolf than Austen. Simply because he is not a Rudolf.'

He had their attention. After a startled moment, Caddie turned within his arm and Hallie turned from the window.

Caddie said, 'What on earth are you talking about, darling?'

Mungay shrugged. 'It didn't seem to matter any more. Especially when Maude and Jack had little Hanover.' He looked at Caddie wryly. 'My own father was elderly – he wanted me to marry. It was the last thing I wanted – committing myself to one woman when there were so many . . . Florence was from a good family. No money. We thought – my father thought – that her family agreed to the match because of our money. My father thought it was a good trade. Buying into an aristocratic family.

364

But it was not so. When we were honeymooning on the Island, she told me she was pregnant. Her lover was in the Army – he was an officer and a gentleman. I was not. She did not wish me to come near her. And I did not for six years . . . and then Maude was born. My daughter. As mad as any Rudolf had ever been.' He looked down at Caddie. 'She loved Austen. She knew he was different from her, but she loved him. And for her sake I tried to. I never told him he was no kin of mine. I might even have fostered his cleverness towards Rudolf ends. Sometimes I thought he was more of a Rudolf than I was myself. But, without realizing it perhaps, I was forcing him into a mould that was quite foreign to him.' He looked at Hallie. 'I don't know, Hal. I really don't know any more.'

She lowered her head and stared at the carpet. For the first time since the trip to Barbados she felt an aching compassion for Austen.

Caddie said, 'Why did Florence hate you, my dear? You gave her respectability and luxury and still she—'

He held her tightly as if he expected her to run from him.

'It was after Maude . . . I – I forced myself on her that night, Caddie. I'm sorry, my dear. I was drunk and bitter.' He shook his head. 'I am not a good man, Cadiz. But I do love you. That I promise.'

She put her own small hand in his and said, 'And that I know.'

They stood there, the two women digesting what he had said. The awfulness of it; the terrible sadness.

Mungay said, 'Ask me anything you want to know, Hal. I will tell you.'

She was silent, shaking her head slowly.

After a while she said, 'I must go home. Perhaps . . . later.' She went to the door and then turned. 'I am glad now that Austen told Hanny about Jack. You should have told Austen about his father a long time ago.'

Mungay waited until she had gone and then he said,

'I couldn't do that. Florence did not want it. Austen's father was killed in a shooting accident.'

Cadiz put her forehead on his jacket lapels and said, 'Oh God.'

'Yes.' He looked over her head into the past. 'I dealt with it like all Rudolfs, Cad. But poor Florence—'

'No! No, you must not say that.' She straightened fiercely. 'She could have had a good life! She chose to make it unhappy.' She kissed him hard. And then said, 'And if Hal does the same thing, I will – kill her!'

Austen drove slowly along the Jarama Valley through a country that had so far been untouched by war. He had rations and a dozen cans of petrol in the back of the car. This would have been confiscated immediately in the Nationalist area, Red Cross or no Red Cross. When he stopped for a glass of wine at one of the tiny villages on the road, there was no fear of that.

He reached Cuernca on the borders of Aragon and found a room in an inn without difficulty. The whole of this eastern side of the country was still held by the Republican Government; the war was spoken of as an 'army mutiny'. Other things were discussed over mulled wine by an enormous fire. He was able to ask about the places marked on the map Travers had given him. A small factory, a coal field, smelting works. They were all running as before; no devastation as in the Nationalist area.

Austen drove on to Valencia the next day. There was tension along the coast. The Balearic Islands were all held by the Nationalists. He went to the English Club and found several bewhiskered ex-patriates prophesying defeat for the Republicans.

'Politically, they are a mess. They need more help than the Russians can give them.'

The speaker was one of the lesser officials from the Consulate. He glanced over his shoulder.

'You know Baldwin is virtually supporting Franco?

Now if we'd got that Attlee fellow holding the reins, it would be a different story.'

Austen thought of his carefully drafted proposal for a Government Commission to investigate the situation in Barbados. Would it hang so tenuously on who was in power?

He said, 'I believe the ordinary British people are in favour of helping the Republicans. If only to send food and supplies over.'

'All the bloody ports are blockaded,' the man told him. 'Nothing we can do about it. I've applied for a transfer. All right for you with that—' He nodded at the red cross on Austen's sleeve. 'You can afford to sit on the fence and be objective.'

Austen smiled wryly accepting the indictment. He slept badly that night and let himself think of Hallie. He had sat on the fence so comfortably throughout the five years of his marriage. Until that night in October.

The next morning he stayed long enough to write a detailed report and leave it in the diplomatic bag at the consulate. And then he started back. There was snow on the high ground overlooking the valley and it was bitterly cold. He prayed Tilly would have talked Jack into leaving. Bilbao was still an open port. If Jack took Austen's papers, there was nothing to stop the two of them reaching Basque country and just up the coast was the blessedly normal French resort of Biarritz. Jack needed long-term care and decent food. And Hallie needed Jack.

Austen arrived back at the war zone on 1 February. The last leg of the journey had been miserable, torrential rain had swollen the Jarama and flooded several places along the main Madrid–Valencia road, and twice he had to get out and manhandle the car out of the mud. But it was more than that. On the outward journey there had been a sense of immediate normality as he left the city and drove into established Republican territory. That had gone. It was as if the deserted muddy stretch of road had suddenly been abandoned. Austen stopped twice and found no-one in the tiny villages. It was eerie. And very ominous.

He left the car in the compound and took the keys into the office. There were papers to sign, thanks to be given – none of it easy when no-one could speak each other's language. And then he made for the corrugated living quarters.

He opened the door and looked down the long dark passage to the stove in the centre. It was lit and belching smoke as usual. Various items of clothing adorned its flue. No-one was about. He opened the door to Tilly's cubicle; no-one was there either. Tilly had doubtless had to return to duty by now and probably taken Jack with her. Austen dumped his bag beneath the bed once again and went to warm himself by the stove and dry off his boots and socks. Two Swiss nurses came in, smiled and disappeared into their cubicles. An orderly lugged some cans of water down to the latrines. He was used to all this, yet the hairs on the back of his neck refused to lie flat.

When it was completely dark he went to the wards to see if he could be of use and to check on Tilly and Jack. The Sister, a smiling Belgian girl, pointed to the theatre. Austen nodded and pointed to his watch raising his eyebrows questioningly.

She pointed to the eight, nodded at him then shook her head when he pointed to himself and bustled down to her office.

So there had been no unexpected influx of wounded; he was not needed tonight. And Tilly would be off duty in half an hour.

He could have visited the Englishmen who were in the top part of the ward, but suddenly he was too tired. He would wait for Tilly and find out where Jack was located, then they could make arrangements for sleeping. The feeling of urgency was still there, heightened

368

more if anything, yet he knew he must sleep before embarking on anything else.

Tilly woke him gently at eight-thirty. She had peeled off her gloves and carried her operating cap and gown in a roll beneath her arm. She looked terrible.

He whispered, 'What's up?'

She said, 'You haven't heard then? Jack was recalled. Two days ago.'

'Recalled? He had gone absent without leave – he should have been arrested if anything. Not recalled.'

She put a hand on his arm and led him outside. 'Austen, I am so tired . . . I have to lie down. Can you boil these for me?' She stood still, face up to the freezing rain. 'He has gone, Austen. I have accepted it. Don't make it unbearable again.'

'I—' He wanted to ask questions, protest to her angrily that she should have kept him by her side. Instead he accepted the bundle. 'Yes, all right. Sleep, Tilly. We'll make plans tomorrow.'

He went to the laundry shed, his mind boiling. He would have to find Jack. Take him home by force if he had to. They had been within an inch of leaving – Jack could not do this, he could not do it.

Thankfully the orderly at the wash-house was English and had been at the wedding.

'Bad news, guv,' he said. 'That young Jack Martin – he had to go, you know. His CO – the British Battalion who are with the Eleventh have a regular CO – good 'un he is too – he said as how he put Jack down for compassionate leave. Knowing as how Dr Tilly was at the Red Cross base like. But now these new plans are afoot, he'd have to go back. Poor devil. He didn't want to go. You could see that a mile off. Just married and all.'

Austen poked at the seething boiler with a paddle. 'What new plans?' he asked.

'We're not supposed to know. The Nationalists want to cut the Valencia road. And we – that is the

Republicans – want to get them away from Madrid. Diversionary tactics.'

'We're strictly neutral,' Austen said automatically.

'I know, guv. And we're losing too.' He grinned. 'Maybe that Mr Martin will make all the difference, eh?'

The place was foggy with steam, the men could barely see each other. It did not matter what expression was on Austen's face when he replied, 'Maybe.'

Although Hanny was a day boy he still was part of the house system at Colston's. Mr Baker was his house-master and it was he who telephoned the High House and asked if he could speak to Mr Rudolf.

'Mr Rudolf is in Spain,' Hallie told him. 'Is something the matter?'

'Your son is causing a little anxiety at school, Mrs Rudolf. Perhaps I might have a word with you? Will ten o'clock tomorrow morning suit?'

Hallie would not have dared tell him it did not suit.

She questioned Hanny as soon as he got home that afternoon.

'Are you in some kind of trouble at school, dear?'

'No!' Hanny flashed her a look to discover the reason for her question. 'Why? Has the cottage loaf been moaning?'

'Mr Baker wishes to have a word with me. In the morning,' Hallie said.

'Oh Lor! I should have told you, I suppose. I broke a window. I didn't want to worry you – what with Dad – Uncle Austen – being away and everything. I could have paid for it with my allowance if he'd given me a couple of weeks' grace.'

She looked at his downbent head, knowing there was more to it than a broken window. But he had taken her breath away by calling Austen 'uncle' and she could think of nothing else for that moment.

He said, 'Listen, Ma—' Thank goodness he did not call her Aunt Hal. 'Ma' was the latest at Colston's, being a shortened form of the public school *mater*. Between the boys themselves it was 'the old girl'. She had heard Clive call Marjorie that often and had hidden a smile.

'Listen. If I take the money in tomorrow, you needn't go. I'll explain for you.' He held out his hand. 'Can I have an advance on next month's allowance?'

She said, 'I have to go to see Mr Baker, dear. I have arranged it.'

His face flushed with anger. 'You don't trust me! I'll give him the money for the window! If my father was home, he'd trust me! But you and Uncle Austen—'

'That's enough, Hanny!' She had to raise her voice to override his, and Sully – who had obviously been lingering outside the kitchen door – appeared like a jack-in-the-box.

'Did you call, madam?' He addressed Hallie but fixed Hanover with a beady eye.

'No. Thank you, Sully. Although now you're here – I shall want to be taken down to the school tomorrow morning.'

'Certainly, madam.' The old man touched his forelock like a retainer of old, then said, 'D'you want to see how the latest is coming along, Master Hanny?'

Sully was making a model of a Rolls Royce from matchsticks. He had a great deal of spare time these days.

Hanny tried to outstare him, his lip thrust out mutinously. Then he said ungraciously, 'Yes. All right then.' And trailed through the kitchen door.

Left to herself, Hallie let her breath go tremblingly and turned to put the kettle on. Thank goodness Meg and Cook were elsewhere. They would have reprimanded Hanny openly and there would doubtless have been a shouting match. Hanny needed a man. Sully would do for a while. And then who would it be? Jack was going to be hopeless. And Austen . . . Austen had gone.

She made some tea and took it into the morning room. She felt unutterably lonely.

Mr Baker said, 'He is talking a lot of nonsense about being an orphan, Mrs Rudolf. I have looked at his record and realize he is an adopted child. These spurts of rebellion can happen, of course. But they aren't the root cause of the trouble. In other words, Hanover is using his adoption as an excuse to behave badly.'

Hallie felt terrible. Mr Baker's room was ancient and comfortable and completely masculine.

She said tentatively, 'You see, he did not know before. And then suddenly he did. He is getting used to the idea. I'm sure that's all it is. I'll pay for the window, of course.'

He looked at her over his glasses. 'We are insured for broken windows, Mrs Rudolf. And we cannot seek recompense for a boy who refuses to work.'

Hallie swallowed. 'Once he is properly motivated—'

Mr Baker gave a wintry smile. 'Ah. Motivated. A word used a great deal in the Saunton kindergarten, I believe.' His smile died. 'So. You would consider his teachers at fault in this case, would you?'

Hallie was horrified. 'Certainly not, Mr Baker! I was going to ask you what I could do at home.'

He in his turn looked appalled. 'Please, do nothing, Mrs Rudolf. We find parental interference is very bad for the boys. Indeed it can do the opposite of what is desired – performance falls drastically behind.'

'Then what is there to be done?'

He looked dour. 'If your husband were home, I would advocate caning. As it is . . . be firm, Mrs Rudolf. Do not spoil him.'

'I don't think . . .' She had been going to defend herself, but stopped. Had they all spoiled Hanny? He was the only child for all of them.

That evening she took Hanny into the old library where she had drawn a table up to the gas fire and set out some books.

'It's not the same book as what we use for spellings,' he said defiantly. 'And anyway, I'm good at spellings!'

'Then you will show me.'

They sat side by side, an angry boy of eight years old and a woman of twenty-seven. Sullenly he wrote out his spellings. And then his tables.

'I hate school,' he told her. 'And I wish we could go back to being a proper family. It's since Gramps married Aunty Cad! And Daddy went away!'

There were furious tears in his eyes. She refused to let them move her.

'Look here, Hanny.' She fixed him with her violet eyes. 'I don't know why you're not working at school. But I do know that your Mr Baker made me feel . . . stupid. And I don't like that.'

'I hate him too!' Hanny said passionately.

'I don't hate him. But I want to show him that I can help you at home. Whatever he says.'

He drooped suddenly. 'It's no good, Ma. You didn't do Latin at school, did you?'

'I chose German certainly, but—'

'All they care about at Colston's is Latin. Dad could have helped me.'

'Yes, he could.' Austen had been an excellent Latin scholar. She wasn't so sure about Jack. She brightened. 'And I know someone else who can help you. If he will.'

'Who? Mr Baker won't come to our house! And anyway it would be terrible—'

'Walter Hinch.'

'Mr Hinch? Do you mean Jennifer's Mr Hinch?'

She smiled more naturally. 'I think of him as your Aunt Margo's Mr Hinch. He is Mr Adams' clerk. D'you remember how good he was with the von Gellhorns at your birthday party?'

'Yes!' Hanny grinned and began to look more like himself. 'Is he really any good, Ma?'

'He used to help Margo – her parents insisted on

her doing Latin. He's wonderful. I'll telephone him, shall I?'

'Oh, Ma . . . !'

And so, Walter Hinch came to High House twice a week after his work and gave Hanny tuition in Latin. Hanny did not enjoy it and played up as only he could, until Walter brought Jennifer one evening in February. It happened to be Saint Valentine's Day and Jennifer wore a tiny china brooch in the shape of a heart on her tie.

While the adults were sipping tea and discussing Hanny's progress, he showed her his books with some pride.

'Wouldn't mean much to you,' he said airily. 'You don't do Latin yet.'

'Not till we're eleven,' Jennifer agreed. 'But when I heard Mr Hinch was coming to you, I asked my mother if I could have lessons from him. I go straight after school Mondays, Wednesday and Fridays and he gives me an hour.' She smiled smugly. 'It will give me a good start on the rest of the class.' She twirled around the table and her navy gym slip twirled with her showing navy-blue knickers with a pocket in the leg. 'I'm the top of my year,' she mentioned casually.

'You would be,' Hanny returned resentfully. There was something about Jennifer McKinlay that put him on edge. Literally on an edge. Walking a tightrope.

'I asked if I could come up with him tonight. To see you.' She touched the china heart. 'I wanted to thank you, Hanny dear. I recognized your writing on the card. And I've brought you one in return.'

Hanny stayed very still afraid he might fall off his edge if he even breathed. She gave him an envelope covered in red ink crosses and decorated with an enormous heart shot through with an arrow. 'Go on, open it,' she urged.

He did so. Inside was a padded heart in blue silk fitted into a lace-edged card. She had written on the card, 'Keep me safe always. From your Valentine.'

She was giggling. 'It's a lavender bag. You put it in your handkerchief drawer. So you have to keep it safe.' She saw his face and said quickly, 'It's a joke, silly. It's not really my heart.'

'I know.' He almost told her that he'd had nothing to do with the china brooch. But all he said was, 'It's just so . . . sweet, Jen.'

'And so is this.' She touched the brooch. Then went on earnestly, 'The thing is, Hanny, I would have been your sweetheart – all the girls have them and you would have done nicely – but I've fallen in love. Properly in love. So this—' she nodded at his card '—it's just being friendly.'

He was amazed. He simply could not keep up with all this.

'Who . . . ? I mean . . . is it Lionel Barrymore? Or Errol Flynn?'

She laughed. 'Idiot! Of course it's not. It's a real man.' She looked around conspiratorially. 'Promise you won't tell a soul? He's married so it will have to be unrequited. Which somehow makes it more heartbreakingly beautiful, don't you think?'

'I – er – yes. I suppose it does.'

'Well, of course it does. Have you seen *Bittersweet*?

'No.'

'It was on at the Royal just before Christmas. It was so sad. I cried nearly all the time. That's like my love for Walter.'

'Cripes! I mean, good.'

'It's not good, Hanny.' She looked at him sadly. 'But then you wouldn't understand. Perhaps one day . . .'

He nodded, still unmoving.

She said, 'I think I can hear them coming. I'll talk to your mother while you're having your lesson. Goodbye, Hanny. I'll kiss you just to console you.' She leaned forward and planted her lips on his. He just stopped himself from flinching away. She moved her face around so that their lips sort of squashed and pleated themselves quite painfully. And then she was gone.

He stood there, staring at the gas fire. He had wanted to tell her that his real father had left him when he was a baby and now his adopted father had gone too, so that he was an orphan. He was glad he hadn't got round to it. She might have transferred her adoration from Walter Hinch to him!

But the remembrance of the kiss stayed with him during his lesson. And he determined that he would beat Jennifer McKinlay at Latin . . . and everything else.

The Jarama Valley campaign began on 5 February and continued until 23rd. In those eighteen days 16,000 men were killed. In a single day the British battalion lost 400 of its 600 men. The river ran red with their blood. And there was no victory for either side.

One of Jack's fellow soldiers brought his watch and the ring Tilly had given him over to the Red Cross hospital. The definite news of his death was almost a relief to Tilly and Austen. They had known that men were being killed in hundreds every day and they had dreaded that Tilly's nightmare would come true and Jack's mutilated body would be brought to the hospital still alive, still breathing, but damaged beyond repair. As Tilly said over and over again, 'He couldn't have stood being blind. Or maimed. He couldn't have stood that, Austen, could he?' And Austen, holding her quite naturally now, murmured, 'It would have been harder for him, my dear.' And above her head he closed his eyes and wondered what was to become of them.

Throughout March there was fighting around Guadalajara. The Republicans broke the Italian lines somehow and the Nationalists retreated to their old positions. Against all the odds, Madrid was holding its own.

But the price to pay was seen clearly at the hospital. The work load saved both Tilly and Austen from the depths of grief. They returned to their old ways, using the iron bed turn and turn about, sitting together at the beginning and end of each shift, smiling slightly, saying little.

And then a convoy of lorries arrived containing not only much needed supplies, but a new team of doctors and nurses. And mail.

Austen opened two letters from Hallie; they were like the kind of reports he was sending to her. He folded them carefully and put them inside his bag. The other letter was from Cadiz. He scanned it briefly, then made a small sound in his throat and read it again.

'Anything wrong, Austen?'

Tilly looked up from her mother's spidery copper-plate. The sudden movement of her head made the tiny cubicle spin around her. She dropped her chin to her chest and closed her eyes.

Austen said, 'Tilly! Are you all right? Lie down.' Austen stood and swept papers on to the floor, Cadiz' letter with them.

Tilly allowed him to lift her legs on to the bed. She put one hand beneath her cheek and kept her eyes closed.

Austen took the newly charged tea-caddy and went out to the stove to make tea. He knelt by her spooning it between her colourless lips.

'Was it bad news?' he asked when she opened her eyes at last.

She moved her head slightly in negation. 'They're fine. So are Hal and Hanny – in case she didn't say.' She smiled slightly. 'We can go home now, Austen. They'll take us back to Bilbao in the lorries.'

He picked up the letter from the floor and sat by her. They were both moving like elderly people.

He said slowly, 'I'm not sure about me, Tilly. You must go, of course. But Cadiz has sent me some rather startling news. It seems I am not a Rudolf.' He smiled at her. 'Isn't that rather ironic, my dear? All these years

377

I have behaved like a Rudolf and now I discover that my mother was expecting me before she married Mungay Rudolf.'

Tilly took his hand. 'The albatross has gone, Austen. You are free.'

'Quite.' He turned his own hand and held hers. 'Free to do what, Tilly? It makes no difference to Hallie and me. So it looks as if I am free to stay here and do the work which I seem to be able to do well.'

She gripped his hand. He said, 'I've told you so much, Tilly. You may as well know that without Jack, there is no point in my returning.'

'You and Hal—?'

'What we had . . . it's gone.'

She released his hand and turned her face away from him.

He frowned worriedly.

'Thank God for that convoy. You have done too much, Tilly. You must go home now.'

Tears formed around her lashes. She said, 'Austen, I cannot go alone. Truly. I hate to be a burden, my dear. But . . . I am carrying Jack's child, Austen. Please help me. Please.'

She turned back and picked up his hands. They were as red and raw as her own now.

'Austen, I must not lose Jack's baby!'

He stared at her for a long time. And then he began to weep. And after a little while, so did she.

Twenty-one

The lorry was closed with heavy canvas, which flapped like a sail as the convoy bucketed over muddy roads towards Burgos. Tilly looked ghastly. She was sick so often the food she managed to swallow was not inside her long enough to provide any nourishment. There were ten of them in the lorry, and eight of them sat tightly along one side to give the other side to Tilly. She lay with her head cradled by Austen, her emaciated body swathed in Red Cross blankets. For two nights they carried her into roadside hovels and made her as comfortable as they could. By the third day the sickness had abated, but she slept most of the time in a kind of delirium, waking to say wildly to Austen, 'Is the baby safe? I must not lose Jack's baby!'

The French doctor who had himself lost an arm during a bombing raid, was not optimistic. 'She is doing the best thing – to be lying. But during the day, the bumps—' He gesticulated graphically with his remaining arm. 'Not good.'

The third night they slept in an inn in Segovia.

Old Castile, the stronghold of Catholic Conservatism and Fascism, had fallen to the Nationalists back in the summer and the city was garrisoned and well organized. They were treated suspiciously – the Nationalists did not believe in neutrality – but well enough. Tilly was given a separate room and a girl brought a stone hot-water bottle and a glass of hot milk. The milk stayed down and Tilly managed to smile and reassure Austen.

'I feel better.' Her voice was on two levels, the top

register roughened. 'Austen, I would never have survived this without you. How can I ever—?'

'We have been together, my dear.' Austen chafed her hands between his. In spite of the hot-water bottle she was very cold. 'There is no question of thanks between us. You know that.'

She sighed acceptance, then said, 'It's all gone terribly wrong, Austen, hasn't it? You came out to take Jack home. And perhaps that would have helped you and Hal. And now Jack is dead and you are left with me – sickly and pregnant.'

He smiled. 'Listen. If we can get the baby home, it will be a victory. And if we cannot then we shall have saved ourselves and there will be work for us to do.'

Her eyes began to close. She whispered, 'D'you realize, I am Hanny's stepmother?'

It had not occurred to him. For some reason it made them laugh. He bent his head and kissed her fingers and heard her murmur, 'A courtier, no less.' And when he looked up she was asleep.

At Easter the family migrated to the Flower House. It had been Charles' suggestion; he was lonely at St George Street and found that visits to High House were not as they had been: Hallie was taking her pregnancy badly.

'To my surprise,' he told her, 'Mungay and Cadiz are all for it! I thought perhaps Hanny would like to invite Clive Maxwell.'

Hallie said, 'It will mean interrupting his Latin coaching.'

'Goodness gracious! Walter Hinch can come out to Clevedon, surely? There's a good enough train service and you are paying him well!'

Hallie looked at her father, surprised by his irritability.

He said, 'Well . . . really, Hal. You make so many difficulties about . . . everything lately!'

She flushed suddenly. 'Papa – I'm sorry. Truly. Of course we'll come. Walter will be here this evening and

I'll put it to him. He'll probably be pleased. Did you know Constantia von Gellhorn is staying with the Adams for a few weeks? Walter does not like Connie!'

Charles chuckled. The incident of the compost bin had gone down in the family annals by this time.

'Can't say I blame him. And what about Clive Maxwell?'

'I'll ask Marjorie. I'm sure she'll be delighted.'

'Excellent. Excellent. The sea air will do you good, my girl! Brisk walks along the esplanade every day, mind!'

She smiled dutifully. 'Very well, Dr Martinez! If you say so!'

'I certainly do. And maybe some of Cadiz' happiness will rub off on you too!'

'I hardly think—'

'I know – I know! Different circumstances. I just hoped that this bomb old Mungay has exploded about Austen would help you. You've been sounding off about him being a typical Rudolf as if it were a sin—'

'Father, I have not sounded off about anything!'

'Well . . . I got the impression from your aunt that you had reviewed his actions and discovered them to be—'

'I may have said to Aunt Cad – just once—'

'And now he is not a Rudolf at all! So surely you can think again about his motives?' He registered her expression and continued hurriedly, 'Never mind that. Putting my foot in it again. Just let us go to Clevedon for two or three weeks and act like normal human beings!'

Hallie swallowed convulsively. Then nodded.

That evening Jennifer McKinlay accompanied Walter to High House and was present when Hallie put forward their Easter plans.

'So we wondered, Walter, whether you would consider travelling to Clevedon two or three evenings to continue Hanny's coaching? It seems an imposition somehow but—'

'Not at all, Mrs Rudolf.' Walter was all smiles. 'I wonder whether I might bring my wife and the two children? They would thoroughly enjoy the airing.'

'Well, of course. In fact I'm sure Mr Mungay would be delighted to arrange for Sullivan to drive you down.'

'Really – I've no wish to be a bother—'

In the flurry of deprecations and reassurances which followed, Jennifer turned to Hanny.

'Will you invite me too, Hanny? We could have such fun. Crabbing and playing on Wain's Hill.'

'Ma says I can have Clive Maxwell.'

'Have you asked him yet?'

'No. She thought she'd better sound out his *mater* first.'

'Good. Then tell her you'd rather I came down with you.'

'But—'

The voices above them began to settle into normality. The adults were fixing dates and times.

Jennifer kept a polite smile nailed to her face. 'Look here, Hanny, you owe me something. Remember?'

She had never allowed him to forget. Recently she had discovered the words for what she had done. She had 'provided him with an alibi'. Her grandfather Adams had given her that one.

He said sullenly, 'Yeah.'

'This is when you pay up. I'm coming to Clevedon so that I can go on seeing Walter Hinch. Is that clear?'

As if to reinforce her statement, she took his hand and began to squeeze. Her grip had strengthened since they attended Margo at the wedding. He winced.

'It's clear,' he said hurriedly.

She turned, glowing, to Hallie.

'I say, Mrs Rudolf. Hanny's just invited me to come with you to Clevedon! Isn't that marvellous of him? I know I'll simply adore it!'

Hallie stared at her son. He seemed to be growing away from her quickly. She had no idea he had a penchant for Jennifer McKinlay. In fact, she would have sworn just the opposite.

'Well . . . I'm sure you will,' she said lamely. And then she added, 'In fact, you and Hanny could take your lessons together. If that would be all right with Mr Hinch?'

'Certainly.' His smile stretched from ear to ear. Coaching was turning out to be a profitable side line for the Hinch family.

So the six of them shared the Flower House and Mrs Hayle stayed with her daughter and came in daily to 'do' for them. Hallie enjoyed the rest of the practical house-keeping: since news of her pregnancy had been confided to the staff at High House, Meg and Cook had made such a fuss of her she was barely allowed to make her own tea let alone polish the brass and silver. It was one more thing that isolated her and she had taken to lying down in the afternoons until it was time for Hanny to come home.

At the Flower House, the kitchen was hers once Mrs Hayle had gone home. She concocted suppers and used the china her mother had used and discovered that there was still enjoyment to be got from doing quite ordinary things.

Cadiz had brought her precious ledgers with her but complained that Mungay 'seduced' her from them.

'We haven't come down here to do work,' he said robustly. 'This is our Easter holiday. And when the sun shines, we go outside! Is that clear?'

Cadiz looked roguishly at Hallie.

'What am I to do?' she asked, mock-plaintively.

This was more than Hallie could stand.

'Look,' she said tartly. 'Let me have them. You all insist on me taking a nap after lunch. I can lie on the bed and check them for you.'

383

Cadiz became serious. 'Darling, I was joking. Mungay is right. The blessed things can wait!'

But that afternoon, just as she was going downstairs to make the afternoon tea, Charles tapped on her door.

'Hal, it's me. And I've got those ledgers.'

'Father!' She opened the door and waved him inside. 'Surely Cadiz hasn't agreed to share her holy writ with useless old me?'

Charles put the three books on to her dressing table.

'Hal, I know you were good at figures at Saunton. All right, you loved poetry and singing and all the rest, but you were good at figures too. I think you should take an interest in what is happening.' He sat on the edge of her bed. 'Listen, my dear. Caddie was the driving force of our business. I admit it – I'm not proud of it, but I admit it.' He waited for a protest which did not come. So he cleared his throat and continued. 'Caddie's lost interest. You can see how it is with her and Mungay—'

'Yes.' Hallie looked at the ledgers without enthusiasm.

Charles said, 'Someone is going to have to know exactly what is happening. To help Hanny take over.'

She stared at him. 'Pa, what are you saying?'

'Dearest girl. I am saying that if you are right and your marriage is over – you will be bringing Hanny up for Jack.' He made a face. 'Even if he remarries, which is more than likely, he will want you to mother the child. Hanny is going to need you to train him, Hal. Can't you see that?'

She continued to stare at him. She had told him – and Caddie – that her marriage was over. And yet . . . and yet . . . there was a faint hope, just a hope, that she and Austen might have reconstructed something, however pitifully small . . . Her father's acceptance of the inevitable came as a shock.

He saw that and said urgently, 'Hal, even if you do patch it up, Hanny will no longer belong to him. How can he with Jack around? He will be your responsibility in the end.'

She nodded slowly.

He went on, 'Learn the business, Hal. You can do it. And – one day – you may well need to know every detail of sherry importing.'

She faltered, 'Oh, Pa, I'm no businesswoman.'

'Darling Hal, you could try. For Hanny. And for this baby.'

She looked from him to the ledgers. And at last she nodded.

'I will try.' she said.

Jennifer panted, 'Quick, you get in first! They'll never find us here!'

Hanny was very much afraid she was right. He wedged himself into the tiny fissure just below the cliff as awkwardly as he could.

'There's no room for you,' he said as if disappointed.

'Of course there is!' She fitted herself behind him so that he was practically sitting in her lap. He tried to hold himself apart.

'There.' She said with satisfaction. 'When they walk along the top path they'll never see us here.'

'They wouldn't see us if we were standing in front of them,' Hanny told her. 'They're always stopping to kiss and cuddle. It's disgusting!'

She giggled. 'And you, a Rudolf, saying that!'

'What?' he asked suspiciously.

'Oh, you needn't pretend not to know. I know girls grow up quicker than boys, but you're almost nine. You must have heard about the Rudolfs!'

'That they sell sugar?'

She almost exploded with stifled giggles. Then, without warning, she put her arms around his waist and held him close into her.

'That they're absolute devils when it comes to ladies!' she said.

It was as well she couldn't see his face. It was the picture of sheer astonishment.

'Pa? And Gramps?' He relaxed and puffed a laugh. 'You don't know what you're talking about!'

She squeezed him tighter still. She would surely be a wrestler when she grew up. Her muscles were like mantraps.

'Your gramps is the worst. There's a house in Hotwells Road where the ladies do nothing all day but kiss men. He goes there.'

Hanny could not stop laughing now however hard she squeezed.

'You're doolally!' he spluttered.

'Shut up, idiot! They'll hear us!' She put her mouth close to his ear. 'And your pa has only gone to Spain to stretch his wings.'

'Stretch his wings? What d'you mean?'

She hesitated then admitted, 'That's what my mother told my father when *he* wanted to go. He said if Austen Rudolf could do it, so could he. And she said Austen Rudolf had only gone to stretch his wings.'

'Oh.' Hanny was properly nonplussed now. What was more, so was she.

Her breath was tickling his ear but he could not move. It had been a blistering scramble down the cliff face to this crack in the rock. She had done well. She could do everything as well as he could. Except Latin. He grinned to himself recalling the marks from their last test. And he did not really mind having his back pressed into her tummy like this. Once he was used to it, it wasn't entirely unpleasant.

She felt him relaxing and suddenly bit his ear and he exclaimed.

'Shut up!' She was frantic. 'They're coming!'

Sure enough, just above their heads they could feel as well as hear, footsteps approaching. Then they stilled. Hanny and Jennifer held their breath.

Aunty Cad's voice came to them sibilant, yet loud, like the whispering gallery at Gloucester Cathedral.

'Oh, my dearest, dear . . .'

386

Then Gramps said, 'Caddie, I want you to hold these moments inside you. Later – they will make you happy.'

'Don't speak like that, Mungay. Please.'

'Darling, I believe what I am saying. It is possible to absorb happiness. Like blotting paper. Retain it.'

She began to weep. 'I don't believe you. Mungay, I can't bear it if you leave me now.'

And he said, 'I am not leaving you now, you goose. But I am twenty years older than you, Cad, and in the very nature of things I should go first.'

There was another silence. Hanny could imagine only too well what was happening. It was absolutely sick-making. No wonder Ma hadn't been keen on this holiday.

And then, when both children had started to breathe very carefully, there came a small laugh from above.

'We behave like a couple of lovesick schoolchildren,' Aunt Cad said, but without any shame at all. 'And we'd better get on. Hanny and Jennifer move fast. We must catch them up.'

Gramps must have made an attempt to detain her because there came sounds of scuffling and much laughter and then the footsteps began again and moved on.

Hanny oozed out of the 'cave' swiftly. Jennifer stayed where she was, eyes unexpectedly full of tears.

'What's up?' Hanny said apprehensively. 'Did I squash you?'

'No. It's just so . . . lovely.' Jennifer looked at him. 'It makes me realize . . . the whole world is filled with it, Hanny. It's wonderful.'

Hanny admitted cautiously, 'It was fun. It'll be funnier still when we creep up behind them.'

'I don't mean *fun*!' she snapped scornfully, emerging at last, tears forgotten. 'I mean *love*!' She eyed him consideringly. 'I even felt love for you then, Hanny Rudolf.'

'Cripes!'

She smiled. 'Don't get above yourself. My heart still belongs to Walter. But – occasionally – in the years to come – I may take pity on you.'

'Cripes!' he repeated.

She began to scramble back up the rock face. Her socks ended at her knees and above that was lots of white leg covered in a down of golden hair. Her knickers were covered in flowers to match her dress.

She turned and hauled him up. She was a terrific climber.

'Come on. Let's get over the hedge on the other side and go to the top of the hill. We can look down on them. I bet they're kissing again!'

This struck Hanny as both boring and tasteless, but he knew better than to argue with Jennifer McKinlay. He needed all his powers to beat her at whatever they were doing.

He was first on the bare scraped-grass summit of Wains Hill. Below them Gramps and Aunt Cad were standing on one of the seats shading their eyes, looking to where the path curled on to the beach. Jennifer joined him and dragged him behind a tree.

'They're bound to look up here, you idiot!' she said. 'Keep out of sight, for goodness' sake!'

The wind was amazing up here. He wanted to shout at Aunt Cad and run down to meet her and be swung by Gramps. But Jennifer had other ideas.

'They'll go back. And they'll see where we climbed down. And they'll think we've fallen into the sea!' She hugged herself gleefully. 'They'll go absolutely potty! Fire brigade. Coastguards. It'll be a hoot!'

'But they'll worry,' Hanny bleated.

She rounded on him. 'Don't you dare spoil it all now, Hanny Rudolf!' She caught his arm and nearly tore it off. 'This is like Tom Sawyer. When he went to his own funeral!'

That put a different face on it. He and Clive played

Tom Sawyer and Huck Finn quite often; especially now that Clive thought he was a great actor.

They slithered and crept down the hill to hide behind the hedge which gave them front seats for what followed. Aunt Cad behaved exactly as Jennifer had forecast. She went completely potty. She was the first to find the broken earth at the lip of the path and within three seconds she was weeping and wailing and wringing her hands like someone demented. It was bad enough to see his brisk business-like aunt going all cow's eyes over Gramps, but this was too much to bear. He broke cover and flung himself on them both. There was a great deal of shouting and hugging; Gramps telling him off, Aunt Cad saying she didn't care so long as he was safe, Jennifer standing to one side looking at him like the angel of death.

When they walked – barely six yards ahead and very sedately – back to the house, she said, 'You certainly know how to ruin a good joke, don't you, Hanover?'

He tried to explain. 'It was so horrid when my father told me he wasn't my father, Jen. You don't know. Honestly. It was. And Ma isn't really my ma. But then I thought, I am their family. My mother was my father's sister and my father was my mother's brother.' He looked at her, baffled by it all. 'And Aunt Cad and Gramps *are* Aunt Cad and Gramps. Before and now. So I couldn't do that to them, could I?'

She considered it.

'Cripes—' It was a word boys used and she determined it was now her word. 'Cripes. If I found out Aunt Margo was my mother and Uncle Otto my father, I think I'd kill myself!'

'Well, I didn't know my mother, of course. But she sounds better than your Aunt Margo. And my father is English.'

'Yes.' She looked at him, seeing him in a new light. 'Actually, Hanny, I've always looked after you, haven't

I?' She sighed deeply. 'It looks as if I'll always have to.'
And she put her arm through his and held him tightly.
Too tightly.

He heard Aunt Cad whisper to Gramps, 'Look at that.
Isn't it sweet?'

But he didn't mind too much. Because he kept
thinking of Aunt Cad going potty when she thought he
was dead. Whatever happened, they still wanted him.

They reached Burgos in mid-March and there they
stuck.

The Republicans still held the coastal strip which
included the port of Bilbao; General Mola was planning
an all-out offensive on this front and the authorities in
Burgos refused to allow the convoy through until the
attack was over.

The French doctor tried to explain it to Austen.

'It is true we are neutral and that we all have our Red
Cross papers. But the argument in the town hall is that
our safety is the responsibility of the Nationalist government – New Spain. And that cannot be guaranteed until
Bilbao has fallen.'

'But the convoy entered from Bilbao! The passage out
was guaranteed by both sides!'

'That is so.' The Frenchman put his one hand on
Austen's arm. 'If there is to be fighting, my friend, it is
better to stay here. Have patience. Dr Martin needs the
rest. And the weather is now good.'

They were housed near the cathedral in comparative
luxury, each with their own room, a bath between
no more than six people. It was obvious, orders had
gone out to make a good impression. When they arrived
in Geneva they were supposed to report that the
Nationalists had arranged their safe passage.

Austen fretted at first, but as the days went by it was
obvious the French doctor was right and the enforced
delay was good for Tilly. She came downstairs for meals
and on a particularly sunny day at the end of the month,

she walked with Austen to the cathedral to view the tomb of El Cid.

The enormous nave with its gilded angels was awe-inspiring after the devastation of Madrid. They walked down the central aisle, through rainbows, of light cast from the stained windows, Tilly leaning slightly on his arm.

He said, 'We're like tourists. It is all so unreal.'

'That has been the case all along,' she murmured. 'The small area of neutrality around the hospital. In the midst of that . . . frightfulness.'

He felt her shudder and led her into one of the pews to sit down. It was a canopied pew. In front of them the old oak had been carved with careful initials.

'Choristers.' He ran his fingers over grooves that spelled E.C. 'They're the same the world over, it seems.'

'You can't blame them here.' She smiled, looking around her. 'They can't be seen at all by. the congregation. They could get up to anything!'

'She's got an eye on them.' Austen nodded at a Madonna apparently fixing them with a stern gaze. 'I wonder they had the nerve to get out a knife and hack away under that stare!'

'Ah. Perhaps they were famous. For instance, E.C. could have been the man himself!'

Austen raised his brows at her.

She said, 'El Cid!'

They both laughed, then stopped abruptly as the big west doors were opened and blocked with door stops.

Tilly peered around the edge of the canopy.

'Gorblimey,' she said in the cockney she had picked up from the Settlement. 'Nobs is a-coming, guv! What do we do?'

'Stay put. We can't be seen.'

Austen too leaned forward to look down the long aisle at the burst of sunlight from the double doors. 'Must be important to open them up. Everyone else has to use the postern.'

She said, almost like the old Tilly, 'I say, Austen. This is rather fun, isn't it?'

He focused her and grinned with pleasure. 'Fun. Yes. That is what it is, isn't it? Fun!'

The arched doorway was manned by ushers, and then a man in full uniform appeared with another man in morning dress.

'Gorblimey,' Austen mimicked Tilly now. 'It's only the Generalissimo himself!'

'Franco?' she breathed.

'Franco,' he assented. 'And I think . . . yes, it is . . . the other man is von Faupel. The German ambassador. I've seen him a couple of times in a closed car. He presented his credentials just before we arrived.' He looked at her again and turned down his mouth. 'Something's afoot, Tilly.'

'Had we better show ourselves? We might be shot for spies if we're discovered.'

She was smiling but half serious. However, there was no fear of them understanding anything that was said. There was a great deal of genuflecting towards the altar and the two men, trailed by a retinue of wives and guards, spoke through an interpreter, obviously making polite comments rather than plots.

They turned into the transept to view the tomb of El Cid; the women drifted away examining various pictures, obviously very bored. The two in the choir stall kept very still and quiet. Austen closed his eyes and thought about the news in Caddie's letter. He had set it aside for the past three weeks but now he thought of his mother with new understanding. He wondered what Hallie made of it all. She had finished with him whatever his name or breeding. It did not seem to matter as much as it had. Jack's death and Tilly's safety weighed on him too heavily to permit any room for other anxieties. He no longer knew what he wanted from life. He had conquered his fear of war, he had failed to bring Jack home; he was doing his best by Tilly.

He heard Tilly's intake of breath and looked at her sharply.

She was leaning forward; too far forward. He pulled her back.

'Look!' she mouthed at him. 'Look at that woman!'

Very cautiously he peered around the canopy. And saw Margo.

It was so unexpected he nearly let out a shout of recognition. It was most definitely Margo; no doubt about that. She was standing stockily in the centre of the aisle, listening to another woman who was evidently pontificating on the icons. Margo was nodding, turning her head in the direction of the pointing finger. Austen was shocked at her appearance. She had always had a round pretty face, now she had developed jowls and bags beneath her eyes.

As they both stared, undecided whether to make themselves known, the men reappeared and the women coagulated behind them and began to move towards the sunlight. Von Faupel turned and said something over his shoulder and one of his retinue spoke and was translated for Franco's benefit. The Generalissimo nodded, evidently well pleased and they all went through the door. Margo fell in with the ambassador's man. Which was natural because Austen now saw he was Otto von Gellhorn.

Tilly breathed deeply, stretching her shoulders as if she had been imprisoned in stocks.

'Why on earth didn't we go and say hello to Margo? We're not at war – we must be mad!' she exclaimed, angry with herself for having made the incident into a conspiracy.

Austen shook his head. 'We'll look her up – I'll make some proper enquiries. It would have embarrassed her terribly if we'd leapt out when she was doing her stuff.'

He handed her down the chancel steps and she said, 'But what is she *doing* here?'

'Accompanying her husband, I suppose. It would be interesting to know what *he* is doing here.'

Tilly said, 'We can find out. We invite her round to the hotel and we ask her.' She grinned suddenly. 'She'll be absolutely amazed to see us!'

'I wonder. She must know you're here. Hallie would have written. Perhaps she's come to find you.'

Tilly made a rude noise with her teeth. 'She was going off me when I was there for Eva's birth. She hadn't really thought about my being Jewish till then.'

Austen smiled at her. It was good to hear her talking so normally again.

They thought they had missed her because the next day the Generalissimo returned to his military headquarters in Salamanca and von Faupel went with him, accompanied by three aides. Austen grappled with the telephone in the foyer and to his surprise eventually heard Margo's voice on the other end.

He said, 'Margo? We thought you must have left Segovia this morning. This is Austen Rudolf.' There was a pause and he said, 'That is Margo von Gellhorn, is it not?'

'My *God*!' Her voice exploded across the line. 'Austen? Is it really you? Where are you? Are you phoning from home? Oh my God, is Hal all right?'

'Yes. As far as I know. It's all right, Margo. I am phoning from the old Alcazar. The hotel next to the cathedral. We saw you there yesterday and have been trying to get in touch—'

'You're in *Burgos*? You and Hal? Oh, how wonderful! I've been so miserable and it's all so hopeless and now, suddenly, there you are!'

'Not Hal. Tilly. Tilly and I are with the Red Cross convoy trying to get home. We've been here for some time. Why don't you come and see us?'

There was a small silence. 'Tilly? You and Tilly? What about Hal?'

'Don't be silly, Margo. Hal could not have left Hanny even if she'd wanted to.'

'But you and Tilly . . . I mean . . . have you run away or something?'

He had forgotten how aggravating she could be. He repeated slowly, 'We are with the Red Cross, Margo. Tilly is a doctor and has been working in the Red Cross hospital in Madrid. And I have been doing some work on the wards.'

She was honestly bewildered. 'But why? I mean . . . both of you. Why?'

He forced a laugh. 'Why don't you come and have tea at the hotel and you can ask Tilly all the questions you wish?'

'Not you?'

'I'll wait and see you then I can make myself scarce. I've had to do it in the past when you girls want to talk.'

'Well, all right. It will be marvellous to see Tilly. Yes. All right.'

She arrived an hour later, her well-upholstered linen suit in striking contrast to Tilly's skimpy summer dress.

She could not get over how ill Tilly looked.

'My dear, you've been working too hard!'

Tilly smiled. 'Yes. I have actually. But I'm going to have a long rest. And I'm all right. That's the main thing.' She suddenly put her arms around Margo and hugged her. 'I am so lucky, Margo. I am all right.'

Margo returned the hug but drew back almost immediately.

'Is it catching? What has been the matter?'

Tilly stared and then burst out laughing.

'Oh, Margo – you'll never change!' She shook her head at Austen. 'You won't catch what I've got. Anyway you've had it four times already!'

Margo frowned and then opened her mouth and eyes together.

'My God. You're not pregnant?' She looked aghast at Tilly's nod. 'Oh my God, you poor darling! Austen—'

Austen laughed too. 'Tilly is married, Margo! It's all quite above-board and Bristol-fashion!'

Margo dropped head and shoulders in relief. Then she sat down, dimpling suddenly so that it was possible to see the Margo Adams beneath the Margo von Gellhorn.

'Darling, you've come to the right person. I can give you advice, help, get you out of this hole, find you a hospital – if you're with the Red Cross you'll know there are some wonderful nursing homes in Geneva—'

Tilly did not take her seriously.

'There are over forty of us, Margo! And now that the offensive has begun we're resigned to waiting. The weather has been continuously wet until the last few days. And what with the fortifications around Bilbao and the mountains . . . I think it will become a stalemate like Madrid. In which case, we should be able to drive through the lines once everything has dried up.'

Margo smiled. 'It won't be a stalemate, Tilly. Not for long. That's why we're here.'

Austen had been on the point of leaving them for the past ten minutes. Tilly put her hand on his arm.

'Sit down, Austen. Perhaps you should hear what Margo has to say.'

He obeyed her. He had thought the unlikeliness of this meeting and Tilly's marriage to Jack, would have demanded time and privacy. Apparently Margo needed neither.

'Weren't you – aren't you surprised to see me here?' She sounded like an excited schoolgirl with a secret.

Tilly said drily, 'Obviously more surprised than you are to see us!'

'Well, I'm astounded – of course! But I might have guessed . . . good-works Tilly. Married, pregnant – I suppose Hal sent you out to bring her back, Austen?'

He looked at the full face which seemed to him quite vapid.

'Something like that,' he agreed.

'I don't do good works.' She dimpled again. 'Only for myself!' She put her hands on the table and pushed herself back into her chair portentously. 'Otto landed the contract to supply ammunition to the Condors!'

Austen and Tilly recalled the bombing raids carried out by the crack German squadron over Madrid. They were silent.

Margo went on enthusiastically, 'We were in the Führer's box you know, for the Olympic Games. It was spectacular. I cannot begin to tell you. Anyway, he'd already decided to help Spain – even then. His foresight is staggering. We were invited to a soirée and the deal was done. Otto has large interests in Krupps Munitions and has been angling for this deal for ages.' She leaned forward. 'But the best thing was, he fell for me! The Führer! He said I was pure Aryan. I told him how much I should adore to see Spain and he turned to Otto there and then and said why didn't he go with von Faupel to advise him, and why didn't I accompany them!' Her eyes were sparkling. 'My dears, what could Otto do? If he could have made me pregnant again – but I've found this wonderful cream he doesn't even know about . . .' She glanced at Austen and apologized quickly. 'I'm sorry, Austen, I forgot how straitlaced you are. Anyway, here I am!'

He said, 'And what makes you think you can arrange for us to leave Spain?'

'Well, not me exactly. The Condors, my dear! They're going to blitzkrieg one of the coastal towns. As an example. The Republicans will cave in immediately – it's much better that way. Saves time and lives in the end. I would say the roads will be cleared in a week.' She hesitated. 'Maybe two.' She leaned back again. 'I'll find out for you. How's that?'

Tilly had gone very pale again.

Austen said quietly, 'Are you all right? Would you like to lie down?'

'No.' She leaned forward in her turn. 'Margo, is it

397

possible – remotely possible – that you could stop this bombing – this blitzkrieg?'

Margo laughed. 'Don't be silly, darling. I'm the wife of the arms supplier. Not Mata Hari. And don't look at me like that, all holier-than-thou! I didn't start this war, you know. The Spanish are doing it to each other. And the sooner it's brought to an end – the Führer says the end always justifies the means, and in this case . . .'

Austen said, 'Tilly, she's right. She cannot stop it and neither can we.' He slowed his voice emphatically. 'There is nothing we can do. Nothing.'

Margo nodded. 'Darling, I know it's all ghastly, but Austen is right. We're outside all the plotting and planning – you must not let it upset you!'

Tilly said harshly, 'Then why have you come? To watch the raid? Austen and I have seen plenty. It's not terribly good entertainment.'

Margo blanched. 'Tilly – my dear – you sound as if you hate me! Do you really think I've arrived in some baggage train to watch a battle? My dear, I came with a definite purpose. I came to find Jack Martinez.'

'You what?'

'I came to find Jack. Hallie put the idea into my head when she stayed with me for little Otto's birth. She was so worried. Jack had sort of disappeared and she was afraid he might be in the hands of the *Falangistos*.'

Austen cleared his throat but Tilly got in first. She said very clearly, 'Jack is dead, Margo. He was in the battle of the Jarama Valley. The British Battalion of the Eleventh International Brigade was practically wiped out. Before the battle we were married. And I am now expecting his child. That is why I am so thankful to be well again.'

If she had thrown a bucket of water over Margo she could not have silenced her so completely. She stayed exactly where she was, filling the chair to overflowing, her head sunk into her neck, her hands on the table before her. And then, as the silence became unbearable, tears flowed effortlessly down her cheeks.

Austen said, 'Margo – please—'

She shook her head almost irritably. 'Shut up, Austen. You don't understand. Tilly does. She knows what she has done to me.'

Tilly said, 'Jack and I were in love, Margo. That's why we got married.'

'Rubbish. You probably nursed him in that hospital of yours. And we all know that wounded men fall for their nurses.'

Austen said irrelevantly, 'Tilly is a doctor, not a nurse.'

'Shut *up*!' Margo repeated. 'Whatever she is, he did not love her. Not properly. He loved wild women. He loved your sister. And he loved me.'

Austen felt Tilly shrink slightly. He said, 'I was there, Margo. I have never seen two people more deeply in love than Jack and Tilly. And I shall never forget it. I am thankful – deeply thankful – that if he had to die, he had had that wonderful time with a wonderful woman.'

Margo was silent again. Then she held out a hand. 'Hanky,' she said.

Austen placed his pocket handkerchief in her gloved palm and she dabbed at her eyes. He tightened his hold on Tilly.

Tilly turned and smiled at him. 'Austen, it's all right. Margo and I are old friends and we shall . . . accommodate this quite quickly. You can go for your walk now.'

He said, 'I'm not leaving you.'

Margo blew her nose. 'Oh, for goodness' sake, Austen! D'you think I'm going to scratch Tilly's eyes out? I'm crying because Jack's dead, not because he married one of my best friends.' She looked at Tilly. 'I know I couldn't have him. I suppose if I could have chosen anyone . . .' She blew her nose again. 'Oh God. Just to know he was somewhere in the world was . . . something. Now – what is left?'

'I thought like that too.' Tilly put a hand on her abdomen. 'But there's the child, Margo. And you have four!'

'Oh God. The children. You don't know what you're saying. Yet.'

Tilly turned to Austen meaningfully. 'Why don't you go and talk to Benedict,' she said brightly. Benedict was the French doctor who had taken charge of the convoy.

Margo said, 'For God's sake don't tell him what I have told you, Austen. It's more than my life is worth.'

But Tilly was pressing his arm.

He said, 'All right.' And went to find the Frenchman.

Margo sighed. 'How do you stand him? How does Hal stand him?'

'He's a wonderful man.' Tilly smiled. 'Strange how things work out. If Jack hadn't been out here, Austen wouldn't have come to find him and I'd never know how lucky Hal is.'

'No. Neither of us liked that match did we? I still don't. Hal was as miserable as sin when she stayed at the *schloss*. All his fault.'

Tilly kept smiling but changed the subject firmly.

'How are you? How are the girls? And the boy – little Otto?'

'And he will be the last one, I assure you of that!' Margo continued to dab with Austen's handkerchief but her face was smooth again. 'Otto isn't delighted, of course, but he's got his son and that's all he worries about.'

Tilly's smile widened slightly.

'And Connie?'

Margo put the handkerchief in her lap and sighed.

'I knew Connie's nose would be put out of joint by little Otto. Poor baby. *Grossmutter* got to the nursery in time, of course. And we've had bars put over the windows. But Connie has gone to stay with my parents for a while. In Bristol.'

'You mean—?'

'She tried to throw him out of the bloody window. Yes.'

Tilly almost laughed. She had been to the *schloss* several times. The nursery was in a turret. She did not dare pursue the matter for fear of exploding into unseemly giggles. It must be hysteria.

Margo said lugubriously, 'Otto's not keen, obviously. He's afraid Mummy and Daddy will spoil her. But he's less keen on her murdering his son and heir so—'

It was too much. Tilly put her hands to her face.

Margo said anxiously, 'Darling, I didn't mean to upset you. It was just a schoolgirl crush I had on Jack. I'm really pleased . . . oh, Tilly, don't cry.' She herself began to hiccough on sobs. 'Darling, I know how you feel. Poor Jack. Oh, the sooner this horrid war is over the better. Surely you can see that, Tilly? And after it's all done with, I'll come to collect Connie, and we can get together like old times and – and – be happy!'

And she clutched Austen's handkerchief to her face and broke down completely. And behind her hands, Tilly wept with laughter.

Twenty-two

Hanny started his summer term on 15 April and arrived home that evening with a smile from ear to ear.

'I'm in the Junior Second Eleven!'

Hallie, almost obsessively involved with the new duties on wine imported from Germany, was slow on the uptake.

'Is that good?' she asked.

Hanny was outraged. 'It's not good. It's – it's – absolutely top-hole! It's a record. No-one has played cricket for Colston's until they're nine! They just let them go into the nets for practice and to get used to the pads and everything! But because Daddy – Uncle Austen – coached me and Sully bowled those slow googlies, I'm good enough for the Seconds! It means I shall have to play away, Ma! We go in a charabanc and if we win they let us sing songs on the way home – it's – it's—'

'Absolutely top-hole,' Hallie supplied, smiling comprehension at last. 'Congratulations, darling.' She picked up his satchel busily and risked adding, 'Takes me back. My brother was cricket mad.'

Hanny was still. 'Do you mean my real father?' he asked slowly.

'Yes. He played for all the villages between here and Clevedon.'

'Oh.' Hanny tugged at his tie which was halfway around his neck. 'Do I take after him, Ma?'

'Well, in that you do.' She smiled at him. 'And he was no good at Latin.'

Hanny brightened suddenly. 'Well, I am!' He took his

satchel from her and unbuckled it. 'We had a test. And old Cottage Loaf couldn't believe it! Look – here it is. Top marks!'

'Hanny!' She was delighted. Somewhere, somehow Hanny had found that precious motivation Miss Bush had been so keen on.

Then he said smugly, 'So I take after Pa for that, don't I?'

She stared at him caught off guard for a moment.

He said casually, 'It's quite good really, isn't it? Having two fathers I mean. Between them they're bound to be pretty good at everything, aren't they?'

She swallowed. 'I suppose so.'

He gave his lovely schoolboy grin and suddenly hugged her.

'Trouble is, I've only got one Ma though!' he said. And as if it were the biggest joke in the world he went into helpless laughter.

Hallie began to think things were looking up. Dr Hesterman was satisfied with her and thought the baby would be born on 15 July. Until the holiday at Clevedon she had thought she was completely uninterested in the baby. She had even wondered whether she would hate it. But some time during those three weeks in unexpected sunshine, with regular walks and the company of her family, the bump in her abdomen had swelled into something that could not be hidden by a full skirt. Cadiz took her into Hill Road to buy some smocks. It had been more exciting than any shopping she had done before. She had always been terribly shy about buying clothes, trying them on quickly and refusing to emerge from the changing-room to show them off. Now she postured before the mirror on the thick grey carpet of Edgar's, putting her hands in the big patch pockets and holding the smock forward like the models did on the London catwalks.

'I'll wear this one now,' she told the assistant. She

smiled at Cadiz. 'Don't you love these big white daisies on the dark-blue background?'

'Yes.' Cadiz smiled, liking it all very much indeed. 'But you don't need a smock yet, darling. Your figure has hardly changed.'

Hallie raised astonished brows. 'I'm enormous!' she maintained. 'Besides . . . I want people to know about this,' and she patted her stomach like Margo had done. Proudly, even smugly.

'So you should,' Cadiz agreed stoutly. 'And the blue exactly matches your eyes.'

As the assistant went to wrap the other ones, Cadiz hugged her niece delightedly. 'You are looking so beautiful, Hal. Do you realize that?'

'You don't think I'll go like Margo? All sort of stodgy?'

'No. I most certainly do not think you will go like Margo.'

Cadiz was finding a new angle in her relationship with Hallie. She was delighted by Hallie's determination to get the hang of the wine importing business. During their last week at the Flower House the four adults sat over the ledgers and talked about the future of the House of Martinez.

Hallie said, 'You sound as if we are starting afresh. Carlos Martinez started this ball rolling a long time ago! About the same time as your Hanover Rudolf got involved with the South Sea Bubble, Mungay!'

It was Mungay who said, 'We're all going to have to start afresh. If Germany continues to expand as they are doing now, there will be another war.'

She said quickly, 'Austen is too old now—'

His dark eyes lifted quickly to hers and she stopped speaking.

He said quietly, 'Yes. But it might not be that soon, Hal. In nine years' time Hanny could go to war.'

'Oh no!' the protest was like a cry for help and Charles put a protective arm around her shoulders.

'It'll never come to war. Not again. They learned their lessons in 1918.'

No-one answered him.

Cadiz said after a while, 'What we need to do is to import from as many different places as possible. So that if half of them are cut off by – by any kind of crisis – we still have the other half. And –' she smiled at Hallie '– we should explore the possibility of British wines. That is something you could do, Hal. You and your father could go to Devon and Cornwall this summer and find out who is growing grapes – offer help – some kind of deal – for sole rights—'

Hallie said, 'There's a man near Porthmeor. He's supposed to be a bit eccentric. But he makes wine from his own grapes and we tried a bottle one year. We both liked it.' She heard herself talking like any married woman and looked up at her father almost defiantly. 'Father, you've never been to Porthmeor, have you? It's delightful. We could take Hanny for Whitsun perhaps.'

'Or sooner,' Cadiz looked at the smock-covered bump. 'We could look after Hanny.'

Mungay said thoughtfully, 'We could do the same with local sugar growing, of course. There are beet fields in East Anglia. If we could put money into some of the farms we could encourage home-produced sugar—'

'Are you suggesting I go up to East Anglia too?' Hallie asked, laughing.

'Why not? You're so patently honest and straight-forward, Hal. You could convince the people on the ground – literally – that we're offering them something worth having.'

Hallie was suddenly frightened. 'I'm not sure about leaving Hanny for so long. It's a bit tricky with school and everything.'

Mungay said, 'We could move into High House. Heaven knows I'm familiar with the ropes there.'

Cadiz agreed enthusiastically. 'I've never lived on the Downs. We could take Mrs Hayle with us as we have done here and close up Dowry Square for a while.'

Hallie thought quite definitely that things were moving too quickly now. She took a deep breath, could think of no more objections and said, 'Why not?'

When they were preparing for bed – almost demurely because the window was opened on to the upper verandah and Jennifer McKinlay was in the room next to theirs – Cadiz said exultantly, 'We should have done this ages ago!'

Mungay said, 'Done what? Undressed ourselves instead of each other?'

Cadiz stifled a laugh. 'You – wicked old man!' She sobered. 'No. I meant we should have pushed Hal. She was in a pit and she needed help to get out of it and we all ignored her.'

Mungay stared at the trouser press gloomily. 'She wouldn't have accepted help. Not till now.'

'You mean since Charles forced her to look at my ledgers?'

'Not only that. Since she began to feel better about the baby.' He watched her as she took the trousers from him and put them in the press. He said, 'You know, it's Austen's child as well, Cad. She mustn't try to forget that.'

'Do you think she is?' Caddie looked up from the trousers.

'I don't know. Perhaps we could talk about him more. She doesn't. Neither does Hanny.'

She hung up the press consideringly, then said, 'You sound sorry for Austen, Mungay.'

He gave a small self-deprecatory laugh. 'Strange thing, Cad. I'd made myself forget – over the years – that Austen wasn't my son. And I didn't like him all that much. He seemed . . . alien. Now that I've admitted to you – and to myself – that he is nothing to do with me, I can understand him. And, yes, I think I am sorry for him.'

She came to him, put her arms around his waist and her cheek on his chest.

'My darling Mungay. Nobody knows you. Not really. You are so sensitive.'

He threw back his head and shouted a laugh immediately stifled because of Jennifer.

'But really, Cad! Sensitive? Whoever heard of a Rudolf being sensitive?'

There were tears in her eyes as she looked at him. 'I did. I heard.' She drew his head down and kissed him. 'Don't worry, my dearest dear. Hanny and Hal might not speak often of your son, but he is very much in their minds.'

He stared into her dark wet eyes. 'My son?'

She kissed him again. 'I think you qualify,' she whispered.

So, for the last two weeks in that sunny April, Sully drove Hallie to Denmark Street and she worked through the present figures with Charles and Cadiz, checked the orders from the Harz vineyards, the increase in imports from the Loire district to compensate for the loss of the Castillo grapes, talked to the blender, watched the casks being loaded on to the drays and drove ahead of them to the goods depot in Bristol where they were loaded on to special flat wagons all painted 'Martinez' destined for a dozen different destinations. She emerged from the cellars festooned with cobwebs, she went into the stables with a supply of carrots and got to know the horses as well as she'd known them as a small child. When Cadiz protested – 'You look like the Witch of Endor and you smell like a drain!' – she laughed and said, 'You think I should wear your sombrero and leather skirt and order people about?'

Cadiz opened her eyes wide. 'You are becoming very pert since your tummy grew!' she declared vulgarly. 'Talking of which, you wouldn't get into my leather skirt!'

Hallie laughed again.

Hanny was playing his first cricket match for the school that afternoon; he continued to do excellently in Latin and Mr Baker had telephoned congratulations only the day before; she herself felt so fit she was doing a full day's work and enjoying every minute of it. And surely, surely, Austen would bring Jack home very soon and they could sort something out. She did not let herself think further. Jack would want her to keep Hanny; she was sure of that. She blotted out anything past there.

Sully picked her up at midday so that she could rest before going to Colston's for the cricket. And when she reached home there was a letter on the hall table from Austen. It was thicker than usual and as she fitted the paper knife into the envelope she discovered she was trembling. The last letter had told her that Tilly and he planned to bribe their way into Madrid and fetch Jack out by hook or by crook.

This one was dated 15 April, the day Hanny had started his summer term. It had taken only fifteen days to reach her which was a record.

She took it into the morning room and sat by the window in a bar of sunlight and imagined Austen touching this same paper, writing these words, his dark face, which she had always considered typically Rudolf, bent over it seriously. Perhaps imagining her.

Dear Hallie,
We have been in Burgos for two weeks now and Tilly has improved enormously. I really think we shall arrive home with the baby safe and sound. It has become an obsession for both of us.

Hallie looked up, frowning. She knew nothing of any baby.

It is possible we may be forced to stay here another week, even two. The Nationalist offensive on Bilbao is bogged down by very wet weather and there is apparently no way our convoy can get through.

Hallie's frown deepened. She glanced at the date again. Beneath it was the stark word, 'Burgos'. So they were being sent home in a Red Cross convoy.

We know quite a bit about the battle because you will be amazed to hear that Margo is here also!

Hallie exclaimed aloud and lowered her head closer to the sheet of notepaper as if she could read between the lines.

She is accompanying her husband who is himself attached to General Franco's staff. He is supplying arms to the Nationalists – did you realize he is something to do with Krupps, the munitions factory in Germany? Tilly and I are horrified, of course, but have accepted that there is nothing Margo can do about it. Meanwhile she is a valuable source of information. She has told us that the Condors will be bombing Bilbao quite soon. We are appalled and depressed. Margo keeps assuring us that the means justify the end and a quick conclusion to this particular campaign will save lives. You can imagine this philosophy cuts very little ice with Tilly. I am going along with it as I do not wish her to become over-anxious again.

On a better note, I am pleased to tell you that Margo did not come to Spain with her husband in order to watch any battles. She came to find Jack. When Tilly told her that Jack had died at Jarama, she was devastated. Even more so that Tilly and he had married and Tilly is now expecting his child. All credit to her, she quickly swallowed her own grief and . . .

Hallie had indeed cried out this time. Meg arrived at a gallop but was waved away. Hallie sat for a long moment trying to marshal her thoughts coherently, then looked again at the letter.

'. . . Jack had died at Jarama . . .'

Jack had died. Jack was dead. And had been dead for some time.

She closed her eyes and squeezed them tightly until the muscles ached. Then opened them and went to the desk in the corner. She removed a sheaf of newspaper cuttings and spread them out. One of them was headed, FOUR HUNDRED BRITISH DIE AT THE BATTLE OF THE JARAMA VALLEY. The newspaper was dated 23 February.

She stared at the cutting. It was obvious that at least one of Austen's letters had gone astray. Yet if Jack had died over two months ago, she would have known. She would have felt the pang of loss. He was her brother and they were linked in some way and if that link had been broken . . . she shoved the cuttings into a drawer and went back to the window.

'. . . Jack had died at Jarama . . .'

She forced herself to speak the words aloud and then to continue reading.

she was devastated. Even more so that Tilly and he had married and Tilly is now expecting his child. All credit to her, she quickly swallowed her own grief and now seems determined to look after Tilly. It is terribly important to the three of us, that Tilly should bring Jack's baby back to Bristol. I know you will understand this, Hal. I do not intend to be a trouble to you. When I learned that I was not a Rudolf – had never been one of the Rudolf clan – I could feel only relief. Tilly has called it my albatross. Well, the albatross has gone. But it also means that I have no home, nowhere to go. Yet I must stay in Bristol to give Tilly what help she may need. I can take a room somewhere. But this may well be more of an embarrassment to you than if

I took up my quarters in High House. I will do whatever you think best. I am like a man with a lost memory. Yet not lost, just laid aside, somehow not my memory any longer. I have to make a new life and new memories. It will depend on you what life and what memories.

Yours very sincerely, Austen.

Hallie stood up and opened the french windows on to the terrace. In spite of the sunshine, it was very fresh out by the flower tubs. They were full of daffodils and the trumpets were all pointing one way in the wind that funnelled up the Gorge. She stood by them, staring over the wall on to the Downs. Inside her body her baby moved convulsively and she gasped and laid a hand on her abdomen.

She said, 'Oh, Jack . . . You will have two children who will never know you . . . oh, Jack.' Tears gathered in her eyes and ran coldly down her face.

From the open windows Meg said, 'Will you have a nice cup of tea, Mrs Rudolf?'

Hallie did not turn her head.

'Yes please, Meg. And some cheese sandwiches too.'

The windows closed and she said, 'I am having a baby too, Jack. And I must keep mine. Oh yes, I must keep mine.'

And she went to telephone her father and aunt. And then to drive to Colston's to watch Hanny in his first cricket match. And as she realized that Jack would never see his son play cricket, the tears began.

On 26 April the German Condor Legion bombed the small town of Guernica. The Basque parliament with its symbolic oak tree remained intact. Everything else in the centre of Guernica was a heap of smouldering rubble under which lay hundreds of dead and wounded. High explosives rained down, followed by incendiaries; any remaining citizens were strafed by machine guns as they

411

ran helplessly like ants looking for shelter, dragging their dead with them. The brutality of the blitzkrieg was numbing; triumphant reports from the Nationalists were tempered by newspaper photographs the next morning.

It was the first day Margo did not make an appearance at the Alcazar.

'She's ashamed,' Austen said, studying some photographs distributed by Benedict, presumably purchased from a journalist.

'She's frightened,' Tilly replied simply. 'All the Red Cross people know who she is. She might get into the hotel, she wouldn't get out.'

'Nobody here would jeopardize our departure now, Tilly.'

'They would. Benedict would. He's left his arm in Spain, it would not take much to persuade him to leave the rest of his body here.' Tilly spoke bitterly. 'Come now, Austen. If it weren't for this –' she patted the front of her summer dress '– we could well start our own little war.'

'I don't think so. We might be asked to help out in Guernica, however. They must be short on hospital staff.' He glanced at Tilly. 'Frankly, I don't want anything more to do with it, Tilly. I don't think you're up to it for one thing. For another . . . I just want us to get home.'

She shrugged. 'I don't expect anyone will ask our opinion.'

And they did not. Benedict called them all into the dining-room that evening and told them that he intended to volunteer his services at one of the field hospitals. One by one the various nurses and orderlies nodded and joined him.

He turned to Austen and said in English, 'It is impossible for Dr Martin to offer her services. But I think she will have to wait until this present emergency is over. And Mr Rudolf is not – strictly speaking – one of us—' He smiled. 'But he too will have to wait and

412

while he is waiting he could help us as efficiently as he did in Madrid.'

Austen said curtly, 'It depends where you are sent. If the hospital is at the Front, I cannot leave Dr Martin. She is my first priority.'

'Certainly.' Benedict spoke smoothly and immediately turned away to talk in rapid French to the others.

Two days later, escorted by Nationalist armoured cars, the Red Cross convoy pulled out again to set up their own field dressing station on the outskirts of Guernica itself. The disinfectant, bandages, drugs and anaesthetics had all been supplied by the Spanish. The soldiers who had paraded so proudly in the town only a week before marched with eyes front and set expressions. Spain had not reckoned on the kind of help Herr Hitler was supplying.

Burgos was strangely empty once they had left; the Alcazar quite literally so. Tilly and Austen wandered the echoing cathedral and sat in the square and felt the true ennui of being left behind. Their conversation was desultory and meaningless.

'Odd to think it is summer here in Burgos. All that wet and mud in the mountains.'

'Spain is a country of extremes.'

'Yes. I think . . . in different circumstances . . . I could have loved it.'

Austen moved a stone with the toe of his shoe. 'It seems to me to be entirely dangerous.'

'That is why Cadiz was so suited to it.'

'She enjoys danger, do you mean? I don't know her very well.' Austen smiled. 'Tended to avoid her in the past.'

Tilly smiled too. 'If you hadn't come out looking for Jack, she would have come herself. Look at the way she rescued me from that unemployment march. And her affair with that young subaltern in the war—'

'I heard gossip, of course—'

'She didn't care about gossip. And now . . . marrying your father. Isn't that dangerous?'

Austen smiled briefly. 'He's not my father, remember. But, I suppose, marrying a man with his reputation – a business rival – older by some twenty years . . . yes, that *is* dangerous!'

They both laughed and Austen moved the stone back again.

'You are very like her, Tilly. I hope you have her stamina.'

Tilly stared at the azure sky. 'I hope so too,' she said quietly.

By 4 May the news arrived that the Fourth Navarre Brigade had occupied what remained of Guernica and was attacking the 'Iron Belt' around Bilbao with renewed ferocity.

Austen said nothing to Tilly, but he foresaw that Benedict would move his unit with the advance and end up in Bilbao ready to embark on the first ship that put in. There would be no thought of the two of them left behind in Burgos. And if there was, it was going to be difficult to send for them amid the kind of devastation happening now. He would be unwilling to risk Tilly in an unprotected vehicle without some kind of escort.

Then the next day there was a telephone call from Margo.

'Austen? Is that you? Can you be ready in two hours? I'll pick you up right outside the cathedral. All right?'

'Ready? Where are we going? Ready for what?' Austen had had enough of Margo. Quite enough.

She laughed shrilly and nearly split his eardrum.

'Ready for the picnic, silly-billy! You know, the one we planned over a week ago?'

'I cannot quite recall—'

'Darling Austen! So forgetful. You know what walls have, don't you, dear? Ask Tilly. She'll remember.'

And she rang off.

Austen repeated the exchange faithfully. Tilly looked at him, big-eyed.

'She cannot mean – surely she cannot mean – she can get us out? She's obviously worried that the conversation could be overheard so she had to make up the picnic thing. In which case she has something to hide. Is she going to get us out, Austen?'

The wild hope on Tilly's long horse-face was pathetic. He said, 'It's possible, I suppose. Listen, don't raise your hopes. I'll stick some of our bribe money in an envelope for the hotel bill. Tell them not to open it until tomorrow, just in case Margo is talking through her hat. We'll take one bag and what we stand up in—'

'We haven't got much more!' Tilly was laughing, childishly excited that at last something was happening.

'And we'll go along with Margo's little mystery and stroll past the cathedral as we have been doing for the past few days—'

'Four weeks. It's been over four weeks, Austen.'

'I know.' He took her hand and mimicked Benedict. 'Courage, *mon enfant*!'

They were ready to leave in fifteen minutes. Tilly wore one of her two summer dresses and left the other in her room. Her old straw hat, not unlike one that Cadiz had worn so it would bring them luck, was pulled well down over her eyes to shield them from the sun. Her leather sandals had been hand-made three years before by a self-support group in the Cotswolds. She had gone bare-legged for some time now and her toes peeping out of the leather thongs looked oddly childish. She carried her doctor's bag.

Austen said, 'No wonder you're a good doctor. I know you are a turmoil inside, and yet you radiate calm and assurance.'

Tilly was surprised. 'Do I? I was thinking exactly the same of you.'

He was equally surprised, then inordinately pleased. 'I say. Really? In that case . . .'

415

'What?'

'If we get through this lot, Tilly, I want to train like you did. I want to be a doctor. What do you think?'

'Austen! How absolutely marvellous!' She held out her hand. 'Shake on it!'

They shook hands solemnly, then laughed. They were both terribly on edge.

It was much too early to set out, yet they could not stop in the hotel any longer. Austen handed over the envelope and they strolled into the dusty sun-baked street.

Tilly said, 'There are a lot of people about. D'you think something big is afoot again?'

'No. And there are no more people than usual.'

'I should have gone to the bathroom. I feel horribly sick.'

'It's because we haven't eaten. Let's cross the road to that little—'

'No! I couldn't eat a thing. Let's just walk.'

So she was leaning heavily on Austen's arm, when a closed car drew up at the pavement.

The windows were tinted, one was down. Margo's head appeared.

'You look like an old married couple!' she said with her usual lack of tact. It was an anti-climax. Austen suspected suddenly that this really was going to be a picnic.

They scrambled on to the back seat and Margo tapped on the glass partition. The car moved off again.

'Don't worry. We're going slowly like this to avoid suspicion.' Margo turned to them; her face puffier than usual; she had been doing a great deal of weeping. 'I've had the devil's own job to persuade Otto . . . anyway never mind all that. Have you got your stuff? We can't go back even if you haven't.'

Austen said carefully, 'What is happening, Margo? Where are we going?'

416

'There's an airfield – never mind where.' She looked away. 'It's used by the Condor Legion.'

Tilly breathed, 'Are you going to get us home, Margo?'

'Eventually. At the moment all I can do is to get you out. But once we land – which will be in Munich—'

Austen said, 'We're flying out with the Condors?'

Margo said hurriedly, 'It's in one of the transport planes used last year to get the Moroccan troops from Africa on to the mainland. It holds twenty and there were two spare seats. Von Faupel needs to report to—'

Austen said suddenly, 'We cannot travel with the German ambassador, Margo. Presumably he is responsible for what has happened to Guernica. You must know how we feel about that.'

Margo turned on him fiercely. 'I suppose you think I don't feel a thing? I probably saw the pictures before you did! I heard them laughing! Gloating! The success of the blitzkrieg here means the success of the blitzkrieg elsewhere! Probably in Bristol!' She sobbed suddenly. 'Do you realize that, you two? It is quite possible that Bristol will be used as an example – just as Guernica was!'

There was a deathly silence in the car. It moved slowly and inexorably out of the city centre into the suburbs.

Austen said, 'How did you persuade them to take us on board?'

'I made a bargain with Otto. If he would get you out of Spain, I would guarantee that you would bring Constantia back to the *schloss* within a month.'

'And then we will not see you again?' Tilly added in a low voice.

Margo's silence was confirmation enough.

Austen said incredulously, 'Is that true? He will wall you up in that castle—'

Margo said, 'It is my home now, Austen. My children are there. I get on well with—'

'*Grossmutter?*' Tilly supplied drily.

417

'Everyone. I am liked because I am fair with blue eyes and can trace my ancestry back to the Saxons!'

There was another long silence. They were driving through a village now. Through the dark glass they watched someone herding goats down a long street.

Tilly said in a small voice, 'I want to go home. So much. Austen, I know how you feel and I feel the same – it's all so awful. But I want to go home.'

Austen said, 'Then we will make a bargain with you, Margo. We will come with you – and be grateful. Very grateful. But when we arrange our flight from Munich, we will book three tickets.'

Margo looked at him, her eyes wide.

'Austen, what are you suggesting? That I leave Otto?'

'Yes,' he replied unequivocally.

She continued to stare at him for some time. Then gave a small whimper. 'Little Otto . . . the girls . . .'

'He will make sure they're not yours even if you stay. You know that. He will alienate them. If there is to be a war, his pride in your Aryan forebears will be dimmed by shame for your Englishness. You will be practically a prisoner in the *schloss*. The children will probably go to governesses—'

Margo breathed quickly and put out a hand to silence him. Then she turned and stared out of the dark window. After a long time, she sat back.

'It is in the laps of the gods,' she said. 'If I can come with you, I will come. But Otto is clever. And Constantia is his first-born.'

Austen had to be satisfied with that. He sat back in the car and reviewed all that had happened to him since he landed in Cadiz at the end of last October. Six months ago. He had spent six months in the land which had produced the Martinez clan. Perhaps it had helped him to understand . . . something. He could vouch for Spanish courage, bravery, stupidity. He and Jack . . . they had liked each other. That was important. Perhaps in the future he could tell Hallie that he and Jack had

418

been – just for a few days – brothers. Brothers in arms.

And meanwhile he could try to bring Hallie's friends back home; he could close his eyes to principles and use Margo's philosophy: this means would justify that end.

Suddenly he smiled and put one arm around Tilly, the other around Margo.

'I'm a lucky man,' he said, as Jack might have said, rallyingly, teasingly.

'How?' Margo asked.

'I know some pretty top-hole women!'

Margo sobbed on a laugh, but Tilly held his gaze and said softly, 'And I have known some great men.'

The car slowed and then turned off the dusty road and on to a barren tract of land where it bumped down a track which opened on to a hastily prepared airstrip. There was a clutch of hangars, a tower mounted by an airsock and three aeroplanes.

For a moment Austen's resolve failed him: the swastikas painted on the side of the aircraft gave him a sense of doom that was almost overpowering. The Third Reich. First the Holy Roman Empire, then the German Empire and now . . . What would this third regeneration bring to the world?

As if she knew his thoughts Margo turned to him and said fiercely, 'If you can get me out of Germany, I will come with you, Austen. I don't want . . . any of this!'

And he grinned at her as if he were some latter-day Scarlet Pimpernel and the next minute they were getting out of the car and hurrying towards the large transport plane.

They were in their seats when the German party arrived. Margo stood by the door, smilingly awaiting her husband, shielding them from more than cursory glances. They pretended to be asleep: exhausted refugees from the Red Cross hospital unit who had worked so hard for the Nationalists . . .

Neither of them had been in an aeroplane before and as it bumped over the field during take-off, Tilly's fingers gripped Austen's very hard. He cradled her and though physical contact had become second nature to him now, still he knew a conscious pleasure in the comfort of human closeness.

And then the noise of the engines increased maniacally, Spain dropped away from them, and, already, as they climbed away from the sun, the Atlantic glinted in the distance.

Twenty-three

Charles was completely devastated by the news of Jack's death.

'I know I've not seen him for eight years . . . oh God, eight years! Your Aunt Cadiz was the link, of course . . . but I should have gone over myself. I should have gone, Hal. I was his father – he was my only son – Hal, I simply cannot believe that all that – that mischievousness is gone! We depended on him to – to—'

'Make us feel alive.' Hallie put her arm around her father, understanding so well, yet with the thought of the child inside her and the child inside Tilly, unable to share the awful dreariness of being without Jack. Grief, yes. Hopelessness, no. After that first dreadful day when she had cheered Hanny with the short sharp 'hurrahs' acceptable to the dignity of his first game, and left him to his friends while she drove down to St George Street, she had discovered that the joy of her pregnancy and the interest in the business had not diminished. In a strange way everything had intensified, become more significant, more important.

Cadiz had told her this was wonderful.

'It's what sacrifice is about,' she had sobbed. 'Jack . . . giving his life . . . to make ours more – more—' She had broken down. 'Oh God, Hal. This will finish Charles! If I didn't have Mungay, it would finish me! Jack – was many things, Hal, but he was so alive!'

'I know, Aunt Cad. I know.' It was what they kept telling each other. He was so alive.

And now, her father, helpless against the maelstrom of grief, wanted a memorial service.

'He's in some muddy trench in a foreign land—'

'Not foreign to him, Pa. He loved Spain enough to—'

'I know. But he deserves a proper send-off. I'll see the Dean. He'll fix—'

'Darling Daddy.' She tightened her hold on his shoulders. 'You can't do that.'

'Why?' He peered around at her. 'Why not? I know he hardly ever darkened church doors, but—'

'It's Tilly's decision, my dear. She is his wife. And she is having his child.' She smiled at him as if he too were a child. 'Doesn't that bring you some hope for the future? Jack will have two children, darling. They will both need you.'

He stared at her silently for a moment, then broke down completely again.

She cradled his head and rocked him gently. And prayed that the next generation of Martinez would bring him comfort.

There was no more news from Spain. Hallie made sure that she was busy the whole time. In moments between one task and another, she would be consumed with sudden terror that they were dead. Tilly and Austen entombed in rubble somewhere; gone for ever. And then she would receive an order for a case of Heartland or the new vintage, Vin de Coeur, and there would be bills of lading to write, transport arrangements to be made.

Cadiz, finding her deep in the cellars one day, asked anxiously whether she was overdoing it.

'You've gone from one extreme to the other, Hal. The idea was to give you an interest in the business, not yoke you to it permanently.'

'I know. But it's much more than that, Aunt Cad. It's – it's my salvation!' She laughed at herself. 'Sorry to be so dramatic, but I've been pampered all my life—'

'You're the one who has done the pampering! When

422

I think how you took over that mausoleum on the Downs and made it into a home—'

'But I've never had to stand on my own feet. I've had you, Father, Austen. Now I feel that if I had to, I could earn a living – keep Hanny and myself and the baby – oh you, of all people, must understand!'

'I do, oh I do. But I still think you are denigrating your real vocation, Hal. Which is to make people happy.' She smiled. 'How awful that sounds! Our little ray of sunshine!' She hugged her niece, half embarrassed.

But Hallie laughed. 'Dear Aunt Cad! I hope you're right. But . . .' She sighed. 'I need, first of all, to make myself happy.' She shook her head. 'Maybe not even happy. Just give myself a bit of – self-respect.' She looked at Cadiz ruefully. 'My self-respect is pretty low, Aunt Cad. Always treated as a child – a little ray of sunshine. Try to help me grow up, Cad. Please.'

They had emerged from the cellars now and Hallie was indeed standing in a ray of sunshine beaming through one of the windows high up in the store-room. Caddie stared at her for almost a minute. Then she said, 'Right. In that case, have you done anything about planning a visit to Cornwall? Or East Anglia?'

Hallie laughed again and nodded.

'I need some news of Tilly first.' She left Austen out of it. 'But immediately I hear she – they – are safe, then I'm off.' They walked slowly up the stairs on which Caddie and Mungay had confronted each other not so long before. 'Hanny wants to know what we are going to do about his ninth birthday. I suggested we spent it at Porthmeor – he has two weeks for Whitsun. Guess what he said?'

She spoke over her shoulder but Caddie did not reply until they were in the office.

Then she said, 'I know exactly what he said. He wants to take Jennifer with him.'

Hallie's face was wide with surprise.

'Did he tell you?'

'No. But I've got eyes in my head and the proprietary way Jennifer treated him at Clevedon leads me to think he won't be able to do much without her in the future.' She smiled ruefully. 'Do you remember a Clevedon girl – some years older than yourself – called Sybil Vallender? She used to play with you and Jack on the beach.'

'No.'

'She moved to London when you were five and Jack eleven. But she took Jack over rather like Jennifer is taking Hanny over.'

'History repeating itself?' Hallie sat down carefully. 'Is it a bad thing?'

'Not at all. Especially for Hanny at the moment. He needs all the support he can get.'

Jennifer and Hanny sat beneath a knee-hole desk in the library of High House awaiting Walter Hinch. Since the Easter holiday in Clevedon, Jennifer had decided that they should take their extra Latin together. She explained to Hanny that Mr Hinch was still paid for two lessons but got them over in one hour instead of two.

'He can get back to his wife and family quicker that way,' she said piously. 'And it's less tiring for him. I thought he looked very tired just before Easter. Then he seemed better.'

'It was the sea air,' Hanny said mundanely. 'He loved being brought out by Sully.'

'That as well,' she agreed judiciously. 'And I think it's up to us to help him as much as we can.'

'Righty-oh.' Hanny did not mind at all. It was another opportunity to show Jennifer – without overt boasting – that he really was doing rather better than she was. Besides, there was something about Jennifer McKinlay. You never quite knew what she would do next. She made life . . . interesting.

They were very squashed beneath the desk and he could feel her thigh warm against his. She was wearing

424

the Saunton summer uniform which was a gingham frock. He liked it better than the winter tunic.

He said, 'I fixed it with Ma. About Porthmeor.'

'You did?' She almost sparkled. 'I say.'

'She'd let me do anything at the moment. Because of my real father being killed in Spain, you know.'

Suddenly Jennifer turned with some difficulty and looked at him from two inches away. He saw that her eyes were brimming with tears.

'It's just too wonderful,' she breathed, her voice snagging on sobs. 'Two fathers . . . both heroes. You must feel so – so proud!'

He felt faint. Her breath smelt of the aniseed balls she had shared with him earlier.

'Your father was a wonderful man. Grammie Adams told me that everyone was in love with him when he was younger. Aunt Margo. Aunt Tilly. And then your – your mother.'

'I never saw him,' Hanny said with his first sense of regret. Suddenly he too wanted to cry.

'You've got his blood in your veins,' Jennifer said, pressing closer.

Hanny said in a small voice, 'I just hope Daddy gets home safely. I mean . . . my uncle.'

Jennifer whispered passionately, 'He will. I promise you, he will.'

'How can you know that?'

'Because he's like the Scarlet Pimpernel. And he's a dark horse too.'

'Who said so?'

'My daddy said he was a dark horse and then Mummy said he was like the Scarlet Pimpernel and my daddy was just jealous.'

Hanny felt his eyes overflow. Of all things in the whole world this was the worst. To be seen crying by Jennifer McKinlay was not on.

She wriggled again and produced a handkerchief. And then she whispered, 'Hanny, I think you've got something in your eye. Let me have a look.'

They emerged from beneath the desks and when Walter Hinch came in he found them standing decorously by the window with Jennifer poking painfully into Hanny's eye with the screwed-up corner of her handkerchief.

'Really, Jennifer, sometimes I think you are a sadist,' he said crossly seeing that Hanny's eyes were streaming.

Quite uncharacteristically Hanny spoke up.

'Is a sadist a doctor, Mr Hinch? 'Cos I reckon she will be the best doctor in Bristol!'

Hallie was superintending Hanny's packing when Meg came upstairs and told her Mrs Gelling was downstairs.

'Mrs Gelling?' Hallie's mind was elsewhere. 'Look here, Hanny, if you're taking your fishing stuff you'll have to carry it! Is that understood?'

'I want to carry it, Ma!' Hanny was indignant. 'You can't *pack* fishing tackle! And I want people to see it on the train too!'

'You're nothing more than a show-off!' But Hallie was laughing. 'And what is Jennifer supposed to do when you're fishing?'

'Cutting bait for me in the sand. Bringing me sandwiches. Things like that,' he replied airily.

She turned away exasperated. 'I won't be around most days – if you drive your grandfather mad I shall be most annoyed!' She looked at Meg. 'Mrs Gelling. Morning room. Is she after donations?'

'Could be, Mrs Rudolf. Bit shabby like.'

'Oh dear.' Hallie looked back at the unwieldy suitcase on Hanny's bed. 'Could you give him a hand, Meg? I'll be about two minutes.'

In the event she was two hours. Because shabby Mrs Gelling turned out to be the Countess von Gellhorn, blowsy, in disarray and considerably distressed.

'Hal! Is it you? My God, you're pregnant too! Oh my God – I didn't think you could – oh dear Lord—'

She flung herself on her friend, weeping copiously. Hallie held her, patting her shoulder, her mind a whirl of surmise.

'I had to come straightaway, Hal! I didn't know about the baby – Austen didn't say a word! He's just gone on and on about Tilly being pregnant and having to get Jack's child back to England!' She wailed again, then went on, 'Austen and Tilly dropped me at Mama's and she was out with Constantia and so was Pa and Walter Hinch told me that you were off to Cornwall at any moment and – I just got a taxi and came immediately! Oh, darling, I'm glad to see you, but . . . what have I done, Hal? What have I *done*?'

Hallie manoeuvred the considerable bulk towards the sofa and they both collapsed upon it. Margo was weeping uncontrollably now and Hallie could barely understand what she had said. However, there was no need for a response.

'Austen said he would only get on the aeroplane if I promised to come with him to England when we landed! So, of course, I promised – I had to get them out, Hal! They'd be there till the end of the war if I hadn't! But they were both so stubborn because of Guernica!' She put a hand over her mouth and stared at Hallie with swimming eyes. 'Don't misunderstand me, darling! I felt the same about Guernica! And it was our doing really – Otto's and mine! Because, after all, I am married to Otto, so what he does . . .'

Hallie took the trembling hands and held them tightly.

'Now . . . just stop talking for a complete minute, Margo. Breathe deeply. I'm going to ring for some tea and you're going to drink it and then you can start again. From the beginning.'

Margo's face worked uncontrollably but she nodded somehow and Hallie released her hands and went to the bell. Cook entered so quickly it was obvious she had been outside the door. Hallie asked for tea and toast and then went back to her friend and held her again.

'Now. Let me tell you what I know. Jack is dead. Tilly is having his baby. They met you in Burgos.' She swallowed. 'I had no idea you were going to bring them home. Where are they now?'

'The Hestermans'. Park Street.' Margo controlled her breathing with difficulty. 'Hal, I'm so sorry about this. Barging in when you're so obviously *enceinte*. If Mamma had been in – or even Constantia – but finding no-one there . . . it was just so terrible. I felt I'd burned my boats for – for nothing!'

'You mean you're not going back?'

'Otto wouldn't have me.' She looked up her eyes drowning. 'Would he?'

'Margo, how can I say? Did you actually leave him?'

'Well, I thought I was going to – I thought I might have to run across the airfield or something stupid. But when it actually happened, he was taken off by von Faupel in the diplomatic car and I – I simply turned around and went with Austen and Tilly . . . no, I suppose I did not actually leave him. At least . . . he doesn't know I did.'

'But you intended to?'

The tea arrived then and Margo was silent until Cook left them. She was shaking too much to hold a cup in her hands and Hallie held it while she sipped and breathed in the steam.

'Oh, that's better. There's nothing like an English cup of tea . . .' The eyes began to fill again and she rushed on, 'I've missed everything so *much*, Hal! And some of the things that happened in Spain – and will happen here – it's just so awful! Austen made this bargain with me and I suddenly thought, Why not. If they're going to be bombed I'd rather be bombed with them.' She scrubbed at her eyes . . . 'You see, Hal, I felt so *ashamed*! When I thought I was looking for Jack, it was all right. But when they told me Jack was dead and he'd married Tilly – Tilly of all people! – then I felt sort of pushed out. Part of them and what they were doing. I can't explain—'

'I understand, Margo. I really do. It's finding out that you can't be neutral. You can't sit on the fence. You have to be one side or the other.'

'Yes. That's it exactly,' Margo said eagerly. 'But now I'm here – everything looks so – so ordinary! No servants and Walter still pottering around like an old woman and – and – I've got little Otto and the girls back at the *schloss*.' She dashed away more tears and said, 'Hal, I don't know what to do. I really don't!'

Hallie smiled her quiet English smile.

'You just give it time, my dear. From what you say, you haven't burned a single boat. After all, if Austen persuaded you to come back to collect Constantia that merely shows your true maternal instinct. Otto might disapprove but he's hardly going to condemn you for it.'

Margo thought about it while Hallie refilled her cup and cut some toast into fingers.

Then she said, 'Oh, Hal. You're such a comfort. You really are.' She picked up her plate and nibbled delicately. 'Darling, when I've had this quite delicious tea and toast, d'you think I could possibly have a bath?'

'Of course. And then I will telephone Queen's Square and Sully can take you back in time for dinner. You must be absolutely exhausted.'

'I am. Aeroplanes are so dreadfully noisy, Hal. And Austen spends all his time worrying about Tilly and doesn't seem to think I might need a little care and attention!'

Hallie watched her eating the toast and said casually, 'I suppose Austen will arrive at any moment?'

'Darling, I haven't got the remotest. He said something about taking a report to London. Someone called Travers. But he'll probably do that in a day or two, won't he?'

'Probably.'

Margo finished the tea and they went upstairs together. Hallie ran a bath and heard the story properly

429

and retold it to Hanny who was outside on the landing hopping from one leg to the other.

She was surprised at Hanny's intense excitement.

'Let's telephone Dr Hesterman! No, better still, let's go with Aunt Margo and tell Sully to take us on to Park Street and give him the biggest surprise of his life!'

He had forgotten the awfulness of Austen's departure last October.

She said, 'I think we must wait for him to come here, darling.'

'Why? It would be such fun to pop up—'

'Aunt Tilly is not very strong at the moment. Shocks and surprises are not good for her.'

'Daddy always likes a bit of fun though.'

She noted wryly that Austen was Daddy again.

'They've had a dreadful time, Hanny. You can see the state Aunt Margo is in. Let's just wait and see what Daddy wants to do.'

'We can't go to Porthmeor tomorrow, Ma! I'll have to tell Jennifer—'

Suddenly she was certain of one thing.

'If Daddy does not contact us we shall be going as planned, Hanny. He has to go to London to deliver some reports. There is no point in us hanging around.'

'We must tell him where we are! He can come down and we can build our usual channels in the sand.'

'Perhaps.'

She knew he would not do that. And if she and Hanny weren't around, he could occupy High House until such time as he had decided what he wanted to do.

Porthmeor was as beautiful and as peaceful as ever. The last few days of May went out in wonderful sunsets and fresh clear mornings. In the afternoons Charles put his deckchair on to the bottom notch and felt guilty because there was still so much contentment in dozing in the sun and watching Hanny and Jennifer throwing water at each other. Sometimes, with a comfortable red glow coming through his closed eyelids, he would try to imagine Jack in the trenches. The Jack he remembered would not have been interested enough to fight a battle so far from home; would not have been serious enough to fall for someone as good and kind – and plain – as Tilly Hesterman. So Jack had changed. He had gone back to his roots and found something worth dying for. The thought made Charles' eyes warmer than ever; he wished with all his heart that he had known the older Jack.

On their third day in the hotel, Hallie left the children with him and went off in a hired Austin eleven to find Derek Aitchison who grew grapes down in Roseland. It meant that Charles had to forgo his deckchair and play with the children in spite of their reassurances.

'It's all right, Grandad!' Hanny shouted as he tore through the shallows clutching his plywood surf-board importantly. 'You can't drown with one of these! You just hold on and—' He disappeared ignominiously beneath a wave and Jennifer screamed with laughter.

Charles felt definitely flustered.

'Hold on there, Hanny – I'm coming!'

He stumbled through the surf wetting his rolled-up trousers and was even more flustered when Hanny appeared practically between his legs.

'Told you, Grandad!' The boy was spluttering and laughing triumphantly. 'You just hang on to the board and you've got to come in!'

'For God's sake, Hanny!' Charles remembered suddenly how often he had wanted to smack Jack when he had been this age. 'I thought you were damned well drowning!'

Jennifer arrived at a gallop.

'Don't you worry, Mr Martinez. I'll keep an eye on him,' she comforted. 'Anyway we're coming out now. Could you buy us some icecreams? And some of that soda-pop stuff?'

The small beach shop was at the top of the cliff path. Charles took it very slowly, pausing occasionally to watch the two children cavorting about on the sand and wondering how he was going to get through a whole day of being solely responsible for them.

So when he reached the top of the path and saw Tilly coming from the hotel, he gave a shout that was doubly joyful. Because, of course, Tilly Hesterman was no longer just Hallie's schoolfriend, she was Tilly Martinez, and she was his daughter-in-law.

She was conscious of this too. Her smile was strained as she put both her hands into his and let him draw her close.

'Mr Martinez – I wondered – I wasn't sure whether to come – how welcome I would be—'

He said, 'My dear girl. My dear, dear girl. How could you doubt for one moment that you would be less than—?'

'Austen wanted to see Hallie, of course. As soon as we heard about the baby. And I – I wanted to see her too. But it was you. I wanted to see you. So I risked coming unannounced.'

He was terribly moved. 'Oh, my dear, I am so honoured that you felt like that.'

'Hallie wasn't there, you see – they said she'd gone out. And Austen was determined to find her so I said would he leave me to talk to you.' She flapped her hands helplessly. 'We didn't know about the baby. Nobody told us.'

'No. She wanted it kept quiet. In case it influenced Austen – brought him home earlier than he really wanted . . . you understand.'

'Not really. I wish so much, you see, that Jack had known about his baby.'

Charles felt his whole face working uncontrollably. He managed to blurt, 'But he knows – he surely knows, Tilly.' And then her arms went round him and they held each other close.

She whispered eventually, 'I know you're right. It's just that . . . it was so good that Austen was there and

432

knew. And now it's good that you and Hallie know. And Cadiz. You – the four of you – sort of encapsulate him.'

'Oh, Tilly . . . Tilly . . . I'm so glad – so happy to see you. You've always been part of our family and now—'

She said into his neck, 'Jack always called you Pa. Could I call you Pa?'

He held on to her and it was as if Jack was there with them. He felt her tears run inside his collar; for a moment it was balm to stand there together, weeping.

Then he said urgently, 'You mustn't cry, my dear. It's bad for the baby.'

And she laughed through her tears and said, 'You and Austen – you see me simply as a receptacle for this child!'

'No. Never that.' He fumbled in the breast pocket of his linen jacket and produced a pristine handkerchief. 'But I would like to look after you a little. As Jack would have done. It would please me so much if you would allow that.'

She nodded, smiling up at him with her nice ordinary face raw in the May sunshine. He felt such a tenderness for her he thought he might explode with it. And he knew that the answer to the riddle of his son lay here, in his son's wife. He said, 'I look on you, quite literally, as Jack's other half, Tilly. And I want you to talk to me about him. Tell me what he was like during those last few months. Because he must have changed.'

She nodded. 'He had changed, of course. We all changed out there. But underneath, he was the same.' She smiled. 'Jack was always kind, Pa. I remember once Margo said I looked like a horse and he swung me round and said most horses were much nicer than people.'

It was so typical of Jack that Charles laughed and then so did she and they stood together, sniffing and smiling.

And at last Charles said, 'I've come to get icecreams for Hanny and Jennifer. I'm not really up to the two of them together. Think you could help me?'

'I'd like that. I haven't been much help to anyone since

Madrid.' They went together to the small shop. 'I'll tell them about Jack and Austen, shall I?'

'Yes. Yes, my dear, do that. Hanny has a right to know that he can be proud of both his fathers.'

Carne-in-Roseland had been a mixed farm until ten years before when a London businessman had bought it and retired there determined to become a recluse. But Derek Aitchison had discovered that although he could not live in company, he became very bored with his own. He needed a rich man's hobby rather than a poor man's livelihood, and he turned to growing grapes and making his own wines during his first summer at Carne. He became totally fascinated by the whole process; he had to share his success somehow, so he began to sell the wines. A dozen bottles here, half-a-dozen there. British wines were not popular; his extensive cellars were almost full.

It was in 1934 when Austen and Hallie had taken Hanny down for his usual summer fortnight they were offered a bottle at the Porthmeor hotel. Austen had enquired the date and on discovering it was 1928, the year of Hanny's birth, had ordered a case to be sent to High House. They had intended visiting Carne and meeting Derek Aitchison personally, but the following year they had gone to Barbados.

Hallie discovered that Mr Aitchison did not possess a telephone so that day's visit was something of a shot in the dark. Charles had wanted to come with her. The hotel could have made arrangements for looking after Jennifer and Hanny. But Hallie had pointed out that the two of them may well pose a threat.

'He's supposed to be terribly shy,' she reminded her father. 'And I look pretty harmless on my own.'

'I don't like it,' Charles said, already dreading the day ahead alone with the children. 'He's meant to be an oddity. And you might look harmless but you also look about fifteen!'

But Hallie, remembering Mungay's words about her obvious honesty, knew that this was one time her annoyingly schoolgirlish looks could be advantageous.

The car was like a very large box on wheels, the window-winders did not work and by the time she had double declutched up and down the hills of South Cornwall she was sweating profusely and wished she had clipped in the waterproof dress guards which went with the blue silk frock she had chosen to wear.

After an hour of steep lanes she drove thankfully into a small, mean mining village and drew up beneath a creaking sign which announced the Tinners' Arms. She sat for a few minutes, the car doors open to the beautiful May morning and let herself and the car cool down. Nobody appeared. She had no notion of opening times but presumably people lived in the Tinners' Arms; she left the car, doors still open and knocked on the door.

A head appeared from an upstairs window.

'Open midday,' it said.

'I just wanted to ask—'

'Open midday.'

'Where is Carne-in-Roseland, please? I'm looking for a Mr Derek Aitchison.'

'You passed it down the road.'

'I looked at every name board—'

' 'E don't advertise isself. Dun't wanna be found. Mile down the lane. Five-barred gate. Granite cairn just to one side. 'S why tis called Carne, see.'

'Oh.' Hallie beamed up a smile. 'Thank you very much.'

The head emerged further. It belonged to a woman, the flat hair was pulled back into a plait.

'We're having a lie-in. We do a nice pasty about one o'clock.'

Hallie smiled again and left, well pleased. If she could charm something out of that landlady surely she could break through Mr Aitchison's seclusion.

But no-one had told her that Mr Aitchison was not only a recluse, he was a misogynist.

She found the cairn without difficulty. Two giant standing stones leaning towards each other were one side of an unmarked gate leading to a muddy track. She parked the car as close to the Cornish stone hedge as she could and clambered over the bars. The track led through the vineyard itself; quite small and on a steep slope elegant trellis ran in strips alongside the track. Each strip had its own irrigation canal. It was incredibly neat and well ordered. They had told her at the hotel that Mr Aitchison employed no help; this was one man's work.

But it seemed she was not even to meet that man. Her diffident knock on the front door of the low granite farmhouse was greeted by furious barking, stopped, just as furiously, by a man's voice.

'Who is it? If it's milk, there's a ten-bob note under the stone.'

'It's not milk.' Hallie had not expected such aggressiveness. Nor a dog. She moistened her lips nervously thinking of the baby. 'My name is Harriet Rudolf and I am here to place an order with you. For wine. A regular order. I represent the House of Martinez and—'

'Get out!' The man's voice rose to a roar. 'Get off my land immediately! I will not have a woman set foot on my property! Do you understand me?'

Hallie started back, shocked.

'But I was hoping to do business with you, Mr Aitchison. My husband and I sampled your 1928 vintage a few years ago and found it extremely palatable—'

'Get out!' The voice rose even further and held a note of hysteria. 'Get out else I'll set the bloody dog on you!'

Hallie realized that the man was obsessed with his horror of women. There was absolutely nothing she could do about it.

She said, 'I'm sorry, Mr Aitchison. I will leave immediately. And perhaps – my father will write to you—'

The man screeched at her again and she turned tail and almost ran down the track to the gate.

And there, emerging from another car, taller than she remembered, much thinner, dark hair showing threads of grey in the pitiless sunshine, was Austen.

She hung on to the gate, out of breath, looking more distressed than she actually felt. And because of that he did not greet her but said urgently, 'Hallie. Cadiz told us what you planned. What has happened? Are you all right?'

And she replied just as directly, 'He told me to get out. There was a dog. I was . . . a bit bothered.'

He vaulted the gate and was halfway up the drive before she could stop him. She tried to call but she had no breath left and in any case was too surprised by the suddenness of his action. She doubted whether the old Austen could have vaulted a five-barred gate; certainly he would never have tried. She stared after him before he disappeared over the rise. He was wearing old flannels, a white sports shirt and a navy-blue pullover. Austen rarely dressed so informally even on their holidays down here. He always wore a jacket; his Harris tweed usually. And his trousers were . . . old. They looked as if he had washed them himself. She frowned. Perhaps he had not gone to High House to pick up his clothes. Perhaps he had come straight from London to see her. And . . . do what? Suggest a separation? A reconciliation? The kind of marriage they had before?

Her heart was still beating uncomfortably and she took two or three consciously deep breaths. Certainly he was interfering. She had not asked him to go leaping up the track to harangue Mr Aitchison. She was suddenly furious with him for arriving when she had failed in her first big project.

She went and sat in the car, her mind in a complete whirl. He did not appear. She checked her watch and saw he had been gone just over ten minutes. And he had been to see Cadiz. He had said 'Cadiz told us' – so he was with someone. Could it be Tilly? How close was he to Tilly? According to Margo his sole concern was Tilly's welfare. She wished she could stop shaking. She put her hands over her abdomen and cradled it comfortingly.

'It's all right . . . all right,' she murmured.

In her rear-view mirror she saw the gate move and then Austen's form appeared leaping it again. She had had no idea he was so athletic.

He came around the car and looked in on her.

'He wishes to convey his apologies to you, Hal. And if you will do as you said and write to him he will consider doing business with the House of Martinez.'

She looked at him, suppressing her resentment.

'Thank you, Austen,' she said formally. 'I expect Cadiz told you of our idea to market home-produced—'

'Yes. And when she said you were in Porthmeor I knew you would come here, of course.' He was looking at her carefully, she could feel his dark eyes on her. She glanced up again. He was so thin he looked cadaverous.

He said, 'We went to the hotel and were told you had left the children with your father and gone out for the day. So Tilly went to find him and I came here.'

'So I see.'

He was with Tilly; it was true, he could not bear to let Tilly out of his sight. She did not know what to say to him. It was incredible; they were strangers. He stayed where he was, one arm along the open door of the car, a foot on the running board. The silence sang like a violin string.

He cleared his throat. 'We should talk, Hal.'

'Yes.' She wanted to stare at him as he was staring down at her. She put her hands on the steering-wheel and held tightly. 'But there seems nothing to say.'

'I don't agree. I have some questions and I would be grateful if you would give me some answers.'

Her heart thumped. The baby was so obvious and he had said nothing.

'Very well.' She risked an upward glance. He was

438

aureoled in the sun, she could not see his eyes. 'There's a pub about a mile on from here. It's called the Tinners' Arms. They open at midday and serve pasties.'

He said, 'Will you lead the way? Are you able to drive?'

She snapped, 'I would hardly be here, sitting in a car on my own, if I hadn't driven it!'

She felt his surprise. He said, 'You have changed, Hal.'

And, still angry, she said, 'Yes. I am no longer . . . meek.'

She made the word sound loathsome. And then pulled the self-starter to indicate the exchange was over.

Sedately, in convoy, they drove towards the Tinners' Arms.

Twenty-four

The public bar of the Tinners' Arms was low ceilinged and looked as if it had been both smoked and pickled. There was no lounge bar.

'We'll eat outside,' Austen said decisively. 'May I take out a comfortable chair for my wife?'

The landlady, who now wore her plait coiled around her head, smiled at Hallie.

'Did you find that queer cuss, missis? And did 'e give you what for?'

Hallie said ruefully, 'He did, rather.'

'Look,' the landlady lifted the bar flap and came round to their side, 'why don't you have your dinners in the parlour? I know the weather's fine, but it's still only May, and in your condition—'

She opened a door and led the way down a passage, then stood aside and let Hallie go into a small room, heavily net-curtained, overlooking ploughed fields. It was as neat as a pin, white-painted and completely private.

Hallie smiled. 'This is *nice*. Isn't it, Austen?'

He stooped and entered. 'Very. Thank you, Mrs . . .'

'Stevens,' that lady supplied. 'And what will you drink with your pasty?'

Hallie looked doubtful.

'How about a nice pot of tea?' Mrs Stevens had obviously decided to take them under her wing. 'Something warm for the baby.'

Hallie glanced at Austen.

'Fine for me,' she said.

He nodded and Mrs Stevens left them; they settled themselves either side of the round table. Hallie noted that Austen did not fuss with her chair as he'd always done in the past. She did not know whether this was good or bad. She did not know anything any more.

He said quietly, 'How do you feel about the baby, Hal?'

She looked at him. Just for a moment her anger made her want to say childishly, Oh, so you've noticed, have you? And then, for some reason, the sight of him, so familiar – yet paradoxically so unfamiliar too – made her anger drain away. She had had nightmares about their last night together – their only night together. The man in her nightmares did not look like this man.

She said honestly, 'I was low at first. There seemed no future for the baby. And then, around Easter, something happened. My father inveigled me into going through the sales records and Cadiz took me shopping for some maternity clothes . . . and I started to feel excited.' She held his gaze with some difficulty. 'The thing is, Austen, I am all right. So the baby . . . it must not make any difference to . . . to what happens to us.'

'What do you want to happen to us?' he asked.

Her gaze dropped. She faltered, 'I don't know.' The table was of fumed oak with a flamboyant false grain varnished on to its surface. She followed one of the shadowed lines with her thumb. 'What do you want, Austen?'

His laugh was so unexpected she looked up again. His dark eyes stared into hers with a kind of helpless amusement.

'I don't know either,' he admitted.

'And that is funny?' she said with a momentary return of resentment.

'Sorry, Hal. It's just that . . . I am so glad to be back – Tilly safe – to see you again, to smell English air. And the baby – it is all so amazing! I thought everything had finished and here it is beginning again!'

The door opened then on Mrs Stevens bearing a laden tray. They leaned back with relief at the temporary respite while she put the tray on a sideboard and proceeded to fit a protective felt cover over the table and flap a snowy cloth over that.

'Can't be too careful,' she told them. 'Hot plates do leach the finish off anything decent.' She placed cutlery carefully. 'Sent for this table, I did. From one of they mail-order lists. From London.'

Hallie met Austen's dark gaze again and looked away before her smile could become obvious.

'There. Dun't that look nice?' Mrs Stevens stepped back to admire the set table. Then she plonked two pasties on the waiting plates and edged some more space at the side for the tray of tea.

'Gissa shout if you want hot water for the pot. I don't believe in drowning it,' and she was gone.

Austen let out his held breath.

'She's taken a shine to you, Hal.'

Hallie could no longer restrain her smile; it seemed incredible that she and Austen could be smiling.

'I think she feels guilty. She directed me to Carne, but she did not warn me that Derek Aitchison would not see me under any circumstances.'

'Listen, Cadiz told us that you intend to do this kind of thing all over the country. You're going to hunt up local sugar beet farms for Mungay too.'

'Yes. In view of the situation with Germany, it seemed wise to try to decrease importation.'

'Yes. But write to your contacts first, Hal. People who just roll up on one's doorstep are never entirely welcome. Whereas if you've made them a good offer in writing first and they've decided to have a look at you, you'll probably be very welcome indeed.'

She nodded wryly. 'Yes. That's a lesson I've learned today.' She cut into her pasty and watched the steam rise from it. 'Look. I haven't thanked you for what you did back at Carne. It would have been a shame to miss out on that particular supply source.' The steam was making a safety barrier between them. 'D'you remember how much we enjoyed that first vintage back in . . . whenever it was?'

'Thirty-four. The year before we went to Barbados.'

'Yes.'

He said quickly, 'Hal, I'm sorry you were so hurt. I thought . . . I mean I didn't think . . . you minded the kind of relationship we had.' He isolated a piece of turnip and speared it with his fork. 'We were good friends, Hal, weren't we?' he asked the question almost pleadingly but she did not immediately respond.

When she did it was after consideration and she spoke very objectively.

'Yes. We were. It was a static friendship, but I think for a time we were both happy. You might have been happy like that for ever. I wanted to . . . develop, I suppose.' She chewed thoughtfully. It was as if she were talking of someone else, two people she did not know all that well. 'I wanted you to treat me like a woman. Not like a child.'

'I'm sorry, Hal. I was so full of self-disgust. You were a symbol of something . . . better. Much better. I had to keep you like that.'

'Pure.' She smiled again and he smiled back. How could they be smiling when they were discussing the awfulness of what had happened?

She said, 'I *was* a child, of course, Austen. That's why I reacted as I did.' She took another mouthful of pasty and said indistinctly, 'I've talked to Tilly's father about this. He explained something. Medically. I mean, I thought you were impotent and then I thought you weren't and he said it could be a reaction to . . .' She swallowed a piece of gristle and was silent.

'I see.' He laid his knife and fork down. 'I don't think I can finish this. It's very filling.'

'Austen, you must!' She forgot her objectiveness in sudden concern. 'For one thing you are much too thin.

And for another Mrs Stevens will be cut to the quick if you don't eat her pasty.'

He took out his handkerchief and laid the pasty on it. 'There. Will that do?'

'Put mine with it.' She shovelled the remains of hers on to the handkerchief and he wrapped it up quickly. She took the bundle and put it into her bag.

'That's better. Now we can enjoy the tea. But you should eat properly, Austen.'

'I do. And I hope you do too.'

She nodded and poured the dark brown tea.

'Cook and Meg between them make certain of that. Apropos of which – you asked where you should live when you came home. It is ridiculous to assume that High House is no longer anything to do with you, Austen. If you wish to stay there, of course you must.'

He accepted his cup and stirred it slowly.

'Ridiculous? But surely you understand, Hal. I am not a Rudolf. *None* of it has anything to do with me. I don't have to plot and connive any more. When I think how I engineered those adoption papers for Hanny and led you to think I was some kind of philanthropist – that was me trying to be a Rudolf! And after the war when I thought that my nightmares would cease if I behaved like all Rudolfs behaved and spent more time in brothels than anywhere else . . . Hal, I cannot tell you what a relief it is to have nothing. No hereditary traits. No expectations to live up to. No money. Nowhere to live—'

'Austen! Mungay will not hear of you—'

'Mungay gave me a home and name, Hal. But I don't want them. He can have them back.'

She stared at him wide-eyed. He really was a different man.

He smiled. 'Don't look so worried. I'm not being as ungrateful as I sound. Mungay and I never got on. He will be as delighted as I am that there is no need to make any further efforts. And I shall manage.'

'What will you do?'

'I'm going to train to be a doctor.'

'But . . . how will you live?'

'Tilly's father is going to lend me some money.'

She was silent, swallowing her tea too quickly and burning her throat. Her eyes watered with the pain of it.

She said, suddenly angry, 'I am still your wife. And what is mine is yours – that is what I said at the wedding service and I meant it. A third of the Martinez business is mine, and therefore yours. You owe it to Jack to use that money! I insist that you use it! And live at home!'

He was surprised again. 'Very well, if that is what you want. I said in my letter if it would be easier to put up a front, then that is what we will do. We owe it to the baby as well as Jack.' He sighed. 'But you are right, I owe a lot to Jack.'

She thought her cup might break between her hands. She held her voice steady somehow.

'Is that why you want to be a doctor?'

'No. I thought – when I got to Madrid – that the nightmares would begin again. Trenches. Smells. Bombs . . . but they didn't. Because I found, when I worked on the wards there, I had an aptitude. Something I could give – do—' He laughed diffidently. 'I don't know what it was, Hal. I want to go on doing it anyway.'

'But Tilly? She is a doctor.'

'Yes?' He sounded puzzled.

'I thought you meant, you owed Jack . . . Tilly.'

He was silent for some time. Then he said, 'I must tell you about Tilly and Jack. She will tell you, I know that. But I was an onlooker and sometimes onlookers see more. I think it will help you – and Cadiz and Charles – to hear about it. Because . . . he was happy. *They* were happy. Against all the odds, they were happy.'

She looked down at her hands clenched around her cup. He made her feel ashamed.

He said, 'Jack and Tilly taught me something, Hal. Spain taught me something. I think it is this ability to –

445

to care for people. That is why I want to go on doing it. It is not something I must forget. Ever again. That is my debt.'

She whispered, 'I'm sorry, Austen.'

'Sorry? What for? Why?'

She looked up and forced a smile. 'When we sat down first, you said you did not know what you wanted to do. It seems you do know.'

'Becoming a doctor? Yes. But I was not thinking of that and neither were you.' He stirred his tea again; he had not touched it. 'If it weren't for this baby, I would probably not be here, Hal. And neither would you. You say I am not to take the baby into consideration, but how can I not? We made this child between us.' He leaned across the table. 'When Mrs Hesterman told Tilly and I that you were to have a baby in July, Tilly turned to me and said, "That's spared me from a great deal of talking, Austen." ' He smiled. 'She was determined we should try again at being married, baby or no baby. But, of course, she had no idea what she was asking.' The smile died and he leaned back again. 'Well . . . you are going to have the baby and you will be a good mother – Hanny will vouch for that. And you will work at the House of Martinez and become very good at that too. So we both know what we are going to do with part of our lives. But the other part . . . you . . . me. What are we going to do about that, Hal? What are we going to do about us?'

'I still do not know, Austen. I am sorry.'

He placed his teaspoon on the saucer with great care. His hair was too long and it fell over one eye now as Jack's had always done.

He said, 'We are able to talk so honestly. That must be good, surely?'

'But we always could. At one level.'

'Yes. Now we have to go deeper.' He held on to the edge of the table. 'We are going to have to talk about our last night together. Hal, I know I forced

446

myself on you that night in October. I am deeply sorry.'

'I—' She felt her face redden like a schoolgirl's. 'I – thought I had – I mean, I was so – I mean, you did not force yourself on me, Austen. At all.'

'But you hated me, Hal. You told me to go.'

'I was so ashamed. That second time . . . I was ashamed.'

'Why? We were close then to making love! The first time all we made was anger and frustration. But then . . . we were learning, Hal.'

She said nothing, her embarrassment so intense she felt faint with it.

He said in a low voice, 'Can we – could we possibly – go on learning, Hal?'

She almost whimpered, 'I don't know! I really don't know, Austen!'

He smiled, suddenly more certain of himself.

'Well, at least you did not say no!' He put his hands around hers and they held the cup together. It became like a chalice. 'Hal, we've got time! D'you realize that? And we can still talk to each other. And there's so much to say. Let's leave your car here and go for a drive. I'll tell you about Jack. And Tilly. And Margo. Does it strike you as strange that I know your friends so well now? And I want you to tell me how Hanny is getting on at Colston's. And why he has brought Jennifer McKinlay down here instead of Clive. And how your aunt is getting on with Mungay. And how you felt when you knew I'd failed you with Jack.' He tightened his hands on hers. 'If only I could have brought Jack home . . .' She gave a small sob and he went on quickly, 'Then we'll come back here and drive back down to Porthmeor in time for dinner. What do you say?'

She smiled up at him, a curious upside-down smile.

'I'd like that,' she replied simply.

Jennifer lost interest in Hanny the moment Tilly appeared that morning.

'Aunty Tilly! You're back! From the fires of hell! Rescued by the Scarlet Pimpernel!'

Tilly's long thin face broke into a smile.

'You know you're very like your Aunt Margo,' she said, hugging the lanky nine-year-old affectionately. 'You're constantly playing to an audience!'

Jennifer laughed unaffectedly for once. 'You – and Mr Rudolf – you always *know*, don't you? That time I said Hanny was in the bedroom when really he was throwing Constantia on the compost heap – you knew then, didn't you?'

Charles ho-ho'd knowingly and Hanny yelled, 'Traitor!' And then shouted, 'Where's Pa, Aunt Tilly? Is he with you? Is he all right? Where is he?'

Tilly, half strangled by Jennifer, put her hands over her ears.

'You're noisier than the aeroplane we came home in—'

'An aeroplane?' Hanny was stunned. 'You came home in an aeroplane? And Pa?'

'And Aunt Margo.' Tilly managed to get an arm around them both. 'Come on, sit down and I'll tell you a story that is true.' She wedged herself carefully into a deck-chair and Charles sat by her. The children sat on the sand, their chins on the nearest knee. She said to Hanny, 'Your father and I drove down at the crack of dawn. He's gone to look for your mother.' Tilly glanced at Charles. 'We thought we might have a little holiday all together. Is that all right?'

He said gruffly, 'What could be better?'

And Tilly began to tell them about Jack. And how Austen had rescued her. And how Margo had smuggled them on to a German aeroplane and then decided to come with them.

They sat more quietly than Charles would have dreamed possible. And when Tilly was silent, so were they.

Until Hanny said gloomily, 'I suppose that means

Connie will be staying in Bristol all the time now and we shall be expected to look after her.'

And Jennifer looked at him and replied, 'She is my cousin, remember. But you can help me to bring her up.'

He pulled a hideous face. 'Oh, *thanks*!' he said ironically.

'Yes. But properly,' she said with emphasis.

He looked at her and a smile dawned. 'Oh. Thanks,' he said without the irony.

Later, building a fortress against the incoming tide, Jennifer said matter-of-factly, 'Will you go and live with Aunt Tilly now?'

He was so startled he only just missed his bare toe with his new spade.

'Why should I?'

'Well, she's your stepmother. And she's having a baby too. It will be your half-sister or brother. You should look after it.'

He resumed digging furiously.

'I've got to help Ma look after our baby!' he said. He remembered a phrase of Meg's. 'I can't be everywhere at once!'

She said, 'No, I suppose not.' She filled her bucket with wet sand and turned out a perfect pie for the top of the fort. 'You are lucky. You're going to be a really big family. Lots of company. I like lots of company.'

Hanny looked over the top of the sand pie to the blue of the Atlantic.

'So do I,' he said with quiet satisfaction.

They spent the afternoon at Porthcurno sitting among the seapinks and using Austen's binoculars to watch a family of seals playing in the sea far below them. They had been here before on previous Porthmeor holidays, sat like this, talked easily, basked in the sun. And yet everything was different now. They were different.

Hallie spoke her thoughts diffidently. 'Isn't it all so

449

terribly fragile, Austen? We cannot control what happens
to us. Sometimes we – the whole thing – seems like an
enormous accident.'

'Does it?' Austen picked up her left hand and turned
the wedding ring slowly on her finger. 'I can see a pattern
– an inexorable pattern. Overriding my scheming – my
petty plans.'

She let her hand lie in his, very still.

'How?' she asked.

'I wanted to grab the House of Martinez. I told myself
that was one of the reasons for marrying you. But the
two families were already joined over in Barbados – a
long time ago. I plotted to make Hanny ours, but Jack
gave him to us – trusted us completely. And Maude's
death drove Jack to Spain and something beyond anything he'd dreamed of.'

'His death?' she asked with some bitterness.

'I was thinking of his marriage, Hal. I'm sorry. Somehow Tilly and the baby . . . they are what has come out
of Spain for me.' He fitted his fingers carefully between
hers. 'Does that sound heartless? I feel that the important
things are right here – in small trivial things. The
enormous events grow from there.' He closed his fingers
on hers. 'That is why you will be good in the business.
I started at the top and – imposed my will on what was
to happen. You will discover the names of the draymen
first—'

'The horses actually.'

They both laughed and without thinking he released
her hand, put his arm around her shoulders and hugged
her to him. They stopped laughing.

For a moment he thought he felt her withdraw from
him and he held on to her and said, 'This is how I started
in that Red Cross hospital outside Madrid, Hal. Not
even a name. A touch. Some of them knew me by my
touch . . . my smell.'

He felt her sob and turned her into his shoulder.

'I'm sorry, Hal. So sorry,' he murmured into her hair.

She said, 'Don't talk now! Let us know each other by our touch!' And she lifted one hand and put the palm against the side of his face. They stayed like that, he holding her hard against him, she cupping his cheek until, very gradually, the tension went from her and she relaxed into the protection of his body and let her perceptions take over.

And then, at last, she spoke.

'Yes. I would know your touch. It is very strong. You would have made a good St Christopher carrying people across the water!'

He breathed a small laugh.

'I'm no saint, Hal,' he said.

'No. But then, who wants to live with a saint?' She squinted up at him. 'I'm no angel, Austen. I'm not the pure innocent you wanted me to be. I tried to kill you that night last October.'

'Did you?' He smiled down at her. 'I'm glad you didn't.'

'So am I.' She smiled, moving her hand as if to smooth the lines around his dark eyes. 'And I'm not ashamed any more, Austen. That second time . . . I'm not a bit ashamed now.'

And she drew his head down to hers and kissed him on the lips very slowly. And they clung together on that Cornish cliff top and knew that for that flickering space of time, they were the centre of the universe.

The reunion that evening was almost hysterical.

They were late for dinner and the other four were already in the dining-room, suddenly anxious, the children overtired and beginning to squabble. Tilly saw the two cars negotiate the gravel sweep and make for the yard at the back, but thought it wise to say nothing. It was Hanny, facing the glass-panelled door which looked on to the reception desk, who spotted the couple leaning over the visitors' book. He did not immediately recognize them. The woman was wearing a loose, sleeveless dress which looked very like one of Jennifer's sun frocks. The tall thin man with his arm around those bare shoulders, looked like one of the many hikers who were all over Cornwall that year, using the hotel for one night and gone before breakfast the next morning.

And then the man turned to kiss the top of the woman's head and she looked up so that she could return the kiss. And the dark face was his father's, and the fair one was his mother's. And there was no prevarication with aunts and uncles this time. He leapt from his chair, his glass of water flying one side of him, his cutlery clattering between his legs, and he shouted at the top of his voice, 'Mummy! Daddy!' and launched himself past Jennifer and between the tables as if he were a rocket.

He was closely followed by Jennifer who was determined not to be left out, and more decorously by Tilly and Charles. And there in the foyer they hugged and kissed in a way they had never done before; because, after all, there were no words for an occasion like this.

Afterwards, it seemed everything was new and different. The other diners smiled at them, the waiter hovered assiduously, the food tasted wonderful, they laughed and then suddenly filled up and patted each other as if giving and receiving reassurance. Hanny realized that no-one was going to tell him off that particular evening and he risked a joke about sitting between two fat ladies. His mother and Aunt Tilly hugged each other around him; it was Jennifer who whispered furiously, 'You – you – absolute oaf!' so that he felt terrible and did not know what to do about it.

Hallie, looking at her friend, felt a deep thankfulness that somehow, against all odds, Jack had seen her properly and had done something about it. Tilly was thin, thinner than Austen, so that the small bump beneath her summer frock was more obvious than it should have been. But she had already assured Hallie that her father was 'downright delighted' with her and said she was going to have an easy birth and a strong baby. Hallie smiled and murmured, 'Tilly Martinez . . . It sounds so *right*.' And Tilly smiled too and responded, 'Like Harriet Rudolf.' And Hallie nodded slowly but certainly.

Austen, surveying all of them, felt, for the first time, a sense of achievement. The long weeks of waiting in Burgos, fretting over Tilly, trying to fill empty hours purposefully . . . that was all over. They were safe. That would still have meant very little if it hadn't been for Tilly's obvious happiness, Hanny's excitement, and . . . Hallie. After all, it had been for Hallie; if she had not accepted that, the significance of the last seven months would be gone. He began to follow that particular line of thought: was it possible for a personal act to achieve significance purely on its own merit, or did it depend on somebody else's recognition of it . . . ? Then he smiled and banished such theorizing. It was good to know that for the next few years he would be working hard. And coming home to Hallie and his family.

Charles lifted his glass.

'A toast to all Rudolfs and Martinez,' he said. 'Where-ever they may be.'

They lifted their glasses. Hanny made himself think of his real father and wished it weren't so difficult. But then thought of how it would be at Colston's next term; two fathers, both heroes. He smiled at Jennifer who was still looking at him coldly.

Austen lifted his glass to his wife. And she thought of Amos and wondered if she could talk Mungay into giving him the plantation.

Charles put his glass down.

'Tilly and I have been talking. I suggested that she should come to live in St George Street with me.' He looked across the table. 'I would like that. A bit of life in the old place again. And Jack's family . . .' He cleared his throat. 'And she has agreed to it.'

Hanny let out a sigh of relief.

'Then you can look after the baby, Grandad!' he said.

'I thought I might have to offer to live with Aunt Tilly. But if you'd rather—' He could get no further for the gales of laughter at his expense. But he didn't mind.

Tilly said, 'Is that all right with you and Austen, Hal? I felt I would like to be in Jack's old home and with his father.'

Hallie and Austen beamed at her together.

Hanny chipped in again. 'Tell you what. I'll sleep in your room with you tonight, Aunty Tilly. Daddy can have my bed in Mummy's room and keep an eye on her. And I'll keep an eye on you.'

The adults all looked very happy with this plan. Even Jennifer who leaned over Tilly again to hiss, 'You're not quite such an oaf, I suppose.'

Austen pushed the twin beds together and overlapped the sheets deftly.

'You've done this before,' Hallie teased, watching him in the mirror as she brushed her hair.

'I've made up beds in some very unlikely places,' he agreed. He came across and took the brush from her. 'I've done this before also.' He moved the brush very gently through her short thick hair. 'I remember wanting so much to feel your hair between my fingers, like this.' He let it fall over the back of his hand. 'But there was electricity between the brush and my hand. I did not dare let it go further.'

'I remember you stopped as if you'd had a shock. Quite literally.' Hallie put up her own hand and covered his. 'There were so many times like that, Austen. We'd look at each other and find we could not look away—'

'And the time you flung yourself on me – at Hanny's birthday party – and I stood there coldly—'

'And before that – when poor Maude was having Hanny—'

He was suddenly still. 'Oh, Hal, you will be all right having our baby, won't you? Perhaps this afternoon we should not have—'

She stood up so suddenly the brush fell to the floor between them.

'Don't talk like that, Austen! Don't make barriers where there are none!' She put her arms around his neck. 'There will be difficulties we shall have to get through together, but not that one. I love you. And I want you. If it were harmful to make love Tilly would have told us!' She kissed him hard. 'Nothing must come between us in that way again, Austen. Nothing!'

He held her to him, adoring her sudden desperation, letting it rush them into the passion they had so gently consummated out there on the cliff. And after it was spent, they both knew the joy of being together in each other's arms, as sleep closed over their heads.

Amelia Rudolf was born very quickly indeed on 12 July 1938. Hallie had backache the day before and then sudden tingling sensations during the evening. At ten o'clock she went to bed early feeling tired, yet could not sleep for an unaccountable excitement. Austen wanted to send for the doctor but she demurred.

'How can we send for the doctor? I've not had a single pain – sorry, contraction! I don't want Tilly's father to think I'm a fusspot!'

And then, at two o'clock, out of the blue she had an enormous engulfing pain that terrifed her and at the end of it her waters broke.

Panting, sweating and considerably distressed she looked at Austen through a kind of haze.

'Darling – get him quickly. If that goes on for long . . . oh, Austen, no wonder poor Maude . . .'

Austen was gone and she pulled the wet draw sheet from beneath her and fell back on the rubber sheeting.

There was another searing, tearing bout of agony while she was alone. Somehow she remembered the books she and Tilly had been reading. She breathed fast, forcing her knotted muscles to relax against their will.

Austen returned with a rush.

'He's on his way. What—' He saw her face. 'Oh, Hal. Another one. What can I do?' He was horrified at his own helplessness. He had coped when Hanny was born. This time he felt bereft of his wits.

But she was suddenly in control. 'Sit on the end of the bed. Take my hands – let me put my feet on your shoulders. When I say pull – pull!'

'Darling, not yet – it's too soon.'

'No it's not. Do as I say – quickly—'

Ten minutes later, Amelia lay between them, yelling lustily. Dr Hesterman arrived to cut the cord and give Hallie some gas and air while he stitched a small tear.

She said, 'Is that it?'

'Yes. There's your baby. What more d'you want?'

'May Hanny come and see—'

'Hallie, it's three-thirty in the morning. He can see when he gets up.'

'I can't believe it. All that time waiting and then suddenly, here she is!'

'She's so beautiful,' Austen doted, bending over the papoose of shawls and gazing at the tightly closed eyes, stubby lashes sprouting from the wrinkled lids. 'She is just so beautiful.'

Dr Hesterman had heard all this before. 'I'll call in the morning with the midwife. Meanwhile, try to sleep.'

Hallie laughed. 'How could we possibly sleep?' She looked at Austen. 'Oh, darling, you've got classes in the morning. I'd almost forgotten. *You* must sleep.'

'Silly girl,' he said fondly.

He took the doctor downstairs and came back carrying a tray of food.

'Shall we have a midnight feast?'

Hallie looked at him. This was the man who had not known about fun, who had been frightened of physical contact. And yet, all the time, had loved her.

They ate water biscuits spread with Gentleman's Relish and picked green olives out of a jar. And as the daylight grew stronger, Amelia opened her eyes and gazed at them consideringly. They stared back at her, breathless. And then she closed her eyes again and sighed.

Hallie whispered, 'We passed the test, darling!'

'So we did.'

He took her hand. And together they waited for Meg to knock on the bedroom door with morning tea and alert the household to the new arrival.

'I'd like to see Father and Aunt Cad and Tilly first,' she said. 'Perhaps Margo could wait till this afternoon.'

'I'm sure she could.'

They both smiled anticipating Margo's endless anecdotes about her own experiences of childbirth. Now that Hanny and Jennifer had taken Constantia under their wing, Margo was much happier 'in exile' as she dramatically put it. She had managed to lose some of her weight and one of her father's colleagues was squiring her around Bristol these days. Otto was pulling strings to divorce her for desertion and though they would have to wait seven years she did not mind too much. She quite enjoyed being the Countess von Gellhorn when the Count was unavailable. And without the support of servants and nurses, one child was quite enough to give her a certain status. Margo was as happy as she would ever be.

Hallie took Austen's hand. 'Aren't we lucky?' she said. 'If things had gone according to plan, I'd be in the nursing home and you would have been most definitely outside the door! As it was . . .' She gazed down at the baby still sleeping. 'As it was, Amelia wanted to greet us both together.'

And Austen nodded. He knew he was indeed one of the luckiest men in the world.

And then the door opened unceremoniously and Hanny stood there.

'You're not in the bathroom, Dad!' he said belligerently. 'Just what's going on?'

And then he saw the baby and registered just what was going on.

'I'm so glad it's a girl,' he whispered, gazing at her with popping eyes. 'I'm getting good with girls.'

He looked witheringly at his parents as they clutched each other, helpless with laughter.

'You're hopeless!' he said. But he said it smugly and though he pulled away when Hallie kissed him, he grinned sheepishly.

He decided it wasn't a bad life.

Twenty-five
June 1944

The Rudolf–Martinez clan were at Porthmeor for D-Day.

Hanny had asked if he and Jennifer could spend his sixteenth birthday down there with Grandad Charles as sole chaperone and, after a tense stillness during which he knew his parents were studiously avoiding each other's eyes, his father put forward the unusual notion that if everyone went it was as good as being completely unchaperoned.

'I don't get it,' Hanny said flatly.

'Well, what Dad means . . .' his mother leaned forward with her usual enthusiasm for anything 'Dad' suggested, 'is that if you went down – the two of you – with one chaperone, it would be like having a gaoler. Constant attention. But with all of us down there, you'll be lost in the crowd.'

Hanny eyed them both with disfavour. He had known he hadn't a hope of them agreeing to his request – Jennifer's demand actually – but sometimes their sweet reasonableness was a bit much to swallow.

His father said, 'If you're worried you'll have to look after Amelia and Jack all the time—'

'You know it's not that!' Hanny protested. He wished suddenly he and his family could go down alone. Without Jennifer. Without Tilly and Jack even. Just the four of them so that he could dig channels with Amelia all day long and no-one would laugh at him and he could see the world through her startlingly blue eyes.

'I was only going to say, we can delegate them to

Connie. Keep her out of your hair at the same time.'

Hanny groaned loudly and covered his face with his hands and at last his parents looked at each other and fell about laughing. Their laughing was another thing he had to contend with. They often laughed at things that weren't in the least funny. Jennifer said it was the most romantic thing in the world, and Clive said it was sex.

Hanny spoke through his fingers, 'I'd forgotten Con the Terrible!'

His father pretended complete astonishment. 'How could anyone forget Con the Terrible?' he asked blankly.

Hanny balled his hands into fists and tried unsuccessfully to control his grin.

'Oh . . . *you*!' was all he could find to say.

So they went down on the last day of May, had a proper dinner party for Hanny's birthday and were still there when the news came through of the allied landings in Normandy.

Hanny was always first in the lounge for Alvar Liddell's six o'clock broadcasts on the big radiogram in the corner. On 7 June when the report of the landings came through, he was alone. He was still in the khaki shorts he wore on the beach, his long legs were tanned so deeply the hairs showed up as a golden aureole. He sat on the carpet to remove a pebble from inside his sandal as the pips went. And he stayed there, his one leg crooked, the other straight on the carpet, his brown hair flopping over one eye.

Jennifer came in through the swing doors.

'Oh, there you are! I thought you must have gone up to change for dinner—'

He shushed her furiously and for a moment she was miffed then heard the name 'Eisenhower' and came to sit by him. Bomber Command had prepared the way with 'strategic bombing' and British troops under Monty were attacking Caen. She put her hand on his bare foot and slid it towards his knee. The weather conditions had

460

been right and allied landing craft had been unopposed. Jennifer's hand left his knee and travelled down his thigh. With the victory in Rome three days before, this would appear to be the final stages . . . Hanny picked up her hand and crushed it in his. There was no question any more of who was the stronger physically.

She whimpered, 'You're hurting.'

'Good.'

'Darling!' She pouted deliciously. 'What is the matter? You usually like little Jen to—'

He said with terrible disappointment, 'The war isn't going to wait for me. It's not going to last another two years.'

'Thank God!' She launched herself at him and kissed him frantically. 'I don't think I could have borne that, darling.'

He released himself and stared at her. He knew she was exquisitely beautiful and he was the envy of Colston because she was his, but he also knew that he was not hers. He often wished he were; it must be good to belong to someone.

He said, 'Wouldn't you like me to do something brave – something really difficult—'

'Not when it might end up with you being dead!' She tried to kiss him again but he held her off.

'For God's sake, Jen!' He inclined his head towards the damask front of the radiogram. 'This is important!'

She was angry at last.

'And I'm not? Thank you very much, Hanover Rudolf!' She scrambled to her feet and he had a close-up of her bare knees. They were exquisite.

'It's the old story, isn't it? You've had what you want and now I'm cast aside like an old glove!'

Anything less like an old glove was difficult to imagine. Alvar Liddell was quoting a message of congratulation from Winston Churchill in Hanny's left ear, but he was looking above Jennifer's knees, under her cotton skirt to the secret places she had shown him a long time ago –

461

had it been on his ninth birthday when his father and Aunt Tilly had turned up? He could hardly remember. Seven years was a long time and a great deal had happened since then.

He said, 'Stop acting, Jen! If it's a kiss you want come here and I'll give you one. And then just shut up and let me listen to what is happening in Normandy!'

But she was seriously annoyed and flounced to the door.

'I'm seventeen this autumn!' she fulminated, turning to look at him with pretended disdain. 'I'm old enough to get married! Why I waste my time with a schoolboy, I'll never know!'

He did not reply. The estimated casualties of the first day's fighting were being announced.

After supper Tilly and Hallie went upstairs to put Amelia and Jack to bed and Con suggested table tennis.

Jennifer said, 'Count me out. I promised Dalesford I'd give him a game of chess.'

'Dalesford?' Hanny looked at her sharply and she smiled, well pleased. Dalesford Williams sat at the next table with an elderly aunt. He was Welsh, had a place at Oxford for September and had let it be known that he was a distant relative of Dingle Foot and intended going into parliament himself after university.

'He has a wonderful intellect,' she said casually. He was also very good-looking, but she did not rub that in.

'I'll partner you, Hanny,' Con said immediately.

'Against us?' Cadiz looked at Margo who hated table tennis but was, after all, quite a bit younger than Mungay and Charles. She worried about both men lately.

Margo groaned, so did Con. Hanny merely looked trapped.

Austen said smoothly, 'Look, could you partner Grandad Charles, Con? I want to talk to Hanny.' He did not wait for refusals but turned to his tall son. 'Sorry, old man. It's rather important. Shall we take a walk over the West Head?'

Hanny tried not to beam. 'Why not? If it's fine enough for the Normandy landings—' It was a pointless remark but he wanted everyone to know that he and his father could discuss the progress of the war.

Con grinned at Charles. At thirteen she was a strapping girl, quite unlike her mother, already famous on local hockey fields. If anyone told her that her father was a Hun, she could use her hockey stick for other purposes. There had been a terrible fuss the year before when a girl from Badminton School had been sent to the infirmary with a suspected fracture of the tibia. Con had been removed from the school hockey team for the rest of the season.

She said, 'We'll show 'em, eh, Grandad Charles?' She looked at Mungay. 'D'you want to put money on it?'

'Why not?' Mungay ignored Cadiz' protests and went to the writing desk. He scribbled industriously. 'I'm going to put a pound note in here with the name of the pair I'm backing. Not to be opened till the game is over!' He looked at Con. 'Your Aunt Tilly can umpire when she comes down.'

'Sounds fair to me.'

The tide was in so that when they reached the tip of the headland they were practically surrounded by the Atlantic Ocean.

'I did want to be in the Navy, Dad.' Hanny stared out to sea feeling the vastness of it flow into his veins. 'I mean . . . I shall enjoy helping Ma with the business – don't get me wrong. I like meeting people and talking to them and there's a lot of that, isn't there? And I'm looking forward to seeing Amos out in Barbados and going over to Spain to see about the Castillo. But I might have been a hero like you. I wanted to be a hero. I wanted to – to—'

'Be totally committed,' Austen supplied quietly.

'How do you mean?'

'So deeply involved in something – life-and-death probably – that you forget about yourself.'

'I suppose so. I hadn't thought of it like that.'

Austen looked around, found a bastion of rock and leaned into it.

'Funny thing, Hanny. When I thought I was a Rudolf, I never felt . . . committed. When I knew I belonged to no-one, then – then was when I began to belong to the human race.'

Hanny fidgeted. When his father got philosophical he never quite knew where to look.

Austen laughed. 'Sorry, old man. You'll know what I mean one day. You couldn't have more roots if you tried, could you? You're hedged in with them. And yet . . . you don't commit yourself . . . you don't give yourself. You don't know what the hell I'm talking about. But one day, when you *do* give yourself . . . then you'll think, Oh that's what poor old dad was trying to tell me!'

Hanny said, 'Well, I definitely don't want to commit myself to Jen McKinlay. I'll tell you that for nothing!'

His father tipped his head back against the rock and laughed unrestrainedly. And after a moment, Hanny joined him.

And then they were quiet for a while, staring out at the sun which was balanced on the horizon. Hanny tried to imagine the Normandy beaches, perhaps like Porthmeor, but cluttered with amphibious vehicles, guns, men . . . bodies.

Austen said suddenly, 'I know how you feel, son. But I am deeply thankful you are still sixteen. I remember France. Nothing heroic about it.'

Hanny said nothing. He could not explain himself further.

Austen said, 'Well . . . I wanted to ask you if you'd take over from me for the next week.'

'Take over?'

'I'm wanted back at the hospital, old man. I'll have to go tomorrow.'

'Dad! It's not fair! You work harder than anyone else—'

'Not true.'

'And Ma will hate it – you were supposed to have ten days and you've had five!'

'Better than nothing. Can you manage?'

Hanny knew this was mere lip service. He said, 'Gramps and Grandad are here.'

'It's the kids. Amelia and Jack. And Con the T.'

Hanny snorted another laugh.

Austen pressed him. 'Seriously, old man, can you take them all on? Your Aunt Cad is concerned about Gramps. Your mother has to keep the peace between Tilly and Margo—'

Hanny said gloomily, 'I reckon Margo has lost her lid. I wish Ma would be firmer with her like Aunt Tilly.'

'It's not easy for Margo. She and Con could easily have been interned, you know.'

'Wish they had been,' Hanny said.

Hanny waited for his father's laugh and when it did not come, he looked round at him.

Austen managed a wry grin. 'All right. I know what you mean. But I feel responsible for Margo – and therefore Con.'

'That old tale she tells about you ordering her to leave her husband!' Hanny scoffed robustly. 'Come off it, Dad! Everyone knows she wanted to come home! Margo never does anything she doesn't want to do!'

Austen looked slightly more cheerful.

'True. It's the other children. She has two daughters and a son in Germany.'

'She can go to see them after the war. And that won't be much longer!'

Austen clapped his son on the shoulder.

'We're back to where we started, eh, old man? Your chance for heroism will come, never fear. Meanwhile –

will you keep an eye on Amelia and Jack and Con?'

'Sure thing,' Hanny said like Oliver Hardy.

'And that will mean permitting Jennifer McKinlay to dally with Dalesford!' Austen reminded him.

Hanny laughed remembering that this holiday had been meant for him and Jennifer.

'I don't mind, Dad. Not one bit,' he said.

His father took a breath and seemed to make up his mind about something.

'Listen, Hanny. Your mother doesn't want this known just yet, so keep it under your hat – where she is concerned too. She's expecting another baby. That's why I don't want her worried with the children.'

Hanny was amazed. 'Another one? At her age?' he said.

Austen hugged him suddenly. 'Yes, son. At her age. Thirty-five. Incredible, isn't it?'

Hanny recognized his father's sarcasm when he heard it.

'I didn't mean . . . but you know, Amelia's nearly seven so I thought—'

'So did I. But Mother thought differently. So you see I'd be extra grateful if you'd be responsible for the kids.'

'Sure thing,' Hanny said, but not like Oliver Hardy this time. 'I say, Dad . . . This is pretty stupendous. Makes you feel . . . different somehow.'

'About what?'

'Well, I don't know. Everything. Going to war, for one thing.'

Austen laughed and looked relieved. He whacked Hanny's shoulder again and they set off for the hotel.

Hanny could not stop thinking about his father and mother. They must have done what Jennifer called 'going the whole way'. Jennifer wanted him to do that and he said no because of babies and this proved he was right. Even so, just the thought of it made him fairly sure that they would be doing it quite soon. His heart beat hard at the thought. He lengthened his stride to his father's and felt almost old.

Con was the snag, of course. If it had not been for her, Hanny would have enjoyed this new arrangement completely. He had wanted to be able to spend time with Amelia and his father had practically ordered him to do just that. He told Jennifer the evening of the table tennis, that for the next five days he would most definitely be otherwise engaged. She did not appear to mind that much. Dalesford had beaten her – not too easily – at chess and was well on the way to becoming enslaved. Already he had reached the stage of trembling if she brushed against him accidentally.

So the next day he shook hands with his father at the station and told his mother not to worry and took Jack and Amelia down to the beach to dig a castle which would survive the tide when it began to come in after lunch.

It was a long way out and the flat wet sand was ideal for digging and reinforcing with pebbles and decorating with green seaweed and multicoloured shells.

Amelia said, 'Hanny, it's just beautiful. Will it really stand firm when the sea comes?'

'For a little while.'

Jack brandished his spade. 'We'll keep making it higher and higher so that we can stand on top like St Michael's Mount and the water comes all round and—'

Con appeared from nowhere and put a foot on the top of the castle.

'Like this?' she said and pressed.

Amelia wailed despair and Jack shouted some obscenity of his own. Hanny knew she did it so that he would chase her off and he started to do exactly that and then changed his mind and made a grab for her long blonde pigtail.

She screamed satisfyingly. He pushed her to her knees.

'Right. Beg forgiveness,' he ordered.

He had never actually attacked her before and she sobbed with pain.

'You're supposed to be looking after me—'

'I have your welfare at heart.' He twisted the pigtail and put his knee in her back.

'Say after me – dear Amelia and Jack, I humbly beg your pardon—'

She twisted and turned and yelled again and eventually screeched, 'Amelia and Jack—'

'*Dear* Amelia and Jack,' Hanny prompted.

'Dear Amelia and . . . You're hurting so much I can't remember . . .' He hurt more and she remembered.

'Right. Now stand up and come and help us rebuild,' he ordered.

'If you think I'm going to play with a lot of kids—' She screamed and stood up.

'We are playing with the kids,' he said softly in her ear. 'You. And me. Got it?'

She was suddenly still in his hold. And then she turned slowly, still squinting with pain, and tried to focus him.

'You mean . . . like you and Cousin Jennifer?'

'Except that she knows how to behave herself and you don't.'

'I do. But I don't choose to.' She went on staring at him. 'She's gone off with Dalesford and you're jealous.'

He smiled as evilly as he knew how.

She swallowed.

'All right. I'll help with your silly old castle.'

He made Amelia and Jack stand aside while she repaired the damage, but Amelia couldn't resist showing her where the mother-of-pearl shells went.

'Like lighted windows, Con. At the top where the bedrooms are.'

Con glanced up at Hanny and said, 'Yes, I see. Good idea.'

And later when the tide did, in fact, wash the castle away, it was Con who said, 'Look. It doesn't matter. We'll do another one tomorrow. I'll get some of those really huge pebbles and we'll make an outer defence wall.'

She turned a bright face to Hanny for his approval. He sighed. He could see that Con as an ally was going to be as much hard work as Con as a foe.

But the next day she was as good as her word and laboured all morning on her outer defence wall. Jennifer, strolling past with Dalesford, interrupted his speech on socialist values to mention that it looked like a concentration camp.

Con picked up one of the larger pebbles and glowered at her. Dalesford said in his sing-song Welsh accent, 'When I get to Oxford I intend to join the—'

Jennifer said, 'Of course, you'd know all about concentration camps, I suppose.'

Dalesford looked surprised. Con said, 'You – you cow!' Amelia and Jack squatted in the moat around the castle and did not look up. They did not understand what was being said, but their mothers had told them to ignore such comments.

Hanny laughed and threw a wet, sandy arm across Con's square shoulders.

'A couple of Jerries together, aren't we, Con?' He lifted his free arm suddenly so that Jennifer had to step back. '*Sieg Heil!*' he shouted.

Jennifer stared at him; her face reddened slowly but inexorably. Dalesford said, 'Good Lord! I say! Rather good, eh?'

She said, 'Bloody good! A bit too bloody good!' And turned to take his arm and march him off.

Hanny turned to Con, forcing a laugh. He knew that he had burned his boats with Jen; maybe not for ever but for the rest of this holiday anyway. It made him feel deeply miserable and a dull ache started in the pit of his stomach. She had been part of his life for so long . . .

Con said fervently, 'You were wonderful, Hanny!' Her face too was bright red. 'Thank you. I thank you from the bottom of my heart.'

469

His own heart sank to meet the stomach ache. He said brusquely, 'Come on. We haven't got all day!' And bent to pick up what looked like a pebble and turned out to be a rock. He strained at it; it became a matter of personal pride that he should lift it on to the defence wall. It surrendered its hold on the sand and came up with a sucking sound. He lugged it into position and Amelia and Jack cheered. Con's face had never been so red nor so happy. He was the only one who felt awful.

After a picnic lunch and the prescribed rest period, during which Con told him about her hockey prowess at some length, and Jennifer ostentatiously went to sleep, they all went down to bathe. The two grandfathers had retired to the hotel for lunch anyway, and the four women aligned their deck-chairs so that they could keep an eye on the distant sea. The tide was at its lowest ebb; a game of cricket gathered momentum on the wet sand; the two airmen convalescing at the hotel stumbled slowly down the cliff path and took their places as fielders. Hanny glanced at them longingly as he swung Amelia over the pools. Con had taken Jack in hand and promised to teach him to swim. Jennifer had gone on ahead and was overarming her way to the rocks where Dalesford sat on a towel composing his next speech for the debating society of Wales. Hanny wished his father had not sworn him to secrecy about the new baby. He wanted to tell his mother to rest more. He wanted to tell Jennifer about it.

They drew level with the sandcastle.

Amelia said, 'Hanny, I don't think the sea can possibly break that castle, do you?'

He squatted by her and they looked at the edifice appreciatively.

He said judiciously, 'The trouble is, Mell, that everything there belongs to the sea.'

'But we made it!'

'The sea let us make it. The sea gave us everything

we needed to make it. It will let us do the same tomorrow.'

'But it's so unkind of the sea to break it up!'

He looked at her. He knew that it was only himself and his parents who thought Amelia was beautiful. Apart from her very blue eyes she was quite a plain little girl. Her hair was dark like Dad's and her face was round like Mum's and her legs were like sticks – her arms too when she was wearing a bathing costume. But for him she stood out in a crowd like a diamond would among these pebbles. He never had difficulty in finding her when she was in the kindergarten playground.

He wanted to comfort her and did not know how.

'The sea doesn't exactly break it,' he said doubtfully. 'I mean, it kind of . . . dissolves it. Ready for the next time.'

She sighed, accepting one more inexplicable fact. Like Con. And Jennifer and Dalesford Williams.

He straightened. 'Would you like to swim now, Mell? It's not cold.'

She grinned. 'It is cold!' But she nodded enthusiastically then stared out to sea. 'Oh. Look where Con has taken Jack.'

Hanny shaded his eyes. Con had towed Jack almost out to the rocks. Well out of his depth. He would kill her when she got back.

'Don't worry,' he said. 'Let's swim out to meet them.'

'I can't go that far, Hanny. I might go under water.' Amelia was terrified of going under.

'I won't let you. Promise.' He got down in the knee depth water. 'Climb on my back.'

She giggled and did so. He began to move out very slowly. Even her weight pushed him under the surface. He stood up with some difficulty; Amelia clung to him like a limpet.

'It's all right, Mell. You're still in depth.' He lowered her gently but not before she had seen that Jack was in some difficulty. He was wriggling frantically in Con's arms as if wanting to get away. And at last he did, shoving himself off with some force and putting at least two yards between them.

'He can't swim, Hanny! He'll drown!'

There was a shriek of laughter from Con and then suddenly Jack was doggy paddling maniacally towards them.

'See!' Con shouted. 'He's swimming!' And with a flourish she waved something above her head. It was Jack's costume knitted lovingly by Tilly and much too loose.

'Throw 'em in at the deep end! Everyone knows that's the best—'

Hanny shouted furiously, 'You damned fool! He's not seven years old yet!'

But Jack was grinning from ear to ear as he came towards them head bobbing, arms and legs working frantically.

Con shrieked again. 'Even better when you throw 'em in naked!'

Hanny thought longingly of the compost heap in the garden of High House as he reached out and scooped Jack to him.

'Don't lift me up, Hanny!' Jack could hardly talk for giggles. 'Con tickled me out of my costume – she kept tickling and tickling till I said I'd swim and then—'

'Yes, all right, old man,' Hanny held him protectively and shouted at Con, 'Get yourself and that costume over here! Now!'

She loved it, swimming towards him obediently, her china-blue eyes sparkling. He prayed to God that Jennifer could not hear this exchange from the rocks. She must have seen. And water carried sounds.

He hissed, 'You stupid, callous, hopeless little—'

But she and Jack were laughing so hard as she taunted him with his costume the words were unheard. And even Amelia was smiling up at him and saying, 'He can swim, Hanny! Our Jack can swim!'

And into the middle of his frustrated annoyance, two planes appeared from behind the West Head. They swooped low over the beach. Something dropped from the first. And then the second. The next moment the Dunes hotel lifted itself from the top of the cliff and began to crumble in mid-air. And then the gas works erupted in a sheet of flame.

Jack screamed. Amelia put her arms around Hanny's waist and gripped hard. Con said, 'Jesus Christ Almighty! It's Jerry fighter bombers!'

Even in that moment of horror he felt a twinge of admiration at her language. Thirteen years old and she could swear like a trooper.

It was as if they were playing statues. Everyone on the beach stayed exactly where they were, all gazing at the hotel and the gas works, motionless, transfixed. Jack sobbed loudly. Hanny could feel Amelia shaking through his own body.

And then, far up the beach, the four women rose in unison from their deck-chairs to run down to their children. And, again in unison, like puppets controlled by only one hand, their feet, trapped beneath the bar of their chairs refused to move and they all fell flat, face down on the sand.

It probably saved their lives, because incredibly the two planes appeared again from the sun; this time they roared across the beach and their cannon fire spurted the sand. One of the airmen outfielding the cricket match went down like a skittle. The cricketers converged on him. Amelia was sobbing now.

Con said, 'Quick. Let's get up to the beach huts. Oh, quick – Mummy—' She disentangled Jack forcibly and started wading strongly to the shore.

Hanny shouted, 'Don't get out of the water, Con! They're coming back!'

He could follow the roar of the aircraft now. They were making a huge sweep on the little town.

He turned and shouted at Jennifer and Dalesford, 'If

they come again, get under the water! D'you hear? Get right under! Bullets will ricochet over the surface!'

The noise of the planes was dying away behind the town. Con turned and came back to him. She was crying helplessly, her nose running unheeded into her mouth.

He snapped, 'Did you hear me? If they come back, underneath. Both of you. Con – you take Jack. I'll take Mell.'

She was looking up at him, her eyes drowning with terror.

'I can't go under, Hanny. I just can't—'

But the planes had erupted from behind the West Head again and they were now raking the shallows with cannon fire. He picked Amelia up and held her close to his chest. And he sat on the sea bed. He opened his eyes and watched her hair floating around her face. And then, quite suddenly, she too opened her eyes and looked straight into his. He gripped her hard expecting her to begin to fight. She did not move. After a split second, she smiled at him.

They saw no bullet splashes and when Hanny surfaced cautiously, the planes had already disappeared over the East Head. He listened. They were not circling the town again. He held Amelia aloft. Con and Jack bobbed up. The rocks were empty and after a moment, he spotted Jennifer's white bathing cap moving towards him. 'They've gone,' he announced.

Pounding down the beach came Cadiz, Tilly, Margo and Hallie. They gathered the children to them. Jennifer was weeping loudly, Jack could not stop shivering, Con wailed over and over again, 'The bloody Jerries, Mummy – the bloody, bloody Jerries—' Amelia in Hallie's arms said, 'Hanny saved our lives. Mummy, Hanny is a hero. Just like Daddy.'

It was then that Hanny started to cry. He didn't let anyone see it, of course, but strode back into the water to retrieve Jack's costume which had come adrift again in the maelstrom. But tears poured down his face and he knew at last that he did belong. Completely and utterly he belonged. To everyone, just as Dad had said. But especially to his sister, who was not his sister at all. And for the first time he was deeply thankful for that fact. Because it meant that one day he would be able to marry her and look after her always.

Two fishermen, who were also Air Raid Wardens, clambered down the ruined cliff path and led them across rocks to East Head and from thence back to the hotel. A group of commandos on training took the injured airman off in a boat and then in an ambulance to Camborne hospital.

The hotel was a mess of powdery plaster and broken glass, but at least it was there. The people from the Dunes hotel piled in as well. Ambulances tore up and down the quiet lanes. There were a lot of casualties from the Dunes.

The grandfathers pretended they had slept through it all, but Cadiz insisted they should see the local doctor as soon as he was able.

Hanny said directly, 'Ma, are you all right?'

'Of course, darling. We're all all right, thank God.'

He thought this was no time for tact.

'Dad told me. About the baby. And you went a real pearler down on the sand, didn't you?'

She looked at him. 'So. You know. What do you think?'

'Well. You're a bit old now. But Dad says you should be all right.' He grinned and quoted Constantia. 'If the bloody Jerries leave you alone!'

She smiled unwillingly. 'She's a real hoyden that girl. I don't know where she gets it from – but at least we know whose side she's on now!'

'Are you all right, Ma? Really?'

'Of course. And I gather you don't mind too much? Another baby about the house et cetera?'

'Oh, Ma.' He made up his mind. 'Look. Dad put me

in charge. And I think we should go home. Now. I'll get on the blower and find out about trains and we can pack and be on our way by tea time. What do you say?'

She thought about it and finally nodded.

'I'll telephone your father.'

He went to the kiosk. He felt wonderful. Masterful. In control. He'd get them home safely and he'd look after them all. He could do it.

At his elbow Jennifer said, 'Hanny. You were wonderful. I'm sorry for . . . everything. You know I love you and will always love you.'

The exchange asked him what number he required. He asked for the Penzance station master.

Jennifer was still white and frightened, her wet hair unfashionably sleek. But she was exquisite. Half of him was pleased to have her back. The other half foresaw problems.

He leaned forward and kissed her.

'I forgive you,' he said magnanimously.

He could cope. He knew he could cope.

THE END

DAUGHTERS OF THE MOON
by Susan Sallis

The twins were born in war-torn Plymouth in 1944, two little girls whose parents – touring actors – didn't altogether want them. Their unorthodox childhood, first as evacuee babies in Cornwall, then at boarding school, then living with their Aunt Maggie, made them grow up uniquely self-sufficient. They didn't need anyone else. They had each other.

Miranda was the vibrant, flamboyant one, determined to be an actress, determined never to conform or be dull and conventional. Meg was quieter, more self-effacing. But it was Meg who always knew when anything bad was happening to Miranda.

As they grew up, the bond between them held – until Meg went back to Cornwall to buy a house, to paint, to fall in love. And for the first time events conspired to drive a rift through their special relationship. Their lives shifted – for Miranda found herself trapped into domesticity, and Meg – feeling herself betrayed – had to seek a new path that ultimately took her to unexpected success.

But the link was still there, in spite of all that was to happen, in spite of violence and tragedy, and finally it led to happiness that came when they had ceased to expect it.

0 552 13934 3

AN ORDINARY WOMAN
by Susan Sallis

When Rose was four the scandal broke about her head. She was really too young to understand what was happening – only that her mother was in disgrace and that they were leaving Aunt Mabe in America and returning home to England. The following May, Joanna – 'Jon' – was born.

Rose and Jon were totally different. Jon was vivacious, fun, liked a good time, and always got what she wanted, even when what she wanted happened to belong to Rose. Rose was reserved, controlled, never wanted to leave her home or Gloucestershire, and was – well – an ordinary girl who grew into an ordinary woman.

But as Jon raced from disaster to disaster, from one violent relationship to another so Rose, in her quiet way, salvaged the family, held them together, pasted over the cracks of tragedy and emotional upheavals whilst at the same time fighting her own personal crises.

It was much later – when the children were growing up, when life at last seemed tranquil and settled, that Jon precipitated Rose across the Atlantic and into the most extraordinary event of her life. When Rose finally returned from America no-one could ever again think of her as an ordinary woman.

0 552 13756 1

A SCATTERING OF DAISIES
THE DAFFODILS OF NEWENT
BLUEBELL WINDOWS
ROSEMARY FOR REMEMBRANCE
by Susan Sallis

Will Rising had dragged himself from humble beginnings to his own small tailoring business in Gloucester – and on the way he'd fallen violently in love with Florence, refined, delicate, and wanting something better for her children.

March was the eldest girl, the least loved, the plain, unattractive one who, as the family grew, became more and more the household drudge. But March, a strange, intelligent, unhappy child, had inherited some of her mother's dreams. March Rising was determined to break out of the round of poverty and hard work, to find wealth, and love, and happiness.

The Rising girls are introduced in *A Scattering of Daisies*, and their story continues in *The Daffodils of Newent* and *Bluebell Windows*, finally reaching its conclusion in *Rosemary for Remembrance*.

A SCATTERING OF DAISIES   0 552 12375 7
THE DAFFODILS OF NEWENT   0 552 12579 2
BLUEBELL WINDOWS   0 552 12880 5
ROSEMARY FOR REMEMBRANCE   0 552 13136 9

A SELECTED LIST OF FINE NOVELS
AVAILABLE FROM CORGI BOOKS

14060 0	MERSEY BLUES	*Lyn Andrews*	£6.99
166885 4	THE SILENT LADY	*Catherine Cookson*	£6.99
15034 7	THE ROWAN TREE	*Iris Gower*	£5.99
14895 4	NOT ALL TARTS ARE APPLE	*Pip Granger*	£6.99
14538 6	A TIME TO DANCE	*Kathryn Haig*	£5.99
15033 9	CHANDLERS GREEN	*Ruth Hamilton*	£5.99
13872 X	LEGACY OF LOVE	*Caroline Harvey*	£6.99
14868 7	SEASON OF MISTS	*Joan Hessayon*	£5.99
14332 4	THE WINTER HOUSE	*Judith Lennox*	£5.99
15045 2	THOSE IN PERIL	*Margaret Mayhew*	£6.99
15152 1	THE SHADOW CATCHER	*Michelle Paver*	£6.99
15141 6	THE APPLE TREE	*Elvi Rhodes*	£6.99
15017 7	LYDIA FIELDING	*Susan Sallis*	£5.99
12375 7	A SCATTERING OF DAISIES	*Susan Sallis*	£5.99
12579 2	THE DAFFODILS OF NEWENT	*Susan Sallis*	£5.99
12880 5	BLUEBELL WINDOWS	*Susan Sallis*	£5.99
13136 9	ROSEMARY FOR REMEMBRANCE	*Susan Sallis*	£6.99
13756 1	AN ORDINARY WOMAN	*Susan Sallis*	£5.99
13934 3	DAUGHTERS OF THE MOON	*Susan Sallis*	£6.99
13346 9	SUMMER VISITORS	*Susan Sallis*	£5.99
13545 3	BY SUN AND CANDLELIGHT	*Susan Sallis*	£5.99
14318 9	WATER UNDER THE BRIDGE	*Susan Sallis*	£5.99
14466 5	TOUCHED BY ANGELS	*Susan Sallis*	£5.99
14549 1	CHOICES	*Susan Sallis*	£5.99
14636 6	COME RAIN OR SHINE	*Susan Sallis*	£5.99
14671 4	THE KEYS TO THE GARDEN	*Susan Sallis*	£5.99
14747 8	THE APPLE BARREL	*Susan Sallis*	£5.99
15138 6	FAMILY FORTUNES	*Mary Jane Staples*	£5.99
15032 0	FAR FROM HOME	*Valerie Wood*	£5.99